Beautifully *Damaged*

L.A. Fiore

Montlake
Romance

Published by Montlake Romance, Seattle

www.apub.com

ISBN-13: 9781477817506
ISBN-10: 1477817506

Cover design by Laura Klynstra

Library of Congress Control Number: 2013916310

Printed in the United States of America

For my children: Don't wish upon a star, reach for it. Go after your dreams and never give up.

———◆———

For my husband: Thank you for giving me the opportunity to try for my dream. I love you.

———◆———

For my sister: You have always been there with your unwavering support and love. You're the best.

Part One

"No one who, like me, conjures up the most
evil of those half-tamed demons that inhabit the
human beast, and seeks to wrestle with them, can
expect to come through the struggle unscathed."

—Sigmund Freud

Chapter One

I t really wasn't my scene: the dark, smoke-filled nightclub; the heavy bass beat; the bodies, shoulder to shoulder; and the voices, the eye-bulging, brain-numbing voices that dissolved into incoherent shouting. The sleek, black bar top spanned the whole side of the place. It was littered with glasses and some of the most beautiful people that I'd ever seen in real life. Yes, I was definitely way outside of my comfort zone.

Lena was meeting the boy she liked here and wanted me to tag along just in case. Though I was shy, I also valued my friendship with her, and being in a place like this was proof of just how much this friendship meant to me.

We pushed our way through the crowd as my toes got stomped, my hair got pulled, and I couldn't help but think that I could have been at home, sipping a glass of wine and reading *Jane Eyre*. We somehow managed to reach the bar when Lena grabbed my hand.

"Look, Em, there he is."

I followed Lena's gaze to the blond standing near the bar. He was tall, maybe six feet, and his hair was perfectly cut. Even in his khakis and oxford shirt, you could tell his body was built like a runner's with long, lean muscles. When his face turned in our direction, I saw that his eyes were hazel-green in a face that was classically handsome.

"What do you think?"

I looked up at Lena and realized that she had been studying me while I studied him.

"He's very handsome. What's his name?"

"Todd."

Todd started toward us. His eyes sparkled in greeting as a smile curved his lips.

"Hello, Lena. I'm so glad you made it." He stepped into Lena and pressed a kiss on her lips and I couldn't help the pang of envy I felt at their greeting, but immediately my mind switched gears to Todd as Lena made the introductions.

"Todd, this is my best friend, Ember."

We'd been best friends since we were in middle school, and our friendship endured high school and separate colleges. He reached for my hand to shake it. Handshakes were big with my dad, yet Todd's was one of those half-girlie shakes. His hands were too smooth and soft—softer than mine. For my dad this would have been a serious red flag, but I pulled my thoughts from that when Todd smiled at me.

"Nice to meet you, Ember."

"You too, Todd."

A favorite song of Lena's came on. "Let's dance." She grabbed Todd's hand. "Are you coming, Em?"

"No, you go."

"Okay." And just like that they disappeared into the crowd. A stool at the bar emptied, so I sat down and flagged the bartender. He looked to be in his thirties and his eyes were friendly. He stopped just in front of me and set down a napkin.

"What can I get you?"

"Cabernet, please."

"Sure thing."

I watched him pour the ruby-red wine into a glass, then I pulled out a twenty and moved it across the bar to him just as he placed my glass in front of me.

"Keep the change," I said.

"Thanks." He threw me a grin as he moved down the bar and I took a sip of my wine.

I turned in my stool and looked out at the sea of people. This place wasn't like the clubs we used to hang out in during our college years—it was way swankier, but it was still a place to see and be seen. And though I tried to mingle like Lena so often encouraged me to do, it was hard for me to strike up a conversation, since the mere thought of talking to a stranger made my stomach fill with butterflies and my palms go sweaty. No wonder my dating life was so anemic. Although I had the ability to attract a man, keeping him interested when I fumbled over my shyness—not so much.

I took another sip of my wine, caught a flash of Lena's auburn hair before she was pulled deeper into the crowd, and then a stir across the dance floor pulled my attention. There were at least six ladies dressed in the shortest, most revealing dresses that I'd ever seen. Every one of them was gorgeous, but it was the man walking in their midst that had my complete attention. He was dressed in faded jeans, a black tank, and boots. He had to be at least six four. His short, spiky black hair framed a face of sheer beauty, but it was the tattoo sleeve that covered his left arm that captivated me. The design was indiscernible from my distance and, never really having a feeling about tattoos one way or the other, I found it to be both beautiful and sexy as hell. Maybe I was moved in this case because of the arm; it was a spectacular arm with a wide shoulder, thickly muscled bicep, and a powerful forearm.

He moved through the crowd, which parted for him to pass—like Moses and the Red Sea—and appeared just to my right with his bevy of babes giggling and tossing their hair. I turned from the scene, since the man clearly wasn't wanting for female attention. The women at the bar—dates be damned—strained their necks for a glimpse of him. I looked down at my jeans and black, sleeveless blouse as a grin curved my lips—nothing sexy about that. My hair, my greatest feature, was long and thick, but instead of blond or red as most men preferred, it was brown, the same color as my eyes. I was definitely not in the same league as the beautiful people just down the bar.

A sudden shove at my back almost made me spill my wine; when I turned to face my assailant, I knew immediately that he was drunk out of his mind.

"Hey, babe. Want to dance?"

Dance? This guy was barely standing up, swaying like a high-rise in a strong wind, so it was rather ambitious of him to even consider walking to the dance floor, let alone actually dancing. I didn't want to offend him, but I sure as hell didn't want to dance with him either, so I smiled and replied firmly, "No, thanks."

He grabbed me, and considering his drunken stupor, I was surprised at the accuracy of his movement.

"Come on, babe." His hands moved down my arms to my hips; I pushed at him, but he was strong and his hold remained steadfast. My annoyance turned into fear.

"Let me go." My voice wasn't quite steady as I tried in vain to pull away from him.

"Let her go." I turned my head toward the bartender, who was getting ready to jump over the bar, but he stopped when a shadow fell over us. It was tattoo-man looming over me and my would-be assailant. The drunk looked over his shoulder, saw who was standing behind him, and immediately dropped his hands before taking a few steps backwards. "I meant no harm, man."

I pulled my eyes from the avenging angel before me and looked into the terror-filled gaze of my unwanted suitor as my fear was rapidly replaced with anger.

"No harm? I said no!"

His eyes flickered to me and I saw the heat flash in them. I could see that he wasn't repentant at all and that just pissed me off. Before I knew my intention, I balled my hand into a fist and connected a solid hit to his jaw, leaning into it with my body just like I had been taught. At the sight of his head snapping back, my jaw dropped because I had just punched someone in the face. What the hell possessed me to do that?

"Bitch!" he howled.

He planted his legs, readying himself to go after me, but faster than my mind could process it, something flashed before me, and my attacker's eyes rolled into the back of his head as his body dropped to the floor. I looked over at tattoo-man, who was steadily watching me and, though I knew the punch had come from him, you'd never know by the way he was casually standing there.

"Are you okay?"

"I think so, but thanks for . . ." I gestured to the man currently lying unconscious on the floor as I held tattoo-man's stare, "that."

"No means no, right?"

I smiled before I replied, "Yes."

His finger ran down my arm before he reached for my hand and when he lifted it to his lips, his eyes stayed on mine.

"Trace Montgomery."

"Ember Walsh." My hand burned from the contact.

He said, "It's nice to meet you, Ember."

Before I could even think of a reply he released my hand and disappeared into the mass of bodies. I didn't miss the nasty stares that his fan club threw at me, but I couldn't focus on them, since I was too busy trying to remember how to breathe.

My attacker was still out cold on the floor as two bouncers came to drag him away. I just watched them, unsure if the previous few minutes had actually happened and, had it not been for my throbbing hand, I would have been more inclined to believe that I had hallucinated the entire scene. A hand touched my arm and I turned and looked up into concerned gray eyes. They were the bartender's, and he gently led me back to my seat as he hunched down to look me over.

"Are you okay?"

"I think so." I looked back at the now vacant floor and asked, "Did that all just happen?"

His chuckle immediately pulled my attention back to him. "Yes."

He reached across the bar for a full glass, then pressed it into my hand.

"Drink this. It's water."

"Thank you. I'm Ember."

"Luke."

I took a sip and realized that I was really very thirsty, so I drank the whole thing in one long swallow before Luke took the glass from me and placed it on the bar.

"Can I offer you some unsolicited bartender advice?"

"Sure."

"Trace Montgomery—I'd stay clear of him."

My inked rescuer—stay clear of him? I doubted the man would even recognize me if he saw me again. "I don't understand."

"He has a way with women. I see him night after night and they just flock to him. Thing is—he doesn't do relationships; he's a love-them-and-leave-them kind of guy. Any night of the week he'll be here with someone different. It's just who he is."

I expected as much, what with the flock of hens all poking around him, but I'd be lying if I said it didn't disappoint me. It didn't matter, since I never expected to see him again after that night anyway.

"Thanks for the advice."

He studied me for a minute and seemed to like what he saw as he smiled and stood up.

"Can I get you anything else?"

"Another glass of water would be nice."

"You got it."

An hour later I was ready to leave. Having not seen Lena since we first arrived, I tried texting her, but I got no answer. I said my good-byes to Luke and left my spot to search for Lena and Todd in the crowd, but the place was packed, which made my search point-less. I eventually made my way to the back near the restrooms and tried texting her again. While I stood there waiting for her reply, I noticed that I wasn't alone. Though it was a fairly dark corner, I had no desire to stick around to witness the lovers' tryst.

I had just started to move away when one shadow's head moved into the light and I saw that it was Trace. His back was to the dance floor and pressed between him and the wall was a woman. She was moving, pushing her hips back and forth, and it was only then that I noticed the hand of his inked arm was lost between their bodies. I couldn't pull my eyes from them because it was the most erotic thing that I'd ever seen, but sanity eventu-ally returned and I started away from them. I didn't get far—when I took one last glance at Trace, I found a pair of steely-blue eyes looking right at me. My feet just stopped as I stared back. He didn't stop his ministrations and, based on the sounds that his friend was making, she was getting close, but his eyes never left mine.

I couldn't help but imagine that he was bringing me to climax and the thought made my body clench hard with desire. It was the tingling of my body, the warming of my blood, and the sharp pang of want that pulled me from my lust-induced haze. With the return of reality came shame, and I turned and fled at the exact moment Trace's friend found her release.

⸻

In the morning I woke and just lay there thinking about the previous night. I really didn't get the club scene, but I was obviously in the minority considering how crowded Sapphire had been. I thought about the drunk guy and how, if I had said yes to his charming invitation, he'd have learned a valuable lesson this morning regarding the negative correlation between drinking and perspective since he'd obviously been wearing beer goggles last night if he was interested in me. And then, of course, there was my sexy hero. Being pawed by a drunken idiot had been worth it to get an opportunity to meet that man. I thought that I'd probably never see him again, but damn, he really was something else. I tended to avoid the opposite sex after my one and only sexual relationship had gone so horribly wrong, but Trace Montgomery could be my cure for that.

I didn't like thinking about my ex, the Creep. I refused to acknowledge him by name because he had made it his job to tell me all the areas in our relationship where I was lacking. He claimed that I didn't take initiative, wasn't bold or responsive enough, which was why he was unable to seal the deal more times than not. I know now it wasn't me who was lacking, but there was still a part of me that believed him.

I climbed from bed and made my way down the hall to the kitchen. Lena was sitting at the table having breakfast.

"Hi, Lena. Morning."

"Morning."

I reached into the cabinet for my granola bars, my standard breakfast, when Lena offered, "I ate the last one."

"Oh, okay. Did you have fun last night?"

Lena leaned back in her chair as a smile curved her lips. "I did." And then her focus zeroed in on me.

"What did you think of Todd?"

I really hadn't had an opinion on Todd considering that as soon as the introductions were made, I didn't see him again for the rest of the night. In fact, I ended up coming home alone. True, I was walking quickly for the door after "the incident," but still, I'd come with Lena. She could have at least told me that she was leaving. It was rude of her not to.

"He's very handsome and he seems quite taken with you, but what happened to you last night?"

"Todd wanted to leave."

I was on my way to the refrigerator for my coffee beans when she said that. It wasn't just what she said, but how she said it. Todd wanted to leave and the fact that she had come with me meant nothing?

"You could have told me you were leaving."

When her eyes found mine, she actually looked a bit annoyed before she said, "Oh, right. Sorry. I honestly forgot you were with us. You can't blame me, Em, since you act like a wallflower whenever we go out."

I just stood there looking at her as she blamed me for why she and her boyfriend had left me. I couldn't lie, that annoyed me, but she was excited about her date so I let it pass.

"I met the most incredible guy last night. Did you see him: tall, black spiky hair, tattoo down one arm?"

A strange look passed over her face. "No, Todd and I were busy." She grinned. "Did you get his name?"

"Trace Montgomery."

"So, did you hook up with him?"

"It wasn't like that."

"Right, you're still tender from the Creep. You should dip your feet back into the pool." She wiggled her eyebrows at me before she stood. "You're older now and less closed off, so whatever was lacking before probably no longer is."

She stood and started down the hall to her room and I just watched her as what she didn't say screamed in my head: whatever *I* was lacking.

———————

That night I had to work at Clover, a restaurant where I waitressed. I stood at the pass in the kitchen waiting for Chef to add the mango confit to the scallops as I marveled—and not for the first time—at how anyone could afford an eight-hundred-dollar dinner. It boggled my mind, but then, as I was raised the daughter of a Philly dockworker, so did most things in Manhattan.

Mom died when I was three and, having been so young, I didn't remember her, but Dad was really good about keeping her alive in our thoughts. Even my name was a reminder of her, modified from her middle name, Emmeline. I was their Ember, the lingering and enduring proof of their remarkable love. And she was the love of his life. When she was taken so suddenly by a hit-and-run, he vowed he'd never remarry.

It was a bit awkward—especially during my adolescent years—learning about my period and the birds and the bees from my dad and his dockworker friends, but they also taught me how to cook the basics, throw a punch, change a tire, overhaul an engine, and play a mean game of poker. I also developed a love of movies from watching them with my dad. He shared all of my mom's favorites with me and I felt closer to her when I watched them. It wasn't really a surprise that her favorites became mine too. Lena didn't always understand my dated movie references, but equating my life with movies that had made an impact on my mom's life was my way of keeping her with me. After graduating from the University of Delaware, I made the hard decision to pick up and move states to New York City, because I wanted to be a writer and the never-ending font of material that the city provided was just too tempting. I spoke to my dad nearly every day and we saw each other on every holiday, so it hadn't been too bad.

Chef pulled me from my thoughts. "Ember . . . before it gets cold."

"Sorry, Chef."

I walked out into the elegantly appointed dining room with dark walnut paneling, crystal chandeliers, stone fireplaces, and hardwood floors. The starched, white linens provided the backdrop for exquisite flower arrangements, sterling-silver flatware, Royal Crown Derby dishes, and Waterford Crystal stemware. Having come from Fishtown, I hadn't known what any of these things were until I started working here and, despite the beauty of the place settings, I still favored my mismatched earthenware dishes, stainless-steel utensils, and vintage McDonald's *Star Wars* drinking glasses.

Clover was located on the Upper East Side, near Central Park, and it felt like a different world when I came here from the fourth-floor walk-up that Lena and I shared in the Garment District. For one thing, there were trees and green grass, and seeing that in the middle of a city made it feel more welcoming and safe.

I liked working here, since I was practically invisible; the less I spoke, the happier my customers were, so when it came to tips, I raked it in.

I stood in the back checking on my tables and couldn't help but wonder what the owner was like. This wasn't his only restaurant in town and not even his most exclusive, so how much money must he make a night when not a table was empty?

I moved to the bar where my friend Kyle Donahue was working as bartender. We discovered we'd each had a relationship from hell and so we bonded, lots of late nights closing up the restaurant and sharing relationship horror stories about the Creep and the Soul Sucker. Kyle became the brother I always wanted and I trusted his opinion completely.

He greeted me with a smile. "So how was last night with meeting the Second Coming?"

Kyle was referring to Lena's new boyfriend, a pretty accurate nickname considering how Lena talked him up, but Kyle was calling him that because he didn't like Lena. It was one point in which we were at odds. Kyle thought she was vain, arrogant, and completely out for herself. Yes, she had a selfish streak but I didn't think she was as bad as he made her sound.

"He seemed very nice."

My eyes caught him as he faked a shiver. "Nice. What a glowing review."

"I really can't say more—I was with Todd for all of a minute. Lena's happy, so I guess that's all that matters."

"Naturally," he muttered with a bit of rancor.

"Not now, Kyle."

He rested his arms on the bar and leaned forward. "One day you'll see what I do."

I was prevented from rolling my eyes at him by his question, "So did *you* meet anyone?"

Just thinking about Trace made my heart rate speed up. "I did. It was right after I punched a guy in the face."

Kyle was horrified. "You what?"

"Yep, he wouldn't take no for an answer. I still can't believe I resorted to violence, but in my defense he sort of reminded me of the Creep. All those daydreams of me nailing that bastard in the face came flooding back and before I knew it, I was curling my fingers and swinging."

"I don't know if I should slap you on the back or give you a stern talking to. He could have hit back."

"Yes, well that's when my savior stepped in."

Something dark passed over Kyle's face in reaction to the thought of someone harming me. He replied fiercely, "I like him already."

"He was pretty amazing."

"And?"

"There is no *and*. I won't be seeing him again. We don't move in the same social circles. Besides, he is so out of my league."

"Did you at least get his name?"

"Trace Montgomery."

"Well, that's a start."

"Pipe dream, Kyle."

"All good dreams are, which makes it that much cooler when you achieve them," he said confidently.

"Wise words, Yoda."

He grinned before he straightened. "Get back to work, slugger."

"Yes, sir," I said with a salute and started away from him.

But he called after me, "We aren't finished with this conversation."

I waved my hand over my head in acknowledgment, walked to my next customers, and almost tripped over my own two feet when I saw that they were Todd and Lena.

"Hi, Em. Can you believe it?" she whispered as she looked adoringly across the table at Todd.

"What a pleasant surprise. Can I get you something to drink while you look over your menus?"

Todd turned those hazel-green eyes on me and requested a bottle of Bordeaux. His French sounded perfect but then how the hell would I know the difference? On the surface he seemed quite charming, if not a bit arrogant trying to impress us with his French skills; even so, an uncomfortable feeling of foreboding worked its way down my spine. Throughout their meal I watched Todd and Lena and wondered what exactly he did for a living that he could afford to bring a girl, who he'd only just started dating, to a restaurant that cost more money for one meal than I made in a week. After dinner they stood to leave and Lena leaned over and whispered, "Don't wait up for me, Em."

She smiled as Todd reached for her hand and pulled her from the restaurant. I grabbed the check and noted that Todd had given me exactly 20 percent tip. Why that rubbed me the wrong way, I couldn't say.

When I returned home after work, I was surprised to find Lena there. Based on how she and Todd had been acting at dinner, I wasn't expecting her. I dropped my keys on the counter as I walked into the living room.

"Lena, what's wrong?"

The surprise in her expression mirrored my own when she looked up at me. I had the sense she was so lost in her thoughts that she hadn't heard me entering the apartment. I settled on the edge of the sofa.

"Is everything okay?"

"Yeah, Todd had to cut our date short. He had some business thing to attend to."

A business thing at ten in the evening—not likely. "What does Todd do?"

I noticed that her shoulders tensed and she looked defensive when she offered, "He's an investment banker."

I wondered what was up with her reaction to my question, but I didn't push it.

"Did you enjoy your dinner at Clover?"

"It was delicious."

"That must have been a real treat for you."

"It was. He was really excited about landing a big client, so it was a celebratory dinner."

"Nice."

"It was, which is why I'm a bit sad that the evening was cut short, but I understand; work is work."

I didn't understand what kind of investment banking business would pull a man from a date at ten in the evening, but I didn't say as much.

"I'm beat. I'll see you in the morning."

"Night, Em."

In the morning I dressed and hurried downstairs, where Kyle was waiting. We were heading into Central Park for a jazz festival. It was a beautiful day and as soon as I stepped outside, Kyle smiled big and pretty.

"Are you ready for a day of jazz, Ember?"

"I am."

We started down the street and I could see how excited Kyle was. He was a musician who adored jazz, so for him to have an entire day where he could sit under a tree and listen to it, yes, he was going to be in heaven. I enjoyed the music but my motivation for joining him was more for his benefit. He liked the company, liked to share the music, and it was something small I could do but it meant so much to him. We stopped off for some coffee, then made our way into the park. We found a nice patch of grass and sat down. Kyle actually dropped down onto his back, closed his eyes, and lost himself in the music.

I leaned back against a tree, drank my coffee, and did some people watching. Sometimes the writer in me crafted stories about the people I saw, but today I just observed. There was one couple, hand in hand, giving each other looks of adoration. It was sweet, but I had the sense they had yet to have their first argument.

Another couple walked by with a screaming toddler. There wasn't adoration in their expressions, but complete exhaustion. And then the elderly couple passing by made me sigh. They had to be in their eighties and yet they were holding hands. You could see how comfortable they were with each other after having shared a lifetime together. That was what I wanted: someone who knew me better than I knew myself, someone who knew all the worst parts of me, yet still loved me.

While watching the elderly couple, I noticed a tall man farther down the path, who was walking toward the music. As he approached I saw the spiky black hair and the tattoo on his arm—Trace Montgomery. I just stared, since I couldn't believe I was seeing him again. What were the odds? I wondered if I had the power to conjure him at will, since, if I was being honest, he'd been in the back of my mind since we met. He stopped by a tree, leaned up against it, and listened to the music. I had the strongest urge to go over and talk to him. Considering I usually couldn't get past my nerves to engage a man in conversation, the fact that I wanted to engage him was odd.

I watched as women approached him, but what was interesting was the look on his face as they did. He looked annoyed, which seemed contrary to his reputation as a player of the first order. He didn't actually engage any of them in conversation and it seemed that when asked something, he replied with as few words as possible. You could tell by the looks some of the ladies were giving him that they knew him intimately, and yet there was no familiarity in his expression, just irritation. You'd think he'd be more flirtatious, but with the expression he was sporting, I was surprised women were brave enough to talk to him, let alone sleep with him.

Since I was far enough away from him, I let myself really study his face. He had nice cheekbones, a strong jaw, a poet's mouth with full lips that were definitely kiss-worthy, and a nose that'd been broken a time or two, which kept him from looking too perfect. His face was gorgeous but hard and there was a coldness in those beautiful eyes. I had become so lost in that face that I didn't realize he was looking in my direction, and then to my utter horror I realized he was looking right at me. There was a slight grin on that mouth and, damn, but that grin was sexy as hell. I wanted to stare back, but I quickly turned my head away from him. My heart pounded like a frightened rabbit's, and I could sense that those eyes were still watching me. I smacked Kyle harder than I meant to.

He bolted upright. "What the hell, Ember!"

"That's him," I said bluntly.

"That's who?"

"Trace Montgomery."

Kyle turned his head in Trace's direction, which made me hiss, "Don't look!"

A grin pulled at the one side of his mouth. "Why not?"

"Because then he'll know we're talking about him."

He leaned closer and now he was smiling. "We are talking about him."

"Well, yeah, but he doesn't need to know that."

"I'll be discreet." Before I could say another word he casually turned his head in Trace's direction. I had to give it to him, he was very discreet.

"Not what I pictured," he said honestly.

"Better or worse?"

"Neither, just different." His voice had lost the teasing quality it had had a second ago. "He isn't out of your league, Ember, he's playing an entirely different game. Please make sure you know the rules before you start to play."

There was no real-life scenario where Trace Montgomery and I would ever interact. The notion wasn't even in the realm of possibility.

"I appreciate your concern, but him and me? Never going to happen, so don't worry about it." My look must have conveyed my thoughts.

"Again I say, one day you'll see what I do," he touched my chin with his thumb before he lowered himself back on the grass and shut his eyes. I smiled at him before I leaned back against the tree, closed my eyes, and got lost in my thoughts as well.

A half an hour later I worked up the nerve to look in Trace's direction. The expression about opportunity knocking was rattling around in my head, which was why I decided that if he was still there I was going to walk over to him and thank him for coming to my aid the other night. But when I looked over, he was gone.

For the rest of the day my mind happily lingered on Trace. I had the feeling that he remembered who I was and that knowledge had filled my belly with butterflies. It was foolish for me to think about him, but I couldn't seem to help it. There was something about him that intrigued me. Thoughts of him had taken up residence in my head and I just couldn't seem to expel them—not that I really wanted to. What was the harm in admiring him from afar?

A few days later, Clover was sponsoring a 5K race in Central Park. All the proceeds from the day, including the profits from the restaurant sales, were going to various charities supporting underprivileged children. When I arrived, I was happy to see the turnout for the event. I registered, got my number, and then moved to the side to warm up.

I wasn't there too long when I felt the oddest tickle down my spine and knew that Trace was near, even before my eyes landed on him. I actually felt the air still in my lungs. He was dressed in black sweats and a white tee that was snug across the muscles of his chest and arms. And how so like a man to be able to make sweats look sexy as hell. He was alone, but as he moved through the crowds I noticed the people, mostly women, started to gravitate toward him like magnets to steel.

I turned my eyes from Trace to the women near him and had to resist the urge to scratch my head. Who fixes their hair and applies makeup before going for a run? Their running clothes were not only designer, but they looked as if they'd never been worn. I felt like a bit of a slob next to them, considering my hair was pulled up into a messy knot, my sweatpants had seen better days, and my faded gray T-shirt had shrunk a bit over the years so that the words MAY THE FORCE BE WITH YOU were stretched across my breasts.

It had been only a few days since I saw him at the jazz festival. I was surprised and a touch suspicious at seeing him again in a city as large as this one. I'm pretty sure it was the shock that made me appear almost bold as I blatantly stared at him. As I watched I noticed again how he seemed detached from his surroundings, including the women flocking around him. I thought about going over to say hi, but the mere thought of doing so, in front of his fan club, made my stomach twist up in knots.

He must have sensed someone watching him as he turned those steel-blue eyes right on me. To my utter joy he started toward me. I almost swooned and my knees actually started knocking. He really was the most gorgeous man alive and he had the most excellent swagger. His stride was long and yet he moved with a deliberateness that made my mouth water. When he stopped right in front of me, I got lightheaded and then real-ized it was because I was holding my breath. I released it with a smile just as he spoke.

"Hi."

I had trouble forming words, since my brain seemed to have seized up from shock, but I did manage a simple, "Hi."

He studied me with an intensity that warmed my blood. Unlike the aloofness I had observed both at the bar and the jazz festival the other day, there was a heat in his gaze that made my heart rate speed up. Somehow I managed to say, "I don't know if you remember me from Sapphire—"

I didn't get to finish my thought when he said, "Ember Walsh, I remember."

He remembered my name. I wanted to do a little victory dance. Looking at that face, I couldn't help smiling; he really was altogether yummy.

"Thanks for helping me the other night."

"I think you were doing pretty well on your own, but I was happy to help."

His voice was so deep and hypnotic. I could listen to him all day. I pulled myself from those thoughts before I started to drool or whimper or both.

"Maybe, but I really appreciated you stepping up, so thank you, Trace."

I noticed a flash in his eyes and I had the sense that he was surprised I remembered his name. The man was unforgettable; surely he knew that.

"You're welcome." We just stood there looking at each other and then he asked, "Do you mind if I join you?"

I was surprised and ridiculously happy about his request. "Please."

He started to warm up, the muscles of his torso bunching and cording under his tee. I noticed the slight coloring along his jaw. Clearly, the man had been in a fight since the last time I saw him, but considering he knocked my would-be attacker on his ass with very little trouble, I wouldn't have been surprised to learn that he was a professional fighter.

I watched as he continued to warm up with his face in profile. His tattoo was on the arm opposite from me so I still couldn't make out what it depicted, but I did see lots of flames. I was pulled from my silent study of him when the announcer called us to the starting line. Trace's eyes turned to me.

"Shall we?" When the gun sounded, I expected Trace to take off, considering his legs were so long. He surprised me, though, and paced himself to run at my side. At one point when I looked, he was looking back. I smiled before I turned my head, but knew my face flushed as red as an apple. I knew he saw it too, if the wicked grin he threw me was any indication. I didn't know what it was about this guy, but I felt like a teenager with a crush when I was in his presence. About halfway through, Trace moved a bit closer to me.

"I'll see you at the finish."

My eyes found his before I replied, "Okay."

He held my gaze for a moment and then he took off. The man was in prime physical shape as he moved himself through the masses. In only a short time I couldn't see him anymore. I didn't really expect to see him at the finish. I assumed his parting words were truly that. I was disappointed because I could have spent the entire day with the man and it still wouldn't have been enough. I found that I was very interested in Trace Montgomery and that kind of interest in a man had never happened to me before. Of course, leave it to me to develop a crush on a man who was so out of my stratosphere.

I finished the race, beating my personal best time, and started to warm down. The sky was an amazing blue and the clouds were like cotton balls so I took a moment to lay down on the grass and stare up. I remembered looking for shapes in the clouds with my dad when I was a kid. I always loved looking up at the sky because I couldn't help but wonder what was beyond it. I think it was one of the reasons why I loved *Star Wars* so much. Aside from it being my parents' favorite movie, which was enough to make it mine too, I liked that we got a glimpse into what could be out there in that vast unknown space.

A shadow fell over me and when I looked up, there was Trace. His smile was a nice sight, but obviously he was a figment of my imagination, so even as I smiled back, I closed my eyes and willed myself awake. His deep voice made my eyes snap open.

"Are you okay?"

"You're really standing there."

His smile was more a grin when he replied, "As you see."

"That's just it, I don't trust my eyes," I muttered.

"Excuse me?" he asked.

"Nothing."

There was a devilish gleam in his eyes as he offered me his hand and when I took it, I felt heat burn up my arm as he helped me to my feet. One look at his face and I knew he felt it too.

He seemed to recover before me when he offered rather softly, "It was nice seeing you again."

"You too."

He started away from me and I heard myself calling after him, "Trace?"

He stopped and looked back at me.

"I run here every morning at nine starting at the Gapstow Bridge and after my runs I go to the Starbucks on Fifth Avenue near the park. If you're ever in the mood for a run, I'd welcome the company."

His smile was sheer perfection before he replied, "I'll keep that in mind."

And then he was gone, disappearing into the crowd as I stood there staring after him.

I arrived at home a short time later, fantasizing about a nice hot bath. As soon as I closed the door, I heard strange moaning, which should have clued me in, but I wasn't really paying close enough attention, since my thoughts were preoccupied with the race and seeing and talking to Trace. It was only when I turned and looked into the living room that I blushed and quickly averted my eyes, because Lena and Todd were having sex on the sofa. I started to rush down the hall when I heard Lena's cry of outrage directed at me.

"Ember, really!"

"Aren't you supposed to put a sock on the door, Lena?"

"You weren't supposed to be home until later."

I couldn't actually believe we were having an argument while Todd was still thrusting. Perhaps I had stepped into an alternate universe. Today was just full of surprises.

"Well, go! Are you going to stand there and watch?"

She was pricking my temper, so to be belligerent I walked around the sofa and just stared at her. The fact that I got to see more of Todd was an unpleasant side effect.

"You aren't really giving me shit for walking into my own apartment, are you, Lena? If you and Todd want to get naked in the living room when you have a perfectly private bedroom, then you're going to have to expect interruptions."

I started down the hall and, though I couldn't make out what Todd was saying, I knew that he was talking about me.

I took an extra-long bath; when I finally climbed out, I looked like a prune, but at least my temper had fizzled. I changed into some sweats, dried my hair, and headed out into the kitchen. Lena was there, sitting at the table eating my leftover Chinese food. It was something she did all the time, and usually I let it go, but her selfishness was beginning to grate.

"You're eating my lunch, Lena."

She looked up at me and I could see she was still angry, so I cocked my hip and held her gaze.

"Sex on the sofa with a man you barely know."

She tried for haughty when she replied, "One thing led to another."

"Well, next time lead it down the hall to your bedroom because walking in and seeing your boyfriend's pasty-white ass is not high on my list of must-sees. Hell, it isn't even on my list."

"You're just jealous," she said as she stood, leaving her plate on the table and walking to her room.

I stood there watching her and realized that maybe Kyle did see something I didn't, because my best friend was turning into a bitch.

Chapter Two

For the next few days, I had a little extra pep in my step as I made my way into the park for my run and every day I felt that pang of disappointment when I arrived at the Gapstow Bridge only to find myself alone. On the fifth day, I lay in bed and decided to blow off my run. I felt like an idiot telling a man like Trace that I'd welcome his company—as if he'd want to spend time with me. I blushed every time I replayed that conversation in my head.

I climbed from bed and made my way into the kitchen to brew some coffee and realized I was out of beans. I changed into some sweats and headed out to Starbucks.

I was just down the street from coffee heaven when I felt that odd shiver down my spine and knew that Trace was near. I looked across the street and saw him, which made me feel a ridiculous amount of joy because I thought that he was making it for our run after all. This delusion lasted for only a moment because a younger version of Julianne Moore stepped up next to him and took his hand.

Of course she was stunning—that man together with me would be as comical a notion as Brad Pitt and Mrs. Puff from

SpongeBob SquarePants. Still, a girl could dream, and did I ever about Trace. To be able to touch every inch of that body, to feel those arms wrapped around me, to be pulled close, with the touch of his lips against my skin, and to be the one to make him lose control as he moved so deeply inside of me, over and over again . . .

Someone knocked into me, disrupting my very erotic day-dream, which was a good thing, since I was dangerously close to pulling a Meg Ryan in *When Harry Met Sally* . . . . I realized that I had been staring at Trace during my entire fantasy so I quickly moved it along on legs that had grown surprisingly weak.

Since I wasn't going to get the man, I decided to settle for the most decadent chocolate coffee concoction Starbucks could think up. In addition to my drink and coffee beans, I tacked on four of their cake pops to my order.

I was just leaving the place, coffee in one hand, bag of pops and beans in the other, when the door opened and in walked Trace with his beauty. Ah hell, and here I'd just shoved the entire Birthday Cake Pop into my mouth. I tried to hide in the shadows, motionless, hoping that Trace was like a T. rex and that his vision was based on movement, but when he said my name, my shoulders slumped as I turned, looking very much like a cow grazing in a pasture. And when my eyes finally found his, I was surprised to see tenderness.

"How are you, Ember?"

I put up my finger, giving myself a moment to finish my cake pop, and noticed that though Trace was looking at me kindly, his date—not so much.

"Hi, Trace." I felt disappointed, because when I mentioned this place to him, I hoped that he would come to see me, not bring his supermodel du jour.

But there was something intimate about the way his lips curved up as he held my gaze. Clearly, his friend noticed it too because she wrapped herself around him and pressed her very feminine body up against him."

"Come on, baby, let's go."

Trace's arm moved and, being so fixated on that fabulous appendage, I couldn't stop from watching as he wrapped it around her thin waist, his hand resting on her ass. It wasn't until he squeezed her and she moaned deep in her throat that I managed to pull my envious gaze away, only to find that he was still watching me. It was painful looking at the man you wanted more than a cake pop and knowing you'd never have him, because to do so would mean becoming one of many other notches on his bedpost. He must have seen something in my expression because his changed, ever so slightly. Standing near him was becoming too difficult, so I smiled as I started to walk around him. "It was nice to see you again."

I walked out of Starbucks battling disappointment. I didn't feel like going home, so I found a bench and sat down. There was a part of me—a rather large part—that sat there waiting to see Trace. It was stupid and juvenile, I know, but I was crushing on the man. Later I would have a stern talk with myself about acting my age.

Sooner than I would have thought, he and the beauty queen appeared on the curb outside of Starbucks. I watched as Trace hailed a cab and felt my stomach drop just imagining round two. A yellow cab pulled up to the curb and Trace opened the door for the woman, but instead of entering after her, he closed the door behind her. He didn't even wait for the cab to pull from the curb as he started down the street. Before I could argue with myself one way or the other, I was up and walking down the street after him. It could be argued that I was technically stalking him, but I was just too damn curious. Based on his performance in Starbucks, I'd thought that he and beauty were getting ready to get horizontal again, so the fact that he put her in a cab only moments after I left—I couldn't deny it; I was intrigued.

L.A. Fiore

I clearly was not cut out for undercover work; we hadn't even gone two blocks before Trace realized he had a tail. It was mortifying to lose him in a crush of people only to have him sneak up behind me a minute later. He said my name and I jumped ten feet off the pavement. I turned, knowing I was the color of a fire truck, and was greeted with the most devilish smile that I'd ever seen.

"Are you following me?"

I tried to look outraged, but was clearly as good an actress as I was a private investigator, based on Trace's amused expression. "No, of course not. I was just walking. It's a wonderful form of exercise—walking."

The slightest of grins pulled at one side of his mouth before he offered, "I've heard that about walking."

I didn't know how I managed to hold his gaze. And then I shocked even myself. It could have been the sugar from the cake pops or the caffeine or the adrenaline, but whatever the cause, I opened my mouth and asked, "So what happened to your friend?"

Trace shoved his hands into the front pockets of his jeans and rolled back on his heels. He held my gaze and I swear I saw humor dancing in his eyes before he said, "She was tired."

"I bet," I muttered before I added, "A shot or two of espresso may have helped her with that."

He said nothing, but his eyes were laughing. I didn't want to go; I wanted to stand there all day and talk to him. That was weird—weird enough to have me moving it along.

"Well, I should probably be getting home. It was nice to see you again."

"Would you like me to walk you home?"

"Would I ever," I said and then I realized I actually said that out loud. I spared a glance at Trace, who was full-out smiling at me. This would be a good time for a bolt of lightning to strike me down. I started backing away from him.

"I'm fine, but thanks."

"Hope you have a nice day," he offered with a laugh.

I was beyond words so instead I smiled, turned, and fled. I felt his eyes on me until I disappeared from sight.

<hr>

The following morning as I ate my breakfast, I contemplated my chances of getting into the witness protection program. The idea of changing my identity and disappearing from the face of the earth was oh-so tempting after my ridiculous display from the day before. I was pulled from my thoughts when my phone rang.

"You interested in going out tonight?"

"Oh, hey, Kyle. Yeah. Anywhere that serves alcohol."

I could hear the humor in his voice when he asked, "Why?"

"Because sometimes I can be stunningly stupid." Not only had I stalked a man, but I actually got caught doing so by said man. I didn't think I'd ever been more embarrassed in my life.

"Clearly there is a story there. You'll have to tell me later."

"Not if I can help it." What were the chances that I was going to see Trace again? This thought both delighted me and depressed me.

He laughed and said, "I wanted to check out Peacock. Does that work for you?"

Peacock was the quintessential smoke-filled jazz club, a hole in the wall with watered-down drinks and fantastic music. "Yup, what time?"

"I'll come for you around seven."

"Cool, see you then."

After breakfast I tidied up the apartment and read for a bit. At five, I started for my room to get ready when the door opened and in walked Lena. I was used to Lena being moody but things had been a bit tense with us since that day I walked in on her and Todd. Yes, the apartment was technically Lena's. Only her name was on the lease, courtesy of her parents' divorce and her dad's need to buy Lena's support, but I did pay my share. We split it half and half and so, even though our bedrooms were really no larger than closets, was it so unreasonable of me to expect her to have sex in her room? I tried to keep my annoyance from my tone when I greeted her.

"Hi, Lena."

She looked over at me, again with the odd expression, before she said, "Hi."

"I'm going out with Kyle tonight. Do you want to come?"

"No, Todd and I are going out. He's taking me to the theater." She moved through the apartment toward her room.

"That sounds like fun. What are you going to see?"

She tensed before she looked back at me.

"Why do you care?"

"I'm trying to make pleasant conversation."

She closed her eyes for a moment before she offered, "I don't know what we're seeing. He's surprising me."

I didn't understand how Lena couldn't see that her relationship with Todd was not a good one. It seemed she had changed so radically, so quickly. Or had she? Was Kyle right and I was guilty of seeing only what I wanted to? Had Lena changed or was I finally seeing her without the rose-colored glasses? Now wasn't the time to ponder that thought so I instead said, "I hope you have a nice evening."

And then I disappeared into my room, not bothering to wait for a reply.

———•◦•———

I woke in the morning and wanted to remove my head. Oh man, I felt like crap. It had been open-mic night at Peacock, and Kyle and I had performed but I had had a drink to calm my nerves before doing so. One drink led to another and by the end of the night, I was very calm and very drunk. I was tempted to pull the covers up over my head and sleep the day away, but I knew that once I started my run I'd feel worlds better. I dragged myself from bed, hastily dressed, and left the apartment. Yet when I reached the Gapstow Bridge, my feet just stopped. Trace was there waiting for me. Of all the days the man could have joined me he picked the day when I felt like something the dog dragged in. He turned in my direction as his eyes found mine. A smile touched his lips as he started over to me.

"How are you feeling today?"

Like shit, actually. There was a constant pounding behind my eyes and I was a bit off balance, but the run would help burn off the alcohol still lingering in my system.

"I've been better." I think it was the lingering alcohol that made me ask, "Why are you joining me this morning?"

"I felt like running and remembered your invitation."

"How did you know I would come today?"

"You strike me as a person who likes routine."

How did he know that about me? I wondered as I heard myself reply absently, "You're right."

"You don't mind, do you?"

I was more than likely hallucinating this entire conversation, but there was an edge to his voice, as if he was truly concerned that I didn't want him here. I'd only thought of him every day since we met. Hell, I was even willing to stalk the man. I held his gaze before I replied with stunning frankness, "I was following you the other day."

Heat flashed in his eyes before he offered, "I know."

"I've been hoping you'd take me up on my invitation."

I lowered my head at that admission. I was still mildly embarrassed. He touched my chin with his finger and lifted my gaze to his.

"I've wanted to."

I just stared at him, trying to understand his words. He wanted to, so what stopped him? I was so tempted to ask, but I chickened out. We warmed up in silence, and ran the five miles with Trace keeping pace with me.

While we warmed down, he said, "Are you going for your coffee?"

"Yes."

"Do you mind if I walk with you?"

"I'd like that."

We started out of the park and I couldn't help looking at him from the corner of my eye. The fact that he was here, with me, made my heart skip. My crushing paused when his voice filled the silence.

"There's a club that I thought you and your friend might enjoy. It's called Nocturne and it's in the Village. They have open-mic night every night."

How did he know we liked open-mic nights? I pondered and answered absently, "We'll have to check it out."

"If you do decide to go, would you give me a call? I'd like to hear you perform again."

"Again?"

"I may have seen a bit of your performance last night." Kyle and I often performed at open-mic nights, he on the guitar and me singing. It was an odd activity for me since I tended to avoid being in the spotlight, but I loved it. I got to step outside of myself for just a bit. I always blamed my boldness on my inner diva. Of course it helped that alcohol was involved, a sure way to remedy nerves.

I wasn't sure what to make of Trace seeing us last night. A warning tickled down my spine at how "randomly" we ran into each other. The statistical probability of that was very small and, though

I should be turning and running in the other direction, my gut told me that I was not in danger with this man. It was likely that my libido was doing all the thinking but I just didn't feel threatened. It also explained why he joined me this morning, because he probably saw the drunk idiot I turned into and wanted to make sure I hadn't caused myself harm. He knew what I was thinking when he said, "You were having fun. There's nothing wrong with that."

"I appreciate you trying to ease my embarrassment."

"Did it help?"

"Not really."

A thrill skirted my spine at the look he gave me. "So, will you call me?"

How I managed to retrieve my cell phone to add his number without fumbling it, I didn't know. My voice was barely a whisper when I replied, "I will."

We reached Starbucks and he held the door for me, offered a smile, and said, "See you." Then he was gone.

I immediately dialed Kyle. "Trace gave me his phone number."

"How did that happen?"

"He joined me for a run this morning." I wasn't going to say more, but the words sort of just tumbled out. "He saw us last night."

"He was at Peacock?" I knew what Kyle was thinking, which was confirmed when he added, "That's creepy, Ember. You don't know this guy and for him to be 'showing up' in places where you are as often as he is—he's stalking you."

"I think that's a leap. Seeing him at the charity run and jazz festival was unexpected but they were pretty huge events for the city."

"And Peacock?" he asked.

My reply sounded weak even to me, "Fate."

"I know you're smitten but don't let it cloud your judgment."

"Believe me, I understand your concerns. I'm having them too, but I just don't get a bad vibe from him."

"Yeah, well, serial killers are apparently really charming too, right up until they hack you into pieces. Just be careful," Kyle ordered.

"I will, and thanks. It's nice to have you looking out for me."

"We're friends, Ember, it comes with the territory."

That night I pulled out my laptop. I had been working on a novel for over a year. I had finished the story months ago, but I was forever tweaking it. Stalling because I was afraid to give it to someone to read.

I wish I was less introverted, but growing up motherless had been hard. I was treated with sympathy and pity but always at a distance, as if being motherless was catching. My dad was wonderful, but with him I developed interests that didn't blend with what other girls my age liked. It was just another barrier that kept me always on the outside looking in.

Writing appealed to me because, besides giving me a creative outlet, it was a way for me to share what was in my head. I suppose the healthier approach would have been for me to tackle what I feared by pursuing a career that forced me into the spotlight, but I liked the solitary life.

What was the point of writing, though, if no one was going to read it? This sentiment had been drilled into me by my creative writing professor. We still kept in touch; he had become a second dad, with encouraging and persistent reminders to follow through, to reach for what I wanted. I had told him about my novel and now he was sending weekly e-mails offering to read it when I was done. I'd been procrastinating, but how would I know if it was any good if I was too afraid to take the next step?

I launched my e-mail and replied to his most recent message. My hands shook as I typed,

Dear Professor Smythe,
    I've completed my novel and I would very much like your feedback.

I'm terrified to be sending this to you but
thrilled at the same time. Thank you for your persistent nudges. I know I wouldn't be taking this step
if not for you.

Anxiously awaiting your thoughts,
Ember

Before I could change my mind, I hit send and watched the hourglass with a pounding heart. Unease filled me when I saw the YOUR MESSAGE HAS BEEN SENT notification. It was too late to pull it back now. And though it was scary, I was excited. I wanted to write fiction, stories that allowed people to escape for just a little while, but whether or not I was good enough was another matter. As hard as it would be to hear it, I needed to know if I had what it took. If not, I was going to need to think about what I did next.

I needed a chocolate fix so I shut down my laptop and went in search of Ben and Jerry, my two favorite New England men.

———•———

Three nights later I debated with myself about calling Trace. I wasn't so naive that I didn't see the odd nature of our acquaintance, however, intrigue outweighed suspicion so I left him a message that Kyle and I were heading to Nocturne.

I stood at the bar with Kyle and found myself constantly looking toward the door.

I wasn't up to singing, since I didn't want to indulge in alcohol again, so I was going to accompany Kyle's most excellent guitar skills. I gravitated toward piano because it was a solo activity even when I was playing with someone else. I settled behind the piano and I lost myself in the music as soon as my fingers touched the ivories.

After our first number, the crowd cheered so loudly that we played another and then another. When we finally climbed down from the stage, several people shook our hands and gave us their business cards for potential gigs. Two spots instantly opened for us at the bar and fresh drinks were delivered, free of charge.

We spent the next hour talking and all the while I noticed the pretty brunette down the bar who kept looking over at Kyle. Her name was Cindi and she worked at Clover with us. I knew Kyle saw her too, since he was looking back.

"Kyle, go say hi."

"I don't want to leave you here alone."

"I'll be fine. Go."

A grin flashed over his face. "Okay, I'll ask her to join us."

"So I can become the third wheel? No thanks. Seriously, go."

He dropped a kiss on my head before he stood, grabbed his beer, and walked down the bar to the brunette. I grinned, watching them for a minute, before turning my gaze to my wine. I was disappointed that Trace hadn't come, but I hadn't actually spoken with him earlier—only left a message—and knowing he probably had a very active social life, it wasn't really a surprise.

I finished my drink and looked over to see that Kyle and Cindi appeared to be hitting it off. I was tired anyway so I was going to call it a night. I walked toward them and Kyle smiled as I approached before he said: "Ember."

"Hi." I turned to Cindi. "Great place, isn't it?" I had never noticed how pretty she was with her chestnut-brown hair and bright-blue eyes. I sensed a bit of shyness when she addressed me, but she didn't seem to suffer that affliction when she was talking to Kyle. This observation made me smile.

"It is."

I turned my eyes back to Kyle. "I'm going home."

"Okay, I'll help you get a cab."

"No, I'm fine."

"Are you sure?"

"Yes." Kyle pressed a kiss on my cheek before he whispered, "Be safe."

"Yes, Dad. Good night, Cindi."

"Night, Ember."

I walked through the club and out the front door and as I stepped into the cool night, I paused. At the curb, Trace was just then parking his motorcycle. I couldn't help but smile; it was completely involuntary. I watched as his denim-clad leg swung over his bike and I took a minute to appreciate the motion. He turned and a smile spread over his face.

"Ember."

"Trace."

"I missed you playing, didn't I?"

"Yes."

"Were you leaving?"

"I was."

"I'm sorry I'm late." He reached for my hand. "Will you come with me?"

It wasn't fear I felt at the idea of going somewhere alone with him, but I couldn't deny I was a bit apprehensive. Trace interested me more than any other man ever had. Somehow I knew that this was a defining moment. I could say no, catch a cab, and stay safe within my small, sheltered world, or I could throw caution to the wind, climb on the back of that bike, and make my own magic. It was an easy decision. "Sure."

He pulled me to his bike and placed his helmet on my head. He straddled the black-and-chrome beast so I could climb on.

"Hold onto me."

We flew down the street and rode around for a while, the cool night air feeling wonderful against my skin. Eventually, we pulled into a tight space on the street and I understood the appeal of a motorcycle in the city when you could park in such a small spot. I climbed down from Trace's bike, pulled the helmet from my head, and placed it on his handlebars. He wrapped his hand around mine and pulled me through the doors of a twenty-four-hour diner.

He settled across from me and took off his jacket. My eyes lingered on his left arm, where I could see the depiction of Hades and his realm of Hell with his demons burning in the fires of Purgatory. It was both disturbing and beautiful.

"Are you hungry?"

It was close to two in the morning and I hadn't eaten since five the night before. Before I could answer, my stomach answered for me with the loudest and longest rumble. I hoped that he didn't hear it, but when I saw the smile that cracked over his face I knew that he had.

He ordered enough food to feed a small country. The waitress needed three others to help her drop off the plates of pancakes, scrambled eggs, French toast, hash browns, sausage, and bacon, and I felt guilty that we would be wasting so much food, but I need not have worried about that. Trace plated for me enough food (a small fraction of what he ordered) to feed a three-hundred-pound man and proceeded to eat everything else. There wasn't even a curd of egg left.

"I've never seen anything like that. You just ate your body weight in food. I think you may have broken a world record. We should call Guinness."

He sat back and grinned.

"I'm a big boy."

That comment drew my eyes back to his most excellent form. I had to agree with him, but he was no boy, oh, no. He was most definitely 100 percent man. "So what are your interests outside of music?" he asked, unfazed by my perusal.

"I love reading. I like being transported to another place, to live a day in the life of someone else."

I saw the question before he asked it and added, "I had a difficult time fitting in when I was younger and so I escaped into books. For just a while I wasn't that awkward girl, I was whoever I wanted to be."

He was thoughtful for a moment. "What do you like to read?"

"I like everything: fiction, mysteries, horror, but I am a bit of a romantic, which is why I'm making my way through the classics. Currently I'm reading Charlotte Brontë's *Jane Eyre*."

"Is Kyle your boyfriend?" A shiver worked its way down my spine at that question. It was probably just my imagination, but he seemed very interested in my answer.

"No, he's just a friend. We met at work and discovered we have a lot in common."

"Where do you work?"

"Clover."

I noticed that something flickered in his eyes—a reaction, it seemed—but then he changed the subject.

"You're not a local." He wasn't asking.

"No, I grew up in Fishtown. It's in Philly. I went to school at the University of Delaware and moved here last summer."

"Why New York City?"

"I'm an aspiring writer, thought this was the place to be."

"And were you right?"

"Yes, I like it here. What about you, Trace, what do you do?"

He seemed to hesitate before he offered, "I'm an amateur fighter."

That certainly explained the bruises and his quick hands. I waited for him to offer more, but he didn't. Instead he leaned over and took a lock of my hair between his thumb and forefinger. "I'm glad we met up tonight."

"Me too."

Trace brought me home at seven in the morning and I was so tired I could barely keep my eyes open. I thought he was just going to drop me off, but no, he parked his bike at the curb and walked me to my door.

"I really had fun tonight, thank you," I said.

"So did I."

I wanted him to kiss me, almost puckered up, but he took a step away from me as he pushed his hands into the front pockets of his jeans. I had the sense he did so to prevent himself from touching me, but I *so* wanted him to touch me. Everywhere.

With a good-night I walked inside and turned as a smile touched my lips. I closed the door behind me and, though I couldn't see him, somehow I knew he lingered even after the door closed.

I climbed the stairs to my apartment and walked right into a heated argument between Lena and Todd. Todd saw me and hissed through his teeth as he stormed past me out of the apartment.

"Are you okay, Lena?"

Her green eyes looked up into mine and she appeared angry with me. For what, coming home? Being that it was seven in the morning, I think I gave them the apartment for long enough.

"I'm fine." She blew out a breath before she asked, "So how was your evening?"

My evening was fantastic but it didn't seem right to rub that in when she clearly just had a fight with Todd. "It was good. Nocturne was fun and after I met up with that guy I told you about, Trace."

She looked genuinely concerned when she said, "Trace Montgomery?"

"Yeah."

"Oh, Ember, I think you need to stay away from him."

"Why do you say that?"

"I mentioned him to Todd and he shared some pretty terrible stories about him. He's a pig, Ember, and he has no respect at all for women. He even seduced away Todd's girlfriend. You can imagine how painful that was for Todd to share. Even worse that Trace only wanted her for sex."

There was a note of disgust in her tone when she added, "She tried crawling back to Todd but he told me he doesn't do sloppy seconds."

If Todd thought Trace was such a predator then he'd have to have conceded that his girlfriend was a victim, lured in by a master. You'd think he'd have at least some compassion for her falling prey to such a mastermind. Calling her sloppy seconds sounded more like sour grapes to me. Perhaps the ex wasn't lured away, maybe she ran away. Lena continued on. "For someone like you, so inexperienced and closed off, Trace would make the Creep look like Prince Charming."

"I'm not closed off, I'm shy—there's a difference."

She shrugged, which prompted me to ask, "What's that for?"

"I don't think you're shy. I think you use the death of your mother as an excuse to keep your distance from people. To me, that is the definition of closed off."

She should have just slapped me in the face, it would have hurt less. No words would come—I was taken completely by surprise at her cavalier attitude regarding my mother's death and her arrogance in believing she knew my own mind better than me.

"He just wants sex, Ember, and based on what Todd told me, he can be very charming, but he's a real deviant. He's into some really sick shit, the least of which is doing several girls at the same time. There are a lot of nice guys out there—do yourself a favor and stay away from him. He's a heartbreak waiting to happen."

And then she stood and walked away. I didn't know what was worse, that Lena seemed to derive pleasure from hurting me or the fact that in the back of my head I agreed that Trace was a heart-break waiting to happen. My happy mood immediately soured as I made my way to bed.

I slept until two in the afternoon—I had been up for hours replaying our argument from that morning. I was genuinely shocked that Lena didn't hold me in very high regard. Our relationship wasn't perfect, but I truly believed she knew me. Her comments proved she didn't, which made her warning about Trace fall flat. Her opinion of me was so wrong and she'd had years to get to know me, so how well could she possibly know Todd and by extension his motives for the warning? Todd could just be jealous that his girl left him for Trace. I would have thought Lena would have questioned that but she chose to believe him because she wanted to.

The man Lena described was not the Trace I had come to know. From what I'd seen of Todd, he was the deviant and the one who held no respect for women. Trying to make Lena see that would be a wasted effort. I could tell from the movement in the other room that Lena was awake and there was no point in delaying the inevitable. When I entered the kitchen Lena was sitting at the table with a cup of cooling coffee in front of her. She was absently following the cracked lines in the table, so lost in thought that she didn't even hear me enter.

"Hey, Lena."

Her head jerked in my direction before she stood and walked around the table to give me a hug.

"I am so sorry that I've been such a bitch. I could have found a better way to tell you about Trace. And what I said about your mom, that was out of line. I was just hurting and I took it out on you."

Out of line didn't mean not true. "Are you okay?"

"Yeah, Todd was drunk and upset over losing a big bet."

"A bet?"

"Yeah, you know: poker, sports, ponies. He likes to gamble."

And apparently even though Todd hated to lose he couldn't stop gambling.

"How often does he gamble?"

Her eyes shone like green fire in response to that question. "Not that often."

I could tell by the way her eyes shifted that she was lying.

"Is he like that every time he loses?"

She didn't answer, but then she didn't need to.

"Seriously, Lena, you need to really think about a relationship with him. Do you want to get involved with a hotheaded gambler?"

"He's more than that. Yes, the gambling is unsettling, but it's only a small part of who he is. I like him, I really do. Just give him a chance."

I was not as optimistic and worse, I was concerned that Lena could so easily dismiss what I thought was a serious red flag in Todd's personality. What could I say that would get through to her? Nothing. "Okay."

Lena remained on my mind a good portion of the day. Despite the fact that I was angry at her, I still cared and her situation caused knots in my stomach. We were going through very similar issues. She was falling for a gambler with anger issues and I was fixated on a bad-boy player. Both scenarios spelled doom from the start and yet, like Lena, I was drawn to someone who was not at all good for me. My spirits immediately lifted when my dad called later in the day.

"Hey, Emmie, how's the big bad city?"

"Conquered." It was my standard, ludicrous answer.

"How's Lena?"

"She's dating a gambler, a complete rage case."

"How long have they been together?"

"They just started dating."

"Gamblers are a tough lot, kiddo. Seems to me she ought to pull stakes and get out of Dodge."

"My thoughts exactly, but she wants to try."

My dad was silent for a moment before he offered, "I've been wanting to mention this and now seems as good a time as any. I know you and Lena have been close, since you were in school, but I think you need to look long and hard at your relationship."

"What do you mean?"

"This shyness you think you have . . . baby girl, I've seen you go toe-to-toe against a team of men with whom you've had a disagreement and hold your ground. I think if you spent less time with Lena, you'd discover that others don't see you the same way."

"Meaning?"

"She undermines you, Emmie, belittles you to make herself look better. She feeds off your insecurities and at the same time she uses them against you to keep you insecure. It was tough for you when you were younger, I know, and Lena was like your savior back then. But now I see it sliding the other way. You are accepting the role of the shadow while she stands in the spotlight, and worse, she's convinced you that the shadows are where you prefer to be."

I had to take a seat because this was the very first time I was hearing that my dad wasn't a fan of Lena.

"Why didn't you ever tell me this before?"

"I didn't see it when you were younger, but lately, yeah, it's been bothering me. I wasn't sure how to bring the subject up to you. Just be careful. Lena looks out for Lena and if the time comes when you need her to have your back, I wouldn't hold my breath that she will."

I knew in my gut that my dad was spot on.

"I will, Dad, and thanks for the advice. But you didn't call to talk about Lena, so what's up?"

There was silence for a moment before he said, "Ember, I don't mind that you still have a relationship with your uncle Josh, but could you maybe not call him so often? After every call with you, he calls me."

"And you don't pick up." My dad avoided my mother's brother like the plague. I didn't understand what happened between them to cause the rift but it had to be something big. At one time, my dad and uncle were thick as thieves and now they didn't speak at all.

"No, I don't." His tone was unwavering but I pushed anyway.

"Aren't you the one always telling me that life is too short? Don't you think it's time to move past your differences? Stop holding a grudge."

"Easier said than done."

"I'll make a deal with you. I will heed your advice on Lena if you take mine on Uncle Josh."

He didn't immediately answer and then he said, "Tenacious."

"I get it from you."

I knew he was smiling when he said, "All right, you've got a deal, kiddo."

"Was that so hard?"

"Watch it." But he was laughing. "Be safe. I love you."

"I love you, Dad."

Chapter Three

The reply I had been both dreading and anxiously awaiting arrived one week after I sent my e-mail to Professor Smythe. He wanted to meet to discuss my book. We arranged a meeting at a local café and as I sat there waiting for him with clammy hands, my stomach was doing flip-flops. Maybe my book was so bad that he wanted to tell me in person so he could be there with a wastebasket when I threw up. We were only talking about what I wanted to do for the rest of my life, not a big deal at all.

Every time the bell over the door rang, I looked up with my heart in my throat. Just when my nerves had reached their breaking point, in he walked. He looked older, even though it had only been a year since I last saw him. His salt-and-pepper hair had become mostly salt, but the kind, pale-blue eyes were exactly the same. As soon as he saw me, a smile spread across his face.

I stood as he approached because I had lost feeling in my legs so was hoping to get the blood flowing through them again.

He hadn't even reached the table when he said, "I liked it, a lot."

All the blood rapidly left my head and I almost pitched forward. The professor grabbed my arm, steadying me.

"You still with me?" He knew me so well.

"Yes."

He waited for me to sit before he followed. He wasted no time getting to the heart of the matter.

"I think your story is good, but I want to make it great. Tell me, Ember, have you ever been in love?"

I was surprised by both the directness and personal nature of his question, but I answered him. "No."

It was true, I had never been in love. I had liked the Creep, liked him enough to sleep with him, but I hadn't loved him.

"I knew that."

I narrowed my eyes at him and asked, "How did you know that?"

"There is a fairy-tale quality to your story, but it lacks that edge of realism. Even in fiction, people want reality. Good doesn't always win, love doesn't always conquer all, and it's the struggle to find the happiness in between that makes a story great. Your story could be great if you define that struggle."

He regarded me a moment before he asked, "Are you with me?"

I liked fairy tales and happily-ever-afters. I didn't read fiction for realism, I read it to escape reality, but apparently that preference was not in the majority. "Yes, I understand."

"I think you'll discover there's just as many magical moments in real life, if you know where to look. You need to put yourself out there and in order to do that I suggest that you get a job writing for a local paper. This will not only hone your writing skills, but it will force you to see the world in a different light. I have a few contacts who I'll pass your name on to if you're interested."

"Yes, please pass my name on. Trying to hone my style will be scary but I know you're right."

"It really is a lovely story and I'm proud of you for forwarding it to me. I know that was a hard step for you. I'll send you the names of the people I'm contacting on your behalf and then we'll see what pans out."

"Thank you, professor, for helping me."

"Like I've told you dozens of times before, I'm paying it forward. I see a bit of me in you and had I not been encouraged by a teacher I wouldn't be sitting before you now." He leaned back in his chair and took off his glasses and wiped the lenses with his shirt. "So tell me, what else have you been up to?"

For the rest of the afternoon my thoughts kept returning to my meeting with Professor Smythe. I understood his point and he was right that it would do me a bit of good to get more involved in the professional side of writing.

I was concerned about spreading myself too thin by trying to handle a journalism gig in addition to working at Clover, because I wasn't about to give up my waitressing job. How I happened to get the job only weeks after arriving in Manhattan, I didn't know. The tips were unbelievable and since it was expensive living in Manhattan, I needed the money.

That night Clover was sponsoring a benefit, this time for battered women and children. The menu included our most popular dish of each course and cost a thousand dollars a seat.

You can imagine my shock and confusion to look up at one point in the evening and see Trace enter. What did he do for a living that he could afford the two-thousand-dollar price tag for this dinner? Fighting couldn't be that lucrative.

His beautiful black suit was clearly tailored just for him and, though he looked elegant, there was no denying the hard, muscular body underneath it. The suit was offset with a charcoal-colored shirt and silk tie and to say he looked exquisite wasn't being fair to him.

The blond on his arm had sharp features hinting at a Slavic background.

I was filled with disappointment seeing him with her, but it was a good reality check. I naively hoped that our breakfast the other night might have been the start of something, but Trace didn't play the game that way. I needed to remember that.

I wasn't thrilled—actually I was downright annoyed that they were seated in my section, but, since the menu was fixed, I only needed to get their drinks and bring them their meals. As I approached, Trace's head moved in my direction.

"Hello, Ember."

"Trace, it's nice to see you."

I looked over at his date, who was watching me with very cold, pale-blue eyes.

"Can I get you something to drink?"

"Patron, neat," she said before she turned her head. The meaning was very clear, I had just been dismissed.

"Dalmore, neat. Thanks, Ember."

I looked over at Trace and saw the grin that was tugging at his mouth, making me smile before I disappeared to get their drinks.

The rest of the evening went the same way. His date remained a cold bitch while Trace was affable and polite. I wondered why he subjected himself to someone as cold as her, but as I watched them I realized that her coldness was directed only at me.

A commotion started across the restaurant where an older couple was being escorted to their table. I didn't recognize them, but clearly I was in the minority because they were causing quite the stir. They were seated at one of my tables and as I approached them, I was struck for a moment by how very familiar the man seemed.

"Good evening. Can I get something for you to drink?"

"Aren't you a pretty young woman?" the wife said. Her husband looked up at me as she continued, "What's your name, dear?"

"Ember."

"Hello, Ember." I almost had the sense that they were dissecting me, and the sensation sent a chill slithering down my spine.

"Are you from around here?" That was an odd question and I wondered why she would care. "No, I'm from Fishtown, Philadelphia."

"How lovely."

"Vivian, order your drink."

The man's voice sounded hard and unyielding, and I noticed the woman reacted to it immediately, like a turtle moving into its shell. She barely glanced at me when she said, "Vodka and tonic, three olives."

"Glenlivet, neat." And then I was dismissed.

I moved to the bar for their drinks and happened to glance over at Trace's table only to find him watching me. My knees went weak. With effort I pulled my attention from him and made myself busy.

When I did return to Trace's table, I found him sitting alone. There was a hardness about him that hadn't been there earlier. I couldn't help looking at the empty seat across from him. "She's in the ladies' room."

"Of course. Can I get you anything else?"

"No, thank you."

Before I could reply, his date returned and mustn't have liked the way Trace was looking at me because she made a production of reaching for his hand as she glared up at me.

"He's taken for the evening so you'll need to find some other stud to scratch your itch."

My jaw almost dropped at her rudeness as my eyes shifted from her to Trace, whose attention was directed solely on his date and from the look of him, he was pissed. I wanted to linger and hear the scathing comment that Trace was surely about to make but I chickened out. I placed the check on their table and hurried away.

It took will power that I didn't know I had to return to Trace's table to collect their check, and thankfully, the table was empty. I took the black leather folder to the register to close out the bill and had to lock my knees to keep from sinking to the floor when I realized that Trace had left me a 50 percent tip.

That night I couldn't sleep, since my thoughts were on Trace. His tip was beyond generous and a part of me thought that I should return it. In truth, though, it wasn't his tip but thoughts of him that kept me up and when I finally succumbed to sleep, I dreamt of him.

To clear my head on my story, I decided to take another run through Central Park. Though it was as muggy as every other day this summer, there was enough of a breeze that the air chilled my skin. My thoughts turned to Professor Smythe. It had only been a few days since we talked, but he'd already sent me an e-mail with the list of names he was going to contact. I didn't think there was a chance in hell I was going to get a job with any of the impressive publications on his list but I was going to keep my fingers crossed.

I wasn't paying close enough attention to my surroundings. I heard someone screaming and by the time I realized they were screaming at me, it was too late. I pulled my focus back just in time to have a head-on collision with a beast of a dog and we tumbled to the ground, our limbs flying everywhere. I attempted to draw breath into my lungs as the dog righted himself and loomed over my prone position. He then started licking me with his huge, wet, pink tongue. Fabulous. I turned my head to avoid the tongue and that's when I saw two pairs of black, scruffy boots. I followed the legs attached to those boots and had a moment of clarity. Trace.

I turned my eyes to his friend, and, honestly, what the hell was in the water where they grew up? Long black hair framed a face of sheer beauty as eyes, green as summer grass, looked down at me with humor. I closed mine for a moment and willed the ground to open up and swallow me. Trace reached his hand down to me.

I couldn't help the little thrill that worked through me. Trace knew I ran this route every morning. So this meeting was not a coincidence. What did that mean?

"Ember."

I accepted the hand he offered and stood up. The dog sat at the other man's side, as perfect as you please. I couldn't help the glare I gave the dog, which only made Trace's friend laugh out loud before he held his hand out to me.

"Rafe McKenzie. I've never seen anyone stop a dog like that."

I narrowed my eyes and had to suppress the urge to stick my tongue out at him. "Ember Walsh, and I was more than happy to play speed bump, but you really should pay better attention to your dog."

"He rarely runs off."

"Really? So today's an exception."

I saw his look of confusion just as Trace started to laugh. Rafe's dog was gone, again.

"Damn it." We all looked to see as the large black blob ran down a path in the distance. I'd walked dogs when I was a kid. I'd have walked more if any of the neighbors had looked like Rafe.

"What's his name?" I asked.

"Loki."

I put my fingers in my mouth and blew a loud whistle, which brought Loki to a halt. In a commanding voice, I called, "LOKI, COME!"

Like magic the dog trotted back to us, stopping just in front of me. I rubbed his head before reaching for his leash.

"Good come, Loki."

My eyes turned to Rafe to find him silently studying me. I handed him the leash as I smiled and spoke to him as if I was talking to a five-year-old, "You want to hold on to that really tightly."

He was expressionless for a moment and then he threw his head back and howled with laughter before turning to Trace.

"I like her."

I smiled. "It was nice to meet you, Rafe." I rubbed the dog's head. "Loki, be a good boy." When I looked at Trace, I found him watching me with an expression that looked remarkably like affection.

"Nice to see you again, Trace."

He reached out and touched his finger to a strand of hair that had fallen from my knot as he whispered, "Thank you."

Being so close to him, I felt my pulse jump, and I knew he saw it. I nodded my head in acknowledgment and then turned without a word and jogged away. I hadn't even made it out of the park when my cell phone rang and when I looked down, my heart skipped a beat.

"Trace."

"Ember. Are you free tonight?"

"Yes."

"I'll come for you around seven?"

"Okay."

I hung up and a smile spread over my face as I floated, not walked, home.

A few hours later I was cleaning the apartment with a smile permanently affixed to my face. When Lena arrived home, I wanted to talk with her about Trace, but one look at her and I could tell she was in another of her moods.

I never knew what was going to set her off and it made things uncomfortable in the apartment. She was turning into a complete stranger and I knew the reason for it was Todd. I told myself I wasn't going to say anything, but she was my friend and I wasn't being much of one if I said nothing. I joined her in the kitchen as she sifted through the mail.

"Lena?"

She looked up at me and I saw the temper behind her eyes.

"What's going on with you? You've been out of sorts lately."

"There's nothing wrong with me. Stop being so sensitive."

I felt my temper stir as I held her glare. "You've been a bitch ever since you started dating Todd. If he makes you so fucking miserable, why are you with him?"

"He doesn't make me miserable. I love him."

"You barely know him."

She leaned up against the counter as a nasty smirk covered her face. "You are going to give me advice on relationships? The twenty-three-year-old who has had exactly one sexual relationship and an unsatisfying one at that."

"And that's not a bitchy thing to say?"

"I don't need your permission or your approval. Stay out of my business."

"Fine, as long as you stop the catty bullshit, because your company lately sucks out loud." And then I turned without another word and walked to my room. What a bitch to throw that in my face! The Creep didn't want a girlfriend, he wanted someone to dominate. For someone like me already struggling with identity issues, when I finally found the strength to get away from him, I drew even more into myself.

It was one of the reasons I was so drawn to Trace: I actually felt almost bold when I was around him and that was not something I'd ever experienced before with guys my own age. Just thinking about him gave me the push I needed to get ready for my date.

Later, as I pulled the door open for Trace, he seemed to recognize something was off.

"Are you okay?"

"Yeah, just roommate trouble."

"Do you want to talk about it?"

I shook my head and he studied me for a minute before he asked, "Are you ready?"

"I am."

He reached for my hand and the heat from the contact warmed me to my core. He walked me to his bike and placed his helmet on my head, then straddled the bike so I could climb on. I liked riding with him, liked having an excuse to be so close to him. I was pleasantly surprised when we arrived at a small cluster of galleries in Far West Chelsea.

"One of my favorite artists has a show," he offered in way of explanation.

"Have you ever met him?"

"No, but I can relate to his work. It's like he's spent some time in my head."

He pulled me into a little gallery and handed me a glass of wine from a passing waiter before we made our way to the first painting. The artist was without question very talented, but his paintings were all very dark. Looking at his work you could all but see the demons that haunted the man and how he tried to exorcise them through paint.

At one point in the evening Trace began studying a particularly disturbing painting that depicted faces, elongated in terror. The eyes were black voids and the mouths had been painted to look as if they were shouting for help. He had become so fixated on the painting that he was oblivious to everyone around him. The look in his eyes broke my heart, a vacant look similar to the eyes in the painting.

I stood there watching him and realized why Trace could relate to this artist. Trace Montgomery had his own demons. My eyes moved to his arm and the tattoo. What secrets was he hiding? I had the strongest urge to wrap my arms around him and just hold him. Who in his life offered him simple comfort? There was far more to Trace Montgomery than met the eyes and I wanted to know him, all of him.

"What do you think?"

"His work is beautiful." And deeply disturbing.

"Are you ready to go?"

"I am if you are."

He took my hand as we walked from the gallery toward the parking garage. Before we reached his bike we both heard something. It sounded like a muffled scream, but the garage wasn't lit very well so it was hard to see anything. I felt Trace tense at my side as he walked me quickly back to the gallery.

"Wait here." Before I could say anything, he turned and disappeared.

I didn't wait and followed after him, but not before I alerted a passing waiter of the potential trouble in the parking garage. As I approached, I could hear the distinctive sound of flesh against flesh. And that's when I saw another part of Trace. He was pounding on some guy; his fist was relentless as he hammered into the man's face. I couldn't move, couldn't tear my eyes from the sight; the look on Trace's face scared the hell out of me.

I noticed the woman then. She was hunched near a car and I immediately hurried over to her.

"Are you okay?"

"I am, thanks to him."

I turned my head just as Trace dropped the now limp guy. When his eyes found mine, I saw a level of rage in him that was frightening.

"You were supposed to stay in the gallery."

"I wanted to help."

I watched as his fists clenched and saw that he was trying really hard to control his temper when he said, "I should get you home."

Was he angry with me? Would Trace ever hit a woman?

At that moment the owner of the gallery came out to see what was happening. Trace walked over to him, and they spoke softly for a few minutes before the man walked over to the woman and helped her to her feet. Two others came out to watch over the unconscious man so he couldn't run off after he came to.

"Let's get you inside and call the police," the gallery owner said to the woman before he turned to Trace and added, "I'll see you when you get back."

I heard the woman offer her thanks to Trace, but looking at him I could tell he wasn't really there anymore. Whatever put that empty look in his eyes continued to consume his thoughts. He walked over to me and reached for my hand as he said, "This was not how I saw the evening ending."

"Why does it have to end?" I asked.

He looked down at me and when he answered, his voice was whisper soft.

"I won't be very good company."

I didn't think, only acted on impulse, as I stepped into him and wrapped my arms around his waist. "You did a good thing here tonight."

I felt his hesitancy and then those arms wrapped around me and held me close. When he spoke, there was anger laced through his words.

"And you did a stupid thing walking into something blindly."

"Talk about the pot calling the kettle black. I was worried about you."

That made him pull away from me so he could look at me incredulously.

"Why?"

I didn't understand his question. "Why was I worried about you?"

"Yes." He acted as if the very notion was completely unbelievable so I answered with all honesty.

"Because I care about you."

He didn't say anything, just continued to look at me like I had six heads. He pulled me back into his arms, pressing me as close to him as possible.

"I should get you home."

"Thank you for tonight."

His lips brushed along my jaw as he whispered, "Thank you."

Chapter Four

I was lying in my bed the next day jotting down ideas for potential story lines, but I couldn't really focus on what I was doing because my mind kept turning to Trace. Yes, I was wildly attracted to him, but it was the lost, vacant look that I'd seen in his eyes at the gallery and the rage I saw later in the parking garage that occupied my thoughts. We'd made plans to meet that evening, and I couldn't stop thinking about him.

Promptly at five, the bell sounded and I pulled open the door to find Trace standing there with a smile on his face.

"You look beautiful."

My heart fluttered in response.

"Are you ready?"

"Where are we going?"

"It's another surprise." There was a dark side to Trace Montgomery. It should be my clue to stay away, but, despite that darkness, my gut was telling me there was so much more to him than the callous womanizer—that there was a really good man underneath.

I let him pull me down the hall. "I like surprises."

We climbed onto his bike and drove outside the city toward Long Island. About half an hour later, I saw the lights in the distance and a smile spread over my face. We parked and as I pulled off my helmet Trace came to stand at my side.

"The fair—we're going to the fair?" I asked and I didn't bother to hide my joy because I loved fairs.

"Yes."

"How did you know I'm a fair junkie?"

"I guessed," he said before he added, "Do you mind if we do the Ferris wheel first?"

I smiled as my heart hiccupped. The Ferris wheel was my absolute favorite. "Not at all."

He paid for the tickets and helped me into the chair. As soon as we were seated, he wrapped his arm around my shoulders and pulled me close.

"Are you cold?"

Being so close to him, I was more likely to ignite, not freeze. "No."

As the ride began its slow, circular spin, I studied Trace and the boyishness about him that I found to be absolutely charming. He caught me staring at him and before I could turn my head, he leaned over and brushed his lips over mine. He seemed almost to hesitate at first and then his hand moved to cradle the back of my head as his mouth settled more firmly over mine. It was a simple kiss, almost chaste, and yet every part of me responded to it. My heart pounded, my toes curled, and parts of my body stirred awake after a very long sleep.

While he didn't take it deeper, he seemed perfectly content to feast on my lips and I felt myself melting into him. He pulled back and his gaze burned with desire, but there was something else there too—something infinitely darker that sent a shock wave of anticipation through me.

Before I could embarrass myself by doing something truly appalling like jumping on him, the ride stopped. We climbed from the ride and, walking hand in hand, we slowly strolled around the fairgrounds.

At one point we passed a cotton-candy stand. "Oh, we have to get some," I said, which was met by a blank stare from Trace. I turned more fully to him and held his empty gaze.

"Have you never had cotton candy?"

"No," he replied and I couldn't have been more shocked by his answer.

"Never? Why?"

"How often do fairs come into the city?"

He was being dismissive, but somehow I knew it wasn't a matter of whether fairs came into the city but rather that he had no one to take him.

"Well, that's a crime. Let me introduce you to spun sugar."

I reached for his large hand, which he wrapped around mine, and I felt a connection to him that went deeper than the physical one. We approached the stand and I held up the money to the kid working the machine.

"One, please."

The mound the kid spun for us was huge, with enough sugar to satisfy even my sweet tooth. Trace and I stepped away from the stand and I held the blue cloud up to him.

"Just pull off a hunk."

As he reached for the cotton candy, I couldn't help the pang of sadness that filled me as I wondered how a man approaching thirty could never have experienced childhood things like cotton candy.

"It dissolves," he said mostly to himself and then he sought and found my gaze, a smile spreading over his face.

"It's delicious!"

I had to kiss his genuine smile.

"Hold this for a second?" I asked. He took the cotton candy from me and I wrapped my hands around his face. I licked his lower lip and heard him growl deep in his throat. His one arm came around me and pulled me close. My tongue sought entrance and when he parted for me, I tasted him fully as I ran my tongue over his. I pulled my mouth away and he responded by tightening his arm around me. I had the sense that he didn't want to let me go and I ran my lips under his jaw, trailing them down his neck before I forced myself to take a step away from him.

His eyes flashed before he pulled me to him and kissed me hard on the mouth. This kiss wasn't chaste like his last one. His tongue demanded entrance and once granted, he swept my mouth, tasting every inch of it. He released me, but it took a minute for my eyes to open because—damn—the man knew how to kiss. I wanted to know what he was thinking at that moment because of the tenderness that softened his features but then he gestured with his hand and asked, "Shall we?"

I smiled in reply and for the next hour we rode practically every ride. The rides were usually broken down when the fair moved from location to location and I must say that I felt scared for our safety when they rattled. Being with Trace, though, feeling his solid strength next to me, helped to alleviate some of my fears.

We reached one of the food trucks and he stopped and looked at me with the most charming expression on his face.

"Tell me, what's it gonna be? Chili dogs or funnel cakes for dinner?"

I couldn't help the smile as I replied, "Can't we have both?"

He pulled me closer. "I was hoping you would say that."

Later that night Trace brought me home and walked with me to my door.

"Thank you for tonight. I haven't had that much fun in a really long time."

A smile tugged at the corner of his mouth. "Me too."

I wanted to wrap my arms around him and kiss him, but I sensed a hesitation in him. A moment passed before he gently brushed his knuckles across my cheek.

"Good night, Ember."

"Night."

He waited for me to enter my apartment before he smiled, turned, and walked away. I was in some serious trouble.

After filling several pages with ideas for a new story, I started to write. I didn't have a clear idea where I was going with the story, but I thought if I just started typing, the story would tell itself. Concentration became an issue because I kept thinking about the fair with Trace from the other night. More specifically, about how I wanted him to kiss me again. A knock at the door was a welcome distraction—especially when I pulled it open to see Trace. Joy turned to anger and worry at the sight of him. He had clearly been in a fight, a particularly nasty one from the look of him. I spoke the first thought that popped into my head.

"We need to get you to a hospital."

"No."

Pigheaded, stubborn man. "Why not?"

"I hate them."

It wasn't so much his words but the fierceness of them that took me by surprise. I held the door open wider as I stepped aside. "Come in. I'll get my first-aid kit and meet you in the kitchen."

I was shaking as I walked down the hall to the bathroom. I grabbed my kit and the peroxide before joining Trace in the kitchen, where I found him bare from the waist up. Despite the fact that I loved his body, I couldn't avert my eyes from the purple welts along his rib cage. I knew he fought in ring matches but this damage was more savage.

"What happened?"

"I had a disagreement with a few guys."

"A few?"

"Four."

"Four against one?"

"It was good odds."

"Wait, what?"

His grin was wicked when he said, "I was the only one to walk away."

"Why did you fight them?"

He shrugged but didn't answer.

"Where did you fight them?"

"In an alley behind a bar."

"Do you mind if I take a look?"

Heat flashed in his eyes, so apparently he was just as eager to have my hands on him as I was. I had learned early how to tell when bones were broken, which was a daily hazard of my dad's job as a dockworker.

As soon as I touched him, he tensed and closed his eyes. I knew that it wasn't from pain but pleasure. His skin was smooth but hard and the muscles were so perfectly defined that I had to consciously remind myself not to linger too long on any one spot. It took effort to remove my hands from him.

My voice was a bit hoarse when I offered, "Well, you've got two cracked ribs and a broken nose. I can wrap the ribs and tape the nose, but maybe you'd like to get a shower first."

The thought of helping him shower, of running my hands over his beautifully chiseled body, was very nice. He seemed to know where my thoughts were when a smile cracked over his face.

"Don't worry, I can manage the shower."

"I'll put out a towel for you. I have a robe; it's one of my dad's old robes, so you can wear that until I get your clothes washed."

He stood as I started from the kitchen but his words stopped me. "Thank you."

I turned back to him to reply but one look into those steely-blue eyes and my words got stuck in my throat. There was pain there but there was something else too, something darker. I managed to hold his gaze as I replied, "You're welcome, Trace."

I couldn't sleep that night, and not just because I was on the sofa, but because Trace was sleeping in my bed. I had envisioned him in my bed more times than I could count but in every one of those fantasies I was with him. I'd insisted that he stay the night because if he was internally bleeding I wanted to be able to get him to the hospital.

I turned over, pulled my blanket over my shoulder, and tried for sleep. It took a good hour before the sandman had his way.

The following morning I woke to the smell of coffee and bacon. I peeled my eyes open and deeply inhaled that lovely combination of scents, and then I sat straight up and just stared. Trace was standing in the living room bare-chested, and thankfully—or maybe not—he had already put on his jeans. It was a nice way to wake, but I couldn't appreciate the view because the man was folding my laundry, my underwear to be more exact. I jumped from the sofa and grabbed the pair he was folding. I couldn't deny that when I wore these I was going to be thinking about his most excellent hands but at the moment I was too mortified to enjoy the visual. I heard him chuckle, forcing my attention back to him.

"I thought I'd fold these for you since you were kind enough to wash my clothes."

I immediately wrapped my arms around the pile of my unmentionables and started toward my room.

"Thank you but I'll finish this later."

I dropped everything on the bed. Trace had even made my bed. When I returned he was in the kitchen, scrambling up some eggs to go with the bacon.

"Are you hungry?"

I moved to join him and I reached for a mug. "Yes. It smells *so* good."

He turned his head to me with a slight smile on his face before he said, "It's just eggs and bacon."

"Yes, well, when your normal breakfast is a granola bar, this is gourmet."

He plated us each a mound of fluffy scrambled eggs and several strips of perfectly cooked bacon, set them on the table, then folded his large frame into the chair across from me.

"This looks wonderful, thank you."

"Thank you for last night."

"How are you feeling?"

"Sore but I'll live."

"Do you want to talk about it?" I asked.

He didn't have to answer since his body's reaction to the question answered for him. No, he didn't want to talk about it.

"Can I ask why you came to see me instead of going to Rafe?"

He held my gaze for a moment before he replied, "It was instinct. I started walking and ended up at your front door."

My heart twisted in my chest as I replied, "I'm glad that you did."

After breakfast, Trace helped me clean up and I wanted him to stay—really wanted him to stay—but he started for the door, grabbing his jacket as he went.

"Thank you, Ember."

"Any time, Trace, I mean that."

He held my gaze for a minute before he turned and walked out the door.

I was just finishing my coffee when Lena came home. I did a double take because she looked happy. I had been getting used to seeing the scowl on her face, but she was actually smiling.

"Hey, Em. Are you doing anything tonight?"

"No, I was going to work on my book."

"Are you interested in going out with Todd and me? It's been a while since we've hung and I miss you."

"I would really like that, Lena."

"Cool, Todd is picking us up around eight."

"I'll be ready."

She started from the kitchen as I called to her, "I've missed you too."

For the rest of the day I felt almost bubbly. I hadn't realized how much the tension between Lena and me had been bothering me. Todd arrived at eight and I was so happy to be out with them that I didn't even ask where we were going. When we arrived at our destination a bit of the happy feeling fizzled out—the place was a dive bar with a definite scary vibe. We weren't there for more than five minutes before Todd disappeared and stayed gone. It was then that I realized we were only there because of a backroom poker game. Did she not see that the love of her life didn't seem all that eager to spend time with her? Or, to be fair, that he liked gambling more than he liked her?

"Does he usually leave you alone?" Could Lena not see that her boyfriend was a loser?

"Just stop. At least I'm dating."

"Sitting here alone hardly qualifies as a date."

Her eyes narrowed at me as she leaned over the table. I knew she was thinking how absurd it was of me to be giving relationship advice to her when I lacked experience, but it didn't take a shrink to see that Todd was all wrong for her.

"I don't claim to be an expert, but I do know that Todd taking you out and leaving you so he can gamble is not a healthy relationship."

"Whatever."

I leaned back in my chair in an attempt to rein in the temper that was stirring to life. She absolutely refused to open her fucking eyes. My dad's warning played in my head. I wanted to leave, but I felt bad leaving her here, alone, in a not-so-safe place. What kind of guy brought his girlfriend to a place like this only to leave her alone to fend for herself? A gambling jackass, that's who. I didn't voice any of this to Lena and instead just sat in silence.

My phone buzzed and when I saw it was a text from Trace, my mind shifted gears and a smile touched my lips.

Are you free tonight?

Yes. I'm at McTaverish's Tavern, but I'm ready to go.

McTaverish? By yourself?

No, Lena and Todd are here.

I'm on my way. Stay with your friend.

So I wasn't the only one who thought this place was dangerous. A shiver of foreboding worked its way down my spine as I looked around the place. The lights were dim so it was hard to see, but I was definitely getting a creepy vibe. Moments later, Todd appeared, red-faced and angry.

"Let's go, babe."

Babe? I knew Lena hated endearments like that, but she made no attempt to correct him.

Todd turned to me.

"You coming?"

"No, babe, but thanks."

I didn't miss the flare of temper that burned in his eyes, but then he shrugged and started pulling Lena away. And Lena never gave me a backwards glance as she obediently followed after him. Nice.

So, there I was alone in this creepy-ass place. I wondered how far away Trace was. Should I text him again? I noticed a few guys at the bar, leering at me. It wasn't my looks, or lack thereof, it was the fact that I was female and alone. I was like roadkill and these guys were the vultures.

The surrounding neighborhood was a bit scary. Should I stay and be a sitting duck? I decided to go to the restrooms and lock myself in until Trace arrived. I stood and made my way through the crowd toward the dark corridor that led to the restrooms when a shadow fell over me and I looked up into very black eyes.

"Hello, there. What have we here? Aren't you a sweet little thing."

"Excuse me," I muttered and tried to move away, but his hand on my arm stopped me.

"Where's the fire, sweetheart? Let's get to know each other."

"No, thank you."

"Oh, come on, don't break my heart."

"I really have to go."

He moved then, pushing me up against the wall, pinning me there with his large body.

"I just want a taste."

I could smell the beer on his breath and the hard length of him against my stomach. My fear turned me numb. I tried to push him away, but that was as effective as the Big Bad Wolf trying to blow down that brick house. His fingers tangled in my hair and his breath brushed over my cheek. "Maybe you'll like it."

He lowered his head, but I turned my head right before his lips touched mine, causing him to press a kiss into my hair. I felt as his fingers tightened on my scalp and he turned my head to hold me steady.

"Just one kiss."

Panic brought my foot down on his instep harder than I planned, forcing him to release me as he howled in pain. His eyes returned to mine and I saw the violence burning in their black depths. He lifted his hand, curling his fingers into a fist, but before he could release the punch, a hand came out of nowhere and grabbed it, yanking him back so hard that I heard the pop of his shoulder.

"Fuck!" he howled as he stumbled to his knees in pain. When he looked up, I saw fear in his eyes as he saw Trace standing just in front of him.

"You dislocated my fuckin' shoulder."

Pain pitched his voice higher.

"Forcing yourself on a woman is bad enough, but hitting a woman is inexcusable." And without further ado Trace moved, with astounding speed, and plowed his fist into the man's face in a quick succession of five blows before the man dropped into a dead faint.

"I told you to stay with your friend."

"They left."

"Son of a bitch," he growled.

I felt the tears prick my eyes just as my body started to shake. Faster than would seem possible, Trace wrapped me in his arms.

His heart pounded against my chest, his body rigid and tense, but his embrace warmed me. In the back of my mind I could tell this hug was just as much to comfort him as it was for me.

"Are you okay?" he whispered.

"Yes."

"You don't belong in this place. Your friends are assholes." I could hear the anger returning to his voice.

He pulled back and looked down at me. I lifted my eyes to his and offered a heartfelt, "Thank you."

Even though his eyes still burned with temper, his lips quirked when he replied, "Rescuing you seems to be turning into a habit. Are you still up for going out?"

"Yes."

Once we were on his bike, cruising down the street, I rested my cheek against his back and I trembled just thinking about that man with his hands on me. Trace saved me again—and just in the nick of time. He really was my own inked guardian angel.

We arrived at a small club and Trace parked and waited for me to climb off. He reached for my hand and led me inside and once we were seated his eyes found mine.

"Are you okay?"

"I am now."

He leaned back in his chair, but I didn't miss the clenching of his jaw. "I'm trying to do the right thing here."

I rested my elbows on the table and asked, "What does that mean?"

His eyes never left mine when he said, "I want you, but I don't want to want you."

I was grateful to have the support of the table between us so he couldn't see how much his words hurt me. My voice wasn't quite steady when I offered, "I understand."

"What is it that you understand?"

I lowered my head before I replied, "You are so out of my league." I had been warned that Trace was a heartbreak waiting to happen but I'd refused to listen. I walked right into this, sadly with my eyes wide open.

His thumb touched my chin and when I looked into his eyes, the emotions I saw burning in them were unfathomable.

I heard myself say, "For the record, I want you too."

He said nothing, but stood and reached for my hand. "Dance with me."

I didn't have to think on that as I allowed him to pull me onto the floor. James Blunt's "You're Beautiful" was playing as Trace turned me to him and pulled me close so that our bodies were pressed together from chest to thigh. His arm came around my waist, pulling me even closer against his hard body, and he rested the hand that held mine over his heart. Our bodies swayed ever so slightly and his grip on me never eased, as if he was trying to absorb me into him. As the song played, he lowered his head so that his lips were right near my ear before he sang along softly.

It was instinct, and a deep want, that made me turn my head to press my lips to his neck, lingering until the song was over. His thumb touched my chin and lifted my gaze to his.

"I can't seem to stay away from you."

He framed my face with his hands just as his mouth captured mine. He tilted my head as he took the kiss deeper, sucking my tongue into his mouth and stroking it with his own. I felt as though my bones were melting and while I suspected I was about to spontaneously combust from the heat burning through me, I knew I would die a happy woman. With effort, his mouth moved from mine. He pulled me up against him and held me there for a good long time.

Chapter Five

It had been four days since I'd last seen Trace and I still had the sensation that I was floating. Complicated didn't even come close to describing him, but I was completely captivated. I moved on autopilot, performing my day-to-day activities as I struggled for focus. Reaching Starbucks after my run, I ordered my coffee. I was about to give the woman a twenty when a hand stopped me.

"My treat."

Goose bumps appeared as I turned to see Trace standing there. "Hello, Ember."

"Trace!" Seeing him had a warmth burning through me.

We started from Starbucks. "Thanks for the coffee," I said as I eyed him from over my cup.

His head turned in my direction and our eyes met and held. "Did you run this morning?"

"Yes. I run so I can feed my cake pop habit."

A grin flirted around his lips. I wanted to kiss him, wanted to throw myself into his arms and feel those lips on mine again. But I didn't. His words the other night—that he wanted me but he didn't want to want me—prevented me.

Walking this close to him I had a better view of the tattoo that ran up his neck to his hairline. "What is that on your neck?" I asked.

"Celtic symbols."

"Does it hurt?"

"Getting a tattoo?"

"Yeah."

"Irritating, but not necessarily painful." His lips turned up on one side before he asked, "Are you inked?"

I almost choked on my coffee at that question. "No, it's so permanent. I'd only do it if I knew with absolute certainty that what I wanted done I'd want forever. How often is anyone that sure?"

"It's just as well. You have beautiful skin. It would be a crime for you to mark it."

The compliment made my heart flutter before I asked, "Can I see the one on your arm?"

I knew I'd thrown him with that question, but he reached for my hand and pulled me from the sidewalk to the shade of a tree before he took off his jacket and pulled his T-shirt sleeve up over his shoulder.

Hades was depicted as half-monster, half-man, sitting upon his throne, naked and aroused. Above him, angels flew, but they were in one of three poses: hear no evil, see no evil, and speak no evil. Below him bodies writhed, elongated and distorted, like the masked dude from the movie *Scream*. They clawed at each other, trying to escape the pit. The entire scene was surrounded with fire: brilliant orange, red, and yellow flames that looked to be dancing up his arm. I ran my finger over one particular flame that started out red, but faded to orange and then to yellow as it grew; the transition was seamless and the work was so flawlessly executed.

"It's beautiful. How long did it take?"

He didn't answer me so I looked up, and when I did, it was into dark eyes that watched me with such intensity that my heart flipped over in my chest.

"Twelve hours."

It took me a minute to realize that he had answered me. I was still holding his arm, and as much as it pained me to let it go, to lose that physical connection with him, I released it and took a step back. A loud honk of a horn seemed to bring us back to reality. He slipped on his jacket.

"Are you heading home?"

"Yes."

"How's the roommate?" He studied me for a moment, taking in my frustrated expression. "That good?"

"My dad warned me of some things, and sadly I've been witnessing firsthand just how right he is. I'm just surprised that I hadn't seen it before."

"What—that your friend isn't much of a friend?"

My eyes widened and I looked up at him. "Yeah, exactly that."

"She's jealous of you."

I took a sip of my coffee as I pondered his comment. "No, I don't think so."

"She's jealous and she has every reason to be from where I'm standing."

I couldn't deny the delicious thrill that his very matter-of-fact comment stirred in me, but I wasn't as convinced. He seemed to know what I was thinking, and added, "If I met your friend and she brought me home and I saw you—no contest. She probably knows that too."

"Well, I suspect you take repeated punches to the head so maybe it's not all working right up there."

He grinned mischievously just before his lips brushed over my ear. "I have a secret—want to hear it?"

My breath left me at his invitation. I could only answer by nodding my head.

His breath tickled my ear, causing goose bumps to rise on my flesh. When he spoke, it was seductively low. "I have a really hard head." And then he pressed a kiss just above my ear before he pulled back.

I spoke what I was thinking.

"I might swoon."

"I'll catch you. I won't let you fall." His strong hand took mine. "Let's get you home."

A week passed and I didn't see Trace once. I knew it was intentional. I knew he was trying to put distance between us. I did, however, run into his friend Rafe. That I just happened on him in Starbucks made me wonder if it wasn't a coincidence.

"How's Loki?"

"Trouble," he said with a grin. As I watched him, his smile faded before he asked, "Can we talk?"

"Sure."

We walked to a table and I watched as Rafe folded himself into the chair opposite me.

He seemed to take an unusual interest in the surface of the table so I asked, "What's up, Rafe?"

He lifted his gaze to mine before he said, "I wanted to talk with you about Trace."

A wave of unease spread through me at the seriousness of his expression before I said, "Okay."

"I've known Trace for a long time. He's a complicated man, but I have noticed a difference in him these past few weeks and I can only attribute the change to you."

I was almost too afraid to ask, "A good change or a bad one?"

He held my stare. "A good one and that's why I'm going to share a bit of his past with you."

"Are you sure that you should?"

"Yes, it might help you understand him better."

He pulled a hand through his hair and stared pensively at me before continuing. "I met Trace when we were fifteen. He was in an alley pounding the shit out of some guy. I pulled him off and I truly believe that if I hadn't, he would have killed the guy. I think he knew it too.

"After that first meeting we started to hang. I think at first he saw me as his reality check, the person who would keep him from going too far. And it was true, I was, since almost every time we were out he would end up in a fight.

"There was so much anger in him, a rage that was nearly uncontrollable. I didn't know then—and I still don't—what fuels it, but it was nearly the death of him. He knew that he needed a better way to vent his anger so he found an outlet by fighting willing opponents."

I paled; I could feel all the blood draining from my face as I remembered Trace in the parking lot and the level of rage in him. The idea of him in some abandoned warehouse pounding the shit out of people scared me. He said he was an amateur fighter but was it more savage than that? Was that why he looked the way he did when he came to my apartment that night? "What, like Brad Pitt, *Fight Club* fighting?"

"No, not really. The fights are legal, held in a gym. There's a ref, even judges, but the method of fighting is up to the fighters, gloved or bare-knuckled. It works for him and it's helped him channel his anger. It gives him a release."

I had already known that he was a fighter, but I was disturbed to learn that he fought not for the love of it or for the money, but as a release for his rage. What in his past fueled it?

"This thing—it isn't just rage in him. He also has a deep-rooted belief that he's a piece of shit. He doesn't think he's good enough for you and at some point he's going to push you away. I hope when he does, if you feel something for him too, that you won't let him."

"I do feel something for him and I really like being with him." I studied Rafe for a moment before I asked, "Does he know you're here?"

"No."

"Last week, I saw a bit of that rage and I won't lie, it scared me. But there's so much more to him than anger. I don't think Trace realizes how much he has to offer. I like him a lot and I want to see where it goes—whatever it is that's between us."

"I don't want to give you a one-sided picture of him. He's been a real friend to me too. I grew up in the system and spent the majority of my youth in trouble. As many times as I've had his back, he's had mine. Yes, he's complicated, but I think you are exactly what he needs."

I couldn't help the feeling of hope that moved through me in response to Rafe's words. "I hope you're right."

<hr>

My cell phone rang and I was tempted not to answer it. I was writing and really didn't want the distraction, but knowing it could be important, I reached for it.

"Hey, is this a bad time?"

I almost dropped my phone. Trace. He rarely called. I wondered if Rafe had told Trace what we'd talked about the other day.

I saved my book and closed up my laptop. "Not at all. What's up?"

"I'm waiting for my fight, so I thought I'd give you a call."

Since he never talked about his fighting, I thought now might be a good opportunity to learn more about it. "Who are you fighting?"

There was a note of humor in his tone when he replied, "Mad Dog Max."

I hadn't meant to laugh, but what a ridiculous name. "That sounds more like a bad malt liquor."

Trace chuckled. "He's had his face pounded in enough that he looks like a pug so the name is actually very fitting."

"Do you have an alter ego?"

"Never understood the point."

"How often do you fight?"

"Several times a week whenever possible. What are you up to tonight?"

It didn't pass my notice his attempt to move the conversation away from him. "I'm working on an idea for a new novel. I'm just outlining right now, jotting down potential plots and characters."

"Have you written others?"

"One, but it needs work, so I'm taking a break from it so I can come back to it with fresh eyes."

"Why do you think it needs work?"

"My old college professor read it and had some suggestions on how to improve the story, most of those suggestions stemming from the need for me to add more realism."

"It's fiction, right?"

"Yes."

"So why do you need realism?"

I laughed out loud before I replied, "That was exactly my thinking, but I do believe he may have a point."

There was silence over the line for a minute. "Maybe you'll let me read it when it's ready."

Whether he really wanted to read it or he was offering to be nice didn't matter. I loved that he asked. "I might just take you up on that."

There was no denying his sincerity when he said, "I hope that you do. They're calling my fight. I'll talk to you later."

"Good luck." I wasn't positive but I was pretty sure he chuckled right before he hung up the phone.

After that first call, Trace would call me several times a week and we'd talk for hours. I hadn't seen him, he hadn't come around, but I found that I really liked talking with him on the phone, since he seemed more at ease. We didn't talk about his past or his family, but he spoke more openly about everything else. Whether he realized it or not, our talks were very revealing, exposing a side of Trace Montgomery that few got to see.

Two weeks after my talk with Rafe, I was sitting in my living room and my thoughts drifted to Trace, as they had a habit of doing. He was a puzzle to me. I knew his reputation, but I didn't see him the way others did—like the man that Luke described on that first night at Sapphire. When I looked at Trace, I saw a man who repeatedly did things for others, helping me out of a few scrapes, coming to the aid of that woman at the gallery, attending charity functions to help those in need. I saw a man who could look at the depiction of a soul in torment and relate.

I was beginning to suspect that Trace's image was not just a product of his low self-esteem, but a means to keep people from looking too deeply at him. I saw a glimpse into the man underneath that hard shell and I liked that man—a lot. Yes, I suspected he was a damaged soul, but he was a beautiful one too. I wanted to believe that Trace avoided seeing me because of his poor self-image, but I also wanted to believe that he called because he felt it too—the connection.

I missed him and as much as I looked forward to his phone calls, they weren't enough for me. I wanted to see him so I grabbed my phone and called Rafe.

"Rafe, it's Ember."

"Hi, Ember. What's up?"

"I want to see him. Do you think that's a bad idea?"

"No, I think it's a great idea. He's been a bit of a prick lately."

"What?"

He chuckled over the line before he added, "He wants to see you too."

I couldn't lie, those words made me feel really good, but then I sobered when I asked, "Do you know if he's home . . ." I almost couldn't get the rest of the sentence out, since I was afraid of the answer, "and if he's alone?"

"Yeah, he's home alone. Let me give you his address and thank you."

"For what?"

"Caring about him."

When the cab pulled up in front of Trace's building, I was surprised to see that we weren't too far from Clover. How did Trace afford a place on the Upper East Side? I climbed from the cab, paid the man, and headed up the steps to the door. Rafe must have called ahead to let the doorman know I was coming since he greeted me warmly before giving me directions to Trace's apartment. I made my way to the fourth floor and down the hall to his apartment. I stopped at his door and took a few deep breaths. I couldn't believe I was here—that I was actually at a man's apartment. I had only ever been in one man's apartment, but this wasn't just any man, this was Trace, and so I knocked.

The door opened and Trace filled the space. The look of surprise on his face made me feel both happy and sad.

"Ember, what are you doing here?"

I held his incredulous stare and answered honestly, "I wanted to see you."

His reply, and the manner in which he said it, broke my heart: It was clear that he was unaccustomed to people visiting him for the sole purpose of just wanting to see him.

"Why?"

"I missed you."

He just stood there and I think he may have been in shock.

"Is this a bad time?" I asked.

"No, sorry, please come in." He stepped back so I could enter and when I got a good look at his apartment, it just added another layer to the mystery surrounding Trace. The place must have cost a fortune. That night at Clover, clearly the two thousand dollar price tag was nothing at all to him. So where did the money come from? I pulled my mind from that and looked around. Though it was sparsely decorated, it was done so with quiet taste. Charcoal-gray walls and walnut floors covered with a Persian rug in deep earth tones were the backdrop for the masculine living room composed of a cognac-colored leather sofa, a dark-oak coffee table, and a TV armoire. The kitchen was against the left wall before the long hallway that led, I guessed, to the multiple bedrooms and bath.

As I moved into the living room, I noticed the walls were bare. There were no pictures of his family or friends. His walls must symbolize his life. He had people around him all the time, but no one that mattered, no one that he cared about, no one he loved, and it was because he hadn't let anyone get close enough. I turned to him. "I like your place."

He was leaning against the door with the strangest expression on his face.

"What's wrong, Trace?"

"I can't believe you're here."

"Do you want me to go?"

He moved from the door and walked over to me to take my hand into his. The look in his eyes made my toes curl before he replied, "No."

He led me to the kitchen before he released my hand.

"Can I get you something to drink?"

"Do you have hot tea?"

He looked at me from over his shoulder as a grin tugged at his mouth. "No, how about coffee?"

"Perfect."

I sat and watched as he started the coffee and then he turned to me.

"I guess I don't need to call you later."

I gave him a saucy smile before I replied, "I've always preferred face-to-face myself."

We settled in his living room with each of us at opposite ends of the sofa, but turned so we could face each other. He still had a funny expression on his face, which prompted me to ask, "Are you upset that I'm here?"

It was surprise that flashed over his face in response before he said, "No, I just can't figure out why you'd want to come here."

I studied him for a moment. "Are you kidding?"

"I'm completely serious."

"I like you, Trace. I came because I missed you."

A smile touched his lips, but the look of disbelief in his eyes hadn't passed my notice. I wanted to ask why he found it so hard to believe that I wanted to be here, but I was too busy soaking up the sight of him. He looked so comfortable, almost relaxed, and the sight of that gave my heart a happy sigh. What made him so beautiful to me was the vulnerable man underneath that handsome face.

"What are you thinking about?" Trace asked, pulling me from my silent study of him.

"You."

There it was again, surprise flashing across his face. I couldn't imagine what happened to make him hate himself so much. I'd ask, but it wasn't the time so I changed the subject.

"So a single man doesn't keep tea in the house?"

Humor danced in his eyes before he replied, "Not this man, but, since I know you like it, I will."

The warmth that burned through me in response to that was completely involuntary. I held his gaze as I smiled. "I like Earl Grey with lavender honey."

"I'll have it for the next time."

So there was going to be a next time; this was progress. The silence stretched out for a few minutes as we just stared at each other. I wanted to touch him, wanted to crawl over to him and curl up into his lap. I wanted my mouth on him and my arms around him, but I managed to control that impulse.

I wasn't battling those feelings alone when Trace moved so effortlessly and pulled me into his arms. His mouth closed over mine and I gave in to my need to touch him and pulled my hands through his hair. He teased me, dipping his tongue into my mouth to taste me, before pulling away and feathering kisses along my jaw. His tongue traced my earlobe and my body's reaction was immediate as delicious little chills shot down my arms. My breasts felt fuller and my nipples grew hard. I sought to ease the ache by pressing myself against him. There was a tingling between my legs and with it came an edginess that made me feel wanton. I wanted to taste every inch of him, wanted to feel him inside me as I stretched to take him. The rawness of my need was both terrifyingly new and deeply arousing.

He gently lowered me onto my back before he moved to cover my body with his own. It was instinctual when I spread my legs to cradle him between my thighs. I felt him hard and thick pressing against the part of me that was throbbing and to my embarrassment and delight I almost came. His hands moved down my body, his fingertips setting off little fires under my skin as they traveled down my arms, over my stomach, across my ribs. He moved to kneel between my legs as his fingers played with my shirt, slowly moving it up my body before taking it off completely. His hands on my bare skin felt so amazing but was nothing compared to the feel of his lips on my collarbone as he pressed kisses there. His tongue licked my overheated skin, moving down my body until he reached my breasts, which were aching for his attention. He kissed under those overly sensitive mounds, around them, and above them but he didn't actually touch them. He worked the front clasp of my bra, flicking it open until I felt the cool air brush over my nipples that were so hard they hurt. His lips were barely touching me as he moved over my breast and then he flicked the nipple with his tongue. Lust shot right between my legs as I grabbed his head and pulled him to me. When he sucked me deep into his hot, wet mouth I moaned in sheer pleasure. He cupped my neglected breast, caressing and squeezing before tugging on the nipple. The ache between my legs was accompanied by a dampness as I shifted my hips, looking for relief. Trace moved his one knee higher so I could rub myself hard against him. I felt powerful and needy at the same time. My hand itched to pull the hard length of him free. I wanted to hold him in my hand, wanted him in my mouth, wanted to push him on his back and sink down slowly onto him as I took him deep inside of me. I wanted to ride him until we both came. Trace seemed to sense what I wanted when he pulled his mouth from my breast and in one fluent move he had my jeans unsnapped and down my legs along with my panties. A heartbeat later, Trace's mouth was right where I ached for him the most.

"Oh my God."

He gripped my hips and pulled me hard against him as his tongue and teeth drove me wild. Lust coiled in my belly as my hips moved against his mouth. I fisted my hands in his hair as I shamelessly ground myself against his invading tongue. The orgasm started slowly until Trace slipped two fingers into me as he sucked on that pulsing nub. I came hard as I cried out from the fierceness of it. It went on for so long as my body pulsed with my release. I felt weightless, sleepy, and sated all at once. It was only after my body came back down that I realized Trace had gone still. I was afraid to look at him for fear of seeing regret. What I saw instead made my heart miss a beat. There was lust and tenderness in his gaze. I was inexperienced but I knew I was the only one who'd experienced the pleasure. I reached for him, wishing to give him what he had given me, but he stopped me and gently wrapped his hand around my wrist.

"Not tonight," he said gruffly.

It felt like ice water being doused over my head. Suddenly I realized that I was naked and I felt completely exposed. I moved with far less grace than I would have liked and started dressing. I had to go. Mortification burned my cheeks and the need to cry was so close that I frantically pulled in breaths to prevent it. I had just reached the door when Trace came up behind me and pulled me back against him.

"Don't leave angry, Ember. You have no idea how much I wanted that."

I couldn't look at him so I focused on the door when I said, "It was one-sided."

"No, it wasn't. It was about giving you pleasure and I loved every fucking second of it."

He turned me to him and pulled my chin up. I saw in his expression that what he spoke was the truth. And then he kissed me and, tasting myself on his tongue, knowing that he derived pleasure from giving me pleasure, I lost a little piece of myself to him in that moment.

"You can stay," he whispered.

"I should go." Despite his words, I couldn't stay, because I was in way over my head with him.

He looked disappointed, but he reached for my hand and started from the apartment. "All right, I'll get you a cab."

Chapter Six

The morning after the most intense sexual encounter I had ever experienced, there was a delivery for me. I opened the box to find two dozen cake pops and a note that simply read, "Thinking of you. —Trace."

My body still hummed from his touch and just thinking about him I ached for his touch again. With the Creep, if he didn't come he got nasty and blamed me for not being woman enough to turn him on. The whole of our lovemaking was all about getting him off. But Trace, all he had been thinking about was bringing me pleasure, even to the extent of denying himself the same.

Or had he? I knew he had been turned on, I felt him, but maybe a man like Trace needed more stimulation or someone with a voracious sexual appetite to bring it home, so to speak.

Or worse, what if he regretted it? What if the reality of me left him wanting? I couldn't think about it or I'd drive myself insane. I grabbed a cake pop and headed to my room to work on my book.

I checked my e-mail first and saw I had two messages from websites Professor Smythe had inquired about on my behalf. Disappointment filled me to read that both responses were the same, a thank-you-but-no-thank-you. It was a long shot, this idea of the professor's, but I tried not to get too discouraged. I launched into my book and lost myself in my work.

There was radio silence when it came to Trace. A whole week with no word. I followed his lead and didn't attempt to contact him either. It hurt. We shared something incredible and then he went off the grid. Lena's warning played in my head—*he only wants sex.* I hadn't wanted to believe her, but I couldn't help it now. It was painful but it seemed my fears were justified, I was just not that interesting to him. Talk about a blow to the ego, he didn't even get sex from me before he backed off.

It was while I pondered that depressing thought that Lena came home. She saw me sprawled out on the sofa and pushed my legs over so she could join me.

"You look depressed. What's wrong?"

"I think you were right about Trace."

"What do you mean?"

I sat up and curled my legs under me. "Last week I went over to his apartment."

"Oh, Ember. Tell me you didn't sleep with him."

My cheeks burned with embarrassment as I replied, "Technically, no."

"What does that mean?"

How did I say in words what he did to me? I answered honestly, "He pleasured me with his mouth."

A naughty smile curved her lips as she settled back against the sofa. "Ah, a little sixty-nine action. I didn't think you had that in you, Ember."

"It was one-sided. He never actually took off his clothes."

Her eyebrow rose slightly before she asked, "And you?"

"As naked as the day I was born," I confessed.

"So what's the problem? Was he not any good?"

"He was amazing but I haven't heard from him since."

"Oh." True concern showed on her face. "Did you get any sense from him that night?"

"I was embarrassed that I had, you know . . . and he hadn't. But he told me he loved bringing me pleasure. He even suggested that I stay the night, but I had to get out of there. He sent me something the next day and at the time I thought it was a sweet gesture, but now I think it may have just been a token, you know, the cliché of roses after a hookup."

"I'm so sorry, Ember, but based on everything that I've heard about him, I can't say I'm that surprised. You're sweet and innocent, not really the kind of woman that would stir the blood of someone so virile."

Hearing my fear repeated back to me was like taking a sucker punch to the gut. Lena didn't seem to notice my reaction as she continued, "Look at the silver lining."

"What silver lining?"

"You didn't walk away empty-handed. You had the best sexual encounter of your life. I think that's enough to make your time with him worth it. Now you need to focus on moving on to someone who's more your speed."

"Why do I get the sense that you have just the person in mind?"

"Because you know me so well. He's a friend of Todd's and I think he's perfect for you. Come to dinner with us, let's do a double date. We haven't had one of those in so long."

"I hate blind dates."

"I know but you need to get out and socialize. The worst case scenario, you just have a good meal with friends, but maybe you and Dane will hit it off. Please come?"

My thoughts turned to Trace and Lena knew it when she asked, "How long has it been since he made your toes curl?"

"A week."

"With no word?"

"Yeah."

"It's time for you to move on because he has."

I knew she was right, so I reluctantly accepted her invite.

Lena and I caught a cab to a popular eatery in the Village where Todd and Dane were waiting. I noticed Dane first since he was looking at me like I was a particularly delicious morsel. I had to curb the urge to look down at myself to see what he was ogling, since I was dressed very conservatively in wide-legged black trousers, a burnt-orange blouse, and black sandals. I forced a smile before I said, "Hello, Dane. It's very nice to meet you."

"Likewise, Ember." His moist handshake left me wanting to wipe my hand on my pants.

As the hostess showed us to our table, I tolerated Dane's hand at the small of my back, but I had to give him credit, he had manners. He pulled my chair out for me before taking his own seat. Orders were placed and then Lena and Todd started whispering, which made Dane look at me expectantly. I silently cursed my so-called best friend before I asked, "What do you do?"

"I'm currently in between jobs."

Unemployed, fabulous.

"Are you from around here?" he asked.

"No, I grew up in Philadelphia."

"Really? So what brought you to New York?"

"I'm a writer."

"Ah, how's that going?"

"To pay the bills I work as a waitress at Clover."

"Clover, nice place . . . too rich for my blood, though." His warm brown eyes sparkled and then drifted lower. Too low. Jerk.

I was curious how he knew of the place. But Todd had taken Lena and probably bragged about it. "Mine too."

"Have you always wanted to be a writer?"

Before I could answer, Lena spoke up from across the table. "Em's been writing since we were kids. I can still see her with her secondhand clothes and knotted hair. Her dad and his friends always loved everything she did."

Could she be any less flattering to me? I thought as Todd asked, "Is she any good?"

Hello, I'm sitting right here.

"Well, she certainly tries really hard."

My gaze met Lena's angelic one, but I didn't miss the contempt burning deep in those green eyes.

"The academic scholarship to college that I won through the *New York Times* would suggest that some in the literary world would put me in high regard."

"Oh, don't get upset, Em, I'm just playing around. Of course you are a very talented writer."

I didn't know why I never saw it before, but my dad and Trace were right. Lena was not acting like much of a friend. Dane reached for my hand under the table and lightly squeezed it and I found the gesture to be oddly comforting.

After dinner we went to Sapphire and while Lena and Todd dry humped against the wall, Dane and I sat at the bar. Luke was working and he winked at me as he made our drinks. Once they were placed before us, Dane turned to me and lifted his glass to mine before taking a sip.

"I hear you play the piano."

"I do, yes."

"I'd like to hear you sometime."

"Yeah, okay." I held his gaze as I asked, "Did you know this was a blind date?"

I saw the grin a second before he answered, "I did, yes."

We spent the next half hour talking and though on the surface Dane seemed like a great guy, he was almost too agreeable, moving right up into my personal space. When he excused himself to use the restroom, I was actually grateful for the reprieve.

"How are you doing, beautiful?" I looked up into the smiling gray eyes of the bartender.

"Hi, Luke. Can I hide behind there?"

"Sure thing."

He leaned over to rest his arms on the bar before he asked, "Blind date?"

"Yes."

"And how's it going?"

"I wish I was home in my pj's eating ice cream."

His laugh pulled a smile from me before he said, "If you want to hide, you better do it now because here he comes."

"My father taught me never to cower," I offered with a little smile.

"I think I'd like your dad. Do you want another drink?"

"Water would be great, thanks."

"You got it."

Dane slid back into his seat with his hand coming to rest on my thigh.

"Are you about ready to go?"

"Ah, I was just getting a glass of water."

"I've got to be up early, but I'd like to see you home, safe and sound."

"Oh, okay. Where are Todd and Lena?"

"They've already left. They're staying at Todd's tonight."

Luke returned then with my water.

"Thanks, Luke," I said as I reached for the glass. I saw the look that Dane gave to Luke. He seemed almost too much in a hurry to leave.

"If you're in a rush I can catch a cab."

"No! I mean that wouldn't be very gentlemanly of me." He's worried about being a gentleman when he's spent most of the night undressing me with his eyes?

There was definitely something weird going on with Dane and I knew I wasn't the only one to sense it, because Luke kept glancing over at me.

I finished my water and as soon as my glass touched the bar, Dane immediately reached for my hand and pulled me from my stool.

"Ember."

I turned to see Trace in his favorite outfit of faded jeans and a T-shirt. And the sight of him made me feel both joy and bitterness. Eyes that looked almost possessive made my bitterness turn into something darker.

"Trace."

He reached up to touch me but I moved out of his reach. I noticed, as he pulled his hand away, that he balled it into a fist as he turned toward Dane. His eyes took on the properties of the metal they resembled, hard and cold.

"Who's your friend?"

As if it was any of his business, but I heard myself answering, "Dane."

"How do you know Dane?"

It was rude to talk about someone when they were standing right there, as I well knew from earlier that evening, but something in Trace's manner made me curious enough to ignore manners and answer honestly.

"I don't, really. This is our first date."

His eyes turned to mine and, damn, I had to give Dane some credit for not peeing his pants because Trace looked positively murderous.

"You don't know him at all?"

He wasn't the only one feeling murderous. Why the cross-examination when the man made it very clear he wasn't interested in me? Or was he? I decided to provoke him. "Not yet."

That answer pissed Trace off even more because he slowly turned his head to Dane and took a step closer to him. "So Dane, are you partial to your face?"

"Seriously, you're going to punch him in the face because I'm on a date with him?"

"Not the sole reason, but it certainly isn't working in his favor."

"How very caveman of you."

He moved until we were nose to nose. "I'm not marking my territory, I'm looking out for you."

I deliberately provoked him again when I asked, "Why exactly?"

"You know why," he hissed.

"I don't know anything of the sort. What I do know is that actions speak louder than words and your actions are crystal clear. Now, if you'll excuse us."

I didn't wait for Trace's reply as I pushed past him and headed for the door. I forgot all about Dane until I heard him say from just behind me. "Maybe we should call it a night."

The icing on the cake, the man I've been trying to ditch all night was now giving me the brush-off. I abruptly turned to Dane and practically shouted at him, "Fabulous idea."

I had just reached the door when I was stopped by a hand wrapping firmly around my arm. I knew by the fire that burned through me it was Trace.

"We need to talk, Ember."

I felt like a belligerent child when I said, "I don't have anything to say."

"I do."

There was a part of me that wanted to run away, the part desirous for self-preservation, but a larger part of me wanted to hear what he had to say. I was once again setting myself up for a nasty fall but I couldn't deny the simple truth: I was falling in love with Trace. He seemed to know I'd acquiesced and his hold on me loosened.

"You can't go home."

I turned to him as my breath halted in my lungs. Damn I had missed him. Disgust replaced longing, knowing that I could be so easily swayed by just a look. I rallied to harden myself to his appeal. "And why not?"

"I overheard Todd in the men's room. His friend, your date, actually paid Todd for an evening with you."

"What?"

"I don't know the specifics, but I do know that Todd guaranteed you were easy and Dane paid for the introduction."

My anger at Trace was trumped by a rising fury I felt when I thought of Todd. I knew the bastard was desperate for cash, but to actually pimp me out! What the fuck? The emotional roller coaster continued as I felt a pang of sadness for Lena. When she found out her boyfriend tried to prostitute me, they'd be over. As much as I didn't like Todd, I knew Lena really did.

"Ember?"

My sadness intensified when I realized that Trace's need to talk with me wasn't at all about us, and neither was his need to rescue me. I had to get the hell out of there before I did something truly appalling like cry. I started past him again. "Thanks for the warning."

"Come home with me."

I was getting whiplash from Trace's moods. "You've done your part. You came to my aid yet again. There's no need for charity. I'm a big girl, I can take care of myself."

There was an edge to his tone when he said, "It's not charity. I would like you to come home with me."

"The last time I was there, it didn't end so well."

He ran his hand over his hair in frustration before he said, "I acted poorly, but I was thinking about your best interest. I was trying to do right by you."

"How is ignoring me in my best interest?"

"You deserve better."

"I completely disagree, but why the change of heart?"

His words were that much more powerful with how simple they were. "Because I fucking miss you."

My heart cracked open and I fell for him the rest of the way. It was stupid and self-destructive but I heard myself saying, "I'll stay tonight."

I had the sense that he was asking me to stay for longer than an evening based on his reaction, but he seemed to know my concession was a victory for him so he stayed silent.

Like I observed before, people parted to let him pass. It made it easier for me to see the looks on their faces, particularly the women, who were not at all happy to see him leaving with a wallflower like me.

When we reached his apartment, he led me down the hall and opened a door to a bedroom with a large oak bed situated in the middle of the room. The walls were painted the same gray as the living room and, again, I was surprised and pleased with the room's quiet elegance. But, I wondered as I had the last time I visited, how the hell did he afford this place? He was asking me to stay with him so he needed to be more forthcoming about himself.

"Trace, how can you afford to live here? There's no way an amateur boxer could make rent on a place like this."

He was uncomfortable, but he knew my question was fair when he said, "My family comes from money."

From the size of this apartment, he wasn't just talking about money, he was talking about MONEY. Montgomery . . . I wasn't familiar with any prominent New York families with that surname but clearly there were some somewhere.

I was pushing it, but I asked anyway. "Why are you so vague when it comes to your life or your past?"

His jaw clenched before he said sharply, "The past is the past and I want it to fucking stay there."

"Fair enough." I wanted to pry more, but Trace was clearly done sharing. My thoughts turned to Lena. She was going to be a mess when she learned of Todd's deviant behavior. I knew I looked forlorn when Trace asked me what I was thinking.

I exhaled rather sharply before I replied, "Lena is going to be brokenhearted when she learns what Todd tried to do tonight."

"How do you know she doesn't already know?"

"Lena may have her flaws, but she's not capable of that."

I knew he didn't agree. "If she stays with him, you can't live there."

"She won't."

"What if she does?" I was about to object when he said more firmly, "Humor me, Ember, what if she does?"

I honestly didn't know. My name wasn't on the lease, so I wouldn't be hunted down if Lena couldn't make the payments on the apartment, but where the hell was I going to live? With what I was contributing for our shit apartment, I would be lucky to get a cardboard box by the river.

"I don't know what I'll do."

"You could stay here."

"I don't think that's such a great idea." My dad was always an option, but it was a point of pride that I wanted to make it on my own. I guess I could double up at Clover to make some extra cash but then that would seriously cut into my writing time. And if I did get a journalism gig, I would have to cut back my hours. There was no entry-level journalism job that would pay what I was making in tips at Clover. I really needed to find a roommate. And the idea of living in close quarters with a complete stranger made my stomach twist into knots.

"It doesn't have to be permanent but it will give you the time you need to figure out your next move. Think about it," Trace said.

I wanted to stay with him. It was crazy, ludicrous even, but I did. Not that it mattered because Lena was going to break up with Todd and she would need me to help her get back on her feet. As wonderful a notion as living with Trace Montgomery was, it was never going to happen.

"I'll think about it."

"My room's across the hall and the bathroom, as you know, is the last door on the left. I'll get you a T-shirt and some boxers to sleep in."

He returned with my sleepwear and I turned to him as he stood there filling the doorway. I wanted him and the intensity of my desire for him, after how our last encounter went, was startling. Though he was still watching me, I offered him a smile before I said, "Good night."

Sleep wouldn't come as I tossed and turned for over an hour. I gave up and climbed from bed. I reached the living room and my feet just stopped because Trace was there sitting on the sofa. "Is everything okay?"

"Yes. I just can't seem to sleep."

"Can I get you something?" He grinned before he added, "I have tea."

A warmth burned all the way down to my toes in response before I said, "That would be great."

He stood and as he walked past me, he reached for my hand and pulled me down the hall to the kitchen. Once I was settled at a stool at the bar, he moved through the kitchen to make my tea.

"Couldn't you sleep either?" I asked.

"I don't sleep much."

"Really?"

He was silent for a minute before he offered, "It's habit."

I held his gaze before I said, "And you don't want to talk about it."

There was the slightest of grins on his face when he replied, "No."

"Okay."

He turned from me to add water to the kettle. "Thank you for earlier."

I saw his shoulders tense. "Todd and Dane are assholes."

"Agreed."

I watched as he lit the gas under the kettle before he turned and leaned up against the counter. "Is that why you can't sleep?"

"I couldn't sleep because my mind won't stop." I studied him for a minute before I asked, "If you rarely sleep then what do you do in the evenings?" And then I answered my own question when I realized what the most likely answer was for his nocturnal activities.

He read my thought when he replied, "Lately, I find myself reading or playing video games."

Lately, like how lately? Oh, man, I so wanted to ask that, but I chickened out. Instead I gestured toward the living room. "So you don't generally sit in the dark and stare at the wall?"

He laughed at that. "No, I was thinking."

"About?"

His eyes flashed hot before he said, "You."

He leaned toward me as his eyes moved to my lips and my heart immediately went into my throat. My response to him was self-destructive in light of our last encounter but I couldn't help the overwhelming need I felt to crawl onto the counter to get to him. The sound of the kettle pulled us from the moment. Trace turned and busied himself with making my tea and I watched, completely unrepentant, at the play on his muscles as he did so.

"Would you like company, Trace?"

He turned back to me. "Yes."

The next morning, smelling coffee, I padded to the kitchen. Trace must have sensed me because he froze with his bare back to me. His jeans hung low on his hips as thick ropes of muscles framed his spine. His shoulder blades were huge and his waist narrow. The tattoo started mid-back and moved up in a swirling scrollwork pattern over his shoulders and up his neck.

He turned to see me staring. As he moved, his muscles made it seem like the artwork was dancing along his skin. His voice, when he spoke, was hoarse.

"Did you get any sleep?"

"I did. It's a very comfortable bed."

Since I smiled and he grinned, I knew that we both had the same thought: us, that bed, naked. He seemed to recover faster than me. He leaned against the counter and pushed his hands into the front pockets of his jeans.

"Would you like me to come with you to your apartment?"

"Thanks, but I should go alone. It's going to be very hard on Lena and she won't want an audience to her breakdown."

"Okay, but if things go south, call me. I'll come get you."

There was a part of me, as terrible as it was to admit, that wanted things with Lena to go south so that I could be here with him. I was sure that made me a horrible person, but if you couldn't be honest with yourself and all that . . .

"Thanks for the offer."

"How about if I make us some eggs?"

It wasn't even a conscious thought as I took a step closer to him and replied, "That would be great."

I returned home to find Lena already there. Based on the look of her, she wasn't aware yet of Todd's disgusting stunt. As soon as she saw me, a coy smile spread across her face.

"So I guess things went well with Dane."

"Actually, quite the opposite."

Her confusion was clearly evident. "Where were you, then?"

There was a smile playing around her mouth. I hadn't seen humor like that in her for a while. This was going to be harder than I thought, but she needed to know the kind of man she was dating. Speaking of which, where was Todd?

"Is Todd here?"

"No, he went home earlier. What's wrong?"

"I'm not really sure how to say this, so I'm just going to say it. Lena, Dane paid Todd so he could spend the night with me."

The flash of anger was startling. I thought I understood her reaction until she said, "That's disgusting and completely untrue."

Her denial took me by surprise before I countered, "It's not. They were overheard talking about it at the club."

"By who?"

"Trace."

It wasn't anger but pity that crossed over her face in reaction to that. "And Trace told you this? The same trustworthy man who fucked you then dissed you. That guy? How do you know he wasn't just being a macho prick? The sight of his plaything with another guy made him lie to you to get you away from the competition. Is that where you were, at Trace's? Did you sleep with him?"

How was this spiraling so far out of control? She was twisting everything around. My temper spiked. "No! Whatever you might think of Trace, he wouldn't make something like that up."

"And whatever you might think of Todd, he would never do something like that."

"How can you say that when the man is constantly gambling, losing more times than he wins, which has him always looking for where the next buck is coming from? Hell, Lena, he takes you out and leaves you in questionable situations to go bet away his savings. His bottom line is money and pimping me out is exactly something Todd would do."

I knew I had gone too far when I saw her expression completely close off. She walked past me to her purse. "I think you need to move out. I'll stay with Todd for a couple of days to give you time to get your stuff out."

"Lena, please don't shut me out. I get that you're mad, but what if I'm not wrong? If he was willing to pimp me out then how long before he does the same to you?"

There was no humor in her laugh. "Do you even hear yourself? Your cunt is so wet for that bastard that you'll believe anything he tells you. He doesn't even like you, he sure as hell doesn't respect you, and yet you're willing to toss our friendship based on his word. His word, Ember, a man with a reputation that makes Lucifer look saintly. You're a fool."

I had never received a verbal slap before and that hurt, especially coming from her. Lena didn't know me anywhere near as well as I thought she did if she believed my motives could be so shallow.

"And you are so confident in Todd and his motives that you have no doubts? You saw Dane eyeing me when we first arrived at the restaurant. He was looking at me as if I was a sure thing. And later when we were getting ready to leave he was acting so oddly that even the bartender picked up on it. He was waiting to get me home, because he had been assured by Todd, and paid for the pleasure, that I would drop on my back and spread them wide for him."

"I don't know what's happened to you but I want you gone by the time I get back." And without another word she slammed the door.

My stomach roiled and I just made it to the toilet before I threw up my breakfast. I dropped onto the cold tile floor and pulled my knees up to my chest as I rested my head back against the wall. What was I going to do? Lena's words were pounding in my head and a part of what made me so ill was the idea that she wasn't wrong. What if Trace had made it up?

The man I thought I knew wouldn't do such a thing, but I didn't know him all that well. He had loved me and left me and only reappeared when I was out with another man. Was it possible that he only approached me last night to mark his territory?

No, I refused to believe that of him. I may not know him well but what I did know was that he had been nothing but a gentleman to me. I didn't believe he would make up something so repugnant just to stake a claim, especially since he could have had me and chose not to. I should have called Kyle and crashed with him but I couldn't make myself do it. As foolhardy a decision as it was, I wanted to take the chance on Trace. I reached for my phone.

"Ember, how did it go?"

"She kicked me out. She said you made the whole thing up. You didn't, did you?"

There wasn't even the slightest of hesitations when he said, "No."

"I don't have anywhere to go," I whispered.

"Yes, you do."

"Are you sure you want a roommate?"

"Yes."

With a sigh of relief I said, "I'd like to stay with you."

"Good. I'll be there in about an hour."

Before I could say another word, the line went dead.

I was in my room piling my clothes on my bed when the doorbell sounded. Trace was standing in the hall with boxes, packing tape, and a smile. "I double parked the truck so I'm going to have to go down in a bit and move it."

He thought of a truck and boxes—in my state I hadn't. I moved into him, pressing my face against his chest. I hadn't meant to cry but I was feeling overwhelmed. His arms wrapped around me and held me close. He didn't offer platitudes, only held me until I pulled myself together. He reached for a few boxes and handed them to me before grabbing a few of his own. "Lead the way."

We spent most of the day packing my room. Under the circumstances, I was surprised to find I was actually enjoying myself. I had forgotten some of the junk I had brought with me and the walk down memory lane became comforting. Trace was across the room packing up my desk. At one point when I turned to him, he was just standing there looking at a picture of my mom. She was young in the picture, maybe in high school, and it was uncanny how much I looked like her. It was my favorite picture.

"What happened to your mom?"

"She died when I was three, a hit-and-run."

He turned to me, his gaze searching. "I'm sorry."

"I was so young that I really don't remember her. Strange, isn't it? Without photos to remind me, I wouldn't be able to picture her face and I don't remember her voice. My dad tells me stories all the time. For him, she was the love of his life and even twenty years later, he still mourns her loss, misses her every day, and loves her just as deeply as he had the day they married.

"She was my age when she died. They had been together for only six years, married for three, but their love was so strong that even the memory of it is enough for my dad. When I was younger, I couldn't imagine loving someone with that kind of intensity, and knowing that the one you're with is the only one you'll ever want."

Trace continued to stare at me. His expression was completely unreadable and his voice was barely audible when he said, "I can . . ."

My heart literally skipped a beat hearing those words from this man. "I can now too."

"I better go move the truck." And then he was gone.

———

It took two full days but we eventually got all of my stuff to Trace's. My new living arrangement was going to be an adjustment, but I secretly loved that I was with him.

Lena hovered in the background of my thoughts. I hoped she learned the kind of man Todd was before the knowledge came back and bit her in the ass. But there was nothing more I could do because she was no longer taking my calls.

Two days after I moved in, Trace was at the gym so I made my way down to the basement. It was huge and a bit creepy, but it was well organized, which made locating Trace's storage unit very easy.

We had moved my furniture in there already but I had a few more boxes of things that I wanted to store. I peeked into Trace's boxes as I attempted to organize my boxes with his and that's when I saw the old newspaper. I pulled it out and was surprised to see the date, 2001. The paper was from someplace in Ohio and the headline story was about a gruesome double murder. I noticed notations along the margins of the paper, but they were done in a form of shorthand I couldn't read. I hadn't recognized the names of the people in the article, but as I read it, I felt my stomach clench at the forensic but undeniably gruesome recounting of the killings. Why did Trace have this? Based on the condition of the paper, it had been read often. Was this what haunted him? I folded the paper and placed it back in the box, but a seed of foreboding planted itself firmly in my gut.

Trace and I tried to find our rhythm, and part of that included weekly chores like grocery shopping, which was definitely an experience. He tended to buy things in bulk and I understood this as I looked at him. Seeing him in all his hard-ass glory while he looked at the nutritional information on a box of cookies was so freaking adorable. His size alone required him to eat at least twice what a normal person would.

"What do you like better, cookies, cakes, or pies?" he asked.

"I like them all, but I rarely eat them, too fattening." My cake pop fetish didn't count, since they were so small they were almost nonexistent. Never mind that I tended to eat several at a time.

He took a step back and, quite intentionally, looked at me from head to toe and back again before a grin tugged at his mouth.

"You could stand to put on a few pounds."

"No way, I'm heavier than I look."

"Really?"

Faster than my brain could compute, he snatched me up over his head like a barbell and repeatedly pressed me as if I weighed no more than a sack of potatoes. Maybe it was my screeching, but he put me down and earned an applause from the people around us, which he accepted with a bow before turning back to me with a laugh. He really was a sight with his dark beauty and his six-feet-four-inches of muscles and tattoos. His humor let me see that boyish part he usually kept hidden. There really was so much more to Trace than met the eye.

His demons still haunted him and influenced how he felt about himself. I wished he would talk to me and let me in, but any attempt I made to talk to him about his past was very efficiently shut down. Could people truly be happy if they were unwilling to put the ghosts of their past to rest? I suspected no.

Chapter Seven

✦

In the weeks after I moved in with him I saw the private Trace who was more open and relaxed. One day he surprised me by asking if I wanted to come see him fight. On the ride over to the gym I had pictures in my head of a dark, dank basement with single lightbulbs hanging from the ceiling by wires. In my head the fighters were covered in ink, muscled, hardened, and tough enough to eat glass. I was pleasantly surprised when we pulled up to a small, brick-front gym. Trace parked his bike right on the curb before we headed inside. It looked a lot like the gym Rocky trained in—small and dingy with a ring against one wall and punching bags and weight equipment against the opposite wall. An audience circled the ring as men stood in their corners waiting for the fight to begin. A white-haired man I assumed was the club's owner, since he had the look of a man very comfortable in his surroundings, engaged the ref in quiet conversation.

I was pulled from my silent study when Trace said, "There's Rafe."

My eyes followed the direction he gestured to find Rafe over by the wall, and as soon as he saw us, he started over.

"Lucien should be here too."

"Who's Lucien?"

"A friend." I looked up at him because there was an odd note to his tone.

"What's that look for?" I asked.

"Lucien's quite the ladies' man."

I almost snorted because I thought he was teasing me but I realized, despite his casual tone, he wasn't teasing. Our conversation was cut short by Rafe.

"So are you going to place a bet on our boy, Ember?" Rafe teased.

My thoughts immediately moved to Todd, but thinking about him and Lena was just too frustrating so I forced it from my head. "Not this time."

"I've got to go warm up." Trace turned to me. "Stay close to Rafe."

There was an edge to Trace, but why? My thoughts took a radical shift when the door of the gym opened and Adonis walked in.

"Yo, Lucien!" Rafe called. Now I understood Trace's comment. Lucien was dressed in all black, with mahogany-brown hair that was long enough to brush his very impressive shoulders. He was thick in the chest, narrow in the hips, and had a smile that would make a nun pant, but it was his eyes, a color not quite blue or green, that were truly spectacular. A ladies' man, oh hell yeah.

He moved through the crowd with the same grace and deliberateness that Trace had mastered. Almost every woman's head turning was proof of his appeal. He regarded Rafe first and then those eyes turned on me. The smile was one I was sure he had bestowed on countless women before me.

Everything about him spoke of control, power, and sex.

"Rafe." His husky voice conjured visions of leather and lace. "And you must be Ember."

For all of his appeal, he didn't hold a candle to Trace. Despite that, I still felt my heart rate speed up before I replied, "Hi."

Hi? What a spectacular opening line.

"Lucien. Nice to meet you."

"Likewise."

The announcer called the fight and Trace appeared, chasing thoughts of Lucien from my head. He was dressed in kickboxer pants, the muscles of his chest and arms bunching and cording as he warmed up. He didn't wear gloves since he preferred to fight bare-knuckled. He was completely in the zone, and then quite suddenly he turned and our eyes locked. I felt that stare like a lover's caress and then he winked at me just before he turned his attention back to the ring. A warmth spread through me in response to that shared moment just as Lucien spoke up. I had completely forgotten he was there.

"He's fighting Ian Campbell. Ian might have size but Trace has the moves."

It was only then that I looked to see who Trace was fighting and gasped when I saw him.

"He's fighting him? The man's a tank."

"Yeah, but Trace is quick on his feet," Lucien said and then added, "He can't hurt Trace if he can't touch him."

I looked at the size of the paws on the beast Trace was fighting and blurted out, "One hit is all he'll need."

"They've fought before." I knew Lucien offered that tidbit as a way to alleviate my distress, but nothing outside of Trace climbing out that ring was going to do that.

The bell sounded and I felt my stomach drop, but it only took a few minutes of watching Trace to understand Lucien's confidence in him. He really was quick on his feet, moving around the ring like a lightweight and not the six-foot-four, two-hundred-and-forty-five-pound man that he was. I'd enjoyed watching boxing with my dad and had often heard him comparing boxing to dancing. I had to admit that there was a elegance about how Trace's body moved. When he connected a punch you could see how his entire body took the shock of it. I knew it had to hurt, but you'd never know from looking at him. Watching Trace I also had to agree with the observation Rafe made that day in Starbucks, that Trace fought to release his rage. There was a ruthlessness about Trace when he fought—as if each punch was purging him, but of what?

He was clearly the favorite since every time his punches landed, the crowd roared in approval and when he took a hit, they cursed.

"Do you see the way he pulls him in and then fakes him out? It's fucking poetry in motion," I heard Rafe comment to Lucien. He wasn't wrong.

The fight lasted eight rounds but after an uppercut to the head and jab to the gut, Ian went down hard. He didn't even try to get up. The crowd roared but I kept my eyes on Trace in the hopes that he would look over at me again. I was not disappointed. And this time, I winked at him.

Most of the fans were gone by the time Trace returned from the locker room. He moved to stand at my side and one look at his face made me reach out to gently touch him. The bruises had already begun to form along his jawline and under one eye.

He reached for my hand and linked our fingers before he turned his attention to Lucien and Rafe. "You up for a drink?"

"Hell yeah, and I'll even pay since you won me a nice chunk of change," Rafe said.

"Is that good with you?" Trace's question pulled my attention. That this was the same man who just pounded the shit out of a walking tank was almost hard for me to believe. The evidence of his savage fight was blooming on his skin and yet now there was patience and what looked like tenderness staring back at me.

"A drink sounds great."

There was a small tavern next to the gym. A long, scarred bar took up one wall and was packed with men drinking beer and watching some game on ESPN. Based on the uniforms of the patrons, the place was definitely blue collar. It was exactly the kind of place my dad and his buddies liked to frequent.

We settled at one of the tables just as our waitress approached. She wore a tight black skirt and a white blouse that was opened low enough to show off her ample breasts. From a distance she looked young, maybe late twenties, but I realized as she grew closer that she was actually well into her forties. At one time she would have been a knockout but now she just looked tired and worn.

"I heard it only took you eight rounds to take down Ian, nice. So what can I get you?"

Trace looked at me, "Beer okay?"

"Yeah."

"Beers all around, Kay."

"You got it."

I watched her walk away and wondered what a day in her life was like. Is that what Professor Smythe meant by realism?

"So how did you two meet?" Lucien's question pulled me from my thoughts.

Before I could answer Trace said, "She slugged a guy and I had a front-row seat."

Like Trace, Lucien's expression gave nothing away. "Really?"

"He was being a jerk."

Lucien's eyes twinkled with mischief before he said, "Nice."

Hoping to change the subject I asked, "What about you guys, how did you all meet?"

It was a fair question, but a slight hush settled over the table. When Lucien finally did answer me, I got the sense he wasn't really telling me the whole story.

"Just moving in the same circles. I've seen a few of Trace's fights, he's been into my clubs."

"Clubs, plural?" I asked.

"Yes."

"So you're an entrepreneur."

There was humor sparkling in his eyes when he said, "Sure. So what do you do, Ember?"

"I want to be a writer."

"A writer. What made you want to do that?"

I fiddled with my beverage napkin as I answered him. "Real life can be hard, so one day I started writing down what was in my head as a means of escape. Writing provided solace even if it was just for a short time."

It was a small revelation but a definite step forward when I realized that Trace and I had that in common, the need to purge what troubled us. Of course, I didn't know what troubled him, really didn't know all that much about him, which was decidedly a major step back.

Trace's focus never left me when he said, "She's got a hell of a voice too."

"A musician. Very nice. Do you play as well?"

"Piano."

"We should play sometime."

That made me turn my attention to Lucien. "You play?"

"Saxophone." He tilted his head and contemplated me for a minute before he said, "You find that odd."

"No, not odd, just surprising. An entrepreneur who also plays music."

"Everyone should have a hobby. I don't trust people who don't have a hobby or a vice. This one . . ." he pointed to Trace, "pounds on people's faces but me, I'm more subtle."

"And you, Rafe?" I asked.

He looked almost embarrassed before he replied, "I like working with my hands, woodworking mostly. It's not just a hobby, it's actually what I do."

I was intrigued since I knew so little about Rafe so I asked, "What do you make?"

"Furniture mostly—tables, chairs, hutches. That kind of thing."

"I'd love to see your work."

"So would I," Lucien muttered.

I settled back in my chair and, for the rest of the evening, enjoyed the company of these three unlikely friends.

At the sound of my cell phone buzzing I pulled myself from my writing and answered it.

"Hey, Ember. How are you?"

"Uncle Josh!" I had spent the past two days since Trace's fight putting in long hours on my new book, so this interruption was most welcome.

"I know this is last minute, but I'm in town and wanted to know if you'd like to go out for dinner."

"I would love to."

"Great, I can pick you up at your apartment, maybe around five? I'd love to catch up."

The apartment. I hadn't yet told my dad that I was no longer living with Lena or that I was now living with Trace. I knew I needed to—and soon—but I just wasn't quite sure how to handle that conversation.

"Actually, I'm not living with Lena anymore. We had a falling out. I'm staying with a friend."

My uncle's damn intuition caught me. "And does this friend have a name?" he asked.

I lowered my voice hoping that maybe he wouldn't hear my answer when I said, "Trace."

There was a moment of silence before my uncle said, "Well, perhaps your friend can join us this evening."

I resisted the urge to bang my head on the desk and replied, "I'll ask him."

"Delaney's, five o'clock, does that work?"

"Yes, Uncle Josh. I'll see you then."

"I'm looking forward to it."

I dropped my phone on the table and moaned. I understood my uncle's concern, but the thought of witnessing the interrogation I had no doubt Uncle Josh was going to subject Trace to was almost too much to bear. I wasn't even sure what was going on with Trace and me, so grilling him for those answers would drive him away from me as far and as fast as possible.

The thought popped into my head to not mention the dinner to Trace and just tell my uncle he was busy, but I was a terrible liar and Uncle Josh was like a dog with a bone when he wanted something. It was what made him such a good private investigator. This fact had me banging my head on the desk, several times in fact, before I stood and made my way down the hall to the living room. Trace was sitting on the sofa reading through some papers when I entered. He looked good, sitting there, comfortable. Maybe Uncle Josh's grilling wasn't such a bad idea because I really wanted to know more about this man and he didn't seem all that eager to share. Maybe I'd even get more insight into the significance of that article in his storage unit.

"Ember?"

"My uncle Josh just called. He invited us to dinner."

There came the slightest of hesitations before he asked, "What time?"

"Five." His expression was clear; he thought that was too early for dinner, but what he didn't know was that Uncle Josh was going to use the extra time to grill him for information.

"Okay."

I settled on the sofa next to him. "Just like that?"

He affectionately tugged on a strand of my hair before he said, "Yeah. So is there anything I should know about your uncle?"

He was teasing me but I answered him anyway. "Well, he'll probably ask a thousand questions, hazard of his job and all."

"What does he do?"

"Private investigator."

An indiscernible look swept over his face, but he offered no insight into what caused it so I continued on.

"He wasn't always. He used to work on the docks with my dad, but after my mom died he became obsessed with trying to learn what happened to her. As a private citizen you can't gain access to most of the sources needed to investigate a case like hers. He always said it was the not knowing that was the hardest. After her case went cold my uncle quit his job and went back to school. Unfortunately, the case is so old that the likelihood of him finding any answers now is very remote even with his increased access."

Trace stood abruptly. "I have some things I need to do before dinner." He reached for his papers and disappeared from the room.

Typical.

We arrived at Delaney's a little before five but my uncle was already there. His back was to us but when he turned, I saw his face; it was so much like the one in the photos my dad was forever showing me, it caused tears to burn the back of my eyes. He was my uncle and my mother's brother, but seeing him made me see her. I couldn't help it when tears started trailing down my cheeks.

As soon as his blue eyes looked into mine, I found myself pulling from Trace and walking right into his embrace. He held me closely and I could hear the tears that he was trying to hold back as he spoke.

"You look so much like your mother."

"So do you."

"God, I've missed you and that pigheaded father of yours."

I glanced up as he looked down at me. "I might not be a private investigator, but I'm still going to find out what you fought about that was important enough to keep you two apart for as long as you've been."

He smiled as he touched my cheek. "I can tell you that now. I told your father that he needed to move on, date, and marry again so that you would have a woman's influence. You were getting older and your dad frequently mentioned how you were struggling to fit in with girls your own age. I thought a mother figure could help to smooth out the transition for you. I knew he loved my sister, but I didn't realize how much until he turned from me—more interested in holding onto a ghost than truly living. At least that's what I thought at the time."

"And now?"

"He loved her—still does. Having never experienced that kind of love, I don't understand it, but I should have respected it. Not to mention that my arrogance implied he wasn't cutting it as your father. I couldn't imagine being a single parent, especially becoming one because of such a tragic loss."

I couldn't help my smile. "Am I sensing a reconciliation between you and my dad in the near future?"

"I hope so."

"It's about time."

I pulled from him, but kept his hand as I turned to Trace. "Uncle Josh, this is Trace Montgomery. Trace, my uncle Josh."

Trace took a step toward us.

"It's very nice to meet you, sir."

"Likewise. Let's get a table." I knew that look. Uncle Josh was just waiting to pounce and he didn't disappoint. As soon as we were seated, he let the questions fly.

"So what do you do Trace?"

Trace had no visual reaction to the question and answered it with the same directness that it was asked. "I fight, amateur status."

"Your address is pretty posh for a amateur fighter."

I was outraged. "Uncle Josh, you investigated him?"

He was completely unrepentant. "Cursory, nothing probing."

Trace seemed completely unfazed. "I have family money and some investments that have done rather well."

I was outraged, yes, but I couldn't lie, I liked learning more about Trace.

"How did you meet Ember?"

A slight smile touched Trace's lips as his eyes moved from my uncle to me. "We were at a club. She punched a guy, I stepped up to make sure he didn't punch her back."

It was Uncle Josh who was outraged now as he turned to me and practically roared, "You punched a guy? What the hell were you thinking?"

"He was being rude."

"So you punched him?"

"It seemed like a good idea at the time."

I could tell my uncle had more thoughts on that subject but he moved on. "What happened with Lena?"

"Her boyfriend's a creep and I didn't want to be near him. She disagreed so I moved out."

"Obviously the CliffsNotes version but I get it. So you're staying with Trace."

"I didn't have anywhere to go, and he offered me a place to stay."

His next question was aimed at Trace. "And your intentions?"

"To make her happy."

My head almost snapped off my neck with how fast I turned to look at Trace. What a thing to say and the sincerity I saw in his expression made it that much sweeter. Uncle Josh leaned back in his chair and smiled.

"Good answer. Let's order, I'm starved."

I wasn't sure what caused the change in Trace but he grew increasingly more distant after our evening with my uncle. The glimpse I caught of a more carefree Trace was just that, a glimpse, and if anything, he was more reserved and brooding than he'd ever been.

Sometimes it felt as if he didn't even remember that he was sharing an apartment with me, but then I'd catch him watching me and I could only describe the look on his face as longing. I really didn't understand why he seemed so determined to keep away from me, when clearly we both wanted the same thing. We lived under the same roof but he had definitely drawn a line in the sand. I had never been in his room. Occasionally he had come to mine, where we would lay in bed and talk for hours. A few times he had even fallen asleep but every morning I woke up alone. But after our dinner with Uncle Josh, he ignored me completely. I wanted to ask him what was causing his change in behavior toward me but he was rarely in the apartment anymore.

One night, two weeks after our dinner with my uncle, I was curled up on the sofa with my laptop when there was a knock at the door. I pulled it open to see a beauty of a woman standing there—the woman from the charity event at Clover.

She looked at me from head to toe and back again, and I could tell she thought me no competition before she purred, "Is Trace here?"

My heart just stopped as a numbness stole over my limbs. It was difficult to talk around the lump that had formed in my throat, but I managed. "No, he's not here."

"He told me seven."

It hurt, that damn organ in my chest, as I held the door open for her.

"Would you like to wait inside?"

She brushed past me as if she owned the place before she settled herself on the sofa, her eyes flickering to my laptop. There was a shrewdness to her when she asked, "Who are you to Trace?"

Good question and one that I didn't have to answer, since at that moment the door opened and Trace walked in. I watched as those eyes moved from me to his date and back again.

"Are you ready, Heidi?"

"Yeah, baby."

He walked to her and reached for her hand, linking their fingers. The sight left tears burning the back of my throat. His eyes stayed on me as he brushed his lips over Heidi's before he patted her on the ass and said, "Wait outside for a second. I need to talk with Ember."

"Hurry," she all but moaned.

I couldn't bring myself to look at Trace so I watched as Heidi sauntered from the apartment. The flatness of his voice reluctantly pulled my attention.

"How's the apartment hunting going?"

That question was like getting my legs kicked out from under me. "I haven't really been looking. I was under the impression you wanted me to stay here."

"You were pretty clear you didn't want to make this a permanent arrangement. I've curbed my lifestyle so I don't make you uncomfortable, but that's not a solution that's going to work for me long-term."

And the hits just kept coming. "Are you kicking me out?"

"Of course not, I'm just offering a nudge. If we come back here, we'll try to be quiet." He looked at me from over his shoulder and added, "But fair warning, Heidi's a screamer."

I stood there long after he left, wondering what the hell that was all about. Two weeks ago he'd said he wanted to make me happy and now he was kicking me to the curb. Shock had my brain muddled but when that subsided I remembered Rafe's warning to me. Was it possible that I was getting too close and Trace was pushing me away? How many people in his life got too close? Only two that I knew of had hung on.

Walking away was safer but nothing worth having came easy. If I was wrong, I'd have a broken heart, but if I was right, there was a chance that if dug in my heels, I may just crack Trace's hard exterior. I was certain that there was something worth the effort underneath.

Over the next week, Trace and I waged a silent war. He continued to try and push me away with his dismissive and callous attitude and I countered by being bubbly to the point of clueless. I wasn't immune to his behavior, but I wasn't about to let him see that. The harder he tried to pull from me, the more understanding I became. He brought Heidi around two more times, but after the last date when I told them to have a good time and if they wanted, I could make myself scarce, he stopped bringing her around. I'd called his bluff and we both knew it. A few times I saw a crack in his outer shell, he who didn't show emotion, and the sight of his annoyance and frustration was very gratifying.

After a week of battling the obstinate and hardheaded man, I needed agreeable company, so I called Kyle. We met at our favorite

Italian place, where I ordered a bottle of wine. I was tempted to ask for a straw, but I suspected that would be frowned upon.

"All right, spill. Are you winning the war?" Kyle was never one to beat around the bush.

"No and it's tiring, but I won't give up because I know his actions and his words don't jive."

"And you are just contrary enough to find a challenge in that," Kyle said.

"I am but I've seen the way he looks at me when he doesn't think I'm paying attention. He isn't indifferent and frankly I think he's worth fighting for, even if it's him I'm fighting."

"So what's the plan?"

"I have no idea. He's so damn pigheaded."

"Seems to me if you called his bluff once then you can do it again."

"Meaning?"

"He wants you to find another place to live, so tell him you have."

"That could backfire."

"Yeah, but you can always stay with me and at least you'll know." He leaned closer before he added, "From what you've told me of him, he's very protective of you, so paint a picture of a living situation that you know he'll object to."

"Kyle, that suggestion is both diabolical and juvenile."

"All is fair in love and war."

I lifted my glass to him in salute. "Amen to that."

———◆———

The following morning, I took Kyle's suggestion. I caught Trace in the kitchen cooking something on the stove and took a seat at the island. "I've been apartment hunting and I found a place I like." I saw his body stiffen, but I just continued on.

"I'm moving out, but I thought you should know that I would like to stay."

A part of me hoped he'd take that moment to say, "Yes, stay," but he didn't so I surged on.

"Thank you so much for letting me stay here."

He remained completely still and if I hadn't witnessed the tensing of his shoulders, I wouldn't have thought he'd heard me at all. I was going to continue with the charade, but based on Trace's lack of response, I wasn't entirely sure I was right about him. Maybe he really did want me gone. "Well, I better go start packing."

I hurried from the room as those damn tears started. I hadn't realized that Trace had followed me until he spoke. "Do you have a roommate?"

I looked up at him and though he looked calm, I had the sense that he was actually more like a hurricane off the coast with all of that deadly energy stirring to life. Hope sprung.

"Yeah, some guy. He seems nice enough."

"You're going to live with a man you don't know?"

"Why not? I'm living with you and I don't know you either. You try really hard to make sure I don't know you at all. Besides, you don't want me here and I can't afford the luxury of living on my own." His hands actually balled into fists and it looked as if he wanted to rip something to shreds. His contrary behavior stirred my own temper.

"What exactly is the problem?"

"You don't even know this guy."

"No, but why the fuck do you care? You parade that bitch Heidi in my face. This is what *you* wanted!"

He was clenching his jaw so hard I thought he might actually break a tooth.

I continued. "Look I get it. There's a whole part of you that you are unwilling to share. You don't want people close and it's easier for you to stay alone so you don't have to be human. You want to be a cyborg? Then be one, but you don't get to push me away one minute and then get pissed the next because I did as you wished. You didn't give me a say. You decreed how it was going to be between us, so now you have to sit back and shut the fuck up!"

The range of emotion that crossed over his face was startling, especially for someone who was so good at hiding behind a mask. For just a moment, I saw past the armor and the indifference to the damaged man underneath. Tears stung my eyes at the look of self-loathing and hatred that burned from those steel-blue eyes.

"God, Trace, what happened to you?"

"I can't hurt you like this. I do want you here."

"Then why are you pushing me away?"

"You deserve better than me."

"Heidi?"

"My attempt to prove that point to you."

"Is that why you're never around, why you encouraged me to move out?"

"Yes."

"Why?"

He moved with startling speed to stand just in front of me. His eyes were dark and wild as he reached for my hand to press it to the hard length of him.

"This is all I have to offer you. Sex is all I'm good for and you deserve more than that, more than a shag from a guy who's fucked half the city."

"All you have to offer or all you want to offer?"

He laughed, but it wasn't a pleasant sound as he moved away from me to pace the room before he stopped to level me with eyes that were filled with conflicting emotions.

"I'd give it all to you—but me—I'm not a good bet. You deserve a man worthy of you. I want you. I can't think straight; I want you so fucking badly, but I'm shit and I always will be."

"What if I disagree?"

"Eventually, you'd come to realize the truth."

"Why do you hate yourself so much?"

"It's what I know."

I walked over to him and took his hands into mine. "I want you too. I want to be with you. Let me in. Let me close to you."

Determination squared his shoulders. He truly believed he was doing this for me, which made me say, "If you don't want to take a chance on me I get it, but you should know the damage is done because for me, it's you."

He said nothing—just stood there looking at me with an expression that broke my heart, and then he pulled his hands from mine, turned, and walked away. It hurt, watching him go. It hurt so much that I had trouble drawing in a breath as I settled on the edge of the bed and let my tears run down my cheeks.

I gave Trace time after our fight. I knew he needed it as much as I did. He hated himself, and by the look he gave me before he left the room, he really truly hated himself. It was that look, more than anything, that made me reach for my phone later that night.

"Rafe, where's Trace?"

It sounded like relief in his voice when he offered, "He's here, at the gym."

I hung up and grabbed a cab. I got to the gym and I could hear the cursing from the street outside. I moved through crowds, but stopped when I felt a hand on my arm. I looked up to see Rafe, but his expression was grim.

"I'm really glad you came."

I felt dread. "Why?"

He gestured to the ring. "He's letting them pound on him."

I turned to see Trace in the middle of the ring with his back and chest covered in large, purple welts. An ugly, blackish-purple mark over his ribs on the right side was clearly the pooling of blood from cracked or broken ribs, but it was the sight of his face that made tears stream down mine. He was so bloody that I couldn't even see his features. I watched as he made no attempt to dodge the blows, taking the pounding over and over again. It was a testament to his strength that he could take that kind of beating and still be standing.

I stood there for ten minutes watching as Trace allowed himself to be hammered and then, as if he'd grown tired of it all, he moved with lightning speed and leveled his opponent with one solid punch to the jaw. The crowd went berserk, but Trace just stood there.

Seeing him standing alone in the midst of a crowd provoked me to go to him. I reached the ring and climbed under the ropes. I didn't know what he was thinking about, if anything—he didn't realize my presence until I reached for his hand. His eyes moved to our hands before he lifted his gaze to my face and it was then that I saw how desolate he looked. I threw my arms around his neck and pressed myself against him. I felt the shudder that went through his body and then he reached up and wrapped his arms around me, pulling me close, before burying his face in my hair.

Rafe helped me get Trace home and made me promise that I'd call him if I needed anything. Trace was standing in the bathroom looking in the mirror when I returned from seeing Rafe out.

"We should get you cleaned up," I said, which made his eyes find mine in the mirror.

"What are you doing here?"

"I'm not willing to let you go without a fight."

"I'm not good for you."

My voice was harsh as I took a step closer to him. "I don't know who it was in your life that made you believe you were worthless,

Trace, but if I ever find out I intend to beat the shit out of them. You are good for me. You are special. You have more to give than you give yourself credit for."

He responded by pulling me into his arms. When he spoke, his voice broke. "I should push you away, far away from me, but I can't."

"I don't want you to push me away."

⚬⚬⚬

In the morning, I awoke in my bed surprised to find that Trace was still in my room. I had asked him to stay with me so I could check on him during the night but I hadn't expected that he would.

"Good morning."

"Morning." I couldn't ignore the one question that kept rolling around in my head: Who'd fucked him up so badly? The fact that he didn't speak of his family made me guess it was either his dad, mom, or both.

"You look beautiful."

I smiled. "Sweet talker. Stay here and I'll whip us up some breakfast."

I started from the bed, but Trace's hand reached up to stop me and when I looked back at him, his expression had turned serious.

"Are you sure about this?"

I sat on the bed, cross-legged, and took his hand into mine. I feared how badly he'd been abused, since the influence of it still haunted him.

"Someone really did a number on you." I felt him stiffen as he attempted to take his hand back, but I held firm.

"Listen to me." He had that look about him, the blank detached one, but he allowed me to keep his hand so I took that as him acquiescing and continued on.

"I don't know what they did to you and I hope one day you'll trust me enough to tell me, but how you feel about yourself is wrong. You say you're only good for one thing. How can you say that when the first time I met you, it was because you saw a man mistreating a woman and you stepped in?

"That sense of right and wrong, and having the courage to act when you see an injustice, is as much a reflection on the man you are as those tattoos. As far as your belief that you are not good enough for me, the only area I see where I have a leg up on you is that I came from a loving family. The fact that you didn't isn't a reflection on you, but on your miserable parents. And sex, I think you use it as a way of seeking value, and as much as I want and plan to have sex with you, I already see your value so for me sex is the colorful ribbon, but you are the prize."

A rainbow of emotions played over Trace's face, but his eyes, when they looked into mine, were wary yet hopeful. "There's some really bad shit in my past, shit that may have you walking out if you knew." I was in love with him. It was too soon and there was so much I didn't know about him, but I loved him, even more so because under that hard shell, there was tenderness and pain. I wrapped my hands around his face and pressed my mouth to his. I showed him without words what I felt for him. For a moment he was utterly still and then his mouth moved under mine. The kiss started out as a tender affirmation, but it had been so long and I wanted to connect with him on every level, wanted him body and soul. He wanted it too when he took over the kiss, taking his time as his lips, tongue, and teeth savored me with their very thorough tasting. He rolled to pin me under him and I felt the pull, deep in my belly. When Trace started to move, hitting the spot that was starting to ache, it felt unbelievably good even through the layers of our clothes.

His hands moved down along my sides right before he fisted my nightgown and lifted it up over my head. His focus was completely on me, and seeing him looking at me with such heat made my entire body hum with desire.

It was the barest of touches as his finger traced my collarbone and down the valley between my breasts. I inhaled sharply. He pulled my panties down my legs and, remembering the last time, I reached to cover myself.

"Don't. I want to look at you."

It was the rawness of the request that made me drop my hands just as he stood and gripped his boxer briefs. He lingered a moment, pulling my attention from the hard ridge pressing against the cotton to his face, only to see the grin that tugged at his mouth as he teased me. And then he was pulling his briefs down his legs so that I saw all of him, gloriously naked and aroused, and all I could think was . . .

Oh.

My.

God.

Before I could react in any other way, strong arms wrapped around me and pulled me farther onto the bed. I had just a moment to see the heat in his eyes and then his mouth closed over mine. It was erotic, his kiss, like he was feeding off of my desire for him. He looked slightly wild when he lifted his gaze to me just as his finger brushed over my nipple.

"You're so beautiful."

I couldn't speak because he was turning me mindless as he rolled that peak between his thumb and forefinger, pulling slightly, which caused an ache to shoot right down between my legs. He lowered his dark head and took my nipple into his mouth. It wasn't even a conscious action when I lifted myself up to offer him more and he took it. He was driving me crazy and with it came boldness.

I wanted to brand him the way he was me, as my hands moved over him, claiming him as I traced the muscles of his abs, the corded muscles framing his spine, the ridges on his arms, his ass.

My hips started to move against him, rubbing the spot that was aching to the point of pain. Trace's mouth moved over me, fanning kisses under my breasts, over my stomach, his tongue taking a moment to lap at my navel. When he reached my inner thigh, he looked up at me with a naughty grin curving his lips just before his tongue touched the part of me that I so wanted him to touch.

He teased the throbbing nub with his tongue, bringing me to the brink of orgasm only to back off. Moisture pooled between my legs and I was mindless to everything but what Trace's mouth was doing to me. I cried out when he pushed his tongue deep inside of me. I grabbed his head to hold him there while my hips instinctively moved against his penetrating tongue.

His fingers replaced his tongue and the intrusion felt mind-numbing. My body grew greedy, wrapping around those fingers as my hips moved to take them deeper. My entire body seemed to draw into itself, like oxygen being sucked from the room just before a flash burn.

"Come for me, Ember," Trace demanded hoarsely.

Our eyes locked just before he flicked the small nub of pleasure with his tongue and just like that, I did. My eyes closed while pleasure moved over me in waves. Like the last time, it was intense and addicting, crave-worthy and, still riding the high, I already wanted to feel it again. I felt sated and so relaxed when I opened my eyes, only to find that Trace was steadily watching me.

I wanted a turn, wanted to explore him as thoroughly as he did me. I felt my cheeks warm just thinking about it because—though I had experience in giving a man pleasure, the Creep made sure of that—I had never before hungered to taste my fill.

"Could I . . . I mean, would you like it if I did that to you?"

He didn't have to answer; the look of stark lust on his face was enough.

He rolled onto his back and I got a really good look at all of him and, wow, was the man big everywhere. I was shamelessly ogling him when he offered softly, "Touch me, Ember, I want you to be as comfortable with my body as you are with your own."

With the Creep I never wanted to touch him for fear of doing it wrong. But with Trace I felt like I was at a banquet and he was the feast. I couldn't decide where to start so I started at the top as I sat up, leaned over, and pressed a kiss on his mouth. I could taste myself on him and damn was that hot. I felt my blood pounding in my veins as I trailed my lips down his neck and over his shoulder. He had given so much attention to my breasts that I wondered if he would like the same. I could taste the salt on his skin as my tongue trailed a line from his collarbone to his pec, where I flicked his nipple with my tongue. I felt the muscles in his chest tighten and took that as a good sign before I closed my mouth over it.

I never knew that pleasuring someone could be so pleasurable. I felt the ache starting again, the knot of lust in my belly, as I moved my mouth lower over the individual muscles of his abs. When I reached his navel, I kissed around it before I lapped at it like a cat with a bowl of milk.

I looked up at him to see he was watching me so intently, but he held himself completely still, allowing me to explore his body in any way that I wanted. That gesture only made me feel more confident—confident enough to move lower down his body. I stared hungrily at the hard length of him and wanted to fill my mouth with him. I was both shocked and turned on by the near-mindless want that I felt for him.

I straddled his legs and wrapped my hand around him, and he inhaled harshly. I immediately removed my hand.

"Did that hurt?"

His voice was raw when he replied, "In a really fucking good way."

I grinned—I couldn't help it—as I continued my exploration of him, running my thumb over the tip before tracing the veins along the shaft. He was so hard but his skin was smooth as silk.

I wrapped my hand around the length of him again and felt his entire body react. I moved my hand up, squeezing him as I did, which made him close his eyes and moan. By the way his hips were moving against my hand, I knew that he liked what I was doing. It wasn't enough, though. I wanted to taste him, so I lowered my head and tentatively licked him. He went still, the muscles in his abs flexing, and I knew he was waiting, eagerly. I was just as eager when I took him into my mouth. He was so big, but I pulled him deep into my throat and sucked, hard.

His hips jerked as the most erotic sound of pleasure rumbled up his throat. His reaction fueled me, like a match to kindling. His hips started moving faster, pushing him deeper. He reached to pull me to him and, desperate for one last taste, I ran my tongue over the tip and tasted a saltiness there.

He flipped me over onto my back before he settled between my legs. His hand moved down my stomach until he reached the part of me that was aching for him. He rubbed his finger over the moist heat for a moment before his fingers slipped inside of me.

His mouth moved to my breast, his tongue playing with my nipple before he moved up my body to linger just over my mouth. He shifted his hips and with a powerful thrust, he was fully inside of me. "Oh God, Trace." He was so big and it felt so good as my body stretched to take him. I lifted my hips and took him deeper. Our eyes never left the other as we moved together and I wrapped my legs around his waist to pull him to me.

I felt the start of the orgasm, like a rope fraying, just as Trace started to move deeper and faster and then I just lost it, the intensity so strong it tore a cry from my lips. Trace continued to move and each thrust prolonged the pleasure. Then he tensed a moment, his face shifted into one of such harsh ecstasy, and his body spasmed with his own release.

He collapsed on top of me. I wasn't ready for him to move away from me and, by the weight of him, he wasn't ready to move. I felt his hard breathing on my neck, the pounding of his heart in his chest, and I couldn't help feeling a bit smug myself because he was as affected by our lovemaking as I was.

"I'll move in a minute," he muttered in my hair.

"No rush."

I felt the curve of his lips against the bare skin of my shoulder before he lifted his head and those eyes looked down into mine. "I didn't hurt you?"

"Only in a good way." And then I wiggled my hips and grinned. "Again."

His smile in reply was breathtaking before he purred, "Minx."

I turned serious when I touched his face. "There is nothing you could ever do that would make me leave you."

There was a note of sadness in his voice when he asked, "Nothing?"

"Well, I can't be one of many. I can't be with you knowing that you are sharing this with others. I'm not made that way."

He reached up and touched my cheek. "Being with you—I wouldn't want to be with anyone else, but are you sure that it's me you want?"

"Yes."

I knew that he wanted to believe me, but he wasn't there yet.

I was prepared to wait him out and then he leaned in and kissed me. And then all I could think about was him.

A week after we made love, I came home from work with more pain than my typical achy feet. The smell of something yummy teased my nose, and I followed it into the kitchen to find Trace standing in front of the stove.

"Smells good."

He turned at the sound of my voice and a smile spread over his face.

"Hi." He placed the spoon on the plate before he walked over and pulled me into a hug, but when I winced, he pulled back with a look of concern.

"What's wrong?" His eyes grew hard. "Did someone hurt you?"

"No, nothing like that. I just, well, I guess it would be easier to show you."

His eyebrow arched slightly in response, but when I took a step away from him and moved to unsnap my jeans, his expression turned into something else entirely as a playful gleam entered his eyes. He rolled back on his heels before his hands found the pockets of his jeans.

"I'm liking this already."

I pushed my jeans down a bit as I lifted my blouse to expose a bandage just below my hip bone. It only took him a second for understanding to dawn on him when he looked back up at me.

"What have you done?"

I removed the bandage and watched as his eyes moved to the spot I had just revealed. The tattoo of the Celtic symbol for everlasting love was done in black and gray and just under it was Trace's name in cursive. I watched him as he stood transfixed, looking at my hip, and then I offered softly, "I knew with absolute certainty that what I wanted, I'd want forever."

His gaze moved up to mine as tenderness washed over his face and then he had me in his arms.

"God, Ember." He buried his face in my hair and breathed me in and when he pulled back and looked into my eyes, I felt tears burning my throat. His voice became a harsh vow when he whispered, "I love you."

My heart swelled hearing those words from him. His lips moved over mine, seeking and tasting as his hands came up to frame my face. I almost whined in protest when his mouth pulled from mine, but then his lips were on my neck, pressing open-mouthed kisses down my throat and along my collarbone, and when he moved back up the other side, his mouth lingered near my ear.

"I love your tattoo."

He stepped back and smiled at me. He loved me. I was delirious, but I could tell he was feeling a little off-balance, so I tried to lighten the mood.

"It's irritating, but not necessarily painful, like hell."

His grin grew wicked. "Ah, baby, I'll kiss it and make it better."

Chapter Eight

Trace and I were out shopping in a part of the city that I didn't often visit. There was a dealer of Schuberth helmets that Trace wanted to visit so he could get me my own helmet, a really safe helmet, for his bike. Were there even words?

Once we picked the one we wanted, I walked outside as Trace took care of the rest.

"Ember, funny seeing you out and about. What, no book to read?"

I stopped abruptly at the sight of Lena and Todd standing right outside the store. Lena wrapped her arms around Todd in what I supposed was a sign of solidarity.

So, apparently, not only had the bridge been burned, but also swept away by a raging current. "Actually, I just finished a wonderful story on karma and how it always comes back around. No one is safe, neither the bitchy and self-absorbed nor the calculating pimps."

Lena's eyes grew wider and her face went pale for a second. "Todd and Dane aren't like that." Our time apart clearly had no effect on where her loyalties lay.

"And you know this because you've been with Todd for a few months so you readily take his word on the matter over someone you've known since the seventh grade?"

"Todd doesn't lie."

"And I do?"

"I didn't say that; don't put words into my mouth. Trace lied and you believed him. Naivety happens when you're socially stunted from spending all of your time alone."

My disgusted disbelief started out as a chuckle, but before long I was roaring, laughing so hard that my eyes filled with tears. I wiped away the tears with the back of my hand as I met, and held, Lena's incredulous expression.

"I can't believe it took me this long to see you for what you really are. My dad had you nailed, but me, I guess I'm not that quick on the uptake."

At that moment the door of the shop slammed open before six-feet-four of towering rage. Trace lifted Todd a foot off the pavement by his shirt. He looked like he was going to commit murder and Todd, it seemed, was about to toss his lunch.

"You're too fucking close, asshole." Trace's voice made the hair at the nape of my neck stand on end.

My eyes stayed on Lena and when she was able to pull her gaze from my spectacularly gorgeous boyfriend, I saw jealousy again in hers.

"This is Trace." I leaned closer before I added, "He really hates your boyfriend. Do yourself a favor and get him away—far, far away."

Trace shoved Todd, causing him to stumble backward before falling onto his ass as Trace took a few steps closer and loomed over him.

"If you get too close to Ember again, you'll need to be carried away."

Todd didn't hesitate to scurry to his feet before he turned and practically ran away, his arms pumping at his sides in his retreat. I turned to Lena as Trace reached for my hand to link our fingers.

"What a real gem you've got there. Actually, you know what? You two are perfect for each other."

With an outraged huff, she turned and followed after her loser boyfriend and though I knew she wasn't, and probably never had been, the person I thought she was, I was still saddened to realize that such a huge part of my childhood had been a lie.

"Are you okay, Ember?"

"I am."

"She doesn't deserve your energy. You know that, right?"

He was right and I said as much.

"Good. Now let's get something to eat because I'm starving."

<hr />

I was working on my book but my focus was off since my thoughts kept returning to the scene with Lena from the other day. When my cell phone buzzed, I welcomed the distraction.

"Ember."

"Hank!" Joy filled me when I heard the voice from home, but it was quickly replaced with fear because why would my dad's friend be calling me? "Is something wrong with Dad?"

"He's okay, Ember, just a little roughed up, but I thought you should know."

"How roughed up? What happened?"

"A really nasty sprain. A crate fell from the lift and your dad landed wrong when he jumped out of the way. He's wearing one of those boots and hasn't stopped bitching about it."

A reluctant smile touched my lips and the fear ebbed since if he was complaining it couldn't be that bad.

"I'm guessing he's home."

"Yeah, forced vacation for a week. Accidents are a part of the job but waiting out the recovery period is always boring."

I needed to see for myself that my dad was okay, but he would feel guilty that I dropped everything to do so. "I'll come down this weekend."

Hank exhaled in relief. "I was so hoping you were going to say that."

———◆———

Trace had left earlier in the day to help Rafe deliver some of his pieces to a client. I didn't hear him come home. He startled me out of packing when he asked, "What are you doing?"

He was leaning against the doorjamb trying to look casual, but he was anything but. I realized how this must look.

"My dad got hurt on the job. It's nothing serious, but I'm going home this weekend to see for myself."

I saw the tension ease before I added, "I would love it if you would come with me, but I completely understand if you don't."

He touched a lock of my hair, rubbing the strands between his fingers, before he teased, "Meeting the parent?"

"It's too soon, isn't it?"

My question hung unanswered between us and I was certain he was looking for an excuse, but he surprised me when he answered with a quiet sincerity, "I'd like to meet your dad."

———◆———

Fishtown, a tight-knit Irish community, was following the example of its neighbor on the west, Northern Liberties, with a wave of urban renewal as new businesses made Fishtown their home. I took one look at our rental as I got in and asked, "Why did you rent an Escalade? It's like a tank."

He spared me a glance, a grin flirting over his sexy mouth, before he offered, "Because it's like a tank."

Understanding dawned as a smile spread over my face. "You're nervous about meeting my dad?"

I noticed his hands were gripping the steering wheel with such force that they were almost white and, when I looked at his profile, I saw his jaw clenching. Hoping to ease his anxiety, I reached over and touched his cheek as he said, "I've never been brought home to meet the family, so it's a bit stressful when the first time I do is with the only one who matters."

"I've never brought a boy home, so it's a first for both of us."

His eyes found mine as a smile touched his lips and we shared a brief moment. I saw humor before his eyes returned to the road.

"Or maybe I'm intimidated. You know your dad and his dock-worker friends."

"Tease all you want but my dad is going to love you and so are the guys. You're going to fit right in, trust me."

We pulled up in front of my dad's row house and there he and his boot were, sitting on the front steps. He looked as he always had with his short-cropped hair, which was the same shade of brown as mine, and eyes that were more hazel than brown. Having worked on the docks, he was built a lot like Trace and even pushing fifty, he was still broad in the shoulders and narrow in the waist. The sight of the boot brought an unexpected pang of fear. My dad was my rock. He was invincible in my eyes but seeing that boot only drove the point home that he was mortal. I shook the thought away just as Trace shut off the engine.

I turned to him in time to see a hint of panic sweep over his expression. Why the sight of that made my heart melt, I couldn't say.

"Come meet my dad."

Trace pressed a kiss in my palm before he climbed out of the car and came around to open my door. My dad moved from the front step and he slowly hobbled over to us. Heaven forbid the stubborn and willful man should show weakness by using crutches.

"Emmie, my girl. You didn't need to come home, not that I'm not thrilled that you did. Hank's turning into a mothering hen in his old age." Before I could answer, my dad wrapped me in his strong, familiar arms.

"I needed to see for myself that you were okay, Daddy."

"Just a mishap with a crate but I'm really happy to see you."

As we pulled away, I reached for Trace's hand and pulled him closer, keeping my eyes on my dad's.

"Dad, Trace Montgomery. Trace, my dad, Shawn Walsh."

I watched as the two most important people in my life took each other's measure.

"It's nice to meet you, sir."

"Call me Shawn, son." My dad's eyes moved to the car behind us; a smile cracked over his face before his eyes returned to Trace's.

"You rented that?"

"Yes."

"Couldn't you find anything bigger?"

There was a moment of silence before Trace threw his head back and howled with laughter. Just like that, all of the tension just drained from him. Trace grabbed our bags and we followed my dad up the steps and into the house.

"Emmie, you're in your room. Trace, I'll put you on the third floor." He stopped halfway up the stairs and turned to Trace before he added, "The stairs creak."

He said nothing more as he turned and continued up the stairs. I couldn't help the chuckle because Trace looked thoroughly chastised.

After Trace placed my bag on the floor near my bed, he followed my dad up to his room. A few minutes later there was a light knock on my door.

"Come in, Daddy."

He pushed the door open, and closed it behind him before he walked over to settle on the edge of my bed.

"So you really are okay?" I asked.

"As you can see. Where did you meet Trace?"

"At a club. Someone was harassing me and he stepped in and knocked the guy's lights out."

I couldn't tell what my dad was thinking, so I started babbling, trying to argue a case in Trace's favor. "He, like you, pegged Lena's character. Something dark from his past has left him believing he is unworthy of love. He's a fighter, a really good one too."

"I know. I've heard of him."

That surprised me, but I moved past that and continued on, "He's good, Daddy. He stands up for what's right and underneath it all, there's a man who is desperate for love, both giving it and receiving it. Next to you, he's the finest man I've ever known."

My heart was pounding as worry over whether my dad was going to like Trace consumed me. I didn't know what I would do if he didn't approve because I loved my dad but I loved Trace too. It was with genuine fear that I asked, "Do you think you could like him, Daddy?"

He reached over to take my hand. "He brought you home in a tank and didn't argue being put up in the attic even though that boy could probably bench press me with little effort." A smile touched my lips as I thought of that one day in the grocery store.

"But mostly, when he looks at you, he reminds me of how I used to look at your mother so, yes, I can see myself liking him."

I threw my arms around my dad and held him close as he whispered in my ear, "Welcome home, Emmie girl."

My dad went downstairs to brew some tea and I continued putting my things away. There was a knock at the door and I called for Trace to come in. I gave myself a moment to look at him filling the doorway of my childhood room.

"How's your room?"

"I think if your dad could have gotten a cot on the roof he would have."

"I'm his baby girl."

"I know and that's why if he had gotten that cot on the roof, I would have slept on it with no complaints."

"He likes you."

His eyebrow rose at that. "How do you know?"

"He told me." I walked over to Trace and ran my hands up those arms, which, sadly, were covered by a sweater, before resting them on his shoulders.

"He said that the way you look at me reminds him of how he used to look at my mom."

Trace's arms came around me then and, when he spoke, he sounded hoarse. "If that look is the one where I can't believe that you're mine and I'd do anything to make you happy, then I'm guilty as charged."

We joined my dad in the kitchen for lunch. I insisted on making the sandwiches so he could sit and rest, which he reluctantly agreed to. I got a look when I pulled the extra chair over to elevate his foot but he needed to suck it up. Once we were settled around the table my dad asked, "How's the writing?"

"I haven't gone back to my first book because the second one is all consuming. I even brought my laptop this weekend because when the story is flowing like this, I don't want to lose momentum."

"If you need someone to read it, I'd like nothing more."

"Thanks, Dad."

My dad turned his attention to Trace. "You're amateur status, right?"

"Yes."

"You have plans on going professional?"

I picked up on the subtle change in Trace's voice when he said, "No, fighting is a release."

"You make enough money to support yourself?"

I tensed even though my dad was justified in asking. "I've got an inheritance and a really good portfolio that keeps the money growing."

"Fair enough." I couldn't tell what my dad was thinking. "If you want to work on your book, I can use the time to show Trace around the neighborhood and introduce him to some of the guys."

"Take him to the docks and throw him in," I said with a grin, but my dad was looking at Trace and shaking his head.

"If anyone is taking a swim, it wouldn't be him. I couldn't budge him with a backhoe. What do you bench?"

Trace's grin was wicked when he replied, "How much do you weigh?"

My dad's laugh was so nice to hear as he slapped Trace affectionately on the back. "Yup, I like you. Come on, let's go scare my buddies."

Trace stood and placed his and my dad's dishes in the dishwasher before turning to me and pressing a kiss on my forehead.

"See you later, love."

"Have fun. Behave, Daddy."

He kissed my head before he replied, "Always."

I was straightening up the living room and dusting when I heard the sound of heavy footsteps coming up the front steps. The door opened and in walked my dad and Trace. Judging from the smiles on their faces, their night together had been a success. Trace saw me first and the look in his eyes made my heart pound in my chest. My dad turned and smiled as he started for the stairs.

"I'm calling it a night. I'm not as young as I used to be." He turned to Trace and put out his hand, which Trace immediately shook.

"Thanks for hanging with an old man."

"Thanks for letting me."

"See you in the morning, Emmie."

"Good night, Daddy."

Trace reached for me and pulled us both down onto the sofa. He wrapped his arm around my shoulders as I rested my head against his chest and snuggled more firmly against his side.

"Did you have fun?"

"I did but it's some male rite of passage so I can't tell you what we did."

"You bellied up to the bar at Bud's and nursed one beer all night while exchanging whose-is-bigger stories."

A smile spread over Trace's face as he reached up and touched my nose. "Exactly."

And just like that his mood changed as he shifted his position so he could frame my face in his hands before he lowered his head to mine.

"Do you think your dad will mind if we make out on the sofa?"

"I've never made out on the sofa before."

"Really? Well, there's always a first time for everything." And then his mouth was on mine as he wrapped me in his arms and pulled me across his lap. What an incredible first time.

Chapter Nine

"Congratulations on your first journalism interview!" Trace's enthusiasm touched me.

One of Professor Smythe's inquires panned out and I got an interview with one of New York City's premier online magazines, *In Step*, days after we returned from Philly.

"How do you think it went?" he asked.

"Really well, but they've got other applicants to consider, so we have to do the waiting game."

His arms wrapped around me and he pulled me close. "Either way, it's something to be proud of just getting an interview. We need to celebrate!"

True to his word, Trace and I went to an up-and-coming jazz bar later that evening, and while he was off getting us drinks, I sat at a table listening to some seriously good blues.

I had difficulty keeping up with Trace's moods from one day to the next. He either came across as the affectionate Trace who was deeply interested in my life, or the closed-off Trace who had no wish to share anything personal about himself and hated me prying.

I knew that he came home to me, that it was I who shared not just his bed, but his life, yet I still in good conscience couldn't admit that it was true. Every time we made love, it was in my room. It was as if his room, like a part of his heart, was off-limits to me. It bothered me way more than I wanted it to. There was this whole part of him, his past, his family, and the dark secrets that still haunted him that he wouldn't share. I was hopeful, though, that in due time, he would feel more comfortable around me and would open up after we were together longer, since it had only been a few weeks since he'd told me he loved me.

A shadow fell over me and I looked up into the pale-blue eyes of a woman. It was Heidi. To know that the deeply intimate acts Trace and I shared in the bedroom had been shared with countless others—yeah, I wasn't having an easy time dealing with that. She really was beautiful, but then she opened her mouth, reminding me that she was also a shrew.

"So, you're Trace's flavor of the month. Welcome to the club." She pulled out the chair across from me and sat down, brushing her long, pale hair behind her so it cascaded down her slim back like a golden waterfall.

"We never officially met. I'm Heidi."

"Ember."

She leaned back, but kept her eyes fixed on me. "So it looks like you reeled Trace in. How exactly did you pull that off?"

"I love him. He loves me."

She waved that off. "He loves all of us, sweetheart."

I got along just fine with Trace's guy friends, but it was the women, the hordes of women, with whom I was having a bit of trouble. It had been hard to watch the familiarity of a girl's hand on his arm accompanied by the knowing look, the one that said, "I've seen you naked." Being forced to talk to one of those women sucked, particularly since Heidi wasn't just one of the horde, she was the specific one Trace used to drive me off. What was so special about her or their relationship that made him choose her over the others? It wasn't a question that I wanted to hear the answer to.

She must have seen me flinch since she leaned up more closely to study my face.

"You don't really think that it's different with you, do you?"

"It is different."

"Well, sure you're living with him, and I give you credit for pulling that off, but Trace has demons, surely you've figured that out for yourself, and his demons hold all the power. He's given you the line, right, that he isn't good enough for you?"

I paled and I knew that she saw it because an evil little smile touched her lips before she forged on.

"He'll never love anyone enough to move past those demons. It's just how he's made. You know that all of those angels on his arm who see, hear, and speak no evil are all the people in his life who knew the secret and kept quiet. You've got to be pretty fucked up to mark yourself with your own nightmare."

How could Heidi possibly know so much about him?

"He is not forthcoming with information on his personal life, yet you seem to have a pretty thorough understanding of the man. How?"

A slight blush tinted her cheeks. I realized that she was embarrassed, but what exactly could embarrass a haughty bitch like her?

"Holy shit, you're stalking him, aren't you?"

"No!"

I tilted my head and really studied her before I leaned back in my chair and laughed.

"Are you the president of the Trace Castoff Club?"

She looked down and smoothed her hands over her lap. "Don't be ridiculous."

"Yet here you are reaching out to me. I'm not arrogant enough to believe that I'm the only one you've done this with. How many others have you treated to this little chat?"

I didn't think she was going to answer, but she surprised me. "Enough to paint a fairly accurate picture."

"And how exactly did you make the leap that he was tormented just from stalking him?"

"I recognized the symptoms."

She didn't offer more. I suspected she was talking about herself, but either way she needed to move on.

"And you care, why?"

She wasn't quite so cocky when she replied, "I'm not used to being unwanted."

"Trace hurt your pride, so you stalk him? You need to get over yourself." I held her stare with a hard one of my own. "I love him. He loves me. It is different with me and I think we both know that. Move on, Heidi, because he has."

She stood then and without another word she was gone, swallowed up in the crowd. Though I knew that everything she said was likely just sour grapes, I couldn't help the feeling that there was more truth than spite in her words.

Trace returned a short time later with our drinks and, as he set my glass of wine on the table, he leaned over and kissed me before taking the seat that Heidi had vacated.

"Are you okay?"

"Yeah, just a little tired."

"Do you want to go?"

"No, the music is very soothing."

"Okay, but let me know if you change your mind."

We sat there in silence for a bit and listened to the music. A steady stream of people stopped at our table to say hello to Trace and through it all, I sat there brooding, playing back Heidi's words in my head. I refused to believe that Trace, if asked, really wouldn't share his past with me, so I worked up the nerve to ask the one question that I needed him to answer.

"Trace, would you tell me about your childhood?"

"When will you hear about your interview?"

I had gotten used to Trace changing the subject when the topic was too close to home, but I wasn't going to back down this time. "You don't talk about your past. Why?"

Irritation moved over his features before he said, "What's done is done. No point in talking about it." His body language made it very clear that the discussion was over. "Do you want to dance?"

"No. I want you to fucking talk to me!"

His face went completely blank and his eyes turned eerily empty. His body tensed, his shoulders stiffened, and I knew before he even answered me that he wasn't going to share.

"No."

"Why?"

His eyes were burning with something dark before he bit out, "Because talking about it doesn't change it."

"Have you ever talked about it?" I tried to reach across the table to hold his hand, but he pulled it away.

"No, and I have no plans of ever doing so."

"And your parents?"

"May they rot in hell. There are things that I don't talk about, ever, and to be with me you need to accept that."

"Is that you in the tattoo on your arm?"

I knew my question caught him off guard. Surprise flashed over his face before he stood, and as he leaned over the table, anger and torment consumed the dullness of his previous expression.

"Yeah, it is. I was one of the masses in the pit, but now I'm the master."

He turned and walked away and as I watched him go, I knew

deep down that Heidi's warning to me hadn't been all sour grapes. I really did believe that he loved me, but I wasn't quite as certain that he loved me enough.

An hour later, he still hadn't returned. I was tempted to go hunt him down at the gym, but I was so angry I was afraid I would say something I couldn't take back.

I didn't go home until close to four in the morning. Kyle, being a really great friend, had let me vent when I showed up at his apartment. I didn't think that Trace would even be home, so I nearly jumped out of my skin when I heard his deep voice coming from the shadows as I closed the door. He came at me from the sofa in a predatory way, and when I flicked on the lights and saw his face, I actually took a step backward. He spoke with a hoarse voice, but I couldn't tell whether it was from anger or something else.

"Where did you go?"

"To Kyle's to cool off."

"Do you not realize the dangers for a woman walking alone in this city?"

"I do and I've had my fair share of trouble, but you left first, not me. Is this how it's going to be, Trace? I say something you don't like, so you walk out?" I was so angry that I spoke the next words without conscious thought. "Will you do the same thing to our children if they step over some arbitrary line?"

His face blanched before he whispered, "I don't want children."

Though I hadn't really thought about having children, that comment effectively took the wind from my sails, since I still liked the idea of having the option.

"Never?"

"No, I won't subject any child to the shit that runs through my veins." He held my stare and asked in practically a whisper, "Are you going to leave me now?"

"Why do you think that I would?"

"Because nothing good lasts."

My eyes moved to the tattoo on his arm and I reached up and traced the man on the throne. He really was fucked up, but I loved him. I loved him enough to stay.

"I love you and that includes all of you. I'm not going anywhere."

His mouth came down on mine as he pushed me against the door. His kiss was almost brutal, stirred by all the emotions that were raging through him. He dropped to his knees and lifted my skirt to pull my panties down my legs and I steadied myself to step out of them. His eyes looked up right into mine as he leaned closer and took me into his mouth. When I felt myself start to break apart, I closed my eyes and rested my head against the door as he brought me to a staggering climax.

My legs almost gave out from under me in utter contentment, until I heard his zipper. Desire again burned through me as Trace lifted me up and onto him. I wrapped my legs around his waist and fused my mouth to his. It was with an almost single-minded determination that he moved deep and hard. He pulled his mouth from mine and pressed his lips to my neck, grazing my throat with his teeth. I felt myself coming apart again and I felt him stiffen as we came together.

After that night we didn't speak of the argument, didn't discuss children (or the lack thereof), and I didn't pry into his past. Though Trace seemed more than happy with our arrangement, I wasn't. We were, for lack of a better metaphor, avoiding the elephant in the room.

Chapter Ten

I arrived home from work one night, a few days after our fight, and I was greeted at the door by Trace, who pulled me into his arms and kissed me—a nice, long, sizzling kiss.

He reached for my hand. "I want to show you something."

We started down the hall, but I stopped when I saw the living room, more specifically the picture on the wall: a picture of me. Trace's walls had always been empty. In my mind it was symbolic of how he kept people at a distance, and yet there I was. I didn't even know he had taken the picture. I can't begin to describe the feelings that burned through me knowing that I rated not just a picture, but the only picture on his wall. I turned to Trace to find that he was already looking at me.

"When did you take that?"

"Not so long ago. You were so absorbed in your book you didn't even notice me."

"Why did you hang it? You don't have pictures," I asked and watched a smile tug on his mouth before he replied.

"After you showed up at my apartment that first time, I knew."

"Knew what?" I asked.

He held my gaze and answered softly, "That you mattered."

I had no words, so instead I leaned into him and pressed my lips to his. He reached for my hand and pulled me down the hallway to his bedroom.

"Was that what you wanted to show me?"

"Part of it." He flicked on the light before moving to the closet and when he opened it, I saw that half of the space had been cleared out. It took me a minute to understand and when I looked over at him, it was to find him watching me silently, almost causally, but I didn't miss the tension in his shoulders or the hardness of his jaw.

"I emptied out two of the drawers in the dresser and made room on the counter in the bathroom. I know you are already living here, but I wanted to make it official that you are living here with me."

I had no words. Trace was sharing his private space with me. He was lifting a part of his armor and letting me in. I felt joy and love fill me with warmth over the commitment he was offering me. My excitement dimmed, though—I didn't know if he was doing this because he really wanted to or because after our fight he felt he needed to make some concession. Was this his way of giving in to me without having to open up? I couldn't answer that question but now wasn't the time to dwell on it because whatever his intentions, the gesture was still beautiful.

I had the distinct impression that he thought I would refuse his offer, as if I didn't want to be here with him, and wondered again what happened in his life that made him think so very little of himself. I smiled a big, goofy grin.

"Consider it official. Being here with you is exactly where I want to be."

His response to that was interesting. He said nothing and started from the room. "I'll go check on dinner."

"Trace?"

He stopped in the doorway, but he didn't turn to me when he answered, "Yes."

"Tell me what you're thinking?"

The silence that greeted my question stretched out for so long, I thought he wasn't going to answer me and then, to my surprise, he turned his head and looked me right in the eyes.

"I just need a minute."

"Why?"

"It isn't every day a wish comes true and you, Ember, are the answer to my wish."

He walked out of the room before I could respond, but I was completely undone by his confession and couldn't even speak. I dropped onto the edge of the bed and just stared at the empty doorway.

We didn't speak about Trace's gesture for the rest of the night. Later, when I was getting ready for bed, he came up behind me and pulled me back against him. His warm breath brushed over my ear. "My bed, every night."

I was about to agree when those hands moved up my body to my breasts, where he caressed me through the silk of my nightgown. He slipped under the silk so he could tease my pebbled nipples, rolling and tugging at them. An ache started between my legs as he ground his hips against me. I pressed back, cradling the growing, hard length of him. The moan ripped from my throat when Trace's finger slipped into my panties, brushing over the sensitive nub before going lower. He pushed two fingers inside of me as his other hand worked my nipple. My head fell back against his shoulder. He pressed a kiss right in the spot on my neck that made my knees go weak. I felt the start of the orgasm just as Trace's hands pulled away.

"Don't stop," I pleaded as he reached for my nightgown and lifted it up over my body. My panties followed.

"On the bed." His voice was gruff and sexy as hell.

That was an order I was more than happy to oblige as I climbed on the bed and fell onto my back so I could watch as Trace removed his clothes. He was exquisite; my focus traveled down his body to see him thick, hard, and ready.

"Flip over, Ember."

Everything below my waist clenched in anticipation.

He straddled my legs so that his erection was pressing against my ass, causing a surge of moisture between my legs. It was the barest of touches as he ran his fingertips down my shoulders, along my spine, over the small of my back. The ache for him was almost unbearable but Trace seemed completely content with his unhurried exploration. He leaned forward to press a kiss on my shoulder blade, which pressed him even harder against me, and I tilted my hips back in response. I felt his restraint slipping when he took himself in hand and rubbed himself down my ass and between my legs. I felt my muscles clenching, desperate and hungry for him to fill me. He moved, keeping his hard length between my legs, and leaned over me and grabbed for my breasts that were pressed up against the mattress. He squeezed as he rubbed himself against me and I instinctively spread my legs and lifted my ass.

"On your hands and knees," he ordered, but his hands were already circling my waist and lifting my hips up as he settled himself between my legs. His hand slipped between my thighs, his finger running up and down the swollen wetness, and I almost came. Too soon his hand was gone, and he gripped my hips.

"Put your hand between your legs and touch yourself."

His words shocked and aroused me and for a moment I couldn't do anything. Never had I been asked to touch myself, to give myself pleasure in front of another, but it was Trace and I wanted it to be different with him. My hands were shaking as I slipped my fingers between my legs and stroked myself.

"Tilt your hips. I want to watch as you push your finger inside."

I felt a wave of shyness at his request even as my body throbbed with lust. I didn't know if I could do that, if I was bold enough to do something so personal in front of him. He seemed to understand my hesitation as he ran his hand up and down my back.

"Close your eyes, Ember, and pretend it's me touching you."

My body shook with nerves but his gentle touch helped as he continued to caress my back. I closed my eyes and thought of him as I rubbed my fingers over my aching flesh. His hand moved lower to stroke my ass and the sensation of his touch, along with my own, had me stifling a moan when I slipped my finger inside, my body clenching around my finger as I slid it deep.

"Pull it out and sink it back in, really slowly." His voice had grown hoarse.

Desire burned through nerves as my hips moved while I worked myself with my finger.

"Another finger."

The second finger joined the first and I dropped my head as my body spasmed with the start of an orgasm.

"My turn." Trace's voice was pure sex. He pulled my hips back and I braced as he thrust forward, sinking himself deep inside me. I came on a scream. I was still riding the orgasm when Trace demanded, "Again."

He pulled all the way out before slamming back into me. In this position he was going so deep, stretching me to the point that it hurt in a really good way. I didn't think I could come again, but the sound of our skin smacking together, his nearly painful grip on my hips as he pounded into me, his finger moving to fondle that pleasure point, had another orgasm quickly following the first. He froze as his orgasm moved through him and the sexiest sound rumbled up his throat. He dropped his forehead on my shoulder before pressing a kiss there and then he moved, rolling onto his side and pulling me up against him.

"Was that too much?" he asked, as if he knew my thoughts. It was wonderful but I definitely felt a little off-balance.

"Ember?"

"I've never done that before."

He touched my chin to lift my gaze to his. "Nothing we do in here is wrong, but if you aren't comfortable, just say so."

What did he like to do? I didn't think I wanted to know. Again he seemed to know my thoughts.

"I'm not into pain and I don't do toys, but your body is beautiful and I do intend to explore every inch of it, repeatedly. Are you okay with that?"

I was surprised at my honest answer. "Yes."

His arms tightened around me and I knew there was something else on his mind so I asked, "What?"

"It isn't my place to ask."

I turned my head to him, "After what we just shared, you can ask me anything."

"Trust me, I understand the irony of me asking this, but how many before me?"

"One and it was a disaster."

I knew he heard me, but he said nothing. Minutes ticked by and my eyelids grew heavy. I was almost asleep when I heard Trace say, "Look, my avoidance isn't personal and if there was anyone I'd share it with, it would be you."

Instantly I was wide awake. Trace continued, "There's someplace I'd like to take you. Will you come with me?"

"Anywhere."

Affection curved his lips before he said, "Lucien sponsors an annual picnic in memory of Sister Anne, a nun who took him under her wing when he was younger. One day each year he brings together the kids from the orphanage where she worked. It's his way of remembering her. The picnic is next week." Silence followed that insight and I thought Trace was done sharing when he added, "The orphanage is where Lucien, Rafe, and I met." He brushed a kiss on my forehead. "Good night."

Tears burned my throat because he had shared a piece of his past with me.

A week after my interview with *In Step*, I was offered the position and, though I would be working from home most of the time, I had to go into the office to meet everyone. I dressed in one of my only pantsuits and pulled my hair up into a twist before adding a touch of makeup. Trace was in the living room when I entered.

"You look beautiful."

I self-consciously looked down at my Jones New York pantsuit before replying, "Thank you."

"Are you nervous?"

"A little, but I am so excited to be getting this opportunity."

"They're lucky to have you."

There was something in his tone that made me tilt my head to study him. "What's wrong?"

He stuffed his hands into the pockets of his jeans and looked down a second before meeting my gaze.

"I'll miss you."

"Could I get a ride?"

His face just lit up before he asked, "Are you sure?"

"Absolutely and maybe I could call you to pick me up?"

The smile that spread over his face was beautiful and to know that he was going to miss me—this tough, strong man—caused a long, slow pull on my heart. He walked over and wrapped me in his arms and just before he kissed me, he whispered, "I would really like that."

The building was located in Midtown, and *In Step* took up two floors of the fifty-seven-story building. I was met in the lobby by my immediate supervisor, a Mr. Stanley Baker, who was one of the people with whom I'd interviewed.

"Ember, so nice to see you again."

"Hello, Mr. Baker."

"There's a staff meeting in an hour, which will be a great opportunity for you to meet everyone on the team. Like I mentioned in the interview, you'll work from home on most days, only coming into the office occasionally for meetings. In the beginning, I'll give you the assignments, but once you get comfortable, you'll have free range to pitch the stories that interest you. We'll monitor the success of those and make changes accordingly."

"Sounds great."

When we reached the office, I was surprised by the number of people milling about, since I assumed that most people would be working from home. As I was led down the hall, people stopped to say hi. Everyone seemed very friendly—well, almost everyone. There was one person who seemed to not like me. Unfortunately she was the editor in chief, Caroline Wiggs. If the editor in chief didn't like me, then how did I get the job?

"Caroline, Ember Walsh is starting today."

Caroline looked up from her writing, but her expression was anything but friendly. "Ember, welcome to the team."

And yet despite her words, she didn't make me feel even slightly welcome. Before I could reply, she lowered her head in a clear sign of dismissal. We continued on our way as Mr. Baker said, "Sorry about that. I'm not really sure what's up with her."

I smiled in response, but kept my mouth shut. No sense in starting off on the wrong foot with everyone.

The staff meeting was awesome: people throwing ideas out, brainstorming, laughing, joking. It was so much fun that I found myself actually looking forward to our next meeting. Before I left I was given my assignment: to write up a film festival that was happening over the weekend. Mr. Baker walked me to the elevators and shook my hand before he said, "Welcome to the team, Ember. It's really great to have you."

"Thank you for the opportunity, Mr. Baker."

When the elevator doors closed, I pulled out my phone and called Trace, who answered on the first ring.

"Hey, how did it go?"

"It was awesome. I'm really going to love this job. My first assignment is a film festival in the Village this weekend. Are you free to come with me?"

"Absolutely. So are you ready for me to come get you?"

"I am, yes."

I walked through the doors out into the sunshine just as Trace said, "Look up, beautiful."

And when I did, there he was, resting against his bike with a big smile on his face.

The festival was wonderful, but the company, Trace, was even better. Trace offered me the use of his office, a place he disappeared into several times a week—but to do what, I didn't know. So on Sunday, after Trace went to the gym, I made my way to the room at the end of the hall. I pushed the door open and my feet just stopped, since there on his desk was a new laptop with a big red bow on it. My journal, which I had taken to the festival to jot down notes, was sitting next to the laptop and a beautiful Tibaldi pen rested on top of it. I moved around the desk and settled in the chair as I ran my hand lovingly over the computer. Demons or not, there was a wealth of love in that man. I then noticed a note sitting next to my journal.

Ember,
The man at the shop set it up with all of the requirements that your Mr. Baker recommended.
Your ID is EmberLove and your password is Mine. Have fun.
Love,
Trace

Was it any wonder why I loved that man so much?

I lifted the lid of the laptop and got to work. I was at it for over two hours before I needed a break. I moved to stand, but as I turned in my chair, I accidentally hit my pen, sending it over the edge of the desk. As I moved to catch it, I noticed a slip of paper on the floor. I retrieved the slip and happened to glance at it and noticed it was a bank deposit slip. My eyes widened to the size of saucers to see the balance in the account. Growing up, my dad was lucky if his savings hit four digits, but Trace's account was well into seven digits. I just stood there, transfixed, having never seen that much money before except in board games. When the initial shock wore off, I placed the slip on the desk and tried not to think about it. Trace's finances weren't any of my business, but when he said his investments were profitable, he wasn't kidding.

"Good work on the festival piece and nice initiative proposing the picnic piece. We might feature that in the main well this next week depending on how that turns out. I like the reclusive orphan billionaire angle. There's also a gallery opening this weekend that I'd like you to cover."

Pride washed over me, but Stanley was not one to linger on compliments so I tucked the moment away. Our phone conversations were usually short and to the point, so I asked, "I've only been to one gallery opening and it was casual, but the ones I've seen in the movies are very elaborate. Which category does this opening fall into?"

"Business casual, but there will be those who are all decked out, which I don't get since you're only looking at paint drying. Can you tell I'm not a fan?"

"Yes, but I'm looking forward to it."

"Good. Keep me posted." And with that he hung up.

The picnic Lucien sponsored ended up a pretty grand affair held on the grounds of the orphanage where he grew up in Hell's Kitchen. The proceeds from the day were filtered back into the orphanage, providing new books, clothes, and food. I knew he was rich and had countless connections but I had the sense that he wanted to keep his professional life separate from this personal tribute. There were sponsors, but they were all organizations dedicated to helping those in need; the YMCA, Brothers and Sisters of America, Goodwill. Was it possible that he feared Sister Anne wouldn't approve of how he made a living?

The picnic was clearly bittersweet for Lucien and I found I wanted to know his story but, like Trace, he wasn't at all forthcoming. I had asked Lucien if he would mind if I wrote a piece on the picnic for *In Step*. The article wouldn't have an effect on the current year, but maybe next year there would be a bigger turnout. He was very receptive to the idea since the more in attendance meant more would be given back to the orphans. Three days after the picnic I turned in both of my assignments.

I was still riding the high over Trace sharing a small piece of his past, but his reveal had only left me with more questions. He had no love for his parents, but to learn he was an orphan surprised and saddened me. That article I found in his storage unit—was it possible that the horrible recounting of those murders was about Trace's parents? I had thousands of questions but I was definitely chipping away at his outer wall.

That night, Trace and I sat in the living room watching the news. Well, I wasn't paying any attention to the news—I was straddling his lap, pressing kisses on his face.

"Did I thank you for the laptop?"

"Repeatedly, and you are welcome to continue thanking me."

I spread kisses down his neck as my hands reached for his shirt so I could lift it over his head and then I took a moment to really appreciate his very fine form. My hands couldn't help reaching out to run over his chest, down his abs, up his arms, and over his shoulders. My exploration of his magnificent body turned his eyes dark with desire.

"Don't stop there, sweetheart."

Trace's expression never wavered as he took my hand and moved it down his body to the large bulge pressing against his jeans. My eyes held his as I rubbed him, but it wasn't enough so I flicked the button on his jeans and unzipped them, slowly, before my hand sought and found him. His eyes closed on a moan as I ran my hand up the length of him, twisting slightly as I reached the tip. It was empowering to render this incredible man weak with need, but I affected more than just him. I was about to rectify that when something on the news made Trace's eyes fly open, and he physically lifted me from his lap. His eyes narrowed and then he was standing, zipping up his jeans, and pulling on a T-shirt.

"Trace?"

"I need to go out."

And then he was gone.

I sat there in mild shock, wondering what had just happened. I turned to the television and reached for the remote to rewind. Some local, Charles Michaels, had announced his intent to run for state Senate. I sat back on the sofa. Who the hell was Charles Michaels to Trace?

Chapter Eleven

With my assignment on the gallery opening done, I was feeling restless, so I decided to take a walk. It was cooler, the crisp air announcing the change of season.

I walked for almost an hour and decided to grab some lunch at a café that Trace favored. Perhaps that would give me some insight into his most recent mood. I was just across the street from the little bistro and was about to cross, but stopped when I recognized part of a couple in the front window. Even from my distance I knew it was Trace—I'd know that man anywhere—but it was his position, sitting across from a brunette, that made all of the air leave my lungs. They were leaning toward each other in a very intimate way, but it was his hand stretched across the table holding hers that hurt the most.

I just stood there and stared at them, feeling like an outsider. I wanted to confront them and demand to know what the hell was going on, but I couldn't get my feet to listen to my head. Deep down I feared what I might hear. I believed that Trace and I were making progress, but maybe that progress was only in my head and I was just fooling myself that things were getting better between us.

Heartbreak warred with anger as I started to walk away. I loved him and wanted to be with him, but I wasn't about to play second fiddle to another. After the news story about Charles Michaels from a week ago, living with Trace was becoming very difficult, but I hadn't expected this. Yes, he had been staying out longer and fighting more often, building a wall between us. But cheating on me?

I couldn't go home, and I found myself wandering around the city. The man I fell in love with was disappearing again, and any attempt I made to get Trace to talk about it proved pointless. In light of what I'd just observed, his behavior at night seemed even more confusing. He was the complete opposite—loving me with such intensity that it almost felt like desperation, as if each night was our last. I knew Charles Michaels was the catalyst.

I tried to learn more about this Charles Michaels by googling him, but outside of learning he was a shrewd businessman and borderline dirtbag, I couldn't find any link to Trace. Uncle Josh could dig deeper.

I hadn't realized how long I had been out until the sky started to turn dark, so I hailed a cab and headed home. I entered the apartment to the sight of Trace pacing like a caged panther. The expression on his face when he turned and saw me was one that I will never forget. He looked broken, but when he spoke there was anger.

"Where the hell have you been?"

"Sorry, I went for a walk and didn't realize how late it had gotten."

He just stood there like he was rooted to the floor. I could tell he was holding himself back, presumably because he didn't know what he would do if he got his hands on me: hug the breath out of me or put me over his knee. My own temper sizzled just below the surface as I held his gaze and asked, "Where were you?"

I saw it for just a second—guilt—before he said, "I was at the gym."

"The gym." A profound sense of disappointment and a stabbing pain in the vicinity of my heart consumed me at that betrayal. I started for the room down the hall.

"Ember?" His voice was so soft—tender even—but I couldn't bring myself to look him in the eye when I spoke.

"A self-fulfilling prophecy. I never really understood that concept, because I never really believed it was possible. I mean the idea of not wanting something to happen so much that you end up acting in a way that brings about exactly what you hoped wouldn't come to pass?" And then I lifted my eyes to his worried ones before I added, "I don't find the concept that absurd anymore. I don't care what secrets you have because the man you've become stems, in part, from those secrets, but I hate what holding on to them is doing to you."

I wiped at my eyes before I started from the room. "I'm going to bed."

Later that night Trace joined me in bed and proceeded to love me so completely and sweetly, despite the fact that he'd lied to me earlier and we both knew it. Afterward, he held me close and as I started to drift off to sleep, he whispered something I wasn't sure I was supposed to hear. The words and how he said them stuck with me because they sounded more like a good-bye instead of a vow of love.

"In my life I will never love anyone like I love you."

———•◦•———

"Are you thinking about giving up?" Kyle asked while we sat in his living room the following day. Thank God Kyle was not just a great listener, he also gave some pretty great advice. I was feeling so conflicted.

"No. I love him. With him I feel like I'm on a roller coaster—thrilling and terrifying and I crave it."

"But?" Kyle asked.

"It's also exhausting."

"Well, that's the thing with roller coasters, Ember. Part of what makes them so fun is that you get to choose when you ride and for how long. You might not be able to save him. This, what you're going through now, might be all you have to look forward to. Do you think you can handle that for a lifetime?"

I felt the tears burning the back of my eyes. "I honestly don't know."

When I returned to the apartment later in the day, I heard muffled voices coming from Trace's office. My feet stopped at the sound of a male voice that was not Trace's.

"I hope I can count on your support."

The rage in Trace's voice was undeniable. "I want you to stay the fuck out of my life."

There was frustration in the other man's voice when he said, "I'm part of your life whether you like it or not."

"Bullshit."

"This is clearly not a good time."

"Damn straight. For you, there is never a good time. Get the hell out of my apartment."

As soon as the man appeared in the hall, recognition slammed into me. I hadn't realized it from the pictures on TV but seeing him in person, he was undeniably the man who had come into Clover, the one whose presence caused such a stir—Charles Michaels. He looked tired, but when he saw me, a politician's smile curved his lips. Before he could speak, Trace appeared, his dark energy sucking the air from the room. I thought it very wise of Charles to hold his tongue and exit the apartment as quickly as possible.

I turned my eyes on Trace and almost gasped at the sight of him. He looked livid. His attention didn't leave the door when he said, "You can't outrun your past no matter how far and fast you run." And then he turned his focus on me and my heart broke because he looked resigned. "You can't save me and if you stay, I'll only bring you down with me."

There was a callousness to Trace I had never seen before, and I felt a surge of panic. Was this the end? But I rallied before I said, with quiet conviction, "I'm not going anywhere. I love you."

Sadness passed over his face. "And that's why you have to let me go."

———◆———

Two weeks after Charles Michaels's unexpected visit, my hope of a happily-ever-after with Trace was fading fast. It made the issues we'd had before look like a speed bump. He was never home except for very late at night and even that was rare. On most nights, I couldn't sleep, lying awake in bed worrying over him.

When he did come home, the sound of his heavy footsteps down the hall would make my heart pound because I knew he would enter the room and quietly undress before climbing into bed and holding me close. I'd feel his breath against my neck and the soft kisses that he'd place there, as he buried his face in my hair and breathed me in. It was during those precious moments that I knew, regardless of what was going on with him, his feelings for me hadn't really changed.

It was because of that revelation that I sought him out during one of his fights. The small gym was packed with people and a month before, I wouldn't have hesitated to work my way through that crowd and stake my claim on Trace, but the man he'd become in the prior few weeks was just not someone I knew anymore. I had turned to leave when Rafe walked over to stand at my side.

"Ember, I'm really glad you came."

"I'm wishing I hadn't." I had spotted Trace standing in the center of it all. Women were huddled all around him, but rather than being indifferent, Trace was actively flirting. I couldn't help but think of that woman from the bistro. How many others had there been?

"Why?" And then he saw Trace and seemed to answer his own question.

"He loves you. I understand why you might doubt it, but he does."

"I really believed that once. I'm just not so sure anymore."

"He's pushing you away just like I told you he would. Don't let him."

"He's not the same man. Look, I know that there's more to his story, but no one seems willing to share it with me. I'm not really seeing the point in my fighting when the one I'm fighting for isn't interested any longer."

Rafe's expression was incredulous as he asked, "You don't honestly believe that, do you?"

"I do, yes."

"Talk to him." Rafe reached for my hand and squeezed. "I'll get him."

I watched as Rafe made his way through the crowds. He leaned into Trace to whisper and Trace's head snapped up. I watched as those eyes turned to me before he moved from the crowd and made his way over. He reached for my hand and pulled me with him down the hall until we were in what I assumed was the office of the gym's manager. He closed the door and leaned against it.

"You wanted to talk?"

"Ever since Charles Michaels's visit you've changed. What is happening to us?"

"You knew the kind of man I was when we started this."

"What's that supposed to mean?"

He replied with a shrug.

"Damn it! I want an answer. You're backing away, putting distance between us and shutting me out. Why?"

He looked as if he was going to blow the question off, but then changed his mind.

"I warned you—staying was only going to pull you down with me. I've tried to be the man you think I am, but I'm not that guy. You'd see that if you'd only open your eyes."

"You're never going to trust me enough to let me in, are you?"

Something flashed in his eyes in reaction to that and he said, "It's not a matter of trust. I'm not your forever guy. We were never going to have the happily-ever-after. I thought you knew that."

My heart just stopped because I hadn't thought that at all. I loved him and though I wasn't demanding marriage, I saw us as that couple that still holds hands in their eighties. I thought he felt that way too.

"What are you saying?"

"I thought you would have come to your senses by now. Mr. Forever will come along eventually."

"You actually believe I could feel any other way about you? You are my forever."

"You're not mine." Those words were barely loud enough to hear and yet the impact of them was devastating. He started to pace as he pulled a hand through his hair and then he exhaled with a hiss. "Why are you making this so hard? I tried to be monogamous, tried the relationship thing, but that's not me. There are things I want to do to you, see done to you, that would disgust you."

"Like what?"

His voice dropped to a seductive whisper when he asked, "Have you ever tasted pussy?"

All the blood drained from my face.

"Have you ever been shared by two men at the same time? I want to watch as you are. I like watching, you got a taste of that."

My stomach roiled with revulsion at the images he was forcing me to see. Tears sprang to my eyes that he could cheapen what we had. That he could turn our lovemaking into nothing more than raunchy, meaningless sex broke something in me.

"Those women in there, I've had all of them, used them in any way I wanted." He leaned closer, "I've fucked them individually but I have to admit to enjoying their offerings in a group."

"Stop it! Why are you saying this to me?"

"To force you to wake up and see me for me. You knew of my reputation. I'm sure you were warned off of me. That all I wanted was a piece of ass and any ass would do. You should have listened."

I wanted to run from him and his hateful words, but there was still a part of me that believed he was intentionally being cruel, because I couldn't reconcile this man with the one who held on to me so desperately late at night.

"Funny how your change of heart coincides with Charles Michaels's visit." Where my courage came from I didn't know.

Trace's voice was flat when he said, "He's just the one who held the mirror up to my face to remind me of who I was."

"Maybe I should go talk with him and find out what your connection is to him. Perhaps he won't be so closemouthed."

I didn't even get to finish that statement as Trace's hands wrapped around my arms almost painfully and when he spoke, his voice was frightening.

"Stay the fuck away from him. Do you hear me?"

"Why?"

A horrible sneer covered his face when he replied, "Because he'd chew up and spit out a sweet innocent like you without a second thought."

He released my arms and took a step away from me. "Are we done? I have a fight."

"We're done." I watched him leave as my heart burned. I had already lost him.

———•••———

I sat at the desk in the spare bedroom trying to lose myself in my writing, but my thoughts kept going back to that horrible conversation with Trace from last week. What he described, the thought of him doing that with countless women, sickened me. Is that what Trace really wanted? I had a tough decision to make but I just wasn't ready yet to make it.

Instead of dealing, I focused all of my waking hours on writing. I even sent Professor Smythe a few chapters of my new book with the hopes that his critique would be so severe that it would keep me even more occupied. When I saw his name on my cell phone, my nerves got a jolt. My self-esteem had already taken a hit with not being able to hold my relationship together, but if I learned my writing wasn't good enough, I'd most likely assume the fetal position and cry like a baby.

"Professor Smythe."

"How's *In Step*?"

"You were right, the job is exactly what I needed."

"I've been reading your pieces. Very nice work, Ember. You are really growing as a writer."

"Have you had a chance to read the chapters I sent you?" I held my breath waiting for his reply.

"I have. You found what your first book was lacking. These chapters are brilliant."

My throat closed up. My love life was taking a nosedive but at least I would have my writing to help me pick up the pieces after it crashed and burned.

Chapter Twelve

A couple days later I received a call from Stanley asking that I come into the office. I had to grab a cab, since Trace was gone, again. I didn't want to think on it. The obvious answer for his overnight absence was just not a place I wanted to go. Stanley met me in the lobby.

"We have a meeting with Caroline."

"Do you know what it's about?" There wasn't a staff meeting, so I was curious why she wanted to see me.

"No, but whatever it is, she isn't happy." I wondered if it had anything to do with my last assignment not being good enough.

My heart started to beat frantically as a coldness settled over me.

The short journey from the lobby to Caroline's office felt like an eternity. As soon as we stepped into her office, she pierced me with furious eyes.

"Close the door, Stanley. You, sit."

I took a seat as my knees shook and then Caroline leaned over her desk with a glare.

"I don't know what game you're playing, but I'll not be strongarmed by a conniving little bitch like you."

"Caroline!" I was only vaguely aware of Stanley's protest as I tried to process her words as fury warred with fear.

"What does that mean?"

"I don't know what you've got on him or if it's just that you are fucking him, but I don't like being told what to do. This is my life's work."

"I don't know what you're talking about."

"Don't pretend to be ignorant—Charles Michaels."

I was rendered momentarily speechless at the mention of his name, but then I held Caroline's gaze before I said, "It's not an act. I met him once; he came into the restaurant where I work. He was curt to his wife and downright rude to me." I didn't mention his visit to the apartment or that he was also somehow tearing my relationship apart.

"What does he have to do with me?" I asked.

Caroline's voice grew softer, kinder. "You really don't know, do you?"

"No, please tell me."

"He's the reason you got this job. He called and strong-armed me into giving it to you and then he called today offering *In Step* the exclusive coverage of his campaign, but only if you were our correspondent."

I stood and began pacing the room. "I don't understand. I don't know him."

Caroline leaned back in her chair as a different person than the one I met when I entered and said, "Well, he apparently knows you."

I knew I had to talk with Trace. "I've got to go. I'm really sorry about all of this."

I gathered my coat and headed for the door, but stopped as I touched the knob.

"What are you going to do about Charles?" I asked.

Caroline shrugged. "I don't know."

"Can you delay?"

"Why?"

"Because I may just take him up on the offer."

Caroline leaned forward and I could see the wheels turning. "I'll delay then."

———•◦•———

It took me some time to track down Trace. When I finally located him in the weight room of the gym, where he actually was this time, I gave myself a moment to watch as he bench-pressed the weight of a small car. I hadn't even made a move toward him when his head whipped around and those eyes stared daggers at me from across the room. He didn't move from his spot, didn't seem all that interested in finding out what I wanted. My anger went up a notch as I stalked toward him. "We need to talk."

"Not now."

"Put the fucking weights down. We need to talk."

I grabbed his hand and he let me pull him from the room. When I found a restroom, I pushed him in and locked the door before I turned to him.

"Who the hell is Charles Michaels?"

I saw the stubbornness enter his expression and knew he was going to shut me out again, but I didn't let him.

"I just had a sit-down with my editor. It turns out that he got my job for me by calling in a favor and now he's willing to give exclusive access of his campaign to *In Step* as long as I'm the front person. With your reaction to him and your behavior ever since, I know you're connected. Who the hell is he and why is he messing around in my life?"

All the blood drained from his face and for just a second, I saw what looked a hell of a lot like fear flash in his eyes before rage took over. Without warning he slammed his fist into the wall. "Motherfucker! No, not you! Absolutely not you!"

"What? Tell me!"

"Fuck!" he roared as he walked away from me and started to pace. I watched him for several minutes as he worked it all out. When he looked back at me, there was a resolve about him that I had never seen in him before.

"I have to go."

"Trace?" I called after him, but he never looked back.

———•—•———

While Trace brooded privately anywhere that I wasn't, which, according to Rafe, was usually his place, I battled with the idea of quitting my job at *In Step*. I really loved the work, but I hated knowing that I only had the position because of Charles Michaels. Caroline tried hard to persuade me to stay. Not only had she told me that I had proven myself and earned the position, but she spoke out loud the one compelling reason I had privately pondered, that through *In Step* I might learn more about why Charles Michaels was so interested in me. That was reason enough for me to stay. Four days after my meeting with Caroline I saw Trace again. He emerged from his study looking tired and lost. He barely gave me a passing glance as he walked to the front door.

"Trace, are you going to talk with me?"

"There's nothing to talk about. I'm going out."

And then he was gone. When he didn't come home that night, I worried. I tried calling him and Rafe, but I couldn't get through to either of them. I called a cab and headed to the Bronx. When I entered Trace's gym, I saw him immediately in a circle of women. Once again, he was flirting. All the little gestures of affection he had constantly been giving to me, he was now freely giving to strangers. Images of him doing to these women what he described that day had angry tears burning my eyes. I hated myself for caring so fucking much.

Like a wolf catching the scent of his mate, Trace's head jerked in my direction. And then he nodded at me as if we had been only passing acquaintances before turning his attention to the bosomy blond standing to his left. A searing pain exploded in my chest, but I kept my head held high as I turned and left. I'd wanted to make it work with him, I'd really believed that there was someone good underneath the hardened man, but I was done. He'd won.

I stood outside his gym for a minute.

Despite whatever motivated Trace—fear or a need to protect me or himself—what was glaringly obvious was that Trace was unwilling to fight for me. Heidi had said it, had warned me. Trace would always choose Trace. Eventually a cab drove by and I was able to hail it to go back to the apartment.

I sat in the living room waiting for him as I worked out what I was going to say. I needed to leave him, but I had to find the words that would cause as little harm to him as possible because despite his callous attitude, I really did believe my leaving was going to hurt him. I waited so long that eventually I fell asleep on the sofa. When I woke, it was morning and Trace still hadn't been home. I showered, changed, and started the coffee. No Trace. The sun was already setting when I heard the sound of the front door opening and closing. I moved from the kitchen just as Trace was walking down the hall to the bedroom.

"Trace."

He didn't even turn in my direction before he said, "Ember." He reached the bedroom and closed the door behind him.

I wasn't going to follow him, but I had had it with his alpha-male bullshit decreeing how it was going to be between us. I reached the door and turned the knob only to find that he'd locked it. I couldn't even begin to describe how that made me feel. Not once in the months that we'd been together had Trace locked me out. I was already leaving, but in that moment I mentally conceded defeat. Trace and I were over.

I waited for him in the living room. An hour later the bedroom door opened and Trace appeared, showered and changed. He walked right to the front door.

"Are you going to talk?"

He stopped, but didn't turn to me before he replied, "Talk about what?"

I was so angry I hurled a candy dish at his head. That got his attention.

"What the fuck are you doing?" I said. "If you want me gone then fucking say it, but don't act like I'm being emotional and unreasonable when you've pulled a Jekyll and Hyde."

He took a few menacing steps closer before he hissed out, "I want you gone. I'm over it and you."

And he turned and left the apartment.

I discovered that a body could still function when the heart was reduced to nothing but ash. I'd heard that deep depression could actually cause physical pain and I learned that is true. Despite the fact that I was dying inside, I chased after him because, damn it, *I* was leaving *him*. I screamed his name as he climbed onto his bike. He never looked back. I was fuming and wanted to follow him and demand that he talk with me but it was too late for that, he was gone.

I called Rafe and learned that Trace was at Sapphire. A half hour later, I was greeting Luke, the bartender.

He said, "Hey, Ember, how are you doing?"

"Have you seen Trace?"

"Last time I saw him he was in the back."

"Thanks, Luke."

When I reached that dark corner, I had the most unpleasant case of déjà vu as I noticed the shadowy figures in the corner. As I approached, I immediately recognized the larger one—Trace in an intimate embrace. A long slender leg wrapped around his waist and his hips moved with deep, hard thrusts. The sight was so similar to that first time that I gasped. He looked over his shoulder and our eyes met and held before he turned back to the woman. My already broken heart shattered. I turned and started away from him, but stopped as fury burned through me. I walked back to the curvy brunette and my eyes found the tart's brown ones.

"Take off, bitch."

I saw fear as she pulled away from Trace, straightened her skirt, and hurried off. Trace worked his zipper and the sound broke my heart again. He turned to me, but his expression was callous, almost ruthlessly casual. I held his stare before I said, "You fucking coward. After everything, this is how you decide to end it with me? I love you, you miserable fuck. I saw *you*, not the man you want everyone to believe you are. I loved that man, but you don't give a shit. You whine that everyone in your life sees you as a piece of shit, yet you still push me away. I think you want to be miserable and alone. I guess the sob stories get you laid, huh?"

He stiffened and his jaw clenched, but I didn't care. I held his glare as I added, "Well, you go back to your meaningless sex. Continue to live a shell of an existence because you're too weak to face your past and move on. But know this—you will never be free of me. I will haunt you too. I'll become one of your demons, because I was the one who loved you and I would have given it all to you. You had the real deal, but you were too much of a coward to hold onto it."

I started away from him, saying, "You can bring your fuck-mates home, since I'll be out of your apartment and your life by tonight."

Then I walked away. It didn't feel anywhere near as satisfying as I thought it would. With each step I took, my anger gave way to heartache. I didn't remember the cab ride back to the apartment—my mind just shut down.

By the time I'd grouped my bags at the front door, I'd decided to try Kyle's place. Maybe he'd let me crash for a bit. I sat in the dark living room, staring at my picture on the wall as my heart beat painfully in my chest. He wanted to love; he wanted someone close and I really, truly believed that he'd wanted me to be that person. I could even understand him pushing me away. It was scary to fall in love, but for someone who had spent his life being a loner, someone with a damaged past, yeah, it had to be terrifying. But then that hateful, vile conversation came back in all of its horrible glory and I wondered if I had ever seen Trace clearly or if I really only saw what I wanted.

I didn't know how long I sat there—I rose to go just as Trace came home and from the way he was fumbling around as he closed the door, I could tell that he was seriously drunk.

"Trace."

I knew I surprised him, since he stumbled at the sound of my voice before he turned to me. I didn't know what was going on with him, but I couldn't go without telling him the truth regardless of how much it hurt to speak the words. I pulled my jeans down enough to expose my tattoo.

"I wanted this and I always will. There isn't, and never would have been anything you could tell me that would have made me leave you, but I guess I was just fooling myself to believe that it was ever up to me. Was the bitch tonight the first time you stepped out on me or just the only time you wanted to get caught?"

I saw his fists clench at his sides and his jaw tighten.

I couldn't bear to be around him; it hurt too much, so I made my way to the door. Trace stepped aside to let me pass. Being so close to him and feeling the heat from his body made me want him, but I forced myself to keep my distance. I looked up into his eyes and saw that they were overly bright and the sight of that cut me like a knife, but he'd broken us, not me.

"Despite your destructive personality, I really hope that one day you'll love someone the way that I love you—someone you are willing to fight, lose, and hurt for. Whoever that very lucky woman is, I hope that she loves you just as much."

Once outside, I hailed a cab and climbed in, but I wasn't sure what to tell the driver. I had forgotten to call Kyle.

"Kyle."

"What happened?" he asked, hearing my sobbing.

"Trace and me, we're over and I don't have anywhere to go."

"You'd better come straight here. That a-hole."

I exhaled in relief. "Thank you."

"That's what friends are for. I'll meet you at the curb."

I hung up and gave the cabbie the address before resting my head back on the seat. I was numb and, though I felt my heart beating in my chest, I was dead inside. Visions of Trace and me together crowded all of my thoughts.

How could someone with so much to give close off so completely? How could he know love to the depths that we did and walk away from it? I'd told him I'd haunt him, but he was going to haunt me too. He was always going to be there in the back of my mind. I knew that any other man who came into my life would be compared to Trace and that every one of them was going to fall short because for me, it was Trace. I tried to save him from his demons and instead he became my own personal demon.

The cab stopped, but I made no attempt to move. I couldn't seem to get my body to listen to my brain. Seconds later the door opened just as a hand reached for me and pulled me out. I looked up through teary eyes into Kyle's worried ones. He said nothing as he pulled me into his arms. I fisted the back of his jacket as I pressed my face into his chest and cried for the loss of the man who, I realized in that moment, I never really had.

Part Two

"Being deeply loved by someone gives you strength, while loving someone deeply gives you courage."

—Lao Tzu

Chapter Thirteen

❖

B reathe. I just needed to breathe. Silent tears rolled down my cheeks, dampening my pillow. It would pass, this pain, and until then I just needed to breathe. I survived the past two days and only had a lifetime left. The buzz of my cell phone filled the silence: the sound had become almost comforting. Dozens of calls had gone into voice mail. Talking had been beyond me when I was trying to remember how to breathe but, though I felt dead inside, I wasn't dead. With effort, I reached for my phone to answer the call. Tears welled in my eyes as I stared blindly at Trace's name. I brushed my finger over the display, seeking a connection to him and knowing it was lost forever. My tears fell harder when I declined the call.

I learned a few things about myself and about life after that very painful day. I discovered I could relate to all those sad songs about heartbreak and that sitting with a pint of ice cream and watching *When Harry Met Sally* . . . really did provide a measure of comfort.

The five stages of grief were real and for me, I lingered a good long time on the anger phase. Visuals spontaneously popped into my head of how Trace would come to an untimely death. They were really very gruesome, horrifying, and oh-so satisfying, which led to the next thing I learned. I had a flair for the dramatic.

Lastly, I learned that heartbreak makes you stupid. After that horrible conversation and then seeing Trace with that woman, all rational thought left my head. My relationship with him became defined by those two moments. My brain was completely unable to get past the fact that he had knowingly and intentionally broken us. It was later, when rational thought returned, that I questioned his intentions. Yes, he told me he was over me and that he wanted unattached and raunchy sex with as many partners as possible, but then he also held onto me late at night as if I was the only thing keeping him from falling into that pit with his demons.

If I learned anything during my time with Trace, it was that he was a walking contradiction and more, he was forever undermining himself with the image he projected. I knew all these things, but when your heart is broken, when you can't find the strength to get out of bed or find the will to function on any level beyond crying yourself dry, thinking logically is just not going to happen.

Christmas came only weeks after the breakup and going home, when I was hurting so much, was exactly what I needed. I invited Kyle to join me, since he usually spent the holidays alone. I hadn't gone into the details with my dad about the breakup, but he knew the major points. As soon as we pulled up in front of his house, he was there opening my door and reaching for me.

"Ember," he whispered as he held me so tightly. "This will pass, I promise, and until it does I'm here."

The tears that were always just under the surface fell freely down my face. I nodded my head in reply.

"Let's get you both settled and then we need to go in search of a tree."

As soon as I stepped inside, I was taken by surprise at the wave of anger that washed over me as I remembered Trace being here and how sincere his affection for me had seemed. Had any of it been real? I pushed all thoughts of him from my head. We were over and the sooner I came to terms with that the better.

Hunting for a Christmas tree in Fishtown wasn't as Norman Rockwell as hiking through a tree farm in the glistening snow. Instead you searched the various lots that were set up in parking lots and gas stations around the area, but I still loved the tradition.

My dad and I had a yearly battle when it came to trees. The fighting started days before and lasted right up until we selected the tree.

On the car ride to the lot my dad tried to engage me in our standard fight over tree size—he liked them short and fat and I liked them tall and slim—but I just didn't care. It was amazing to me how difficult it was to do the simplest things when your heart was broken—climbing out of bed, eating, sleeping, holding intelligible conversations—all were almost too taxing.

"Ember, I know the wound is still fresh, but you've got to put one foot in front of the other. You can't shut down. Believe me, I know that is far harder to do than say, but for your own well-being you need to try."

He was right, of course, and because I could hear the worry in his tone, I tried to make an effort.

"Considering my emotional state, you're going to concede and get a tall, slim tree, right?"

My dad's eyes met mine in the rearview mirror. "Hell, no."

That night we decorated our medium-size tree. Many of the ornaments were ones that my dad and mom had purchased together. I looked over at my dad as he and Kyle hung the lights.

He had lost the love of his life and yet life went on. If my dad could survive the death of the love of his life then I could endure the breakup of mine.

Later, after my dad had gone to bed, Kyle and I stayed up drinking spiked eggnog and watching a movie. Out of the clear blue he turned to me and said, "You're different."

I studied him for a minute. "What do you mean?"

"Less afraid, more confident. I'm sorry about what happened with Trace and I know it hurt you, but I think the silver lining from the experience is that you're coming out of your shell."

I was feeling almost mellow from the eggnog. The constant pain in my chest was only a dull ache. "I'm all for silver linings."

He touched my hand as his eyes held mine. "You never told me and I didn't ask, because I didn't think you were ready. What happened with you?"

"I thought I could save Trace—thought that I could conquer his demons by loving him, but I was wrong."

Kyle watched me with knowing eyes before he said, "You're still in love with him."

"I am. He was it for me."

"I'm sorry, Ember. That's hard."

"Yes, but I'm stronger than I was and with time, I will move on and this will be a lesson learned."

"Didn't he try calling you?"

I looked down as I remembered the hope and unbearable pain I felt at seeing his name on my phone that day right after our breakup. Every missed call had been Trace. He still called but I never answered. "Yes."

"He wanted to talk. Aren't you even a little curious as to why?"

I took a sip of my eggnog to soothe the ache from the tears that burned the back of my throat.

"His method for telling me it was over was for me to find him fucking some woman."

"Jesus, Ember, I'm sorry. That was really shitty of him."

"Well, he wanted me gone and he did the one thing that he knew would make me go."

On Christmas Eve we went caroling—another family tradition that had started with my parents. Every year a group of our neighbors walked along our street offering tidings of good cheer through song. It became a social activity since those we sang to usually joined the caroling until we all ended up at one house to eat Christmas goodies and drink spirits.

My dad was a terrible singer but for some reason he believed that the louder he sang the better he sounded. My ears were bleeding by the time we finished and as we entered our neighbors' house, Kyle leaned over and whispered, "You're smiling."

And I realized that I was and it had taken no effort at all to do so. I knew then that I was going to be okay.

On Christmas morning there was a package waiting for me. My dad looked just as surprised as me when he brought it in and placed it on my lap.

"Who's it from?" I couldn't contain my excitement.

"I don't know. There's no return address."

My first thought was that it was from my uncle and then I unwrapped it and my heart stopped for a moment when I saw the old copy of Charles Dickens's *Great Expectations*. I studied the beauty of the book. The royal-blue embossed cover with the weathered green spine and gold embellishments was exquisite. I flipped open the cover: the texture of the leather felt wonderful against my fingertips and the smell of old parchment filled my nose. I was so lost in the beauty of the book that it took me a moment to see the inscription written in a cursive script with which I was very familiar: Trace's.

I'll tell you what real love is. It is blind devotion, unquestioning self-humiliation, utter submission, trust, and belief against your-self and against the whole world, giving up your whole heart and soul to the smiter.

It was a quote from the book—words spoken by Miss Havisham to Pip. I remembered that night from long ago at the diner when I told Trace that I was reading my way through the classics; he remembered that too. I sat there looking down at the greatest gift I had ever been given, which was given to me by a man who claimed to be over me. A smile touched my lips as my heart whispered, *liar.*

My dad came into my room later that morning and settled on the edge of my bed.

"I don't condone what Trace did or how he treated you. In fact, I'd like to inflict pain on him for hurting you, but I suspect he's hurting too. Most people go through their entire lives and never find what you and Trace had. Before you walk away from something that precious and rare, be sure you're doing it for the right reasons."

"He broke us, not the other way around."

"You've told me that he pulls you close one minute then pushes you away, usually when the situation gets too personal. The man who came here that weekend with you wouldn't have stepped out on you. It's just too coincidental that Trace performs a one-eighty right after a mysterious man from his past comes calling. Just be sure that he's guilty of whatever you think he did because I can tell you that spending your life without your soul's mate is very hard."

⸻

Kyle and I returned home after Christmas and I found it was easier to lose myself in the routine of my life so I wouldn't think about Trace. I spent hours every day writing and the familiarity and comfort of it was soothing.

Kyle told me not to rush getting an apartment because he had the room and actually really enjoyed having a roommate. I couldn't lie; I wasn't ready to be on my own. I really liked being with Kyle and having someone I could come home and talk to. Unlike my experience with Lena, Kyle was an excellent roommate.

In fact, he was such a good roommate that after two months of me camped out on his sofa with my laptop, Kyle had enough.

"You can't hide away in here forever. You do eventually need to get out and socialize and working doesn't count."

"You're right, I know, I just can't seem to get myself motivated to move."

"Why? Are you afraid of seeing Trace?"

Despite his gift and the gesture behind it, I was afraid to see him. The thought of seeing him back to his old ways with women everywhere—no, I couldn't stand it, especially after he put such graphic details into my head about how he spent his time with those women.

"Cowardly, isn't it?"

"He hurt you, I get it. Avoidance is natural, but you can't stop living your life. You need to confront him or move on, but being in limbo isn't an option."

I hated it when he made sense and I said as much.

"How about we go out to dinner?" Kyle wiggled his eyebrows before he added, "My treat."

I didn't realize how right Kyle was about me hiding out until I found it almost difficult to move from the sofa. I was using my writing as an excuse to disengage from everything. He was right, I'd moped long enough. "Dinner sounds great." I gathered my belongings. "You're a really good friend."

"Likewise, Ember, now go get dressed. I'm starved." I was halfway to the bathroom when he called, "And take a shower because you're beginning to get ripe."

The place Kyle suggested was quaint but packed. As we were being led to our table, Kyle said, "I ate here the other night and the lasagna was smack-yourself-in-the-face good."

"I know what I'm getting then."

Once we were settled Kyle seemed to hesitate before he said, "I've seen him around you know."

A coldness swept through me as my heart stopped. "Trace?"

"He looks about as good as you do. I'm not a betting man, but if I was, I'd say he was taking your breakup as hard as you." He leaned closer before he added, "I know you, Ember, and you've got it in your head that the man's back to his wild ways. But he's been trying to reach you—maybe it's time you give him a chance to explain."

I didn't reply, but Kyle knew me well enough to know I was thinking about it. After our delicious dinner we started for home but Kyle's words were still knocking around in my head. I knew what was holding me back: fear. I was afraid there was more truth than spite in his words. Afraid that though he may love me, he was off appeasing his various appetites with countless women. I could stay afraid and in the dark or I could do something about it.

"I want to go somewhere, will you come with me?" I said.

"Yeah, where are we going?"

"To see Trace."

Kyle hailed a passing cab before he said, "Progress."

People spilled out onto the sidewalk near the gym, smoking. It was in between fights, so the noise level was really loud. Somehow we found a spot inside against the flow of the crowd. It took me only a moment to spot Trace and when I did my heart started to race as involuntary chills of excitement made the hair on my arms rise. He was standing near the ring with Lucien and he had obviously already fought, based on the look of him, but he was getting ready to go again. The ref moved up into the ring and announced the new fight but I didn't watch the two in the ring because my attention was completely on Trace. Women approached, putting their hands on his arm, touching his chest, but it was his response to them, or lack of response, that had my heart pounding to the point of pain.

"Are you satisfied?" Kyle's question got my attention as I turned to him.

"Satisfied about what?"

"Whatever it was you needed to see."

He knew me so well. "Yeah. We can go."

We started for the door when I felt a heat burning down my spine and I turned right into Trace's stare. The look of joy and pain that swept his face had my soul sighing. Tears burned my throat and my first instinct was to throw myself into his arms, but that was followed with the urge to hurt him. I wanted to hit him and rage at him for breaking us and me. It was only a few minutes that we stared across the room at each other, but it seemed as if time just stopped. The smile seemed to come from my soul, and I knew everything I was feeling was reflected in that simple curve of my lips. His identical smile stayed with me as I walked out the door.

———❖———

What to do about Charles Michaels, the spark that started the downward spiral in Trace and his relationship with me?

Considering that Trace had been dealing with Charles alone, it was time that someone had his back. Caroline had offered me a reprieve after the breakup and allowed me to set the campaign piece aside for a bit because my heart wasn't in the work, but now it was time to get back into it. I picked up my phone.

"Ember, how was your visit home?" Caroline asked.

"It was really great. How about you, how was your holiday?"

"I ate and drank too much, it was perfect. Are you calling for your next assignment?"

"Actually, I was wondering if Charles was still interested in having me for a liaison?"

There was silence over the line for a moment before Caroline said, "Yes."

"What exactly is he offering?"

"Exclusive interviews and coverage of him on his campaign trail, access to him at home and in the public eye, and the complete backstory from his humble beginnings to now."

"And he still wants me?" I knew his interest in me stemmed from Trace, but why? What was he after? I intended to find out.

"Yes."

"Okay, then please tell Mr. Michaels he has himself a correspondent."

"Are you sure? He seems to have an unusual interest in you."

"Yes, I'm sure."

"Okay, come into the office tomorrow and we'll sort through the details."

"See you tomorrow."

My meeting with Caroline led to a meeting with Charles Michaels. I arrived at his campaign headquarters and couldn't deny that I was nervous. Trace's reaction to him had been startling. I needed to be mindful of the potential danger. I was led down a hall to the room at the end. As soon as Charles Michaels saw me, he stood and moved around his desk to greet me.

"Miss Walsh, thank you so much for agreeing to meet with me here." He looked over at the woman who escorted me and smiled, "That will be all, Pam."

The pretty blond smiled before quietly pulling the door closed in her retreat.

"Miss Walsh, won't you have a seat?"

"Thank you, and please call me Ember."

He settled behind his desk before he steepled his fingers and gave me what looked like a genuine smile.

"Ember, it's very nice to finally meet you."

I wanted to comment that he had met me twice before and had been an über dick the first time and a pain in Trace's ass the second, but being confrontational right out of the gate wasn't going to glean me any information. A knowing smile touched his lips.

"You did not catch me at my best. I do apologize."

What could I say to that? I had to give it to the old guy, he was as good a mind reader as Trace.

"You strike me as an intelligent woman. Please let me explain why you are here. Trace is my nephew. He has been on a downward spiral for a long time—thirteen years, in fact. Something happened that changed him and I think it's time he brought that secret out into the light. I realize that he doesn't seem to care, that he's perfectly okay with ruining his life, but I am not okay with that. He's the son of my late sister and it pains me to see him being so destructive. You, Ember, are the only person he's taken an interest in and I'm hoping you can help him."

I felt as if the ground dropped out from under me as I reeled from Charles Michaels's confession: He was Trace's uncle. I hadn't seen that coming. No wonder Trace clammed up and reacted as he had whenever talk shifted to his family. What exactly had his uncle done that made Trace hate him? I pulled myself from my thoughts to ask, "How?"

"I'm hoping you will encourage him to seek help before he's lost to us."

"And your timing for this concern is just coincidental?"

"Like I said, Miss Walsh, you are a very intelligent woman. I won't lie. I have certain aspirations. Trace's behavior could be a hindrance to my success."

Arrogant narcissist. He let Trace suffer in silence until it began to affect him and then he suddenly took an interest. Bastard.

"Why does he hate you so much?"

"I think you'll learn that he hates most people, family in particular."

"That's not an answer. He hates you and I think he may fear you too. Why?"

An odd look crossed over Charles's face before he said, "I failed him."

"Meaning?"

"That's his story to tell, but now I'm trying to make amends."

I didn't understand what he meant, but even so, I believed him—believed that he really was trying to right a wrong. Was Charles's failing Trace related to his demons? Most likely.

"I'm not with your nephew anymore."

"I know, but you still care for him."

"I won't lie to him and I'll be up front about all of it. I'm doing this for him not you."

"Fine."

"I don't know what haunts Trace, but you are a part of why he's tormented. Surely you know that."

"I do."

"And you let him suffer in silence for all these years. You allowed him to face alone whatever it is that has a hold over him. He moved here when he was fifteen, so I'm guessing that he was still a kid when he was abandoned. How the fuck do you sleep at night?"

His tone turned hard when he replied, "There is nothing you can say to me that I haven't already said to myself. I'm a bastard—a selfish bastard and I know it. Yes, I failed, but I am trying now."

"A little late. Every action that your nephew makes is tainted by his past. He's stuck, he can't move forward and he can't go back. Trace has been left alone for long enough." I stood and reached my hand across his desk.

"Yes, I will try to do what you never did."

The insult had the desired effect as a look that could only be described as shame crossed over Charles's face before he took my hand into his own. "Thank you."

Chapter Fourteen

I thought for a few days on how I could reach out to Trace. Unconscionable was the thought of a young Trace left alone to deal with whatever dark secret plagued his past. It was no wonder that Trace closed off to everyone; even his own family had turned their backs on him. Once I came up with an idea, it took me the better part of the day to make it just perfect.

That night I sat on my bed as butterflies took flight in my belly. Kyle had given me a picture right before Trace and I split. It was one he had taken when the three of us were out dancing one night. Trace and I were on the dance floor, slow dancing, but it was the look on our faces that said it all: it was love, pure and simple. I framed that picture and dropped it off with his doorman. I sat in wait for him to receive it, hoping that he was going to acknowledge the gift. As if I willed it, my phone buzzed and I almost dropped it because my hands were shaking so badly. When I read his text, my heart tripped in my chest.

> "All my heart is yours: it belongs to you; and with you it would remain, were fate to exile the rest of me from your presence forever."

Jane Eyre's words, Ember, but my thoughts . . .

I thought about the book he had sent to me and the meaning behind it and realized that my dad had been right: Trace had done what he had to to make me go. He was protecting me from whatever threat Charles Michaels posed and I had believed the lie; I believed the worst of him. I didn't know how long I sat there looking at his text before I replied to it. I wasn't sure that he'd answer me, but I needed to ask anyway.

Why did you push me away?

The fact that he answered almost immediately made me smile. He was doing as I was, waiting and hoping.

In my life, I've never had anyone who means to me what you do. You are the most precious thing in my life and I would do anything to keep you safe.

Keeping me safe from what?

You were protecting me?

I was trying to, but the one I was protecting you from isn't the threat.

That made the warning bells go off.

Meaning?

Are you going for your run tomorrow?

I thought that was an odd question, not to mention that he was changing the subject.

Yes.

Thank you, Ember, for the picture and the meaning behind it. Sweet dreams, beautiful.

I sat up for a good long time trying to figure out what Trace was up to, but when I did finally fall asleep, it was the first night in months that my dreams actually were sweet.

The next day, as I ran, I wondered why Trace had asked me if I would be running that day. Maybe he was going to join me, yet when I arrived at the Gapstow Bridge, he wasn't there. He was stubborn as a mule, used to getting his own way, and apparently convinced that our relationship was not in my best interest. But damn it, I'd stand at his side even though he didn't want me there.

After my run, I warmed down before I went for coffee. My feet moved on instinct, since my thoughts were entirely on Trace. I walked to the counter at Starbucks and before I could place my order, the kid behind the counter asked, "Are you Ember?"

"Yes."

"One minute, please."

I watched as he reached for a large cup and added hazelnut syrup before filling it with coffee. He then bagged several cake pops before reaching for a small ivory envelope sitting on the back counter. When he returned, he handed me the coffee, the bag of cake pops, and the note.

"There's no charge," he offered with a smile.

I was so stunned, I couldn't say anything more than, "Thank you."

I took a step away from the counter and looked down at the note with my name written in Trace's hand. My heart did a long, slow roll in my chest. I placed my coffee and pops down on the condiment bar before I ripped open the envelope and pulled out the card.

I miss you and I want a future with you. If you still want to be with me, meet me at Sapphire on Friday at eight. I'll be there, waiting for you, in the spot where we first met.

A part of me wanted to rip up the note but a larger part of me saw Trace as a young man who was left alone to deal with whatever tormented him. He deserved a second chance, but even more compelling a reason for me to go to him was the simple fact that I loved him. I loved him so much that I could forgive him for just about anything. He was reaching out to me, he was trying to fix what he'd broken, and I had come to learn that my dad was right: living without your soul's mate is very hard.

When I arrived at Sapphire, there seemed to be no line to get in. I wished there had been, if only for the delay. The memory of those weeks prior to us splitting up was very painful and there was a small part of me that thought I was foolish to go down that road again. The valet opened the cab door for me and offered me his hand.

"Good evening, Ember."

I was so surprised that he knew my name I just stared at him, openmouthed. He pulled my hand through his arm and led me to the door before opening it for me with a smile.

"I hope you enjoy your evening."

I felt and probably looked like a lobotomy patient as I managed to mumble, "Thank you."

I stepped through the doors and my feet stopped moving because the place wasn't just quiet, it was completely empty. I was about to turn for the door when music began to fill the silence: U2's "All I Want Is You." I took a few steps and stopped when I saw Trace standing just in front of the stool where I had been sitting when we first met.

Memories of that first meeting filled my head. I had been so sure that he was nothing more than a fantasy, a ridiculously gorgeous fantasy, and yet here he was. Standing there, looking at me with love and apprehension burning in his eyes. He pulled a hand through his hair, drawing my gaze to the tattoo that was so much more than body art.

My heart pounded in my chest as he started toward me. I had dreamt of this moment so often, dreamt of us finding a way back to each other, but I'd never imagined that it would ever be more than a hopeful dream. He reached for me and pulled me close and his mouth covered mine. In that moment I realized that Trace and I were like the last piece of a puzzle fitting into place. I needed him and he needed me and together we were whole. Feeling his arms around me with his mouth on mine, I was home. He pulled back briefly from me and his voice sounded raw when he whispered, "You came."

"How could I stay away?"

"I hurt you. Can you forgive me?

"I already have."

He pulled me to him again and held me so tightly. "God, I've missed you. I see your face—every time I close my eyes, I see the look on your face when I told you I didn't want you anymore." He looked fierce when he added, "That was the hardest fucking thing I have ever done. Holding you is more sexually stimulating to me than a room full of women. I need you to know that. I was intentionally cruel to shock you into leaving me."

He feigned hurt and added, "You didn't have to believe me so easily."

His teasing, for some reason, made me cry in earnest. I buried my face in his chest and let myself just feel. There was a part of me that didn't believe this was real, believed that I was just dreaming, and I wanted the moment to last forever. I took in every detail so that I could replay this happy dream over and over again. It was a while before I looked around and asked, "Where is everyone?"

A slight grin tugged at his mouth before he offered, "We have the place to ourselves for the next hour."

"How did you manage that?"

"I know the owner." He reached up and touched my cheek and that soft touch caused a searing heat just under my skin.

"There is so much I need to tell you, but I just want to hold you. Is that okay?"

"This is really happening, isn't it?"

He looked back at me with affection when he said, "Yes."

He linked our fingers as he started toward the dance floor, then turned me to him and wrapped his arm around my waist. He brushed his lips over my knuckles and placed our joined hands over his heart.

"That woman, I didn't fuck her. I wanted to. I thought if I did I could purge you from me." He touched my cheek. "I wanted to forget you but I can't. You did haunt me every single day." A slight smile pulled at his lips before he added, "All I want is you."

I fisted the back of his shirt. "That feeling is mutual."

We stayed right where we were for what seemed like an eternity, holding each other, body to body, and though we were silent, words weren't needed. When Trace pulled back from me, I was reluctant to release him.

"I don't deserve a second chance, I know that. I hurt you and I violated your trust, but I'm asking you to please give me one.

The one thing I've learned with absolute certainty over these past months is that I cannot live a life without you. I'm ready to share everything with you. Much of what I have to say is going to be very hard for you to hear. All I ask is that you reserve judgment until you've heard it all." He held my gaze as he asked, "Can you do that?"

"Nothing you could say will turn me from you. Telling me, sharing it, will help you heal."

His smile took my breath away. "Will you come with me?"

I was reminded of another time when he spoke those very same words to me. I answered instinctively as I had before: "Yes."

When we reached his apartment building, he shut down the bike and waited for me to climb off before he followed after me, taking my hand and leading me upstairs. Once we were settled at his kitchen table, with wine for me and beer for him, he rubbed his hand over his spiky hair and took a long pull from his beer.

I watched him and could tell how much this talk was going to cost him—telling me whatever it was he needed to—but I needed to tell him about my meeting with his uncle. I needed him to know what I knew before he shared with me. It didn't feel right not to.

"Before you start, Trace, I need to tell you something."

He looked nervous, but his eyes never wavered from mine. "Okay."

"I know who Charles Michaels is. I know he's your uncle."

His fingers turned white as he clenched his bottle of beer so tightly in his hand I thought it might shatter.

"How did you find out?"

"I sought him out, wanted to learn what hold he had over you. He asked me to help you and to get you to open up about something that happened thirteen years ago."

Trace shattered his bottle of beer against the far wall and began to pace like a caged panther. His eyes turned to mine and there was so much turmoil looking back at me.

"Why?"

"Because you could be a potential problem for his plans, but I love you and you've been hurting and alone for long enough." I walked to him and wrapped my hand around one of his balled-up fists as I looked up into his face. His eyes were closed and tears were rolling down his cheeks.

"Tell me. Let me carry some of your burden. Please, let me in."

He wrapped his arms around me as he buried his face in my hair. After a moment, he pulled back, reached for my hand, and led me into the living room before he pulled me down onto the sofa, where he practically held me on his lap.

"One weekend, thirteen years ago, I learned that my dad was hurting my sister."

Dread filled my belly and I looked into his empty eyes. The words that he spoke next reached into my chest and ripped out my heart.

"I thought it was just me."

I went completely numb as rage, disgust, heartbreak, and overwhelming love for this man filled me. He just watched me. Somehow I managed to ask, "How long?"

"It started when I was nine: a late night visit, an inappropriate touch, but it wasn't until I was ten that he actually . . ."

He didn't finish the thought, but then he didn't need to. "But it stopped not long after it started. I knew it had because my sister was reaching the age that he preferred. I stayed in that house for her and still, I failed her."

"Oh God." I could see him as a beautiful little boy and his father . . . I felt the bile rushing up my throat as I ran down the hall to the bathroom, making it just in time, and after, I just knelt there in front of the toilet as tears streamed down my face. I hadn't expected that, hadn't expected something so vile and depraved.

For Trace to be the good, kind, and compassionate man that he was after suffering through a childhood as sick as that one only proved how incredible a person he was. His voice sounded detached when I heard him speak from right behind me.

"I'll understand if you want to leave. Like I said, I'm dirty."

My eyes flew to his as fury burned back the heartache.

"Dirty? You?" I stood and approached him as my anger for his father boiled over.

"You were a child, an innocent soul, who was abused by one of the people who should have loved you most. You suffered alone in silence, dealing with something that most adults can't deal with, and look at you: You are the strongest, bravest, kindest man I've ever known." I grabbed his face and forced him to look at me, "Don't look at me like that. You came to my aid when I was being assaulted, have repeatedly rescued me when I needed rescuing. The only person you abuse is yourself."

He closed his eyes as I continued. "I love you truly, completely, and hopelessly. You don't have to suffer in silence anymore and I swear to God I will never let anyone hurt you again."

He wrapped me in his arms and held me so tightly against him; I felt his tears on my neck. When he pulled back some time later, he reached for my hands.

"I'd like to tell you the rest."

"Okay."

Back in the living room he pulled me down onto the sofa with him and finally spoke his nightmare aloud.

"At the time, I thought I was misreading his intent, though I continued to look for signs and watched her at night. He was more careful with her and I realize now that he was waiting for the nights that I wasn't home."

I looked back at him as he added, "I'd started fucking around early, and I know now I did so because it was my way to have some control. I was out that night getting my rocks off while my dad was . . ." He clenched his fists and I could see disgust and self-hatred burning in his eyes.

"Is that why you believe you're only good for sex?"

"I've been conditioned, since I was a child."

"No, you were abused and don't you take the blame for your father. He and only he is at fault."

I could see he didn't agree with me, so I was intentionally harsh in reply. "So then your sister is also at fault?"

He roared his denial: "No!"

"Why you and not her?" I forced him to look at me. "Neither of you are at fault. Only that animal who's your father is at fault."

He seemed to think on that for a moment before he pulled me back to him and pressed a kiss on my head.

"Thanks for that."

"Tell me the rest."

He inhaled and let it out in a slow exhale.

"That night I begged my mom for help, even knowing that she was completely uninterested in her children. How sad is it that I can't even remember what my own mother looked like? She never gave either of us the time of day. I knew this about her, but still I begged her that night, for my sister's sake, to get us the hell out of there. She didn't, though; she wouldn't even move from the sofa. It was like she was zoned out, so I got my sister into the car with the intent of getting her to a doctor, but I hydroplaned and we crashed into a tree. The next thing I knew, we were in the hospital and I learned that my sister had gone through the windshield. The doctors had thought she was going to die, but she lived, though she was never the same again."

I turned around to face him and wrapped his face in my hands as his tear-filled eyes looked into mine. "That's why you hate hospitals."

He nodded before he added, "I made her the way she is now. Sometimes I wonder if it wasn't for the best, because she doesn't remember the abuse. The mind she has now—she's always happy, childlike in her happiness."

"But you remember for both of you."

"I'm her big brother. It's my job to worry over her."

I reached for Trace's arm and ran my fingertip over his tattoo. "Master of your own hell."

My eyes found his as I reached for his hand, linking our fingers.

"You're not alone anymore." I pressed my lips to his, drawing as much comfort as I knew I gave. And when I pulled back he looked less haunted.

"What happened to your parents?"

"They were murdered that night."

I know my face paled at that announcement as I managed a rather incredulous, "What? Why?"

"The police claimed it was a home invasion, but I know it wasn't. There had been no previous cases of robberies in the area and for there to be one that ended in a double murder, one of the victims being an heiress—no chance. I can't prove it, and I've really tried, but up until quite recently, I believed that my uncle Charles killed them."

And then I remembered the paper in the storage unit. The recounting of those gruesome murders was about Trace's parents. There had been a mention of children in the article, but because they were minors their identities had been kept secret.

"Victoria and Douglas Stanwyck. But your name isn't Stanwyck."

"I changed it."

"That's why you reacted so strongly when you heard about Charles on the news. But why would your uncle take such a risk, especially since he wanted to get into politics?"

"You met him. He's a self-serving narcissist and he believes deep down that he's untouchable. But if he really is a murderer, he'll do anything to keep his secret."

"That's why you feared for me."

He touched my face before he replied softly, "Yes."

"What made you think it was him?"

"He's always had political aspirations and running a political campaign can be quite costly. If something were to happen to my mom and dad, her estate, minus the trusts that she set up for my sister and me, would go to my uncle. Plus, my dad was a sick son of a bitch and not someone an aspiring politician wants in his closet. Taking them out would have solved two problems for my uncle."

"You said that you thought he did it . . . do you no longer?"

He pulled a hand through his hair before he replied, "I'm not so sure now. Ever since you told me that he got that job for you, I've been rethinking it. He's arrogant, ambitious, and callous, but his reaching out could really be just that. I agree with you; trying to help me is self-serving for him, but it's possible that he's just a miserable and self-absorbed human being."

"I came to that same conclusion after my meeting with him."

He studied me for a minute before he reached up to touch a lock of my hair.

"What are you thinking?"

"You really pushed me away to protect me."

Tenderness washed over his features as he held my gaze. "I've lived for so long with the belief that he was a killer, and saw what I believed he was capable of. Knowing you were on his radar because of me sent me over the edge. I couldn't bear the thought of something happening to you because of me." He paused a moment as affection swept across his features before he added, "Even if Charles is innocent, someone murdered my parents and got away with it. With Charles in the spotlight, his family will be pulled into it as well, and the whole scandalous mess is going to get dug up. Whoever killed my parents is very likely going to get very nervous, which means that there's still danger."

"And we'll face it together."

He wrapped my face in his hands. "In my life I've never had what I had with you. I could share my darkest secrets with you because you knew I was damaged and yet you still loved me."

"I do love you."

"And I will endeavor to deserve you every day of my life."

"You do deserve me, always have."

"Where do we go from here?"

"I want to be with you, but it will only work if you don't shut me out or push me away."

"Instinct for me is to do just that and it's going to take me some time to break my habit, but for you I will."

He was watching me and saw the worry that wrinkled my brow. He touched my chin to lift my gaze to his. "What?"

The timing didn't feel right, but we were putting all the cards on the table so I answered, "I want to be more bold with you but I will never be bold enough to sleep with a woman or another man, to share you, or to watch you with another person."

"Of course. That's not to say I wouldn't love watching you bring yourself to orgasm again. But only if you're comfortable doing so and it's for my eyes only."

The memory of it made me feel bold now. "Only if you return the favor."

He kissed me then, as if in promise, before I asked, "Where's your sister?"

"She's in a facility, the best I could find. I visit her every week."

"Did you take her to that bistro you like?"

He looked at me with an odd expression before saying, "Yes, she likes it there."

"I saw you."

"What, when?"

"That day I came home from my walk and you were waiting for me. I was going to that bistro for lunch and saw you with her, in the front window, and my heart just broke. And when I asked you where you were, you said you were at the gym."

He reached for me and pulled me up against him. "I remember. The pain on your face when I lied, it broke my heart. I knew then that I was going to lose you, that I wasn't strong enough to hold onto you."

"You are, though—you are strong enough. You just weren't ready then to share."

"No, but I am now." He reached for my face and cradled it in his strong hands. "I'd like you to meet her."

"I would really like that. What's your sister's name?"

He smiled. "Chelsea."

Chapter Fifteen

R olling Acres was aptly named, since the place was situated among acres and acres of rolling green hills in Westchester. Trace pulled his motorcycle up to a gated parking lot as the attendant stepped out of his booth to greet us.

"Mr. Montgomery, welcome."

"Hello, Sam."

"Please pull right in." Sam hit a button that was discreetly concealed against the wall of the booth, causing the gates to swing quietly open. The long, tree-lined drive brought us to a sprawling stone building that was surrounded by gardens, which I imagined would be filled with color come spring. As Trace parked, I couldn't help but notice that the cars in the lot were all foreign and very expensive.

Trace waited for me to climb off before he followed, taking my helmet and placing it on his bike. He looked down at me nervously, almost awkwardly, and then he said, "Chelsea will just be finishing lunch and after she usually likes to walk to the pond to feed the ducks."

"I like feeding ducks."

He smiled then and the warmth of that smile caused a long, slow pull on my heart. He lowered his head before he whispered, "I like you."

We started into the building and as soon as my eyes adjusted, I was impressed with how elegant yet comfortable the place appeared. The little touches of fresh flowers and potted plants made the place feel more like a home rather than a hospital. Trace led me down the hall to room 114 before he knocked. When the door was pulled open, we were greeted by a beautiful woman with a big smile on her face.

"Trace." She threw her arms around her brother as his came around her. I stepped back to give the two a moment. When Chelsea pulled away from her brother, her gray eyes turned to me and her smile, I noticed, never faltered.

"Chelsea, this is my friend, Ember. I told you about her."

My heart leaped at his words. Even though he hadn't been ready to share her with me, he'd shared me with her.

"She's pretty, just like you said."

And then she held her hand out to me.

"I'm Chelsea. Nice to meet you, Ember."

I took her hand into my own.

"It is my very great honor to meet you, Chelsea."

"I like her, Trace. Can we feed the ducks now?"

He reached for her hand. "Absolutely."

As we walked along, I couldn't suppress the smile because Trace was right; she really was very childlike. She ran around us, skipping at times, telling us stories about making chocolate-chip cookies, watching movies, playing with her friends. She was, I suspected, a few years older than me, but she had the mannerisms of a carefree and happy eight-year-old girl.

I could see in Trace's beautiful eyes that when he looked at his sister he felt responsible, he felt guilt, and that wasn't fair because he had only been a kid himself when he begged for help and had been denied it. He had been only a child of fifteen left to his own devices to seek out that help.

We reached the pond, a beautiful sapphire pool that reflected the sun like thousands of little diamonds resting upon the surface. The mallard ducks swam a bit of a distance away. The vibrant green of the male duck heads met our eyes before the all-over brown of the females, but as soon as the bread pieces touched the glistening water, all of the ducks beelined for Chelsea. She squealed in delight.

"Aren't they so pretty? The girls should have the pretty colors though, don't you think, Ember?"

"I do, Chelsea."

Trace reached for my hand and, for the next hour, we watched her joy as she fed the ducks.

Later, Trace took me to that same bistro and once our order had been taken, he reached across the table for my hand. The gesture was so much like the one that I witnessed with him and Chelsea that it caused a small tug at my heart.

He said, "Thank you for coming with me. I know that Chelsea really enjoyed meeting you."

"She's lovely, Trace."

He turned silent for a minute; his thoughts were his own. "In a few months, she'll turn twenty-six. She should be dating, maybe married with a child of her own, and instead she's perpetually an eight-year-old."

"Did you ever consider that if you and Chelsea had not left your house that night, you two would have died too?"

In response to my words he just sat there, stock-still. I squeezed his hand before I added, "Perpetually eight is far better than being perpetually dead. You saved her, and in more ways than one."

Trace brought me back to Kyle's and parked his motorcycle at the curb before he walked me to my door. I hesitated to go in because I wasn't ready to leave him, but at the same time the past two days had been so emotional that I needed some time to process it all.

His eyes held mine as he reached up and ran his finger along my jaw. "Could I see you tomorrow?"

Oh, to hell with needing time to process, I needed Trace more. "I would really like that."

"I'll pick you up around noon?"

"I'll be waiting."

He leaned into me and brushed his lips over mine.

"Good night, Ember."

I leaned against the door and practically sighed, "Night."

When I entered the apartment, Kyle was waiting for me with a glass of wine. He didn't even wait for me to drop my keys on the table before he asked, "Do you want to talk about it?"

I walked over to the sofa and settled next to him, reaching for my glass as I did.

"You know me so well."

"How did it go?"

"It was wonderful. His sister is beautiful and sweet."

Kyle settled back on the sofa and grinned. "Start from the beginning."

Midday the next day, I was finishing getting dressed when the doorbell rang. I walked out into the living room just as Kyle opened the door for Trace. The tension between the men could have been cut with a knife as we left, but I understood because Kyle was the one to help me pick up the pieces after Trace broke my heart. Kyle had been a good friend.

Moments later we were driving down the street and I tightened my hold on Trace, resting my cheek against his back. I felt the shudder that went through him in response. We drove for a while before reaching our destination and when I saw that we were at Nathan's, love burned through me.

"One hot dog with everything on it," Trace said to me before he leaned back to kiss me. My heart stuttered in response because I had shared with him my love of hot dogs during one of our countless phone conversations and he hadn't forgotten.

"You remembered!"

———◆———

In the week that followed, I spent every day and most evenings with Trace, but he always brought me home at the end of the date, leaving me at the door with a good-night kiss. One night he took me back to his apartment, where we ate popcorn and watched Christian Bale as Batman. Another night, we just strolled through the Village, talking.

I knew what he was doing: trying to reconnect, trying to bring us back to where we had been before he pushed me away. The thing was, I didn't need any of it. As much as I loved every second that I spent with him, I understood why he'd acted as he did. I loved him, never stopped, and more, I wanted him to hold me, to touch me, to love me.

Time for some drastic measures. We were at dinner, a small Greek place, and were just finishing our main courses when I reached across the table for Trace's hand.

"Trace?"

"Yes, love?"

I leaned closer to him so no one else would overhear. "If you don't make love to me, I think I might go insane." His body practically started to hum with want.

"Are you sure?"

"God, yes."

"Check, please!"

We barely made it outside of the restaurant before Trace pulled me to him and kissed me so carnally that my stomach flip-flopped with desire. We broke several traffic laws to make it back to his apartment in under ten minutes.

As we entered his apartment, he closed the door behind us and I turned to find him leaning against the door watching me. The look in his eyes burned desire through my body. I knew he wouldn't make a move; he wanted to, but was following my lead. I wanted him to touch me, I wanted to touch him, so I held his gaze before I whispered, "Make love to me."

That was all it took. He walked across the floor and pulled me into his arms. His mouth fused to mine as his hands sought the hem of my shirt, pulling from me only long enough to rid me of it and my bra. My hands were eager for the feel of the hard smoothness of his skin as I ran my fingers over his heated back, causing those muscles to bunch and cord in response. He lifted me into his arms and started walking down the hallway to his room. I pressed my mouth to his neck, sucking the blood to just under the surface of his skin before I bit him. He growled in response. He tossed me on his bed as he stripped and then he pounced, caging me with his aroused, hard body.

"I can't wait. I need to be inside you." His hands lifted my skirt and pulled my panties off. He touched me and found me ready before he settled himself between my thighs and slowly joined us. I wanted it hard, but loved that he took it so painfully slow.

"Oh God, you feel so good," he growled as he started to move, each stroke causing the delicious tension to build until I felt as if I was being torn apart from the pleasure that ached to the point of pain. I gripped his excellent ass as I urged him to go deeper, harder, faster and when he did, I came apart, screaming out his name. I felt him tense and with two more thrusts, he closed his eyes, threw his head back and roared with release.

When he collapsed on top of me, I thought I'd never move again until he started to roll my pebbled nipple between his thumb and forefinger. Just like that the tension started to grow.

"Trace, we couldn't possibly."

"No?" He rolled away from me and settled back against the pillows. He eyed me, staring a moment longer at my breasts and between my legs before he said, "I could go all night."

I started to throb.

"But if you're sure . . ." His hand moved from over his head and came to rest on his chest. There was a twinkle in his eyes just before he slid his hand lower down his body. I pulled my greedy gaze from his hand to his face. He looked positively naughty. I looked back to his hand; it was just reaching his abs before it stopped.

Lust made me almost yell, "Don't stop there."

"Do you want to watch?"

"Oh my God, yes."

His hand closed over his erection and his legs spread slightly wider. He moved with deliberate slowness, down the shaft and up. He moaned deep in his throat as he slowly increased his pace. His eyes closed as pleasure moved across his features. His hips started rocking slightly back and forth while his other hand joined the first. He reached for the heavy sacs between his legs and started to squeeze. It was the hottest thing I had ever seen in my life. I wanted to watch him bring himself to orgasm, but I wanted to ride him there more. I crawled over to him and straddled his lap. His hands immediately fell away, but his eyes never opened. "Took you long enough."

I moved with the same deliberateness he had as I slowly sank down onto him.

"Fucking sweet." His hand moved to my hips as I started to move. He leaned forward and sucked my breast into his mouth. I cradled his head in my hands to hold his mouth there as my hips moved wildly against him. His hand found its way between my legs and touched me in just the right spot. I felt the start of the orgasm just as Trace tensed and when we came, we came together.

That night, despite happy exhaustion, I had trouble sleeping so I lay there for a while watching the gentle rise and fall of Trace's chest. His dreams seemed to be untouched by the horrors of his childhood. After an hour of sleeplessness, I decided to make myself some warm milk, so I climbed from bed, pulled on Trace's T-shirt, and padded down the hall. As soon as I entered the kitchen, I saw a bottle of wine on the counter and opted to have a glass of that instead.

I took my glass into the living room and settled on the sofa, pulling my legs under me before looking out the window as thoughts fired randomly in my brain.

Trace and his sister were sexually abused as children and the thought of those two precious souls having been violated enraged me in a way that I'd never felt before. Tears filled my eyes thinking of him—both of them—as young, helpless children in a situation that they had no control over. In Trace's case, it explained his behavior as an adult: the plethora of single-dated women, the sex, the fighting. Everything that he did in his adult life, he controlled. Never was the control taken from his hands.

His father got off lightly. He should have been made to suffer the pain and helplessness that he had inflicted on his children. And his mother, what the fuck was her problem? How the hell could a woman bear children and then sit back and allow harm to come to them?

What was his uncle's involvement? More now than ever I understood Trace's reaction to him—and to think I was voluntarily working at the man's campaign headquarters! I might need to have my head examined. I was thankful that Trace finally was able to share his hell. The fact that it was with me touched me and made me feel a connection to him that no one ever had. Maybe, having spoken of it and facing it, he really would begin to heal.

I was so lost in my thoughts I didn't realize that Trace had joined me until he was standing right in front of me. Thankfully, he had pulled on his boxer-briefs, though actually it was a bit more of a tease than if he had been standing there naked.

"I could look at you all day," I said.

He hunched down just in front of me and reached for my glass to place on the coffee table before he rested his hands on my legs. "I like that you're looking."

He ran his hands up my legs and under his shirt that I was wearing before lifting it slightly so his fingers could trace the tattoo on my hip. His eyes followed his movements and then locked onto mine. His voice was hoarse when he said, "You have no idea what this does to me: to know that you marked yourself for me."

"Trace."

I reached for his hand and pulled him up to join me on the sofa as I shifted to curl myself into his lap.

"We need to look into your parents' deaths."

"I know."

"Uncle Josh is very discreet."

He ran his fingers through my hair and the feel of those strong fingers caressing my scalp almost had me purring.

"I'll call your dad tomorrow. I need to speak to him anyway."

I looked up at that. "Why?"

His grin was positively wicked before he pressed a kiss on my nose. "That's for me to know and for you to find out."

"Really, there are ways to make you talk."

His eyebrow lifted ever so slightly. "How?"

My fingers dug into his side as I attempted to tickle him to no avail. Then he lifted me from his lap and dropped me on my back as a devilish gleam lit his eyes.

"Oh, love, you shouldn't have done that."

He was a Jedi Master in tickling. When he finally relented and stilled those wicked fingers, I had tears running down my cheeks from laughing so hard. He looked down at me with a combination of humor and desire.

"You're all flushed." He reached for the hem of my shirt and started to lift it as his hungry eyes devoured each inch of bare skin he exposed.

"You're flushed everywhere. I'd like to see how far down the blush goes."

And then he was lifting me into his arms and carrying me down the hall.

I ran my hand over the muscles of his arm. "My, what big muscles you have."

He looked me right in the eyes when he replied, "That's a very appropriate reference, my dearest Ember, since I fully intend to eat you."

My jaw dropped. Again? His lips brushed over my cheek to my ear before he added, "Until you shatter."

The only words that my sexually hazed brain could form were, "Hell, yeah."

*C*hapter *S*ixteen

I can't lie, I'm a bit upset to lose you as a roommate, but I'm glad things worked out with Trace." It had been a month since Trace and I had our heart-to-heart and Trace had asked me if I would move back in with him. I was hesitant, but had to take the leap.

I didn't have much stuff—only a few bags of important things. I had left the rest at Trace's when I departed so abruptly. I hadn't yet retrieved my things since I didn't know how. Luckily, now I didn't need to worry about it. "Thanks for helping me pack the rest of my stuff. I've really enjoyed staying here. How about I order us some Chinese food?"

He turned to look at me as he filled my duffle bag. "Cool."

Once I was all packed Kyle and I sat on the floor in the living room eating Chinese food and drinking wine—something we tried to do at least once a week. Kyle reached for another egg roll.

"Just because you're moving out doesn't mean we can't do this anymore."

"Agreed. We should continue to make it a weekly deal with one week here and one week at Trace's. What do you say?"

"Sounds perfect. How are things with Trace?"

I placed my plate on the table and reached for my glass. "We're actually talking about his past—I understand him better now and it's helping us as a couple."

Kyle smiled. "You saw something in him and you held on. He's lucky that you cared enough to stick."

"I think I'm the lucky one. Knowing all that I do about him, I get why he closed himself off to others—he needed to for self-preservation. That he saw something in me that made him want to reach out is humbling."

Kyle held his glass up to me as a grin touched his lips. "I'm a sucker for happy endings."

It was close to twelve when I finally returned to Trace's. As he requested, I called him and he was standing out front waiting for me. He opened my door and helped me from the car before he kissed me hard on the mouth.

"Did you have fun with Kyle?" he asked as he carried my bags into the building.

"I did. We're going to continue our Chinese takeout night once a week: here one week and there one week. We'd both like it if you'd join us."

Surprise flashed over his face. "I would really like that," he said rather softly.

Trace pushed open the door to his apartment and waited for me to precede him before he followed, closing and locking it. We headed for the bedroom, where Trace dropped everything by the closet.

"We can unpack tomorrow."

"Agreed."

And then he said, "I'm going to give you to the count of three."

"For what?"

He answered by pulling me onto the bed and covering my body with his own.

"Welcome home, Ember."

And then he was kissing me and all was right in my world.

———•———

A few nights later Trace and I went up to the Bronx to his gym, but he wasn't fighting that night; we were meeting with my uncle. I loved crime dramas and, feeling a bit cloak-and-dagger, we thought it best to be discreet regarding our interests in Charles's past. Most who attended these fights were only interested in the fighting. It seemed like the perfect place to meet with our PI.

My uncle had been very receptive to helping us.

Trace gripped my hand firmly in his as we made our way through the mass of people. He had no problem at all seeing over people. I felt the light pull on my arm and knew he had found my uncle.

A few minutes later we reached a clearing in the crowd and there he was.

"Uncle Josh."

He turned and smiled. "Ember." He pulled me into a hug. "I was so happy to get your call."

He turned to Trace. "It's nice to see you again."

"Likewise, sir."

"So tell me what is it you need me to do."

———•———

A week later I was working at Charles's campaign headquarters, when I happened to glance up to see Vivian Michaels walking toward me. As usual, she made the picture-perfect image of a campaign wife with her St. John's blue-silk suit and Tory Burch ballerina slippers. Her blond hair was upswept, her makeup perfectly applied, and huge sapphires hung from her ears. I was curious as to what she wanted.

"Ember, it's so nice to see you again."

"Mrs. Michaels, hello."

"Please, call me Vivian." She settled into a chair next to me with such regal elegance she reminded me of a queen.

"I understand that you are dating my nephew, Trace."

"Yes, I am."

"The conflict between my husband and the last of his family has been going on for far too long. I was so hoping that you could talk with Trace and get him to agree to join us for dinner. We don't have to have it at the house if it would be more comfortable for him to meet at a restaurant." She touched my shoulder before she added, "You don't have to answer right now. If Trace is anything like my husband, I understand your hesitation, but think about it, won't you?"

"Yes."

"Wonderful." She stood, smiled, and rested her hand on my shoulder. Her queenly pose didn't flag for a second.

"I do hope we can all be friends, since we are family after all."

And with that she breezed away—the faint scent of her Chanel No. 19 still lingering in the air. I sat there after she had gone, wondering, what the hell was the real purpose of that visit?

I thought about Vivian's impromptu visit for the rest of the day and later, during my shift at Clover, I made the decision to not mention it to Trace just yet. There was enough going on that he didn't also need to feel the pressure of getting reacquainted with absent relatives who, more than likely, were faking interest as a means to get close to him and possibly cause him harm.

I moved to the guests that had just been seated at one of my tables, and my heart lodged in my throat to see Dane and Heidi, Trace's castoff/stalker. What the hell were they doing together?

As soon as Dane saw me, a smile spread over his face and to say it gave me the major creeps wasn't an exaggeration.

"Ember Walsh, you're looking particularly fine this evening." He didn't bother to hide a healthy ogle of my breasts before his eyes found mine again. "How have you been? You don't call or write."

"Can I get you something to drink?"

He lifted his water glass and eyed me from head to toe. "So professional."

"I was truly sorry to hear about you and Trace. I thought if anyone could reach him it would have been you." Heidi's voice distracted me from Dane and when I looked at her I saw sympathy in her expression. Heidi practically ripped my head off when she was here with Trace and he paid me polite attention, and now her date was openly flirting with me and her response was pity?

What the hell were these two up to? Like she wanted me to make it work with Trace. The woman had a spy network around the man. How did she not know we were back together? A part of me was tempted to inform her, but it wasn't any of their damn business.

Dane's voice sent a chill down my spine when next he spoke.

"You can imagine my delight learning that your guardian is no longer an issue."

His hand shot out and wrapped around my wrist, which made me wince as I tried to pull free of him.

"I have every intention of finishing what we started."

He sounded like a spoiled child. Heidi wasn't looking sympathetic anymore, she looked like she wanted to reach across the table and wring Dane's neck. Kyle appeared then with a glass of bourbon that he "accidentally" spilled in Dane's lap.

Dane jumped up, cursing as Kyle offered an insincere apology. Without another word, Dane pulled Heidi from the restaurant.

What the hell had that been all about?

"Are you okay?" Kyle's concern only served to freak me out further. What did *he* think was going to happen?

I touched Kyle's arm. "Yes, but thank you."

"I don't like the look of him. That's Dane, right?"

"Yeah."

"You weren't wrong, you need to be very careful with that one."

His words echoed exactly what I was thinking when I released on a breath, "Don't I know it."

The maître d' came over then and I thought for sure Kyle or I or both were going to be fired. He surprised me, though, when he also said, "Are you okay?"

"I am, but I'm sorry about the scene."

He looked around the room. "A little spice is exactly what some of these people need." And then he winked and went off to smooth any ruffled feathers.

I wasn't sure I had heard him correctly until I heard Kyle's muffled laughter. "I didn't expect that," he said.

"You and me both. I thought for sure we were canned. Let's get back to work before he changes his mind."

Chapter Seventeen

❖

The following afternoon I retrieved the mail and noticed a card for Trace from Chelsea. I walked down the hall to his office.

"You have something from Chelsea," I said in way of greeting. I reached over to hand it to him and he grabbed me and pulled me onto his lap before he kissed me hard on the mouth. And then he kept me there as he reached for the envelope and tore it open. It was a birthday card and I realized that I didn't know when his birthday was.

"When is your birthday?"

"May twenty-first."

"Good to know." Maybe I could throw a small birthday dinner for him.

"What are you thinking?"

"Nothing."

"Liar." He started to rub my back before he said, "I don't do big birthdays."

"I suspected as much." And then to change the subject I asked, "Trace, would it be okay for me to take Chelsea out shopping and to lunch?"

His hand stilled on my back and I wanted to protest, since he was igniting little fires under my skin, but then he spoke and the tenderness in his voice made my heart melt.

"You would do that?"

"I would love to do that."

"Yes, Chelsea would love spending time with you."

"Great. So, I can just call and make the arrangements?"

"Yeah." Then he lowered his head so his mouth lingered just above my very eager lips before he whispered, "I love you." And then he sealed that vow with a kiss.

<hr>

Trace had ordered a car service for Chelsea's and my day out. She was waiting for me dressed in a lovely sundress in the color of buttercups and her pretty brunette hair was pulled back in a thick black headband. She didn't wear makeup, but then she didn't need to because she was just stunning. As soon as she saw me she jumped up from her chair in the lobby and ran to me and threw her arms around me.

"Hello, Chelsea. It's so good to see you again."

"I can't wait to go shopping with you. I haven't been shopping in forever."

"Is there someplace special you would like to go?"

"Anywhere," she said with a big smile before she reached for my hand to hold.

"Okay."

We walked along Fifth Avenue and stepped into Cartier and Tiffany. Seeing Chelsea's wide-eyed expression at the jewelry was so fun. She fell in love with a daisy necklace with the Tiffany blue enamel, so I bought it for her. I didn't really have the money for it, but I could do some creative financing. The expression on her face made it worthwhile. We watched as the saleswoman wrapped it in the pretty robin's egg–blue box before slipping it into a shopping bag. As soon as we were on the sidewalk outside the store, Chelsea peeled open the box to hold her treasure a moment before slipping it over her head with such a heartfelt thank-you that I was completely and totally undone. After our shopping we went to the Plaza Hotel for lunch at the Palm Court.

Our waitress approached us. "Do you know what you would like to eat?" Chelsea scrunched up her nose and seemed to really ponder the question.

"I don't know."

To be helpful the waitress asked, "Do you like chocolate?"

"Yes."

"We have a frozen hot chocolate drink that is delicious."

"Does it have whipped cream?"

"Of course."

Chelsea's eyes turned to me. "Can I get that?"

"Anything you want, Chelsea."

"Okay, I want that, please."

I smiled at Chelsea before turning to our waitress. "And for her—the chicken lollipops and shrimp cocktail and I'll have the Queen of Berries."

"Sure thing."

As soon as our waitress disappeared, Chelsea said, "I like it here. It's very pretty."

"I like it too. Did you have fun shopping?"

Her hand wrapped around her necklace before she said, "Yes, but you didn't get yourself anything."

No, I had wiped out my cash with her necklace and this lunch but she didn't need to know that. "I didn't see anything that I wanted. Besides, I had fun just watching you enjoy yourself."

"Trace is lucky. He gets to see you all the time." Chelsea said as her eyes grew wide when her drink was placed before her.

I wondered how Trace would feel about having Chelsea come to live with us. I knew she loved Rolling Acres and had friends there, but I wondered if she wouldn't like it more being with her brother. I'd find a way to bring that up to Trace.

We were getting ready to leave when a familiar voice came from behind me seconds before Lena appeared in front of our table. She looked terrible. She was too thin and had purple smudges under her eyes, but meanness poured off her in waves. She looked over at Chelsea and I saw her intent in those spiteful eyes even before she opened her mouth.

"Well, who's your friend?"

Our waitress seemed to pick up on the bad vibes when she suddenly appeared and asked Chelsea, "Would you like to see the kitchen?"

"Hurray! Please, can I, Ember? Pretty please?"

"Absolutely." She led Chelsea away and my smile turned into a sneer as I looked Lena up and down.

"You look like shit. Being with Todd is clearly not good for you."

"Shut up about him. You've no right to speak of him."

"Whatever." I stood and started to collect my and Chelsea's things before I added, "I'd say it was nice seeing you, but it wasn't."

I started around her, but she stopped me with a hand on my arm.

"Who's your friend? What's wrong with her? She sounds like a retard."

"None of your business." I stepped closer to her and pulled myself up to my full height, which wasn't much, but it was a few inches taller than her.

"Call her a retard again and I'll make you eat your tongue."

Fear flickered in her eyes, but it was immediately replaced with loathing. I didn't understand why she hated me and before I realized it I asked that very question out loud:

"Why do you hate me so much?"

"I was supposed to be the superhero and you the hero support, not the other way around."

The *Sky High* reference threw me for a minute, since Lena hated that movie. "Why does one have to shine over the other?"

"Because the shiny always looks better next to the dull."

"I'm sorry you feel that way, I truly am." And then I turned and started toward the kitchen, but she followed after me.

"Don't judge me. You're doing the same thing with your little retard. Unfortunately for you, even she still looks better than you."

We had reached the back near the restrooms so I turned on her and took a few menacing steps closer.

"I warned you." Rage fueled me into action and before I could talk myself out of it, I punched her right in the mouth. She fell backwards into the wall and though she was still standing, she was disoriented so I took the opportunity and moved closer to glare at her.

"Next time you see me, go the other way or I'll leave permanent damage. We clear?"

She nodded her head as her eyes glazed over with pain and, satisfied that I made my point, I turned and walked away.

Four days after my lunch with Chelsea, Lena's meanness had faded in all of the planning for Trace's birthday. I had sent him off to the store while Rafe, Lucien, and Chelsea arrived for his birthday dinner. They must have been hiding in the lobby because it was only moments after Trace left that the doorbell rang. Chelsea threw her arms around me as soon as I opened the door.

"I love birthday parties." And then she saw the balloons and I was immediately forgotten. Rafe and Lucien entered just behind her.

"This was a good idea," Rafe said and Lucien immediately added, "Thanks for the invite."

"I knew Trace would want you here."

"What can we do?" Lucien asked.

"There are balloons and streamers that need to be hung and a salad that needs to be made."

"I'll help you in the kitchen," Lucien offered as Rafe called to Chelsea to get her to hang the balloons instead of batting them around in the air.

"Let's do all pink."

Rafe grinned at her suggestion before he said, "We should probably mix it up."

"Oh, I guess."

The lasagna was in the oven, and I had to say, it smelled really good. I was delighted when Lucien agreed. He started chopping the vegetables for the salad before he added, "This is really great that you are doing this for Trace."

"Birthdays should be special, and I suspect he's had far too many that weren't."

"You're not wrong."

He stopped chopping and stood there rigidly, which told me there was something he wanted to know. So I asked, "What?"

He looked at me with those eyes. "At the risk of getting too personal, how are things with you and Trace?"

I didn't immediately answer as I searched for the right thing to say. "For a time I was really worried that we weren't going to make it. But I think the worst is behind us."

I watched as the tension seemed to slip from him. "I have never seen him more self-destructive than he was after you left. He can be a royal pain in the ass, but he loves you. I'm really glad to hear that the feeling is mutual."

"He's lucky to have friends like you and Rafe."

Understanding passed between us over our shared concern for Trace before Lucien said, "Likewise." And then the moment was over as he started chopping the vegetables again.

A half hour later, the phone rang twice, the signal from the doorman that Trace was on his way up.

"Hurry, guys," I said as I turned off the lights and we waited in the living room. A few minutes later we heard the heavy sound of Trace's footsteps seconds before the key turned in the lock. When the door opened we screamed, "Surprise!"

It took him a minute before a grin curved his mouth. He really looked surprised. He placed the bag of groceries on the entrance hall table. Chelsea ran to him and hugged him.

"Happy birthday."

Trace smiled with every one of his features before he wrapped her in his arms. "Thank you, Chelsea."

He lifted his head and the tenderness in his eyes as he looked at me made my heart flip over in my chest. Suddenly he was pulled away by Chelsea, who wanted to show him the decorations and the cake. Rafe came up next to me and bumped his shoulder into mine.

"I'd say that was a success."

"Agreed."

"I am so happy that you two are back together. He's happier than I've ever seen him."

"He makes me happy too."

"I can see that."

Lucien joined us and he said, "Let's check on the lasagna."

We sat around the table as Chelsea told Trace about our day out; it was four days ago and yet she remembered every moment and conversation as if it just happened. She showed him, for the hundredth time, her new necklace.

She looked so much like him. The eyes were different, his blue and hers gray, but with the shape of their eyes, their noses and lips, and their bone structure—there was no denying they were related. What would she have been like had the accident not happened? Would she have suffered in self-esteem, as Trace did? Would she too have closed off or would they have found their way through it together?

I wasn't really listening to the conversation so was taken a bit by surprise when I saw that three sets of eyes were looking at me, two angrily, which had the alarm bells going off in my head.

"What?"

Trace's voice was so soft I nearly missed his question. "Who approached you at the Palm Court?"

"Oh, that. It was nothing," I said as I stood and started collecting plates. I tried to dismiss his question, since I didn't want the beauty of the evening ruined by Lena, but Trace wasn't having any of that. He slammed his hands down on the table.

"Goddamn it, Ember, who the fuck approached you?"

I was surprised to see that reaction in him. He usually turned disturbingly quiet when he was angry. "Lena."

His expression turned frosty. "Was Todd or Dane there?"

"No, and I handled it."

"What am I missing? Todd and Dane who?" Lucien asked but Rafe spoke almost on top of him.

"Meaning?" I realized that Rafe was just as angry as Trace.

"Let's just say I don't see her bothering me again," I said as I collected a few more plates and started from the room.

"Ember."

"Stop!" I was furious that Lena had the power to fuck things up and not even be in the damn room. "I won't have tonight ruined over her."

I had started out of the room again when Chelsea's voice stopped me dead.

"Ember punched her in the face."

Horrified, I turned to her and asked, "And how do you know that?"

There was guilt on her face when she said, "I had to go to the bathroom."

I put the plates down and moved to kneel next to her chair. "I'm really sorry you saw that."

"She was being mean."

So simple an observation, and yet very true. "Yes, she was, but hitting isn't the answer."

I stood but kept my eyes on Chelsea and waited for the lecture from Trace or Rafe or both, but when it didn't come I looked at them to find them grinning at me. There was a note of admiration in Trace's voice when he said, "Way to go, slugger."

Rafe held up his wineglass in salute to me. "Sorry we missed it."

"Punched who?" Lucien demanded.

"Her ex-roommate Lena who's dating a jackass named Todd," Rafe said.

"And who's Dane?"

"Dane Carmichael—he went on a blind date with Ember that was set up by Lena. He's a real dirtbag."

I snorted before I said, "You're all juveniles." And then I started toward the kitchen again.

I was just finishing stacking the dishes in the dishwasher when Trace entered.

"Thank you for tonight."

"You're welcome."

"I don't want to talk about Lena either, but if Todd or Dane approach you, you have to tell me."

I felt my heart drop at those words as an unpleasant sensation filled me. I somehow managed to ask, "Why?"

He walked to me and wrapped his arms around my waist and the affection in his eyes made my blood warm.

"You are the most important thing in my life and I need to keep you safe. Those two are assholes—I know the type—and that makes me worried for you. If Lena is comfortable enough to approach you then Todd and Dane will be too. I don't want them anywhere near you."

"Okay."

He lifted my gaze to his. "You'll tell me, right?"

I felt like shit lying to him, but I didn't want to ruin his evening. I gave him the answer he was looking for and promised myself that I would tell him in the morning. "Yes."

He lowered his head to brush his lips over mine before he pulled back and grinned.

"Thank you."

Self-loathing filled me as I looked at him and tried for a smile before I asked, "Are you ready for cake?"

After cake Chelsea moved to the sofa to watch television while the rest of us lingered over our coffee. There was a noticeable difference in Lucien since the conversation earlier. I wasn't the only one to pick up on it when I heard Trace ask, "What are you thinking, Lucien?"

"I was surprised to hear you mention Dane Carmichael."

"Why?" Trace asked. "Do you know him?"

"Not personally but I've heard stories. He's on the watch lists at my clubs. He gets too feely, manhandles girls. A few times he's been accused of much worse."

"What you mean?" I asked.

"Sometime back he got involved with a woman who worked for me. Her name was Sabrina. She moved here from Iowa with the hopes of making it on Broadway. She worked for me for almost a year before she finally caught her break and landed a role in an off-Broadway production. That was when she met Dane. He was one of the investors in the show. His family is affluent and patrons of that sort of thing so it wasn't really a surprise that the Carmichael name was tied to the production. He swept Sabrina off her feet. He wined and dined her and, being that she came from meager beginnings, it was all very exciting to her. One night after dress rehearsal, there was a cast party and Dane was there.

"He raped her, though he claimed it was consensual. She tried to press charges but it was her word against his and he had his family to back him. It got to the point that even at work people started talking about her, how she had asked for it, how she was crying rape to get money. It all became too much for her and she killed herself."

"Oh my God," I gasped.

"I remember you mentioning this sometime back. It was Dane you were speaking about?" Trace asked.

"Yeah, at the time it was a horrible story and I took precautions at my clubs to watch him, but I didn't know Sabrina personally. However, with him having a connection to Ember, it seemed prudent to share the story again." His attention turned to me before he added, "Clearly she had issues to go so far as to take her own life, but it was the ease with which his family brushed it under the rug, as if they had practice in these matters, that stuck with me."

"Yet another reason why you need to tell me if either of them approaches you, Ember," Trace said.

Tomorrow was soon enough. "Okay."

Hours later I was in our bedroom getting ready for bed while Trace took Chelsea home. I heard the door open and close, heard the sound of his footsteps coming from down the hall. I looked over just as he entered our room.

"Chelsea's all tucked in?"

"She was talking a mile a minute on the taxi ride back but as soon as her head hit the pillow, she was out." He started toward me. "You're wearing too many clothes."

My legs went weak. He moved until he had me pressed between the wall and his hard body. And then he lifted me into his arms and I wrapped my legs around his waist just as his mouth captured mine. His fingers moved under my nightgown and past the barrier of my panties. "This is going to be fast," he whispered just as he touched me. I worked his zipper to free him.

"I like fast."

He wasted no time and when he filled me I threw my head back and moaned. He moved almost violently between my thighs.

"Oh God, you feel so good, Trace."

His mouth burned a trail down my neck with hot, wet kisses along the column of my throat. Each thrust of his hips rubbing against my core brought me closer and closer, but it was when he sucked my breast into his hot mouth through the silk of my nightgown that I came apart. My orgasm was so fierce it brought tears to my eyes.

I felt him tense and right before he came he growled, "Mine, Ember, you are mine." And then his face froze with pleasure as he continued to push into me to rub out the last of his release. He lowered his forehead to my shoulder and his lips touched my neck before he whispered, "This was the best birthday ever."

Chapter Eighteen

Several days after Trace's birthday I still had not told him about Dane's visit to Clover. I couldn't help but think that Trace was being overprotective. Not that I could blame him, considering what he and Chelsea had lived through. But his overprotectiveness made it hard for me to predict how he was going to react. My gut was telling me this confession was not going to go well but I had promised that I would tell him if Dane approached me. To not do so was wrong. I steeled myself for the encounter and walked down the hall to his office. I rubbed my sweaty palms on my thighs before I knocked lightly on the door.

"Come in."

He was looking up, probably because I had yet to speak, and the smile that spread over his face took me aback. Just two months before he wouldn't have done that: smiled so naturally and unguardedly. He was healing, whether he knew it or not.

"What's up, beautiful?"

I moved toward him and placed my hands on the back of one of the leather chairs that sat just in front of his desk. "I need to tell you something."

He leaned back in his chair but his focus was completely on me when he asked, "Is everything okay?"

"Yes, but I should have told you before and I didn't because I didn't want to ruin your birthday."

Trace stood and moved from around the desk to take me into his arms.

"Ember, just tell me."

I pressed my face into his chest and closed my eyes as I sought additional strength because I knew as soon as the words were out he was going to go berserk. I took a deep breath and said it.

"Dane came into Clover and I had the sense it was specifically to see me."

The gentle stroking that Trace was doing to soothe me stopped as he went completely still. I risked a look up at him and saw that he was clenching his jaw and his eyes had turned hard and cold.

"When?"

"A few days before my outing with Chelsea."

He pulled away from me and put some distance between us, since he probably couldn't trust himself to not throttle me because I kept this from him. He reached the other side of the room before he turned back to me and asked, "What did he say to you?"

"He said that he was glad my guardian was no longer an issue and that he planned on finishing what he started."

Trace was clenching his fists so hard that the tendons were bulging and turning white from lack of blood flow. His voice was soft, menacingly so, when he asked, "Did he touch you?"

"He grabbed my wrist, but Kyle dumped a glass of bourbon on him."

"You should have told me. I asked you to tell me if either of them approached you and the day I asked this of you, you looked me in the face and lied."

"I know and I'm sorry. I just didn't want to ruin your birthday."

"And if he had gotten his hands on you and hurt you, don't you think that would have fucking ruined my birthday? If he had played out whatever sick fantasy he's got in his head, don't you think that would have ruined my fucking birthday?"

He fell silent as his body just pulsed with rage. Trace reminded me of a rattlesnake that was poised and ready to strike. Not at me, I hoped. He grabbed a paperweight from his desk and hurled it across the room with such force that it got embedded into the solid oak door. He started from the room and I knew that if he left the house, as angry as he was, he was going to kill someone.

"Please, stay here."

He moved down the hall with determined strides as I hurried to catch up to him.

"Calm down first. I don't understand why you are reacting like this."

I had never seen Trace like this. I'd seen him unreachable but it was the rage that accompanied the remoteness, a rage that made him appear almost calm, that scared me. I knew that part of what was fueling him stemmed from his past and his inability, at least in his mind, to protect his sister.

"There's more; Heidi was with him."

He stopped, mid-stride, and turned his head to me and I could tell we were thinking the exact same thing: What the fuck?

"For what it's worth, she seemed genuinely upset that we didn't stay together. It was weird seeing them together. I know you're mad, but I honestly don't understand why."

"Because a few days after this you went out alone with Chelsea."

"I didn't then and still don't believe she was in any harm."

He took a few steps closer to me before he hissed, "What would you have done if it hadn't been Lena who approached you that day? What if it had been Dane or Todd or both? You knew what they tried that night at Sapphire. If they're capable of that, who knows what else they're capable of. You didn't just put yourself at risk, you also put Chelsea at risk and she's been through enough."

And then he turned and walked out.

I just stood there staring at the door, unable to get my feet to move because I was really fucking angry too. I suppose if I was being completely truthful, there was a nice dose of hurt there as well. I had always thought myself a mild-tempered person, but Trace had the power to make me deliriously happy, heartbreakingly sad, and really fucking angry. I'd cried more since I'd known him than I had in all of my life up to that point. There really is some merit to the expression, "there is a fine line between love and hate."

I'm not sure how much time passed, no more than five or ten minutes, when the door opened and Trace walked back into the apartment. He closed the door behind him before leaning back against it. The look of contrition burning in his eyes made my heart sigh. He shoved his hands into the front pockets of his jeans as he looked at me.

"I walked away again."

"Yes, and a good thing too, because I was inches from slugging you." I held his gaze and added, "You came back."

A ghost of a smile teased his mouth before he replied, "I suppose that's progress."

"It is progress."

"I'm sorry. Maybe you're right, maybe I'm overreacting, but I failed someone I loved before. I can't make that mistake again."

"You didn't fail her. You were both in an impossible situation, but thanks for caring."

He moved from the wall and walked over to pull me into his arms.

"I need some time to cool off. I'll be in my office."

"Okay."

He pressed a kiss on my forehead before he released me. He was halfway to his office when I called to him, "I know this is hard for you, going against instinct, but I'm glad you came back."

He stopped and looked back at me from over his shoulder. "On the contrary, it was surprisingly easy because I was coming back to you."

My heart swelled with love as I watched him disappear into his office and then I did a little victory dance. Progress.

Later that night I was making dinner when I heard the door to Trace's office open. The sound of his footsteps down the hall made my heart flutter. I turned my head just as he appeared in the door-way. His hands found the pockets of his jeans. The oddest expression washed over his features. He looked uncomfortable, almost nervous.

"What's wrong?"

"I can't be upset with you for not being completely forthcoming when I haven't told you everything either. I called your dad and asked that he and your uncle come for a visit this weekend. There's one more thing that I need to share with you and your family."

I studied him and realized that it wasn't nervousness; it was panic. "Trace?"

"I've been trying to figure out the best way to tell you and I'll admit that I've procrastinated because there really isn't a good way to say what I need to say."

His expression changed as that empty look—the one he got when his past pulled him down—crossed over his features. I won't lie, I wanted to demand that he tell me whatever it was he had to say, but I bit my tongue because of that look. "Please don't look like that. Whatever it is, whatever you have to say, we will deal with it together."

He didn't hesitate to wrap me in his arms before he whispered, "God, I hope that's true."

Friday night arrived and when I heard the bell I started to the door, only to find Trace already pulling it open for my dad and uncle.

"Hello, Shawn, Josh, please come in."

"It's good to see you, son," my dad said and then he turned to me.

"Emmie."

"Hi Daddy and Uncle Josh. What a treat to see you two in the same room."

My dad looked embarrassed before he said, "You get your temper from me."

I laughed as I hugged him.

"Where's mine?"

I couldn't help the grin, since my uncle always had a way of making me feel like a little kid again. I hugged him hard before I led them to the living room. Once they were settled, I started to the kitchen to get the iced tea, but Trace stopped me.

"I'll get it. You stay and catch up with your family."

Trace's remoteness was another survival mechanism. He was distancing himself as a means of protecting himself. What the hell did he have to say that worried him so? I watched him go before I joined my dad and uncle on the sofa.

"It's nice to see you two have worked it out," my dad said as he studied me closely. "You look happy, Ember."

"I am."

"Do you have any idea what Trace wants to talk with us about?" my uncle asked.

"I don't, but I know he's worried about our reactions."

"He sounded a bit off when I spoke to him earlier in the week," my dad said.

Trace walked in at that moment and set the tray on the table. He settled in the chair opposite us and rested his elbows on his knees. His head was down and I had the sense he was working out how he wanted to say whatever it was he had to say. He lifted his head and looked directly at my dad.

"It isn't by chance that I know your family." His eyes moved to mine before he added, "It also wasn't simply that chance meeting at Sapphire that made me interested in you. That meeting wasn't really by chance at all. That night was the first time we spoke, but it wasn't the first time I saw you. I knew you grew up in Fishtown, knew when you got your scholarship to U of D, and I knew the exact day you moved into the city." He looked down for a moment.

"I own Clover and it was through me that you learned of the opening. I didn't get your job for you; I only made sure you knew that there was a position. I should have told you, when we first met, that you worked for me. Telling you only a half-truth was still lying to you. In order for me to tell you the truth, I was going to have to explain how I knew of you to begin with and I just wasn't ready to have that conversation. I am now."

His confession had me almost speechless. Almost. "Go on."

"After my parents died, I moved to Manhattan, a move orchestrated by my uncle. For the first year, I lived at the orphanage with Lucien and Rafe. At the time I didn't understand why he put me there instead of using the money we had to set me up in a different situation. But I get it now. It wasn't like a normal orphanage; it was strict and Sister Anne, for the short time that I knew her, was a miracle worker. I was really fucked up when I first arrived, getting into nonstop fights. She got through to me, probably the only person who could. She helped me work through my pain and after a year of being self-destructive, I pulled my shit together. Got Chelsea settled, got emancipated, was able to do so from a trust fund my mom set up for me. It was then that I started looking into the two people who were my parents. I had no love for them but they were my parents and how they died never sat right with me.

"While I was going through my dad's papers, I learned that in the early eighties he used to work a factory job in Fishtown before he and my mom moved to Ohio. I found an article from years later that was tucked away with his papers about a hit-and-run and when I dug a little deeper, I realized the car that had been seen fleeing the scene matched my dad's. I found receipts from a garage for repairs on that car and it was then that I put it together. It didn't make sense why his car would be in Philly when we lived in Ohio, but I couldn't argue with the proof in front of me."

I felt my heart drop just as my dad stood. His face was turning red and his hands were fisting at his sides. My uncle, I think, was in shock.

Trace didn't seem to notice—he was so lost in his purging. "That was when I sought out your family, sought you out. I felt responsible and, since he was no longer around to make amends, I felt that I should. I wanted to help you but I didn't know how until you got older and then it came to me. I had all of this money, their money, and it seemed only fitting that they fund your schooling so I sponsored your college scholarship. Even when you moved into the city I tried to keep my distance, but I helped whenever I could to make sure you were happy."

He stood and started pacing. "I didn't plan on meeting you that night at Sapphire, but I wasn't sorry that I did. And, yes, I made myself more visible to you after that, because the woman I saw that night was sweet, but brave. You were unlike anyone I'd ever known and I needed to know you better."

He stopped and looked me right in the eyes. "I fell in love with you and by then I was afraid if I told you the truth that you, all of you, would hold me responsible and hate me for it. I don't deserve to find happiness with you knowing how much my family has cost you."

I was having a bit of trouble following Trace, only because his words were causing a long, painful pull on my heart, but I needed to hear him just say it. Before I could ask him to do just that, my dad did so and the tone of his voice was not one that I'd heard before.

"We would hate you for what, Trace?"

There were tears in Trace's eyes as he held my dad's hard stare before he whispered, "My dad was driving the car that killed your wife."

My dad's voice sounded pained when he asked, "How old were you when you put it all together?"

"Sixteen. I should have told you sooner. I never should have slept under your roof and accepted your hospitality knowing what I did. I was terrified that once Ember knew what linked us, I would lose her."

My heart ached. "And as a sixteen-year-old, who was struggling to deal with your own abuse and the medical care for your younger sister, you sought to ease the pain of a little girl you never met because you felt responsible for your dad's actions?"

He turned to me before he replied, "Yes."

I lowered my head because my tears were coming too fast for me to control. My dad and uncle were equally quiet. When Trace spoke, he sounded defeated, which made me look up at him.

"I'm sorry I deceived you, all of you." He turned his focus on me before he said, "I do love you, Ember. I always will."

I grabbed his arm as he tried to walk out of the room.

"My tears are for you, not me."

He looked completely baffled by that comment and the look was so adorable that a small smile touched my lips. I didn't see my dad move until he was standing just in front of him. My heart started pounding. There was only one thing that could make my very reasonable father go over the edge and that was his wife; he had cast my uncle out for three years for merely suggesting that he marry again.

My stomach tied into knots. And then my dad pulled Trace into his arms and hugged him. I was so surprised, my jaw dropped. When my dad stepped back, there were tears in his eyes.

"It was your dad driving that car, not you. The fact that you sought us out and felt responsible speaks to your character, son. You are a good man."

My dad turned to me. "I'm going to go back to the hotel. I need some time. I'll be back in the morning."

My uncle shook Trace's hand before he followed my father out.

"That couldn't have been easy and it took a hell of a lot of guts. Thank you for telling us because, even after all this time, knowing what happened to Mandy brings a measure of closure. I have some news to share with you so we'll both come back in the morning, if that's okay."

Trace walked with me to the door as we saw my dad and uncle off. What a secret to hold on to, but his confession explained a lot, like how I kept running into him when we first met considering we lived in Manhattan. I grinned at the thought. Trace had been stalking me and that fact didn't bother me at all.

"Ember?"

"I imagine you must feel a lot better getting that off your chest."

"Not until I know how you feel about what I said."

I walked to him and reached for his hands. "I don't remember my mother. Knowing who killed her will give my dad and uncle closure, but for me, I made peace with her death a long time ago. My tears earlier were for the young man you had been, who, even coming from the nightmare that was your life, still sought to ease the pain of another."

I saw the tension drain from him as he started to pull me to him, but then he stopped and asked, "Why were you just grinning?"

"I couldn't figure out how we kept running into each other when we first met. You were totally stalking me."

"Takes one to know one." He grinned back at me.

I laughed out loud at that and then I sobered. "That had to be unimaginably hard for you to hold on to that secret. None of us hold you responsible. The silver lining is that we got each other." His lips brushed over mine, tasting and teasing, before he angled his head and took the kiss deeper. My hands came up to grip his shirt as I leaned into him and kissed him back. His tongue swept into my mouth and tangled with my own, making my knees go weak. My hands moved to wrap around his neck so I could pull him closer and kiss him deeper. When his mouth pulled from mine to run hot, wet kisses over my face, I closed my eyes and savored the feeling of being with him.

He lifted me into his arms and walked me to our bed before he placed me down and immediately covered my body with his own. He reached for my hands and pulled them up over my head as his mouth moved over me. He lifted my shirt and ran his tongue around my navel before dipping in, causing my body to jerk as my hips instinctively rose up off the mattress.

"Please, Trace."

"Anything for you, sweetheart."

─────◆─────

The following morning, when my dad and uncle arrived, they both looked surprisingly good. My dad followed me into the kitchen.

"Are you okay, Daddy?"

"I am. Honestly, it's closure and I didn't realize how much I needed it until I found it. How's Trace? That couldn't have been an easy burden."

"He's okay. Part of the hold that his past had on him was keeping that secret and now that he's purged it, he seems more at peace. I think he's finally ready to let go of his past and be happy."

"He deserves that."

"Yes, he does."

A few minutes later, Trace and my uncle joined us in the kitchen. We all settled at the table before my uncle said, "I want to share what I've learned so far." My uncle's eyes moved to Trace. "I need to know how much you're comfortable with me discussing."

Trace went completely still. I reached for his hand that was resting on his thigh. He squeezed my hand before he turned his attention back to my uncle and offered, "I'm learning . . ." he looked at me before he added, "how to deal thanks to Ember." He looked back at my uncle before he added, "Full disclosure is fine with me."

"Very well, but for the record I want to say what your dad did was depraved and how your mom did nothing was just as bad. You were one brave kid and I'm honored and proud to have you as a part of this family."

Trace's throat worked and his eyes looked suspiciously moist. "Thank you, sir."

"Your dad was into some serious shit. He was a gambler, but he wasn't very good—owing markers all over and many of which were to some rather unsavory characters. He had a string of girl-friends, most of whom later claimed that he was abusive, and he couldn't hold down a job because he was hostile and aggressive. Your mother had money—apparently quite a bit of money—that was given to her from her mother's side of the family. Most of the people I talked to had trouble recalling her—she was completely lost behind her husband. My guess is your dad was the target and your mom was collateral damage. I've a long list of people who need a closer look, so when I have more I'll let you know."

Trace asked, "Did you find anything on Charles Michaels?"

"Nothing that throws up any flags. He's ambitious, a hard worker, and unyielding. On paper, he's a straight arrow, but I agree with you that there's more to his story. He's arrogant enough to commit murder and believe he'll get away with it. I'm going to keep digging. I don't believe in a perfect murder. It only takes one little mistake."

Uncle Josh asked, "Your uncle knew what was going on in your house, didn't he?"

Trace sounded menacing when he replied, "Yes, and he let it go on for years. If he killed my parents, it didn't have anything to do with my sister and me."

"The man should be hung up by his short hairs for that, the bastard," said my uncle. "As far as I'm concerned that crime is far greater than murder."

My dad started to rise. "I agree, but enough shop talk. I say we challenge these young folk to a game of billiards."

"Oh yeah, I want a chance to win back all the money that I've lost to Ember over the years," my uncle said.

Trace and I both stood as I looked into my uncle's laughing eyes. "Never going to happen, old man. Not only did you teach me everything you know, but I also have my ace in the hole—Trace."

My uncle and dad continued to talk smack as they made their way to the front door. I leaned into Trace and held his tender gaze before I added, "And I'll never let you go."

Chapter Nineteen

❖

I liked to believe I was in fairly good shape, but Trace made me feel like a sloth during our daily runs. He trained religiously, which seemed to be helping his growing cake pop addiction.

Every day, after our run, Trace took me to Starbucks for my coffee and cake pop. And he never failed to get himself one.

As he ordered, I just stood back so I could watch him. I liked him in sweats: today's were black and rode low on his hips. His white tee was snug across the muscles of his chest and arms—arms that were flexed from the run. His hair was a bit longer, but still spiky around that arresting face of all angles.

He towered over everyone around him and there was a hardness to him when he interacted with people: not mean, but untouchable. Watching him, I was deeply grateful that he allowed me into his heart.

We stopped at the condiment bar so I could add cream to my coffee and then we stepped out into the beautiful morning. We stopped and looked in a few shop windows, but it was when we passed a window for Chanel that I remembered Vivian and her invitation from a few weeks back.

"Oh, shit."

"What's wrong?"

"Vivian Michaels caught me at campaign headquarters and invited us to dinner."

I felt Trace tense, but it was only for a moment and when he spoke it sounded more curious than angry. "From what I know of Vivian, Charles tells her to jump and she says how high. My guess is he put her up to that." He looked at me and grinned. "You know, the whole 'keep your friends close and your enemies closer.'"

A chill went down my spine and Trace obviously noticed it so he wrapped his arm around my shoulders and pulled me up against him. He spoke with quiet conviction when he said, "He won't touch you."

I wrapped my arm around him. "It's not me that I'm worried about."

His grin was cocky. "I can take care of myself, but I do so like having someone worrying over me."

"Well, get used to it," I muttered before changing the subject. "Hey, so tell me, how did you become the owner of Clover?"

I saw the flash of sadness that swept over his features before he pulled it under control.

"My mom had money and my dad liked to spend it and one of the things he spent her inheritance on was a cook. Mrs. Fletcher was a hell of a cook. She could make French, Italian, Greek, and Indian cuisine just as well as she could make comfort food. The house always smelled delicious when she was with us and it was under her watchful eye that I learned how to cook. I developed a real love of food and not just eating it, but also creating and presenting it. I decided, when I got older, to use some of my inheritance to turn my passion into a business."

My heart ached because I realized that I had unintentionally brought up a subject that was painful to him.

"I'm sorry."

"Don't be. I guess you figured out that Mrs. Fletcher didn't last. It was while she was with us that my dad's depravity escalated and I'm pretty sure Mrs. Fletcher discovered his dirty little secret. I really thought she was going to take Chelsea and me away—that she was going to help—but one day she just stopped coming to work."

I absently dropped my cup in a trash can that we passed as I realized something about him. "And all good things come to an end."

"Exactly."

"Have you ever looked her up now that you're older?"

"No, she became one of the angels who saw, heard, and spoke no evil."

I hated that he endured what he had, that there was no one to help him and he was eventually forced to help himself. But I was thrilled that he was so willing now to talk about his past.

"I wish I had been there to help you," I said.

"I don't because he would have hurt you and that would have sent me over the edge. I would have killed him and then we'd have missed out on a lifetime together."

I buried my face in the crook of his neck and pressed my lips to his throat.

He lifted me with ease and moved us from the sidewalk because we were causing a jam in the flow of pedestrian traffic. He placed me on the ground and pulled away from me so he could look me in the eyes.

"I think I may take Vivian up on her invite, but I hate putting you in that man's sphere any more than you need to be. Working at his fucking headquarters is bad enough."

"Please don't ask me to sit out when you know you wouldn't do the same."

His smile was tender as he ran his finger along my jaw. "Fair enough. How about we take them to Clover for dinner?"

"Perfect."

"All right, I'll send Vivian an e-mail and let her know." He reached for my hand as we started down the street again. Thinking of Clover made me wonder about his other businesses.

"What are the names of your other restaurants?"

"Just Coq au Vin."

"You own Coq au Vin?"

"Yes. Why, have you been?"

"No, but I bet it's fabulous." Coq au Vin was the most sought-after restaurant in the city with a six-month waiting list. I had always wanted to go, but, outside of the long wait, it was just way too expensive for me.

"Would you have dinner with me there?" he asked.

"Oh. My. God. Yes!"

He chuckled at my very enthusiastic answer as he reached up and tucked a lock of hair behind my ear.

"When would you like to go?"

"You don't have to wait?"

"No, I have a table."

"Oh." And then the thought of being one of many, just another in the revolving door that was his table at Coq au Vin, dampened my spirits. "It lacks the same appeal when you've brought so many others." He cradled my face in his hands and spoke with quiet sincerity. "I've only ever brought Chelsea to Coq au Vin and that night at the benefit at Clover, Heidi was supposed to be a distraction so you wouldn't realize that I was there to see you."

I stared like he had grown another head as I tried to process his words. He hadn't gone home with Heidi that night and for some reason knowing that made me feel really good. But still . . .

"What about the babe from that first night at Sapphire who you were so thoroughly entertaining?"

He actually paled, which took me completely by surprise, before he said quite seriously, "I watched over you for a long time and in that time I fell a little bit in love with you. I only brought her there because I knew you'd be there. I wanted to see you, but I also wanted to push you away."

A smile touched his lips when he added, "When I caught you following me I knew that the battle I was fighting to keep you from me was a pointless one."

"I never bought your image, never believed you were the man you wanted everyone to believe you were. I'd caught a glimpse of the man under that facade and I liked what I saw, a lot."

"And thank God for that," he said in a near whisper.

"Why Heidi?"

I knew I'd thrown him with that question when he asked, "What do you mean?"

"You aren't a repeat dater but you did with her, even using her to try to push me away. Why?"

"I'm not trying to dismiss your question but there's a lot of shit in my past and trying to explain all of it will only leave you more confused. Can we just leave it at Heidi being a part of my past that I really want to keep in the past? And before you ask, no there was never anything between us but she knows me well enough to feel sympathy toward me and mine. Not that she usually does."

It was more of an answer than I expected. "Fair enough."

I wrapped my arms around him and he pulled me close. "I have a confession." I looked up into his eyes before I continued, "That night at Sapphire, I was fantasizing that it was me you were stroking to climax."

His voice dipped to a sexy purr when he said, "Any time, absolutely any fucking time."

"Oh God."

He pressed his lips to mine for a kiss filled with promise, before he reached for my hand again. It took me a minute to realize he was still answering my original question.

"I also owned Noir, but I recently sold that, since there was another club I wanted, almost irrationally so."

"Really, which one?"

He smiled before he added, "Sapphire."

"You own Sapphire?" I stopped walking and turned to him as I remembered our private hour at Sapphire. I punched him affectionately in the stomach as I grinned at him. "You know the owner."

He laughed as he pulled me closer to him.

"I had to own the place because it's where I met you."

I felt myself going all gooey inside and then I realized that I had an answer to a puzzle.

"That's why you were already at Sapphire that night with Dane."

"Yes, I was finalizing the deal."

"Lucky for me, you were there that night."

"It's more than luck." Before I could ask him to explain that comment his mouth fused to mine and seconds later I forgot my question.

Trace dropped me off at home before he headed off to the gym for a few hours. The man was relentless, but I very much appreciated the results of his working-out efforts. I showered, changed into my comfy clothes, and curled up on the sofa with my laptop. My novel was coming along but at a much slower pace. Professor Smythe was helping me, offering direction on story flow and character development. I was in the middle of reworking a scene when Trace came home. Just hearing the key in the lock made my heart rate speed up. I wondered if I'd always feel that involuntary excitement at the thought of seeing him; I suspected I would even when we were old and gray.

"You look comfortable," he said as he closed and locked the door.

"I am. How was the workout?" I turned in my seat so I could see his face.

"Good, but I am in serious need of a shower."

"Can I make you anything for lunch?"

He walked over to me, leaned down, and kissed me hard on the mouth before he replied, "No, thanks."

I watched him disappear down the hall. I tried to work, but my thoughts were on Trace, more specifically Trace naked and wet. I moved down the hall to the bathroom, but, when I pushed the door open, Trace was already out of the shower with a towel wrapped around his waist. "Took you long enough."

My feet carried me into the bathroom with a mind of their own, stopping only when I was right behind him.

"You're beautiful," I said in awe as I pressed my palms to his shoulders and slid them slowly down the hard ridges of muscle on his back. He turned to me, but he made no move to touch me. I wondered about his restraint until I looked up into his eyes to find that they were burning with desire.

"And you? I see only perfection when I look at you," Trace said.

"No one's perfect," I said.

"You're pretty fucking close."

"Sweet talker."

His hands wrapped around my face as his mouth settled over mine. I reached down for his towel and pulled it from his hips. He whispered against my lips, "Touch me."

My hands wrapped around him as I ran my fingertips up and down the valley of his spine. I felt as his body hummed under my touch as I moved even lower to shape my hands around the hard muscles of his ass. He pressed himself closer to me as my hand found its way to the hard length of him that was pressing against my stomach. He moaned into my mouth but I moved from him, took his hand, and walked to the bedroom.

"On the bed," I ordered.

My stomach twisted with nerves seeing Trace lying on the bed, completely naked, but I had wanted to be bolder. And more than that I had wanted to show him that I trusted him with everything, including my body. I reached for my shirt and lifted it over my head. Our eyes were locked as my hands moved over my bra-covered breasts, my fingers pulling on my nipples through the fabric. I moved one strap teasingly down my arm before working on the second and then I grabbed both my breasts and squeezed.

My body hummed in anticipation when I saw what I was doing to Trace as he grew hard and thick. I flipped the clasp but held the bra in place for a few heartbeats before I let it fall to the floor. I heard him growl just as my hands slipped under my sweats. I was so swollen and wet, and looking at the part of Trace I wanted touching me pulled a purr from deep in my throat.

My sweats dropped down my legs when I pulled the tie free. I stepped out of my panties and lifted one foot onto the bed. My hands moved up my leg to the juncture of my thighs. My body flushed with desire as I stroked myself. I slipped one then two fingers inside as my hips moved against my hand. Trace wrapped his hand around his erection and started moving it up and down as he watched my fingers with hungry eyes.

"You're so wet." His eyes lifted to mine. "You like that."

"I like you watching me. I like watching you," I said as my eyes moved to between his legs where he was still stroking himself. "But I like you inside me more."

"Then come over here."

I climbed on the bed and straddled him before reaching for his hands to press to my breasts. Very deliberately I lowered myself onto him and felt as my body clenched around him, desperate to take more of him, and then I pulled up, my muscles protesting the emptiness.

"Fuck, Ember. I'm going to come on you in a minute."

I rubbed against him very lightly, moving up his length as I teased him. He was fully erect and seemed to grow even larger as I played. I moved against the tip of him as I pleasured the pulsing nub between my legs. Trace closed his eyes as if he was in pain. I spread my legs wider and waited a beat before I sank down on him hard.

"Fuck!" tore from Trace's throat and it was the single most sexy sound that I'd ever heard. I started to move just as Trace's thumb touched my sensitive bud.

The orgasm started low in my belly. I cried out as Trace's grip tightened on my hips, moving me harder and faster to prolong my climax. In the next minute I was on my back as Trace took over. His hips were relentless, causing small orgasms to ripple through me, and when he came, he was loud and slightly out of control.

When he was capable of speaking he said in awe, "You're amazing."

Chapter Twenty

Charles and Vivian ended up being very receptive to dinner and so, about two weeks after Trace and I discussed it, we were being seated at Clover. Charles and Vivian had not yet arrived. Trace held my chair for me before he folded his large frame into the chair at my right. He turned to me as soon as he was seated. "You look stunning tonight."

I marveled over the compliment as a slight blush tinted my cheeks. A lascivious smile transformed Trace's face and he added, "Even more so now."

"Thank you."

Our waitress, Cindi, came over to take our drink orders.

"Hi, Ember. It's nice to see you on the other side of things tonight."

"It's nice to be on the other side of things. Cindi, this is my boyfriend, Trace."

She blushed, clear up to her hairline, and I had complete sympathy for her, since I had a similar reaction when first meeting Trace. I had to give her credit, though; she recovered quickly before she asked, "What can I get you to drink?"

"We'd like a bottle of the 2003 Hundred Acre Cabernet Sauvignon, please," Trace said, which made my jaw almost, but not quite, drop. That was Clover's most expensive bottle of wine. Cindi's expression matched mine before she managed, "Very good."

I watched her leave before turning my attention to Trace, but he was watching only me. He touched a lock of my hair that had fallen over my shoulder as he looked at me. "Only the best for you, sweetheart."

"Have you ever had that bottle before?"

"I have. I taste everything we stock in our cellar. I think you're going to love it."

He smiled, a beautiful smile, but I noticed when it faded. His attention moved to something behind me. Charles and Vivian had arrived. Trace stood as they approached the table; his body was rigid and his jaw was tight. Vivian offered an overly cordial hello, to which Trace responded curtly. He helped seat Vivian in the chair to my left before turning his attention to Charles.

Cindi came over then and the next few minutes were spent with Trace tasting the wine, approving it, and glasses being filled. Charles looked over at me and smiled after Cindi departed.

"Hello, Miss Walsh, it's very nice to see you again."

I couldn't say the same so I only smiled in return. Vivian, oblivious to, or because of, the tension, started talking to fill the silence.

"Charles and I really do hope that this can be the beginning of many gatherings between us."

Trace said nothing and turned his attention to Charles. "So what is it you really want?"

Charles had the sense to recoil; it was slight, but definite before he replied, "I didn't do right by you back then and I'm trying to make amends."

Trace's hand clenched into a tight ball, which made me reach for it and cover it with my own. He immediately turned his hand so he could link our fingers, but his hard stare never left his uncle. I knew what he was thinking because I was thinking it also: too little too late. He said as much when he did finally reply.

"We could have used your help back then—could have used someone then who gave a shit about our welfare."

Charles's reaction to that surprised me, because he looked remorseful and contrition laced through his words when he offered, "I know and I'm sorry."

Vivian looked over at Trace. "Please let's not speak of the past. It was a dark time and we didn't handle it well. I chose not to know your parents but I realize now that I should have made an effort. If I had, maybe I would have realized what was happening in your house and for that I am very sorry."

Trace offered nothing to that, since what could he possibly have said? For the next two hours we engaged in awkward conversation. Charles peppered Trace with questions about the past, details on the night of his parents' death, and what Trace did after he moved into the city, which Trace politely evaded. By the time we were getting ready to leave, I was really glad the evening was over. I couldn't decide if the Michaelses were the most arrogant and self-serving jackasses who ever lived or if they were living in serious denial.

Vivian and I excused ourselves to go to the ladies' room. She clearly was a drinker. She hadn't stopped the entire night, so by the end of the evening she was pretty flagged. We stood in front of the mirror in the restroom as I washed my hands and she attempted to touch up her makeup. It was rather funny watching her apply her lipstick. Her eye-hand coordination was off from the booze.

"I love these Venetian-style mirrors. This one in particular is stunning. I do believe I've seen this before or something remarkably like it."

It *was* lovely, the rectangular, hand-cut, mirrored glass, and I said as much to Vivian, adding, "Shall we?"

"Yes."

Trace was just paying the bill when we returned to the table and I knew, from the wide-eyed expression on Cindi's face when she passed by me, that Trace had been exceedingly generous. Charles reached for Vivian's hand before turning his attention to Trace.

"Thank you for dinner and for agreeing to have it with us."

"Yes, it was so nice to get to know you a little. I do so hope that this is the first of many evenings together," Vivian added.

I knew Trace would have rather said nothing, but manners dictated otherwise.

"Thank you for extending the invitation."

I had to give Charles credit for accepting Trace's words and seeming to understand that they were the only ones he and his wife were going to get. Charles turned to me and brought my hand to his lips, causing Trace to tense at my side.

"It was lovely seeing you again, Ember."

He brushed his lips over my knuckles before releasing my hand. I had to suppress the urge to wipe my hand on my dress. "Good night, Charles and Vivian."

We watched as they walked from the restaurant. By unspoken agreement we waited for a few minutes to be certain that they were gone before following them out. The night was clear and warm as we walked down the street toward home. Trace seemed distracted and I imagined his thoughts were on dinner. At least Charles didn't ignore the obvious, didn't try to brush the past under the rug. I had to give him points for that.

I was surprised when Trace pecked my cheek and asked, "So what are your thoughts on the evening?"

"I'm not really sure. I give Charles credit for accepting responsibility, but I'm still not sure I understand what the point was of that dinner. I feel like I'm missing something."

"It seemed like a fishing expedition."

I thought on that for a moment. "That's exactly what it felt like. What do you think he was trying to glean?"

Trace shrugged his shoulders. "I've no idea, but since he didn't get anything, I'm guessing we haven't heard the last of them."

"Probably not."

"It's still pretty early . . ." he said as he reached for my hand. He hailed a cab passing by.

"Where are we going?"

He waited until we were in the cab before he turned to me and grinned.

"I'm taking my beautiful woman dancing."

He pulled me into his lap and fused his mouth to mine.

When we entered the club, he walked us right onto the dance floor just as "Straight From the Heart" from Bryan Adams came on. He pulled me into his arms and held me right up against his hard body, but we didn't move to the music. He then gave up the pretense of dancing completely to wrap my face in his hands and cover my mouth with his own. My hands moved under his jacket to wrap around his waist and we stayed like that for the duration of the song. Trace pulled from me and grinned as he reached for his tie to remove it before shoving it into his jacket pocket.

"Wait here," he said before he moved toward the bar, removed his jacket, and handed it to the bartender. As he approached me, he was rolling up his sleeves and the sight of his tattoo against the elegance of his attire made my mouth water. He reached me just as "I Gotta Feeling" from Black Eyed Peas started to play.

Trace was an excellent dancer and it was sexy as hell to be led around the dance floor by someone so utterly masculine and yet dressed so elegantly. Howie Day's "Collide" played at one point in the evening, which made Trace pull me into his arms. He didn't kiss me, but his eyes were only for me. Even with a dance floor overflowing with gorgeous women, his eyes never left mine. The song came to an end and he leaned over and brushed his lips lightly across mine. In the next moment, he whispered, "Love isn't strong enough a word."

My heart rolled over in my chest.

Trace kept me close for the rest of the night as he pressed our bodies together at every opportunity. Feeling that hard, muscled body pressed up against mine was making me overly warm because I was seriously turned on. Trace noticed it too, and whispered in my ear, "You're flushed."

I spoke without thinking. "I am so turned on right now."

His eyes sparked hot in response to that before a wickedness entered his expression. "Maybe I should take you home and help you cool off."

"I think that's a fabulous idea."

He kissed me hard on the mouth before he pulled me from the dance floor and grabbed his jacket from behind the bar. When we returned home, I dropped my purse on the sofa and wrapped my arms around Trace's waist. A shudder went through him before he turned into me and fused his mouth to mine. I worked the buttons of his shirt before I ran my hands up his chest, dividing the shirt as I did. I pulled the cotton down his shoulders and arms before letting it drop to the floor. Desire burned through me at the sight of him. My hands continued their journey, running over his abs, up his chest, and under his arms, forcing him to lift them over his head.

"Keep them up," I whispered as the tips of my fingers trailed a line down his body, moving over his pecs and down along each individual muscle of his abs. Trace's eyes never left mine and in his expression I saw what I was feeling looking back at me.

I gripped his undershirt and lifted it up and over his head.

"I love your body," I whispered before I pressed a kiss over his heart. I felt the restraint in him, knew he wanted to take, but he was holding himself back and allowing me the freedom to touch him in any way that I wanted. I was humbled by him and the trust he had in me. My hands and mouth roamed and savored every inch of his chest. I felt as his control started to slip when I pressed a kiss to his naval. He reached for me, but I moved away from him. My eyes never left his as I stepped out of my sandals. His eyes were hot, watching me as I pulled the pins from my hair.

I heard him growl, low in his throat, as I reached for the zipper of my dress and slowly worked it down. The silk slipped off my shoulders and fell in a wave to the floor as I stepped out of it and moved toward him. My fingers worked the front clasp of my bra as I flipped it open and slowly pulled the lace down my arms before allowing it to follow my dress to the floor. Trace was fisting his hands at his sides as his eyes burned into mine and then I was pressing myself against his hard chest. He wasted no time pulling me closer as his mouth sought and found mine. He lifted me into his arms as I wrapped my legs around his waist before he turned and pressed me up against the wall. I heard the sound of his zipper right before his fingers touched me, rubbing and teasing. He slid the swatch of lace out of his way just as he rolled his hips and claimed me. I closed my eyes on a moan, loving the way it felt to be possessed by this man.

Trace's voice was raw when he demanded, "Look at me."

My eyes opened to find Trace watching me with a look that was almost wild. "I love you."

After that vow he started to move his hips with a slow deliberateness that made me ache. He closed his hand over my breast and his fingers teased my nipple, rolling that tight bud, before tugging on it hard enough to cause pain. I tightened my legs around him as his hips moved faster and deeper just as his hand moved down my body and his thumb found that small point of pleasure.

He teased and stroked in time with his thrusts until my body splintered apart from my orgasm. I managed to somehow keep my eyes on Trace so I saw as his face flushed, watched as his eyes glazed over just as his body spasmed his own release, my name ripping from his throat in a voice that was raw with lust.

A few weeks after the dinner with the Michaelses, Chelsea and I opted for another girl's day at Trace's apartment instead of going out for lunch. We painted each other's nails, ate chocolate, and watched movies.

I was on the phone in the kitchen placing our order for lunch with the local Chinese place while Chelsea cued up *Harry Potter.* I entered the living room carrying two glasses of iced tea and noticed that Chelsea was looking at the pictures on the wall. Trace's walls were no longer empty. Granted, most of the pictures were of me, but photos of Rafe, Lucien, and Chelsea had joined the wall, as had pictures of my family. I walked over and handed her a glass as she pointed to a picture of my mom.

"Is that Amanda?"

To say I was thrown wouldn't be an exaggeration.

"Yes, how did you know that?"

"I've seen her before."

"When?"

Chelsea, oblivious to the fact that her words were twisting me into knots, walked over to the sofa and took a seat. She looked up at me with guileless gray eyes.

"She came to the house once when I was younger."

"Your house in Ohio?"

"Yeah. I remembered her because she was the prettiest lady I'd ever seen."

I had to sit because I had a feeling my legs weren't going to hold me up much longer. "Do you remember when this was?"

"Yeah, I had just turned six. I remember because I was playing with my new Strawberry Shortcake dolls: Lime Chiffon, Orange Blossom, and Raspberry Tart."

I felt my heart beating painfully in my chest when I asked, "You were born in August of 1987, right?"

"Yeah."

Oh my God, August of 1993 was when my mom was killed. I needed to call my dad.

"Excuse me, Chelsea, for one minute."

I hurried down the hall to the phone in the bedroom and dialed my dad.

"Ember, how are you, honey?"

"Dad, I've got Chelsea over and she saw a picture of Mom and recognized her—not just recognized her, but knew her name."

This was met with silence.

"She said Mom visited her house in Ohio in August of 1993."

The exhale that came across the line held both shock and pain and then my dad's soft voice said, "What did she say?"

"Not much, but how's that possible?"

"I really don't know. I'll call your uncle."

"Let me know, Dad."

"I will."

Later, I waited in the living room for Trace to return from dropping Chelsea off at home. I'd been thinking about what Chelsea had said as I tried to come up with some explanation to make sense of it, but the only question I kept circling back on was if my mom had been in Trace's house before she died, and she was killed by Trace's dad, then was her death an accident or intentional? I heard the key in the lock seconds before the door pushed open and Trace walked in. He looked over at me and smiled, but his expression immediately faded into a look of concern.

"Ember, what's wrong?"

I was holding my mom's picture as I walked over to him.

"Chelsea saw this today and asked me if this was Amanda."

Trace's expression mirrored mine. "How did she know that?"

"Apparently my mom was in your house the month she died."

"What?!"

"Exactly. My uncle is looking into it."

He squeezed my hand. "You understand what this means?"

"That her death may not have been an accident."

Pain burned in his eyes, but there was something else too, something that looked a lot like panic. "Yes."

I pulled him into the room and placed the picture on the table before I pushed him down onto the sofa and straddled his lap.

"What's that look for?" I asked.

His hands rested on my hips, but he wouldn't look at me. I touched his chin to lift his face to me.

"I love you regardless of what your father may or may not have done to my mom. The son will not be made to pay for the sins of the father. I thought you knew that already, but I'm saying it again. You were eight when she died. You are not responsible."

He pulled me to him, wrapping me firmly in his arms as he buried his face in my hair.

"You are very wise."

"Much like Yoda. Think like he, yes, I do."

The grin that cracked over his face was almost boyish.

"Do you know that I've never seen those movies? Not the originals or the newer ones."

I shook my head in an attempt to get my brain working again. "The originals I like, the newer ones not so much. That's really not acceptable. We must remedy this immediately."

I climbed from his lap and started down the hall.

"Where are you going?"

I looked back at him from over my shoulder. "I'm going to order the Blu-rays and when they arrive we're spending the day watching all three in a row with no interruptions."

"Yes, ma'am."

Chapter Twenty-One

I was sound asleep when I heard what sounded like an animal being tortured. At first, I thought that the noise was coming from my dream, but what in my dream would make such a tormented cry? Another wail of pain and I woke. When the cry came again, my blood turned to ice in my veins. It was Trace, who was beginning to thrash around in his sleep. After Chelsea shared her startling observation two weeks earlier, Trace's sleep had been more restless but the nightmares were new.

I reached for the bedside light and when the soft glow filled the room I hoped it would wake him, but whatever was haunting his dreams had a firm hold on him. His beautiful face twisted in agony and it was heartbreaking to see him in such a state. If his parents weren't already dead, I'd sure as hell like to have a go at them, the fuckers.

I moved to wrap myself around him as I whispered in his ear, "Trace, it's Ember. Wake up, baby, you're safe. I've got you; my arms and legs are wrapped around you. You're safe. Please wake up."

I kept up the soft words for almost five minutes and slowly he started to calm down. I knew the moment he woke because

I felt him tense a moment before his arms wrapped around me. He turned his head into my neck just as I ran my hand down his cheek. I felt a dampness there, which made my heart twist in pain.

"Are you okay?"

His lips brushed over my neck. "I am now."

He pulled my mouth to his for a kiss of such raw emotion that my heart literally skipped a couple of beats. He rolled so that we were lying side by side. His mouth moved from mine as his arms wrapped around me to hold me close. Together we drifted back into sleep.

In the morning I woke to find that I was still wrapped in Trace's arms. I thought he was still asleep and I needed to use the bathroom, so I attempted to move without waking him.

"Good morning."

I turned to find him watching me and based on the look of him, he'd been doing it for some time.

"Good morning."

He brushed the hair from my cheek as his eyes held my gaze. "Thank you for last night."

I could tell he really didn't want to talk about it so instead of asking the questions that were on the tip of my tongue, I replied, "I'm glad that I was here."

Later that day Trace was working in his office and I was eating lunch and working on the campaign coverage in the kitchen when the doorbell rang. Trace poked his head into the kitchen on his way to the door.

"I've got it."

I recognized the voices immediately, so I joined the others in the living room.

"Dad, Uncle Josh." I suspected my uncle would be paying a visit but I was pleasantly surprised to see my dad. "Did you find something out?"

"We're still looking into it, but Josh had some questions for Trace." Uncle Josh and Trace had begun looking over crime scene photos from that night thirteen years ago. I wasn't really listening to their conversation. I was too busy checking out the photos as well. Trace's entire house had been photographed and it was while I was reviewing them that I made a discovery.

"That mirror, you have one very similar to it at Clover, Trace."

He studied the mirror before he said, "Actually, that is the same mirror. It was one of the only possessions of my mother's that I kept."

"Is there another like it?"

He looked up at me before he replied, "No, it's a one-of-a-kind piece. Why?"

"That night at Clover, with the Michaelses, Vivian said she recognized the mirror, but she also claimed to never have been in your parents' house."

Uncle Josh asked, "Trace, before the restaurant, the mirror was in your home in Ohio? But you said it was your mom's, so it came from her side of the family, like an heirloom, so it's possible that Charles could have known about it?"

"Yes."

"So either Vivian saw the mirror when it was still in her husband's family's possession or she lied and had been to your house. It can't hurt to look deeper into her background."

Uncle Josh moved to join me as my dad walked over to talk with Trace.

"I've been asking around at the hospital where your mother worked and some of the nurses remember that right before she died she was agitated about something. They aren't really certain of the details, but they believe she was attempting to cut through some red tape. There is a record of Douglas Stanwyck being treated at Penn Medical Center, but he was treated in the ER. Mandy worked in obstetrics so there isn't a link there. One name came up frequently among those I spoke to, a Darlene Moore who worked with Mandy in obstetrics, but so far I've been unable to locate her. She could probably shed a bit more light on what Mandy was up to. I'll keep looking."

"Can you do me another favor?"

"Sure thing."

"Could you look into a Mrs. Fletcher who worked for Trace's family?"

"Sure, why?"

"Closure."

Chapter Twenty-Two

Trace usually made dinner, but I decided to cook for him for a change. I wasn't as good a cook as he, but there were a few things I was quite adept at making and pot roast was one of them.

I reached for the Dutch oven from the pot rack hanging over the kitchen island. All the pots and pans were All-Clad and Le Creuset. Trace really did like to cook. I wondered if he ever worked the line at Clover or Coq au Vin? I thought that he was certainly skilled enough to do so.

I moved to the subzero refrigerator and pulled out the chuck roast and carrots before reaching into the cobalt-blue bowl Trace had on the counter for the onions and potatoes. I had just finished seasoning the roast and was browning it when I heard the sound of the front door opening and closing seconds before that wonderful voice called my name.

"Ember?"

"In the kitchen."

I heard his heavy footfalls coming down the hall and then I felt the heat that sizzled my nerve endings. I peeked at him from over my shoulder and saw that he was leaning against the doorjamb watching me. It had been two weeks since his nightmare and he hadn't had another, which was a relief.

He pushed off the wall and walked over to wrap his arms around my waist. His lips brushed lightly along my jaw and across my cheek before he took a sniff as he looked at the pot.

"Pot roast?"

"Yes."

"Sounds delicious. Do you need help?"

"Actually, could you show me how you chop the vegetables in that way of yours?"

I turned to him and saw the weird look on his face.

"What's that look for?"

"You want me to teach you to chop vegetables?"

"You don't have to, but you do it without looking and I'd like to learn how to do that."

He was silent for a minute and then he said very softly, "I'd love to teach you."

"Oh, cool. We have to chop some carrots, potatoes, and onion."

He turned back to me after washing his hands at the sink and he looked almost excited. That was when I realized he had learned this gift of cooking and never had anyone to share it with.

I felt the tears burning the back of my throat. He really had been so alone, even with all the women that had come through his life. As he reached for the knives from the magnetic strip on the wall, I walked over, wrapped my arms around his waist, and pressed a kiss to his back. He turned and brushed his knuckles over my cheek.

"What was that for?"

"Just because."

He smiled and then he placed a cutting board in front of me and laid a large knife next to it.

"This is a chef's knife and, personally, I think it's the best knife to have in the kitchen."

Trace turned out to be an excellent teacher.

———•———

That night, as Trace and I snuggled up in front of the television watching *Psych*, the phone rang. Trace reached behind us for the receiver and when he spoke, I felt as his words rumbled up his chest.

"Hello. Hi, Josh . . . really? . . . when? One second . . . Em, you up for a trip?"

I leaned up and turned to Trace before I asked, "What's up?"

"Your uncle located Darlene Moore. She works at a bar in Ramsey, New Jersey. He's with your dad in the Bronx and they're on their way to talk with her and wanted to know if we wanted to join them."

"Yes."

He smiled as he lifted the receiver to his ear. "We're leaving now so we'll see you soon."

Darlene was not at all what I'd expected. She was in her late forties, but she looked much older. I couldn't help but wonder why someone who had been a nurse was waiting tables at a bar. Trace and I arrived before my dad and uncle so we grabbed a table and ordered a drink. Trace was sitting at my side as his fingers lightly brushed over the back of my hand. The action was so unconscious that I didn't think he even knew he was doing it.

"Dinner was delicious."

"That recipe never fails."

He grinned at me as he leaned up and took my hand into his. "Just because you have a great recipe doesn't automatically mean you're going to make a great meal. There is skill involved."

I smiled, since I didn't necessarily agree with him. "You're a wonderful teacher."

He blushed and I leaned closer to him as I ran my finger over his cheekbone. "You're blushing."

"No, I'm not."

"You are and I understand now the appeal of a blush."

He straightened in his chair and tried to look serious. "I am not blushing."

I grinned as I sat back in my seat. "Okay, if you say so."

"I do say so."

"Seriously, though, you really are a wonderful teacher. Did you ever cook at any of your restaurants?"

"I was a sous chef at Clover before I bought it. I didn't like the head chef; thought he was an arrogant jackass who didn't know the difference between sautéing and frying. I replaced him with Chef when I bought the place."

"I like Chef."

"Chef likes you."

"How do you know?"

"He told me."

"Does he know about us?"

"Does he know that you are the very air I breathe? Yes, he knows."

We were silent for a moment and then I asked, "Why don't you still work at one of your restaurants?"

"I like cooking, but I think I like teaching more."

"Have you ever thought of teaching at a cooking school?"

I could tell, from the look on his face, that he had thought of that and then he said, "I always wanted to open my own cooking school, but who wants to be taught by the likes of me? What are my qualifications?"

"I think the only qualification that matters is that you cook like a freaking god."

"It's not really practical, not for someone like me." His tone was one of finality and it was that, more than his words, that made me angry. I wasn't mad at Trace, I was enraged at the lingering impact of his parents' neglect. If his dream was to open a cooking school then, goddamn it, I was going to see to it that he had his school. I had no idea how I was going to make it happen, but it had become my mission. Lucien's entrepreneurial skills would come in handy. I was diverted from my plotting when Trace reached for my hand and pulled me from my chair.

"Where are we going?"

He said nothing, just continued to pull me to an area that I realized was a small dance floor before he turned me to him and held me close. His lips were right near my ear when he whispered, "Have you ever listened to the words of this song?"

"What song is it?"

"'Everything' by Lifehouse."

"No."

And then he started to sing to me as he slowly moved me around the floor. The song was about a man feeling in awe simply because he was in the presence of the one he loved, and hearing those words coming from Trace made me feel almost lightheaded with love. When the song came to an end, he pulled back to look at me only to see the tears that were clinging to my lashes and wetting my cheeks.

"That song perfectly states how I feel for you."

It was the magnitude of love I felt for him that made me speak words that came directly from my heart. "Marry me, Trace."

Shock flashed over his expression at first and then a smile spread over his face as he framed my face with his hands.

"You're stealing my thunder, sweetheart."

It took me a minute to process his answer and when I had my reply, it was anything but eloquent. "Wait, what?"

He only smiled and said, "Yes, Ember, I will marry you." My eyes instantly filled with tears as love for this man filled me.

"You were going to ask me?"

He moved so that his lips were just over mine before he whispered, "I'm still going to ask you."

"But you already agreed to marry me."

And then he was kissing me. After a bit he pulled away and we returned to our table. He held my chair for me before taking his own and his eyes found mine as he reached for his beer.

"I always imagined when the woman I loved asked me to marry her, she'd get down on one knee."

I narrowed my eyes at him and he chuckled before he reached for my hand and brought it to his lips. He kissed my fingertips.

"Teasing aside, you asking me to marry you is the greatest moment of my life. Thank you."

I moved closer to him. "You agreeing to marry me is the greatest moment of my life too."

At that moment, the door opened and Trace's eyes moved from me to just behind me as a smile touched his lips.

"Your dad and uncle are here."

"Are we going to tell them?" I asked.

"Hell, yes!"

Just then my dad came up behind me and rested his hands on my shoulders.

"Hello, Emmie."

He leaned over and brushed a kiss on my head as I heard Uncle Josh's greeting.

Trace stood and reached his hand across the table to shake my uncle's hand and then my dad's before he said, "Ember just asked me to marry her."

I put my head down and started banging it against the table. "Nice segue, Trace."

His response was a grin, a completely unrepentant grin, before he added, "I said yes."

My dad's voice filled with joy. "Welcome to the family, son." He reached for Trace and hugged him.

I sat back and watched as my uncle also hugged Trace, and saw the look on Trace's face, a combination of happiness and embarrassment. And then I was being lifted from my chair and pulled into my dad's arms.

"I am so happy for you," he said.

"When is the happy day?" Uncle Josh chimed in.

"When can I expect grandkids?" asked my dad.

I paled and looked at Trace, who was watching us with a tender smile on his face. "Nine months after I get my ring on her finger."

He didn't want children—confusion filled me. He seemed to understand what I was thinking.

"Excuse us for a moment," Trace said before he walked me to a corner.

"A child that comes from the love we have for each other, a child that is a part of both you and me, how could I not want that?"

I reached up to touch his face. "You're healing."

"I am and it's all because of you."

When we returned to the table, Trace pulled my chair out for me as we joined my dad and uncle at the table. Uncle Josh reached for my hand and squeezed. "Congratulations, Ember."

"Thank you."

Our attentions turned to Darlene as my uncle stood. "She knows we're coming. I'll be right back."

I was watching my uncle, but my dad's voice turned my attention to him.

"Do you have any idea where you want to get married?"

"If Trace doesn't mind, I'd like to get married in the chapel where you and Mom were married."

At that moment, Uncle Josh returned with Darlene. Seeing her up close drove home that the years had not been good to her. Her hair, naturally brown if her roots were any indication, was dyed in an attempt to look blond. She was thin, but seemed malnourished rather than fashionably slim. Both my dad and Trace stood as the introductions were made. Her tired blue eyes turned to me as a smile touched her lips.

"You look so much like her. She loved you so much and used to talk about you all the time. She had a booklet of photos that she would whip out to show anyone even slightly interested." Darlene's eyes moved to my dad before she added, "Both of you."

She looked at my uncle and asked, "What do you want to know?"

"Right before Mandy died she was working on something. Do you happen to know what she may have been up to?"

Darlene sat back in her chair, the lines around her mouth and eyes deepening as she thought on it for a few minutes. "I do remember she was really off weeks before the accident. I never knew what it was that was bothering her, but I do know it had something to do with her friend, Teresa Nolan. Whatever it was, it put an end to their friendship."

My dad leaned up in his chair. "I knew Teresa stopped coming around, but I didn't know it was as serious as all that. What happened?"

"She and Teresa stopped speaking after their huge fight."

"What fight?"

"It was in the hospital cafeteria—I wasn't there at the time. Teresa was visiting some doctor that she was smitten with and something that Teresa said really upset Mandy. They had words and then Teresa stormed off. They didn't speak again after that and it was around that same time that Mandy started acting oddly."

"Meaning?" Uncle Josh prompted.

"She seemed paranoid at times, secretive, and then there was the whole drug thing."

"What drug thing?" Trace asked.

"Mandy developed an unusual interest in the drug benzodi-azepine—specifically the withdrawal symptoms."

"I have to admit I have no idea what that is," I said.

"It's a psychoactive drug, a really powerful sedative among other things. You know she was spending a fair amount of time with Dr. Cavanaugh, the head of the psychiatric department at the hospital. The doctor could probably tell you more."

My uncle looked over at my dad, who was sitting silently, look-ing almost lost in thought. "I haven't thought about Teresa in years. Teresa really wasn't much of a friend. She was more interested in what Mandy could do for her."

His eyes turned to me as a slight smile touched his lips just before Trace said, "Like mother, like daughter."

Darlene looked at us quizzically before she continued. "The thing I didn't understand about Teresa was that she claimed to be in love with this doctor, a man who was old enough to be her father, but the few times I saw her she wasn't with the doctor."

Darlene's eyes moved back to Trace. "In fact, the man she was with looked a lot like you."

I noticed something close to tenderness move across her expression as she looked at Trace.

I looked from Darlene to Trace and saw as he clenched his jaw and the blood drained from his face. My uncle reached across the table with his phone.

"Was this the man?"

Darlene looked at the picture and it was clear that she recognized the face, but what was even more interesting was her reaction to seeing him—her jaw clenched and her lips thinned—before she said, "Yeah, that's him."

Trace's voice was hard when he said, "Douglas."

"Teresa and Douglas. I wonder if Victoria knew?" my uncle said.

"I doubt it, since she was out of it all the time," Trace said softly.

"Wait! Trace, you said your mom was zoned out that night you asked her for help, but what if she wasn't zoned out, what if she was drugged? Think about it, my mom visits your mom and suddenly she takes an interest in the withdrawal symptoms of a powerful sedative."

Uncle Josh pulled a hand through his hair as he shifted in his chair. "It makes sense. How much do you want to bet that Teresa was dating the doctor for the scripts? She was probably bragging to Mandy about her clever ruse that day in the cafeteria. It would be so like Mandy to visit Victoria to confirm for herself if the woman was really in trouble."

I looked at Darlene, saw a flicker in her eyes, and wondered what she was thinking before I asked, "If someone was on that drug for any period of time could it make them almost comatose?"

She didn't hesitate to answer. "Absolutely."

"Do you remember the doctor's name, Darlene?" my dad asked.

"Dr. Richard Grant. He heads up the cardiac division now."

Uncle Josh noted that down as I turned my attention to Trace. He was clenching his jaw and fisting his hand.

"It sounds like something my bastard of a father would do,

drugging his wife to keep her oblivious while he spent her money and abused her children."

"Your mother was as much a victim as you and Chelsea," I said.

Trace's tone didn't improve as he replied, "I know."

"Where is Teresa now?" my dad asked.

"I don't know," Darlene said. "After Mandy died I never saw her again."

It really wasn't my business, but I just needed to know. "Can I ask why you're no longer working as a nurse?"

"I made some bad decisions and lost my license."

She didn't go into detail on how and I didn't have the heart to pry further.

My dad turned to Uncle Josh. "We need to find that bitch."

"Absolutely."

Chapter Twenty-Three

Lucien had gotten us invites for the opening of a very trendy nightclub. The guest list was pretty swanky, so I wondered how he managed it. We were in a cab on the way to the club when I turned to Trace and asked, "How did Lucien swing these invites?"

Trace's head turned to mine and I saw as his mind shifted gears from whatever he was thinking about to focus on me. A slight smile touched his lips before he offered, "Lucien Black is a bit of a gangster."

"What?"

"Yeah, most of his businesses are legit now but they didn't start out that way. Because of his colorful background he's made contacts all around the city.

"Really?"

"Yeah, but that's his story to tell."

He turned to look out the window. I knew he had a lot on his mind, including that he still believed himself somehow responsible for his father's actions. I wished that there was some way I could take that burden from him, but I knew that he'd never truly be free of it until he realized, finally, that he was nothing like his father.

It had been several weeks since the idea formed about starting a cooking school for Trace. I hoped to pull Lucien aside that evening so I could pick his brain about starting one up, since I didn't have a clue where to begin.

The cab pulled up in front of the club and Trace climbed out before helping me out. He paid the cabbie before reaching for my hand and leading us inside. The place was fairly packed, but as soon as we entered, a pretty blond approached us.

"Are you Trace and Ember?"

"Yes," I said.

"Please, this way." She led us deeper into the club until we reached a table that was in a prime location. Lucien was already seated, but as soon as he saw us, he stood. We stopped just in front of the table as Lucien walked around and reached for my hand to lift to his lips.

"It's lovely to see you again."

"Hi, Lucien, likewise."

He was grinning when he released my hand and turned to Trace.

When we settled at the table I asked, "How did you get these invites?"

"Wouldn't you like to know," he teased before he added, "I have friends who have friends."

What Trace had shared with me about Lucien was still rolling around in my head. It was amazing to me that someone who started out with nothing could have accomplished so much. Before I truly knew my intention, I heard myself asking, "If it's too personal, I'm sorry, but how long did you live in the orphanage?"

He immediately sobered and I retracted my question. "Sorry, never mind."

"No, it's fine. I was around two when I was dropped there and seventeen when Sister Anne died. After she was gone there was no point in staying there."

"You miss her?"

"Yeah, for a time she was the only family I had. If not for her, I wouldn't be here. I'd have died in a gang fight or gotten hooked on drugs and overdosed. She was a friend but strict." An absent smile touched his lips as he remembered, "She never hit but she didn't need to. She had the power to make you feel guilty with just a look. She should have been married with kids of her own, but she always said, why bring more children into the world when there are so many already looking for love? She was taken too damn young but that's the bitch of cancer. No one is immune."

He grew silent so I said, "I bet she would be proud of you."

He shrugged. "Maybe now but there was a time, after she died, that I walked the wrong side of the law. I think I was spiting her for dying. Luckily for me I didn't get myself in too deep with the wrong people."

"That's sounds ominous," I said.

Lucien changed the subject and asked Trace, "So when are you fighting again?"

———◆———

I got Lucien alone later in the evening when Trace excused himself from the table.

"How would someone go about starting up a cooking school?"

He looked at me and I saw he was confused by the question. "Why? We've got some really outstanding schools already in the city."

"It's a dream."

"Ah, well, you'd want to do a cost-benefit analysis to justify that the investment is both sound and feasible. After that you'd need to find a location, write a business proposal, find investors, instructors, create a curriculum, go through the steps to get accredited . . ."

My shoulders slumped, because though I already knew it was going to be a lot of work, hearing the steps required was overwhelming. Lucien, being so intuitive, seemed to realize where my thoughts were when he offered, "The other option would be to create a different kind of cooking school, one where people pay for a week or two of hands-on training. For that you'd only need a large enough space with multiple kitchens to accommodate your pupils."

My spirits immediately soared, making Lucien say, "You are very easy to read."

"I know."

"This is for Trace, isn't it?"

"Yes."

"I'd like to help you set it up."

"Are you sure?"

"He's my friend and he deserves to have some good come his way."

"I agree."

Lucien looked past me. "Here he comes. I'll call you tomorrow and we can set something up."

"Thank you."

"It's my pleasure, Ember, it truly is."

That night, Trace and I were in bed when he asked, "What were you and Lucien fraternizing about earlier?"

"Nothing."

"Liar."

And then his mouth came down on mine as he rolled to pin me under him. His fingers gently touched my face before running lightly down my throat. He ran kisses down my neck and lower still to the valley between my breasts before he worked his way back up to settle his mouth over mine again. My arms wrapped around him so I could trail my fingertips up and down his spine. His mouth pulled away as he lifted his head so he could look at me. He didn't say anything, but then he didn't need to.

Chapter Twenty-Four

All the investigating into my mom and the months prior to her death made me really miss her. She'd been gone for so long, only a distant figure to me, yet I felt closer to her than I ever had because now I had more of an insight into the person she had been. It was thinking about her that made me wonder if there might be any clues in her belongings. We knew so much more now—something might shed some new light on what happened to her. Among her possessions were her high school yearbook, pictures she had drawn, even a few journals from when she was younger. I took the yearbook and settled back against the sofa so I could page through it.

I couldn't help the smile as I read the little words of farewell that seemed so standard for a yearbook: "Have a great summer," "You're really nice," "Good luck next year." Teenagers really didn't get the magnitude of graduating high school and moving on. They didn't understand that it wasn't just another day in a life, but truly a milestone. People that you'd spent thirteen years of your life with were going to become nothing more than memories. People whose statuses you occasionally checked on Facebook or saw at a reunion, but who would no longer have any real impact in your life. The words written as our younger selves were very nearsighted.

I stopped on my favorite photo of my mom and dad. In this picture there was no doubt at all how happy they were. My dad was right; what they had was what I had found with Trace, and to know my dad lost her after only six years—it wasn't enough and yet somehow he'd survived. My dad was a very strong man.

I flipped through a few more pages and found a picture of my mom with another woman and it was only when I read the caption that I realized it was Teresa. I studied the photo for a while and couldn't suppress the feeling that I had seen this woman before. There was something familiar in the line of her jaw, the curve of her chin, and her eyes. Her brown hair was long, longer than my mom's, and her blue eyes were shrewd, unlike my mom's, whose face looked happy and carefree. Did this woman have anything to do with my mother's death?

I closed up the yearbook and looked through a photo album and, again, there was Teresa. These photos were from a few years later, but Teresa looked much the same—hard and cheap. I knew in these pictures that my mom was just finishing her degree in nursing, but what was Teresa doing?

I noticed the necklace around Teresa's neck; it was a lovely gold filigree heart pendant with a large diamond in the center. I couldn't help but wonder where she got such an exquisite piece of jewelry when she was dressed in what looked like Walmart clothing. I wondered how she and my mom had met because they didn't seem to fit. Why did they become friends? I couldn't help but think of my relationship with Lena and how very similar it seemed to what my mom had with Teresa. Lena and I became friends because she was the first girl my age to befriend me. Later Lena proved to be selfish and only looking out for her own interests. According to Darlene, Teresa was much the same. Was that how it had been for my mom? Was she awkward too and her friendship with Teresa stemmed from something as simple as a hello? Was it possible that because neither of our relationships were built on anything more substantial they were doomed to fail? We had another similarity, though, a far more pleasant one to ponder. We had both found the loves of our lives. Maybe it wasn't just my looks that I had in common with my mom and this thought warmed my heart.

About an hour later, I was packing up the box when Trace came home.

"Hi, Ember." He took the box from me and gave me a quick kiss. Even just a kiss had the power to make my knees weak. "Where do you want this?"

"Shelf in the closet."

He kissed me again, a deeper kiss. "Would you like another cooking lesson tonight?"

I had asked Trace to teach me to cook, so I could experience his love of cooking. I followed him into the bedroom. I had intended to answer him, but then I got distracted as I watched him put the box away. His T-shirt pulled tight as he stretched, and the muscles of his back showed in relief under the cotton. The fabric separated a bit from the waist of his jeans and that small flash of skin made my mouth dry. Surprise shone on his face when he turned to see me standing there, but when he realized I was ogling him, a gleam came into those eyes.

He started toward me, slowly and deliberately, and then he stopped before he reached for the back of his shirt and pulled it forward over his head. I was like a junkie and Trace was my drug. Then I noticed the bandage over his left pectoral. Desire gave way to concern as I lifted my hand to touch the bandage.

"What happened?"

He was smiling at me, which I thought was an odd reaction to a wound, but then understanding slowly started penetrating my fuzzy brain as I spoke the words he had said to me once upon a time.

"What have you done?"

He said nothing as he reached up and removed the bandage. Love, and something feeling remarkably like possession, filled me at the motion. The tattoo was of a silver skeleton key. The bow was delicately ornate and along the blade my name was worked into the design, but the best part was that the tattoo was situated so that it rested over his heart. A few weeks ago I'd asked him to marry me and he responded by branding himself mine. My eyes filled with tears as I reached out and touched it and I understood what he felt when he first saw my tattoo.

Without thinking, I leaned forward and pressed my lips just above it. I felt the shiver that went through him before I pulled back and looked up into his eyes that were swimming in love.

———◆———

The following day, Lucien picked me up to show me possible locations for Trace's cooking school. The third place we saw was the winner—not far from the apartment, the area was still affluent, and the space was huge. It was going to take lots of money to convert the space into working kitchens, but this was the place. One look at Lucien and I knew he shared my opinion.

"So now I just need to figure out how to fund this. No bank in their right mind is going to give me a loan."

"I wanted to talk to you about that."

I turned my full attention to Lucien and was surprised to see that he actually looked nervous.

"I really like what you're doing here, especially because it's for Trace. How would you feel about me being your only investor? I'd front all the setup costs and once the place starts making money I'd get a percentage until I was paid back. At that point, you and Trace would be sole owners or I could remain your partner and we could adjust my percentage."

I was overwhelmed by his generous offer, so much so that I couldn't seem to find my voice. One look at Lucien told me he had interpreted my silence as something else entirely so I was quick to say, "Yes, but only on the condition that you stay our partner. If you're with us from the beginning then you are with us for the long haul. I won't take no for an answer," I said as I put out my hand.

"Do we have a deal, Mr. Black?"

He took my hand, pulled me in for a hug, and pressed a kiss on my cheek.

"We've a deal, Miss Walsh."

He pulled back and he was still grinning when he asked, "Any idea on what you want to call the place?"

I thought on that for a moment and remembered Trace talking about how he wanted to do more than prepare dishes—he wanted to create and present them as well. I thought of the song that he sang to me during our dance in Ramsey. A smile spread over my face as the answer came to me.

Lucien grinned. "I'm guessing that smile means yes."

"I think we should call it 'Everything' and on the sign, under the name, should be a visual representation of the art of cooking from the raw ingredients to the final, elegantly plated dish."

Lucien thought on that for a minute and then smiled. "I like it. I'll have my lawyers draw up a contract and then maybe you should have your dad or uncle, or both, look it over."

"Okay, I know how shifty you are."

He laughed at that. "Then celebratory drinks are on you."

"So this is the kind of hard bargain you drive?"

Lucien was still laughing as we made our way to his car.

———•———

Chinese food night with Kyle morphed into dinner and game night and the guest list changed as well—including Chelsea, Lucien, and Rafe. Since there were six of us, Trace bought another television, Wii, and all the extra remotes and wheels so that all of us could play at the same time. I hated to be a stereotype, but I was really not very good at driving my race car around the tracks of *Mario Kart,* which was evident by the number of times I fell off the various cliffs. Chelsea, on the other hand, was amazing and it had to be said that she may have even been the best of the lot.

I took a break so I could plate up the desserts that Trace and I had made earlier, but I took a minute to watch Trace and Chelsea. They laughed and joked as they played. Had they ever had a day like this when they were younger, a day where they could laugh and play like children? In my heart, I knew that there never had been days like that for them and being able to witness their joy, and to have a small hand in bringing it about, made me stand a little taller. The phone rang, pulling me from my silent study, and I turned for the kitchen to answer it.

"Hello."

"Hello, Ember, it's Vivian Michaels."

I wanted to groan and then I wanted to kick myself, since I knew it had been a mistake giving Charles our phone number.

"Hello, Vivian."

"Charles and I would like to invite you to our home for a campaign function we're having on Saturday for the *In Step* article."

"What time?"

"It starts at seven and it's black tie. There's no need to bring a date, since you'll be working. Caroline and Stanley will also be attending."

I wanted to ask why I was needed if they were attending, but I didn't and instead said, "See you on Saturday."

I hung up just as Trace came into the kitchen. He took one look at me and asked, "What's wrong?"

"I have to go to the Michaelses on Saturday for a campaign thing."

The look on Trace's face was priceless because his expression mirrored how I was feeling.

"Why?"

"Apparently, they still want me to document his campaign journey."

"I don't like the idea of you alone with those people."

"Me either, but Caroline and Stanley are going to be there too."

"I still don't like it."

"I already told Caroline I would do this so I really don't have a choice."

"I'm coming."

"You weren't invited."

At that moment, Lucien walked into the kitchen looking for dessert. "You can't tease us with sweets and then not bring out the sweets." He stopped when he saw the look on Trace's face.

"What happened?"

"Nothing. Mr. McGrumpy doesn't want me to go to this campaign thing on Saturday, but I have to."

"The Michaelses' thing?"

"Yeah," said Trace.

"I'm going. I'll watch her. I'll even bring her home."

Trace turned to Lucien and I could tell he didn't like it, that he wanted to be there, but then he seemed to relent. "Thank you," he said.

———◆———

On Saturday night, I sat in Charles's study and tried with not much success to keep my eyes from closing. The man was a windbag.

Oh my God, the man really liked to talk about himself. One look at Caroline and Stanley and I knew that they were struggling to keep awake too.

My thoughts turned to Trace's reaction when I walked out into the living room earlier. As soon as he'd looked up at me, his jaw had dropped and then he'd stood and took a very blatant and thorough walk around me, his fingers trailing a line over my shoulder, along my arm, and across my belly. His eyes were dark with desire when he came to stop just in front of me and said, "You can't wear that. Don't you have some shapeless black housedress or, better yet, sweats? No, not sweats, you look hot in sweats too."

"Trace, seriously."

"I am being serious." He actually frowned before he added, "He doesn't deserve to be in your company and it really grates that he's keeping you from mine."

"I'm sorry."

He took my face into his hands. "No, I'm sorry. I just don't want you anywhere near that man."

"I know, but Lucien will be there."

"Yes, and that's the only reason you're going and I don't give a shit if that sounds controlling. I don't trust that prick and I sure as shit don't trust him with the most precious thing in my life."

"I promise to stay close to Caroline, Stanley, and Lucien."

"You do that, and when you get home I'm going to help you out of this dress."

The thought of that promise made my toes curl. Grinning to myself at the memory, I didn't hear Charles, which was bad enough, but worse when I finally realized that he was talking to me.

"Oh, I'm sorry. Could you repeat that?"

He actually looked put out, but he did repeat himself. "I have some more published articles that I would like you to review so you can get a better understanding of my politics."

More articles. Kill me.

I tried for a smile when I replied, "Sounds great."

I'd been recording all of this on my phone, which was good because if I had a pen I'm fairly sure I would have stabbed myself in the eye at that moment. No, on second thought, why should I deprive myself of the pleasures that awaited me at home; I should stab Charles in the eye. When I found myself looking long and hard at a pen on his desk, I mentally shook myself to snap out of it.

He was off again, talking to hear himself speak, so I started looking around his office. There were a few pictures on his credenza and as I studied them my eyes were drawn to one of Vivian. It wasn't Vivian I was looking at, but the necklace that was hanging around her neck. I suspected I was just being fanciful and was seeing something that wasn't really there because Charles was boring me to death.

I almost wept with joy as we were dismissed, and we were most definitely dismissed. I beelined it to the bar for a glass of wine. I was mid-sip when Lucien came up next to me.

"That bad?"

"Worse." And then I turned fully to him and narrowed my eyes.

"What exactly are you doing here anyway? I thought you didn't like Charles Michaels."

"I don't, but I'm also a businessman and I am smart enough not to show my hand until I'm ready."

"You remind me of Shrek, Lucien."

I knew this twisted his nose out of joint. "I'm nothing like Shrek."

"You are, though—lots of layers like an onion."

"Layers like an onion? You suck at flattery."

I grinned and then I leaned over and whispered, "But you look like Apollo."

"Now that, Ember, is more like it."

At that moment, Vivian approached us and I had to take a moment to admire her style.

"Ember, I am so glad you could make it."

She leaned in to kiss my cheek and that was when her necklace really registered with me. I wished I could get a picture of it, but then I noticed Vivian's eyes moving to Lucien. There was no recognition in those blue orbs so I offered the introductions. When Vivian moved away to greet her other guests, he pulled me to the side and asked, "What are you plotting?"

"I'm that obvious?"

He crossed his rather impressive arms over his equally impressive chest. "I can see the bubble over your head."

I resisted the urge to stick my tongue out at him and said, "I would really like to get a picture of the necklace that Vivian is wearing."

He didn't bother to hide his confusion. "Why?"

"I want to compare it to something. Do you think there is any way we can get a picture?"

"Yes, but then you owe me."

I leaned over and pressed a kiss to his cheek. "Deal."

Later, I sat in Lucien's car looking at the picture he had taken of himself with Vivian. I didn't ask how he went about it, and he wasn't willing to share, but I had a picture of the necklace.

"Why are you interested in that necklace?"

He had been such a trouper—I owed him, so I filled him in.

"We think that Trace's father was driving the car that killed my mother. Trace believes that anyway, and so he started looking after me."

Lucien's expression changed, softened, before he said, "How old was he?"

"Sixteen."

Lucien said nothing for a moment and then he offered, "I already knew he was a good guy but that shows a hell of a lot of character."

"I know."

"Please, continue."

I smiled. "Recently we learned that it's possible my mom's one-time best friend was dating Trace's dad. Teresa, that was her name, disappeared after my mom died, but I found a few pictures in my mom's things the other day and in those pictures Teresa is wearing a necklace very similar to this. I'm sure it's nothing, but, based on how our families seem to be linked, I wanted a closer look."

"Makes sense."

———◆◆———

Trace was in the living room watching television when we got back to the apartment, and as soon as we entered he got up. His attention was completely on me and his heated stare made me feel as if I was standing before him naked, but then he noticed Lucien and his expression cooled. Before he could ask, I said, "Lucien helped me do a bit of recon this evening."

Trace's response to that was a slight raising of his eyebrow.

"Meet me in the kitchen," I said.

I hurried to the bedroom and returned shortly with the picture of Teresa. I placed it on the counter and then I reached for my phone and brought up the picture of Vivian. I placed my phone down next to the picture.

"Son of a bitch," Trace said.

"It's a match, isn't it?"

"Sure looks like it," Lucien offered as he continued to study the pictures.

Trace began pacing, his long legs carrying him across the room in four long strides before he was forced to turn around again.

"If Teresa is Vivian, then she's been a very busy woman. She dated my dad, helped to drug my mom for access to her money, I assume, and then later married my uncle. So, when exactly did she and my dad meet and was it a coincidence or was it all a part of their plan to get their hands on the Michaelses' fortune?"

"I need to call my dad," I said.

"I'll call and fill him in," Trace said before he walked over and pressed a kiss on my forehead. He turned to Lucien and held out his hand.

"Thank you for escorting Ember tonight."

Lucien took his hand before he replied, "It was my pleasure."

He left for home while Trace called my dad.

I walked down the hall toward the bedroom only to find Trace sitting on the bed with his head in his hands.

"Trace?"

"Your dad and uncle will be here in the morning"

"Why?"

"Your dad wants to wring Vivian's neck and your uncle wants to interrogate her."

"I hope my uncle goes first." I was teasing but Trace didn't see the humor.

"Are you okay?"

He looked up then and my breath stilled at the range of emotions flashing over his face.

"It's a goddamn clusterfuck."

"Yes, created through greed."

He pulled me to him and wrapped his arms around my waist. "My father was a depraved motherfucker and he got off way too lightly."

"I agree, but if Vivian was Douglas's partner . . ."

"I know, it's very likely that she killed my parents."

The news definitely tempered the mood, but I needed to connect to him, to seek the solace that only he could offer, and I knew that he needed it too. I hiked up my skirt before I climbed onto his lap to straddle him. I pressed my lips to his neck right where it met his shoulder and my teeth grazed him ever so slightly before I licked the spot I'd nibbled. I felt the tension start to drain from him just as his hand reached for my zipper and started to slowly pull it down. He touched every inch of bare skin he exposed, setting off little fires under my skin. I touched his chin to lift his gaze to mine.

"The silver lining is we met because of that clusterfuck."

Trace fused his mouth to mine. He pulled my dress down my arms and then he was lifting me and laying me on the bed; he continued to pull the fabric down my legs, then draped the dress over the back of a chair. When his eyes returned to me to find that I was only wearing a pair of strappy sandals, he stripped in record time and covered my body with his own.

"My sandals."

His voice was nothing but gravel when he said, "No, they stay on."

He wrapped my legs around his waist, took my face in his hands, and as soon as his mouth covered mine he shifted his hips and slid into me. My hands gripped his biceps as he moved so deeply inside of me, and when I felt myself tensing, squeezing him as I did, he moved faster and deeper. I came and he was right there with me. His face was in my hair as his warm breath teased my neck. Even with all that was going on, right now, with him, I felt only serenity.

"Right now, when I'm buried so deeply inside of you and am a part of you, this is my heaven." Trace said.

My heart swelled hearing him speak my thoughts. "You took the words right out of my mouth."

I wrapped my arms and legs more tightly around him. He pressed a kiss to my neck and then he rolled until we were facing each other. My leg came to rest over his thigh as he wrapped me in his arms while my head rested over his heart.

"Good night, Trace."

"Sweet dreams, Ember."

And together we drifted off to sleep.

Chapter Twenty-Five

I woke to the feeling of being squeezed to death. I was having trouble breathing because it felt like steel bands were slowly strangling me. It took a moment for my sleepy brain to wake and for me to realize that I was being crushed by Trace, who was once again trapped in a nightmare.

I moved my head and pressed my lips to his tattoo, the one over his heart. It had been over two weeks and still I couldn't get my fill of it.

"Trace, love, wake up."

I ran my finger across his brow, down his nose, along his jaw, and over his lips.

"Wake up, sweetheart." I pried his arms apart so I could sit up. I noticed my sandals were off, which meant Trace must have fallen asleep after me. I pressed kisses all over his face, which eventually woke him from his nightmare.

"Ember?" His voice was still hoarse with sleep.

"You were having a bad dream."

His eyes opened as he focused on me and smiled. "I like being awakened like that, particularly when you are dressed so beautifully while doing so."

I looked down and wasn't at all embarrassed by my nakedness for the first time. "Are you okay? You know if you ever want to talk about anything that I'm here, right?"

"I do, I know that."

"Any time, anywhere."

His eyes turned hot as he ran his finger over my nipple, turning it into a tight peak. The sensation of what he was doing as he watched himself doing it had my stomach clenching hard with desire.

"You are so beautiful." He switched our positions fast as he pinned me to the bed. He lowered his head and pressed his lips to my tattoo. His eyes were wild when his head lifted and then he moved lower down my body before he lifted my legs and draped them over his shoulders. I waited in anticipation for his tongue to touch me. And when he did, my eyes rolled up into the back of my head. Desire knotted my belly as fire burned down my legs. And as much as I loved what he was doing to me, I wanted the connection, wanted him a part of me.

"I need you inside me." He moved over me, spread my legs farther apart, and slipped into me in one smooth stroke. We moved in perfect harmony and when we came, we did so together. By the time he pulled me into his arms and settled me against his chest, I had already drifted back into sleep.

"Wake up, beautiful. Your dad and uncle are going to be here in an hour."

I peeled open my eyes to see Trace standing before me. He had showered because his hair was still wet, but he hadn't finished dressing.

"Ember, sweetheart, rise and shine."

"No."

He hunched down next to the bed and grinned. "It looks to me like you need a shower to help wake you up."

He lifted me up into his arms and carried me to the bathroom.

"I like sleeping."

"Um," was all he said as he held me in one arm while he turned the shower on. I took a moment to appreciate the fact that he was holding up all of my weight with only one arm, but then he was climbing into the shower with me, jeans and all.

"What are you doing?"

"I'm going to wash your back."

I sat at the kitchen table with a very clean back as I thought about Trace's thorough washing. I could tell when he turned to look at me from over his shoulder that he was thinking about it too.

"What are you making?" I asked.

"A frittata. It's similar to an omelet with meats, vegetables, and cheeses blended into the egg mixture."

"That sounds delicious."

He moved to place the frittata in the oven before he pressed a kiss to my neck.

"It is, but not as tasty as you, sweet." He licked my neck from my shoulder up to my ear, where he nibbled my lobe before he whispered, "Your taste is my most favorite in the world."

Little chills swept through me, stirred by his words, and then the doorbell sounded.

"Saved by the bell," he purred.

We walked together to the front door. As soon as Trace opened the door we were greeted by the sight of two very unhappy men. Teresa had been my mother's friend, and knowing she could have insight about my mom and yet never came forward, yeah, I imagined they felt infuriated and saddened.

"Daddy." I walked over and wrapped my arms around him. He was practically shaking with rage, but when his arms came around me to hold me close, he was gentle.

"Emmie."

Trace shook my uncle's hand and when I turned to greet my uncle, Trace led my dad into the kitchen, where the pictures were still sitting on the counter. Trace and I stood back and watched as the two studied the pictures and when my dad stepped back, his reaction to them was much the same as Trace's had been.

"Goddamn it."

My eyes moved from my dad to Uncle Josh. "Did you talk with Dr. Cavanaugh and Dr. Grant?"

"Yes."

We settled at the table as Trace plated the frittata and a fruit salad and as we ate my uncle filled us in.

"Obviously, Grant wasn't interested in digging up his past particularly, since his actions were unethical. However, after much posturing and repeated promises from me that I didn't give a damn about his actions, he admitted to giving Teresa the scripts. As far as Dr. Cavanaugh—apparently Mandy was asking questions regarding the protection of minors and the steps required to involve Child Protective Services. I called them after my meeting with Dr. Cavanaugh and there was a file opened, but before Mandy could give them all the details, she was . . ."

He didn't finish the sentence, but then, he didn't need to. I felt the tears, but I didn't let them fall because when I looked over at Trace he had that lost look burning in his eyes. My eyes stayed on Trace as my uncle spoke.

"I did a little digging and discovered that Douglas, like Teresa, was a Fishtown local and, more interesting, they knew each other since they were kids. Teresa's friendship with Mandy didn't really blossom until Mandy started her nursing degree."

My eyes pulled from Trace to look at my uncle.

"You think Teresa was looking to use Mom?"

"It certainly fits her pattern. I think that Teresa must have been gloating to Mandy and that's what put Mandy on the scent. I believe she went to Trace's house that day to help his mom, but her focus changed after that visit; she was working to get Trace and his sister out of that house."

Trace's head came up at that—guilt written all over his face.

"The thing is, Trace, the only way that Mandy could have learned that you and your sister were in danger was from your mom," my uncle added.

"What I don't understand is if Mandy's goal was to get Trace and Chelsea to safety, then why kill her? Also, the thought that it was Teresa who killed Douglas and Victoria doesn't make much sense either, since Teresa moved on to bigger fish and landed Charles. She got exactly what she wanted. There's no motive. Douglas coming after Teresa, I can see, since Teresa moved on and left Douglas behind, which could have sparked jealousy, but not the other way around."

This came from my dad, but I was too busy thinking about my mom as a wave of pride for her washed over me. She had been trying to be Trace and Chelsea's avenging angel. Knowing that about her made me feel an even greater love for her. Trace, though, was clearly not thinking along the same lines as he attempted to stand, but my dad stayed that action with a hand on his shoulder.

"I want to say something to you, Trace, and I ask that you please hear me out."

Trace sat back down, but he didn't look happy.

"Mandy was my life. What I felt for her is exactly what you feel for my daughter. We belonged to each other from the moment we met. When I lost her to such a senseless accident, it nearly undid me, but knowing that she was trying to do the right thing—that she died as she lived, with honor and an indomitable sense of right and wrong—I don't know, somehow it makes it easier to accept her death. With that being said, all that I have left of Mandy is in Ember."

"I understand, sir." Trace started to rise again, but my dad stopped him.

"You don't, though, so please let me finish. I love Ember with all that I am; she's my life, and not just anyone will do for her. When you and Ember have a daughter, you'll understand. You will know that no one will ever be good enough for her and you will not allow her to settle. Look at me, son."

Trace did and I saw a flood of emotions on his face as he listened to my father.

"What I'm trying to say to you is that when I look at you I see my wife. I see a person of incredible integrity and honor. What I don't see is the sick son of a bitch who was your father and I don't know how to make you understand that—to make you see that you are nothing like the man who donated his sperm—except for putting it into terms that you can understand.

"You, Trace, are very, very worthy."

Trace just sat there, his head lowered, and then I saw the shaking of his shoulders and realized that he was crying. I stood to go to him, but my dad beat me to it as he wrapped his arms around Trace. When Trace—big, hard, badass Trace—turned and leaned into my dad and really cried on his shoulder, I started crying in earnest because I knew, somehow, that my dad had finally gotten through to him.

My dad and uncle left after breakfast to hunt down Vivian, but my thoughts were on Trace. He was in his office and I knocked on the door. He didn't answer so I walked in and found him behind his desk. He was looking out the window with his back to me, but I knew he was aware of my presence. It wasn't possible for us to be in the same room and not feel the other on every imaginable level.

"My nightmares, the ones recently, they're not about my past or my dad . . ." He turned then and looked me right in the eye.

"They're about losing you. For twenty-eight years I believed I was a good-for-nothing and I was self-destructive, because deep down I believed I wasn't worthy. And then you came into my life. Someone who lost so much because of the depravity of my family and yet it was you, even knowing what linked us, who made me feel good about myself and gave me hope to believe that I wasn't a worthless piece of a shit."

He stood then and came around his desk so he could pull me into his arms.

"Your mom tried to rescue me, but it was you who saved me."

"Fate, Trace."

"I never believed in Fate, but I do believe that you're right." He pressed a kiss to my head before he lowered to one knee.

"This wasn't how I planned on asking you. I intended to make it a grand gesture, but my feelings for you run so deeply that I think this way is more appropriate."

He reached into his pocket for a small, black-leather box. My heart was pounding in my chest as Trace opened it to reveal a beautiful platinum, oval-cut diamond ring. The sight of it being held in his hands made my eyes fill with tears.

"There are so many reasons I could list as to why I want you in my life and the three most important are I respect you, I admire you, and I love you. Marry me."

Tears spilled down my face as I lifted my hand and watched as Trace slid his ring onto my finger.

"Yes, I'll marry you."

He stood and wrapped me in his arms, lifting me up and spinning me around in circles. "You won't regret it. I'll make you happy every second of every day."

"You already do."

Chapter Twenty-Six

Minutes later, I called Kyle.

"Hey, I was just thinking about you. What's up?"

"He asked me to marry him!" I said on a scream.

There was humor in Kyle's voice when he asked, "I thought you were already engaged?"

"Well, yeah, because I asked him, but now he asked me. I even have a ring—it's beautiful."

He chuckled. "Well, then it's official." And then he sobered and added, "I'm truly happy for you, both of you. It's been a really rocky road and I'm glad you guys made it."

"Thanks, Kyle. I don't know if we would have if not for you. Thanks for the nudges."

"It was my pleasure, I mean that. Over a week without a shower is just wrong."

I laughed. "I miss you. Can you come over later, maybe around five? We can have a small celebratory dinner. It wouldn't feel right if you weren't here."

There was a pregnant pause before Kyle said, in a voice filled with emotion, "I'd love to."

Later that day, my dad and I reviewed the contract that Lucien had messengered over while Trace and my uncle went to pick up Chelsea. My dad and uncle had found Vivian, but other than her admitting to being Teresa, she didn't have much to say. My dad was convinced she wasn't telling them everything. I was happy to take his mind from that.

"I think the cooking school is a wonderful idea." He looked at me and smiled before he asked, "Am I going to meet this mysterious Lucien Black?"

"Actually . . ." the doorbell rang. "Yes."

I walked to the door and pulled it open for Lucien. He stepped into the apartment and lifted my hand, but stopped when he saw the ring on my finger.

"Congratulations."

"Thank you."

My dad moved forward. "Ember and I were just reviewing the contract you sent over. Thank you for helping her make this possible."

Lucien's eyes found mine before he said, "It's my pleasure."

My dad chuckled and then he said, "I asked a lawyer friend of mine to look it over and he said it looked good. In fact, he said it was written with Ember's interests in mind, not your own."

"She's my friend."

"So I suppose we can set up those meetings with the contractors," I said.

"Absolutely. We'll work something out."

"We're having a small celebratory dinner, can you stay?"

"I don't want to intrude."

"You're not. Rafe and Kyle are joining us too. Please stay," I insisted.

His smile was dazzling before he said, "I'd love to."

As soon as Chelsea entered the kitchen, she ran right to me and threw her arms around me.

"You're going to be my sister for real."

"Yes, I am."

"I always wanted a sister." Chelsea pulled back and her smile was breathtaking.

"Chelsea, I would like to introduce you to my dad." Chelsea's eyes moved to him and I saw nervousness fill her, but she walked over to him and extended her hand.

"Hello, sir."

The look on my dad's face as he looked at Chelsea almost broke my heart because I knew he was thinking about all that she had suffered. He hugged her and I saw her stiffen, saw as Trace reacted, and then quite suddenly her arms reached up to wrap around my dad.

———◆◆———

Lucien and I sat in our newly purchased building as four different contractors presented their visions to us. I liked them all, but McAllister Associates was the closest to what I'd envisioned.

I looked around the deserted building and I couldn't wait to see the transformation. I couldn't wait to sit in the front row for Trace's very first cooking lesson. The building had at one time been a restaurant, so much of the framework was already in place: electricity, plumbing, even the large air vents for the commercial stoves that would significantly reduce the number of permits we'd need to acquire. Plus, most of the renovation would be focused primarily on cosmetic work, which also reduced the overall time required for the project.

Lucien continued hammering out the details at a level over my head so I found my thoughts detouring to Trace's parents. The night that Trace begged for help, his mom was unresponsive, basically forcing Trace to help his sister himself: an action that took them out of the house on the very same night that Trace's parents were killed. It was just too improbable that it was a home invasion; it was intentional.

Every time I ran the scenarios in my head, the only one that made any sense to me was that Victoria refused to help her children because she wanted them out of the house. She wanted them gone because she intended to take care of her husband, personally. Especially when I learned that she was trying to help my mom save Trace and Chelsea, yes, I thought Victoria killed Douglas, but what I didn't know was who the hell killed Victoria and why?

I had yet to share this suspicion with Trace, but I did pass it along to my uncle and I wasn't surprised to learn that he was thinking along the same lines. Of all the players in the game, none of them had a motive to kill Victoria, so it was more than likely that her killer was still out there—an unknown.

In my mom's death, I knew the evidence that Trace uncovered pointed to Douglas, more specifically his car, but I was still hung up on motive. The man didn't seem that particular. He was depraved, but not picky and, though he was a scumbag, he didn't strike me as a killer. Maybe the hit-and-run really was just an accident and he was too much of a coward to step forward, but the glaring question my uncle and I had was, why the hell had he been in Philly when he lived in Ohio?

From almost the beginning, my family and Trace's were linked. Though the connection was not a good one, without it, I would never have known him. I was deeply saddened for all that he and Chelsea had endured, and for all that my dad, Uncle Josh, and I had, but in the end, I got Trace. I was distracted from my thoughts when I heard Lucien say, "We're all done here."

"Okay."

I stood and started toward him when he said, "Work starts in a week."

"What's their estimate for time?"

"Three months."

"So maybe we can open in early January?"

"Yes."

"Perfect."

———◆———

That night, I stood in Trace's corner with my dad and uncle watching Trace fight and I had to say I really loved seeing my name over his heart, and as petty as it was, I really liked that all the other babes in the room saw it too.

Even better, between every round, he walked right over to me to kiss me hard on the mouth, further staking his claim on me and mine on him. It wasn't even a year that we'd been together, but he was so deeply entwined in my life that I couldn't imagine life without him.

As I considered that, I had a passing thought of Lena. I tried to call her several times to warn her about Dane but if I was being honest I didn't really put much effort into the warnings since I was still pissed. Maybe she wasn't even with Todd anymore. I hoped she had moved on since I'd never seen a more self-destructive relationship. Todd and Dane, on paper, were perfect with their Ivy League educations and prosperous families, yet Trace was by far the superior man and human being. Maybe Trace was finally seeing that—seeing that he wasn't who he was because of his background, but despite it.

Trace approached me in that loose-limbed stride of his. I knew he'd won the match, but I wasn't thinking about that as I wrapped my arms around his neck and kissed him.

Rafe walked over. "I'm the best man, Ember."

I looked at Trace. "You asked him?"

"He didn't really give me the chance. I finally relented because I couldn't take his nagging anymore. We need to set a date," Trace said.

"I'm for as soon as possible, but the first available date is, well . . ."

"What?" Trace asked.

I glanced over at my dad. "October thirty-first."

"Done."

I looked up. "Seriously, you're okay with getting married on Halloween?"

"Absolutely."

My dad hollered like a cowboy as he reached for his phone. "I'll call the pastor."

I was smiling at my dad's enthusiasm when I said, "We only have a few weeks to pull this off."

"As long as you say 'I do,' I don't care about the details."

"I need a dress."

"Why?" he teased.

"You are incorrigible."

"Only with you," he whispered before his mouth covered mine.

Chapter Twenty-Seven

I was planning my wedding. I smiled every time I thought about Trace's proposal; every word of it was etched onto my brain. He may have been aloof to others, but to me he was loving and so very generous with his affection. It really was no wonder why I loved the man to distraction.

A group of us were at Sapphire. Lucien and Rafe went to get us drinks while Trace and I settled at our table.

I turned when Trace spoke my name. Looking into those steel-blue eyes always made my heart beat just a little bit faster. "Halloween can't come fast enough," he said.

"I agree. I'd say we should just elope, but that would break my dad's heart."

"True. Any thoughts on where you want to go on our honeymoon? We could go to Paris or Barcelona or Tuscany?"

"I do actually, but I could be anywhere with you and love it," I said.

"That feeling is mutual, though if you have a preference I want to hear it."

"I thought it would be nice to go farther up north to Massachusetts, since it's going to be fall."

"Anywhere in particular?" Trace asked.

"Marblehead. I've always wanted to go there."

"Done."

"Just like that?"

"Considering that I plan on keeping you naked and in bed for the majority of our honeymoon, any location works for me."

"You have such a way with words, Trace."

He looked like a vaudeville villain in response to that as he brushed his lips over my cheek to my ear and whispered, "If you like those words, I have a few more."

By the time he was finished, I was beet-red and totally turned on. He knew it too, and his mouth settled quite firmly over mine. I was thinking about the first time I saw him. More specifically, I was thinking about him doing to me what he had been doing to that woman. He read my thoughts.

"As much as I would love to take you in the back and have my way with you, you deserve better than a quickie up against the wall."

"On the contrary, I'm thinking that sounds just about perfect."

"I'll take you home and we can do it any way you want: up against the wall, on the kitchen counter, in the shower . . ." his mouth covered mine as he bit my lower lip and sucked it into his mouth before he added, ". . . or all of the above."

"Oh, dear God. I need to go splash my face with cold water."

He laughed as I started from the table. "Don't be long sweet-heart," he called after me.

I was making my way through the crowd, when suddenly a hand wrapped around my arm and pulled me back.

"Don't make a scene." Dane's silky-soft voice purred in my ear and my heart started beating frantically in my chest. I was about to make the biggest fucking scene ever until he added, "I will hurt you if you resist me."

His hold was unyielding. Better to bide my time and allow him to believe I was acquiescing.

"What do you want?"

"To finish what we started."

My stomach roiled as bile moved up my throat. I tried to hide the effect his words had on me when I said, "I'm not interested."

"Doesn't matter. I'm not accustomed to not getting what I want. Besides, I did pay for the pleasure."

He really was like a spoiled child. "Take that up with Todd. He never should have pimped me out."

"It's hardly pimping out when the woman enjoys it."

"I wouldn't enjoy it, trust me."

He leaned closer and hissed, "All women enjoy it."

His grip on my arm tightened as he pulled me toward the back exit. I dropped my purse with the hope that someone would find it. He was calm, almost methodical, nothing like the carefree guy he'd been that first night. If something happened to me, would Trace ever recover from it? That thought had me biting, kicking, and clawing at Dane, but it didn't slow him down.

He pulled me into the dark alley behind the club where a car was waiting. Dane slammed me up against it and slapped me across my face. Holy hell that hurt. "I just wanted to have some fun that night at Sapphire."

He tried to kiss me but I turned my head. His reaction disturbed me because he laughed, like the whole thing was a big joke. It was instinct that made me bring my knee up hard into Dane's balls. I didn't get full contact, but it was enough to get him to release me.

I started to run from him but Dane was fast. His hand grabbed my hair and he yanked me back. I screamed bloody murder before his hand closed over my mouth. I threw my head back and nailed him in the nose. He howled in pain, but he didn't release me and then I felt the blinding pain as his fist connected a solid punch to my kidney. All the air left my lungs as he started dragging me back to the car.

Trace's bellow resonated down the alley and sent chills down my spine seconds before Dane's hold on me disappeared. I dropped to the ground, still attempting to pull air into my lungs. My head throbbed. Suddenly, strong hands wrapped around my upper arms and I flinched before I started wildly throwing punches; it wasn't until I heard Lucien's soft voice that I realized I was among friends and not foes.

"Ember?"

Tears filled my eyes as I looked up into his worried ones and then I saw Trace just behind Lucien. He had straddled Dane and was pummeling him, over and over again. The rage I had seen in Trace that night in the parking garage was nothing compared to what was pouring off him as he hammered Dane's face. If we didn't pull him off Dane, he might kill him. I saw Rafe trying to do just that, but Trace was unreachable.

Lucien gently lifted me to my feet and I gasped at the pain in my back that simple move had caused.

"We have to stop him," I whispered. Lucien supported me as we made our way to Trace. I reached out and touched Trace's shoulder.

"Trace, he's down."

And just like that Trace's hand stilled as he looked up at me. He dropped Dane and moved to wrap me in his arms and I flinched in pain even with the care he took.

"We need to get you to the hospital."

My brain had yet to process the events of the evening and despite the pain shooting down my back all I wanted to do was go home, curl up in bed, and have Trace hold me. I drew him into an embrace and mumbled into his chest, "I'm fine. Besides, you hate hospitals."

His finger touched my chin and lifted my gaze to his, and though I could see the rage burning in his eyes, when he spoke his voice was whisper-soft and patient. "Ember, don't argue."

"Rafe and I will take care of the trash. Trace, you get Ember to the hospital."

Lucien and Rafe dropped an unconscious Dane in an alley near his building. They wanted to drag his ass into the police station, but the charges would have been dropped by morning.

Trace and I returned home at close to four in the morning. The trip to the emergency room had taken hours. I did not have a concussion, but I had a bruised kidney. The doctor prescribed pain meds and lots of rest. Once we were locked inside the apartment, Trace pulled me into his arms and just held me. I felt his powerful body shaking and broke down seeing him so undone. I fisted his shirt as I pressed my face against his chest and sobbed. It had been a horrific experience, but there was a small part of my mind that acknowledged this was as close to closure as Trace was going to get. He had been able to save someone he loved and once the rage settled he was going to realize that. His soft voice pulled me from my thoughts.

"I was coming to look for you because I thought you were trying to lure me to that corner. I had only taken a few steps when I saw your purse and knew. Lucien, Rafe, and I split up, but I just knew you were in the alley." I lifted my head to his and the look on his face held both confusion and awe.

"I don't know how I knew that, but I knew where you were. I'm sorry it took me so long to get to you."

"You came, Trace. You pulled that animal off of me."

His body went rigid and I knew he was seeing Dane punching me, but it was over. We needed to focus on getting that animal off the streets before he could hurt someone else, but we could think about that in the morning.

"Let's go to bed, Trace."

He gently lifted me into his arms and started to our room. He settled me on the bed and helped me to change into my pajamas. I watched as he stripped from his clothes before climbing into the bed and drawing me into his arms. He pulled the covers over us and turned out the light. His hold on me never eased as he held me so closely against him. It was exactly where I wanted to be.

<hr />

A few days after the attack Trace and I went to my old apartment building around the time I knew Lena generally got home from work. I wasn't proud that this was a visit I should have already made but like I said, I was pissed at Lena and so I'd made excuses. After witnessing what Dane was capable of, I needed to warn her. We waited for almost a half hour for her to come home and one look at me made her sneer, "I see your man has some anger-management issues."

Trace tensed at my side just as I clarified for her: "This is the handiwork of Dane Carmichael."

She started to open her door, so I reached for her arm. She jerked away from me.

"Look," I said, "I realize our friendship is over, but I couldn't in good conscience not warn you. Dane is bad news, stay away from him."

"You're still on that? Seriously, get a life, Ember."

"I've warned you, whether you choose to heed it or not is completely up to you."

I turned from her and started down the hall just as Trace reached for my hand.

We were halfway down the hallway when I heard her say, "Thanks." It was so softly spoken but I knew she knew I heard her and that knowledge made me smile.

"What are we going to do about Dane?" I asked later that night while Trace, Lucien, Rafe, and I sat in Trace's kitchen.

"He's untouchable in New York, so we have to change that. We need someone with enough political clout and money to really start putting pressure on the Carmichael family," Lucien said.

"Trace's uncle," I said.

"Yeah," Lucien confirmed. "Based on what we know of the exalted Carmichael clan, the one characteristic they all have in common is self-preservation. Dane is a wild card at best, a liability at worst, and I don't see the family going down because of him. I think if enough pressure is applied, they'll cast him out and when he's no longer protected under the Carmichael name, he'll be fair game."

Trace added, "As far as the family, I agree with Lucien. They should be held accountable for allowing that animal loose. I do believe your boss Caroline would just love to sink her teeth into a story like this."

"There have to be others that he's hurt. We get a few women to step forward about their abuse, about what they remember, and it could be the beginning of the end for the Carmichael empire," Lucien added.

"The women, how will we learn who they are?" I asked.

Trace answered that. "Heidi, for one, and maybe she knows someone and so on. To break the silence it only takes one."

Lucien was practically seething from his spot across the kitchen, which prompted me to say, "Not that I don't appreciate your wish to help, but is it because of your employee Sabrina that you're so determined?"

"Partly her, but it's also the fact that Dane is a predator. I know predators and they don't stop until they're made to stop. Dane thinks he's protected and that makes him even more dangerous."

It was just the tiniest of insights into Lucien and I so wanted to pry for more, but now wasn't the time.

"Well, I'll speak up," I said.

Trace walked over and hunched down in front of me, taking my hands into his, before he said, "I know and I'll be standing right at your side."

Later, after everyone went home, I took a shower and when I stepped in front of the mirror I couldn't help inspecting myself. I saw a nasty bruise over my kidney, one along my ribs, and a splash of purple along my jaw.

I was reaching for my robe when I saw Trace standing in the doorway. Even from my distance, I saw the fury.

"It looks worse than it feels."

"When I saw the bastard touching you, knowing what he intended to do to you, I lost it. You were right, I was going to kill him. But you went up against that bastard and held your own. I don't want to sound condescending, but I am so fucking proud of you . . ."

I moved to him and wrapped my arms around his neck. "Love me. I need you to touch me, hold me . . ." I didn't realize how much I needed his gentle and tender touch to obliterate the ugly memories of Dane. He understood what I was thinking, understood far better than anyone else could, as he gently pulled me closer.

"I wasn't sure that you wanted me to."

I reached up and framed his face in my hands. "I will always want *you* to touch me."

He lifted me into his arms and walked us into the bedroom. He placed me on the bed before he undressed. My eyes moved to the tattoo that rested over his heart. He climbed onto the bed and caged me with his body just as his mouth moved to cover mine.

Chapter Twenty-Eight

Since I was ordered to rest, I found myself with an abundant amount of time on my hands. When Caroline learned of the attack, she ordered me to take a few weeks off. I thought about working on my book but with everything going on, I just couldn't concentrate, so I asked Trace and my uncle for copies of the police reports for both Trace's parents' murders and my mom's accident.

As I settled down at the desk, I flipped open the folder on Trace's parents' murders. The pictures were really gruesome, the subjects practically unrecognizable. The bodies had been found on the sofa in the living room, which was where Trace remembered his mom to have been that night when he begged her for help.

Another shot was of the kitchen. There were dirty dishes on the counter and used pans on the stove, but it was the bottle of wine that caught my eye: more specifically the two glasses sitting near it. I sat for a good long time staring at that bottle and those glasses. Who the hell was Douglas drinking with? I'd bet the farm it wasn't Victoria. Was there someone else in the house that night, someone else who witnessed Douglas's depravity?

Was it Vivian and was it possible that she was the murderer? Vivian was Teresa when my mom was alive, but she died in 1993. Trace's parents were murdered in 2001, at which time Teresa had already morphed into Vivian, but did she still maintain ties to her past? I flipped through the pages, reading the notes from the lead detective, Vincent Gowen, and found the statements from both Charles and Vivian. They both had alibis for the night of the murders: a charity function where dozens of people had seen them. Okay, so if it wasn't Vivian in the house, and it was unlikely that Douglas was sharing a romantic evening with the woman he was drugging, then who the hell was in that house?

As I reviewed the file, I realized the autopsy reports were noticeably absent. In fact, there was nothing in the file that definitively identified the victims. That seemed odd to me, but since the bulk of my knowledge came from crime dramas I decided to call my uncle. I reached for my cell phone and hit three; Uncle Josh answered on the second ring.

"Hello, Ember. How are you feeling?"

"I'm good."

His response was almost inaudible—almost. "Bastard."

"I'm really okay."

"Doesn't make me any less angry."

"I love you, Uncle Josh."

"Ah, sweetie, I love you too."

"I'm calling because I'm reading over the Stanwyck file and there don't seem to be any autopsy reports. Is that odd?"

"I noticed that too and yes, it is odd."

"In fact, I haven't read anything that positively identifies the victims. Even though the bodies were found in the Stanwyck home, it wouldn't just be assumed it was them, would it?"

"No, and it's a pretty blatant exclusion, so it was either shoddy police work or . . ."

"Or what?"

"Or intentional."

"A cover-up?"

"Maybe. I'm waiting on a call back from the investigator on the case. We'll get to the bottom of it."

I planned to interrogate him in person so I let it go.

After I hung up with my uncle I reviewed my mom's file, but if the Stanwyck file seemed light, this file was almost nonexistent. My mom was walking home from the bus stop, something anyone who knew her would know was her routine, when a car came out of nowhere. It's believed that she was dead on impact. There were eyewitness accounts, but it happened so quickly that no one got a good look at the driver and only a passing glance at the car, which Trace believed was his dad's.

I suppose what I didn't understand was why a man would keep the proof that could link him to a hit-and-run? The receipt to the car repair and the newspaper article were pretty damning. Wouldn't the motivation be to put as much distance between himself and the crime as possible and not hoard proof that could tie him to it? Unless, of course, he wasn't hoarding proof, but collecting it to protect his ass from someone.

And it was right on the cusp of that revelation that I made another more glaring one. The cases were believed to be linked through Douglas, but there was someone else, a person who was still alive, who tied the cases together. We were going to need to have another sit-down with Vivian.

I found Trace in the kitchen making dinner. He was standing at the counter chopping onions in that way of his that I found both incredibly skilled and deeply sexy. How out of my head was I for this man that the sight of him chopping vegetables was a turn-on? He looked at me from over his shoulder and smiled.

"Hello, sweetheart."

"Hi. What are you making?"

"Curried chicken."

"Something you learned to make from Mrs. Fletcher?"

Surprise flashed across his face before he answered, "Yes, you remember that?"

I walked to him and pressed a kiss on his back before I answered, "I remember everything when it comes to you."

His hand snaked out and wrapped around my neck to pull me in for a kiss and then I heard the knife hit the counter right before Trace's other hand reached around my waist and pulled me closer. Chelsea entered the kitchen just as I was about to wrap my arms around his neck.

"Hi."

Trace's lips lingered on mine for a moment before he pulled back. I smiled, he grinned, and he pressed a kiss on my forehead before he turned to Chelsea and said, "Hi."

I wrapped my arms around his waist and pressed my face into his chest. God, I loved this man.

After dinner, while Trace and I cleaned the dishes, my thoughts kept circling back to Vivian. I didn't want to believe she was a killer, but, at the same time, she knew more than she was saying. We really needed to talk with her.

"I'd like to meet with Vivian again."

He looked up from the pot he was cleaning, and I could see the question in his eyes before he asked, "Why?"

"She's the common denominator in both cases. I think she knows more than she's saying."

Trace stopped scrubbing and just looked at me. "What is it you're trying to learn?"

"I just can't believe she has no insights from back then. Maybe she doesn't even know that she's holding on to vital information. If we get her to talk, maybe something will shake out."

"You sound like your uncle."

I guess I did. I held his gaze. "There are too many unanswered questions, too many holes, and though your dad was an animal I think your mom and my mom deserve to have their murders solved. And maybe in the solving of your mom's death, you'll find a bit of peace."

His hands were still soapy when he wrapped them around my face and pulled me in for a kiss that was about more than love and, when his eyes found mine, I felt my knees go weak at the depth of emotion looking back at me.

"No one ever has, or ever will, know me the way you do. You're inside me."

I covered his hands with my own. "It's that way for me too."

Chapter Twenty-Nine

Vivian Michaels was a hard woman to track down, being that she was part of so many charitable organizations and committees, but we did eventually lock her in for a luncheon. I couldn't argue that she had come a long way from Teresa Nolan when she arrived dressed to the nines in Armani.

Trace stood and pulled out Vivian's chair. She smiled in thanks as she took her seat.

"I was so happy to get your call, Ember." Her eyes moved to Trace before she added, "And for Trace to be joining us, how delightful."

I leaned over and whispered, "You knew my mother, and you knew Trace's parents; we know this already. You're the only person still alive that can possibly lend some insight into what happened."

She looked positively ill when her blue eyes lifted to meet mine and her reply became nearly lost as she hissed, "Why are you still pursuing this?"

"Because my mother is dead and so is Trace's and we want to know why."

I didn't think it was possible, but the woman paled even more before she managed to ask, "You don't think I had anything to do with their deaths, do you?"

"The thought has crossed our minds."

Vivian lifted her martini, downed the entire contents, and signaled for another before she turned and met our unwavering stares.

"What do you want to know?"

"Were you getting scripts from Dr. Grant to drug Victoria?"

Guilt and shame covered her expression before she answered, "Yes. It was Doug's idea, but yes."

"You and Doug grew up together."

"Yeah. We were dirt poor and then along came the Michaelses and we saw a taste of how the other half lived and we wanted it."

Trace's arms came to rest on the table as he leaned closer to Vivian. "So you planned, from the beginning, to ingratiate yourselves into Charles and Victoria's lives."

"Yes."

His voice grew hard when he asked, "And the drugging of my mother?"

"Doug told me Victoria was having trouble sleeping, but she was too embarrassed to go to the doctor. She didn't want rumors to circulate that a Michaels was a pill popper. I didn't realize what he was doing, I honestly didn't, and then I met Charles and really fell for him. I left Fishtown not long after that and went to New York with Charles."

She leaned over the table and looked almost desperate when she said, "I didn't know what was going on in that house. I swear to you I didn't know. I wanted a different life and that is what I've done. On the few occasions that I reached out to my past to touch base, Darlene never made mention of anything going on, so I just assumed all was well."

"Wait, what's this about Darlene?" I asked.

"Darlene, Doug, and I were like the Three Musketeers ever since the fourth grade."

Trace's reaction to that matched my own.

"Are you saying that Darlene and Doug hung out even after he married my mom?" Trace asked.

"Yeah, she loved him and was really pissed when he married Victoria. She even took issue with Doug and me and we were only ever friends. He told me once that Darlene was getting too possessive and that he was going to tell her to stop coming around, but after I moved to New York they started spending more time together, not less."

"She failed to mention that," Trace hissed.

Genuine surprise flashed over Vivian's face. "You found Darlene?"

"Yes, why?" I asked.

"She just dropped off the face of the planet after Doug and Victoria died. I always wondered what happened to her."

"Did you know about my mother?" I asked.

"I knew your mom had suspicions, particularly after Darlene mentioned that Mandy knew about the scripts. I also knew that Darlene was nervous, scared even, of what Mandy might uncover. I should have paid better attention."

"Did you know my mom was trying to get Child Protective Services involved and that she was trying to get Trace and Chelsea out of that house?"

"No, I didn't. Your mom suspected what was happening?"

"We think Victoria told my mom that she feared for her children's safety, but before my mom could make anything happen, she was killed in a hit-and-run by a car that matched the description of Douglas's car."

Vivian looked downright sick. "Oh my God."

"What?" Trace barked.

"Douglas rode around on a motorcycle. Darlene had been using his car."

"Shit. That explains why his car was in Philly and why your dad had that newspaper article and the receipt to the garage. He really *was* trying to get proof. How much do you want to bet Darlene was blackmailing him? Take out the person who could potentially take away the man she loved and use that crime to bind the man to her," I said to Trace.

Trace slammed his hands down on the table before he hissed, "Goddamn, there's no end to his shit. It's like a fucking house of cards." He turned his attention on me and some of the anger gave way to pain. "I'm sorry for what that bastard did to you."

What could I say to that? So I said nothing.

———————

Uncle Josh called a few days later with news on Mrs. Fletcher.

"She's dead. She died in 1995 in a car crash when someone ran a light." As soon as the words were out of his mouth I needed to sit, since my legs were refusing to hold my weight.

"That seems suspect," I said.

"I agree. Who was she?"

"Their cook. Trace really bonded with her and it was she who taught him everything he knows about cooking. She discovered Douglas's secret and then she just stopped coming to work."

"Jesus," my uncle hissed through his teeth. "He has had more than his share of shit."

My gut told me that Darlene was responsible: another way for her to protect Douglas while at the same time binding him more tightly to her.

Trace and I had not yet shared what we learned from Vivian because once my dad and uncle learned of it, Darlene would be in some serious shit.

It seemed probable that it was Darlene who killed Douglas and Victoria in a jealous fit of rage, but the only thing that kept me from completely getting behind that theory was the police report or, more to the point, the lack of victim identification. We were missing something, and until we knew why Detective Vincent Gowan had withheld certain information from his report, I couldn't take that final step.

That night, while Trace and I got ready for bed, I told him about Mrs. Fletcher.

"Trace? I asked my uncle if he could find out what happened to Mrs. Fletcher."

I saw the tension that entered his body in reaction to my words, but a part of healing was closure and he needed to know that Mrs. Fletcher wasn't one of the angels who saw, heard, and spoke no evil. I wasn't sure how to break it to him, so I decided to just come right out and say it.

"She died in 1995 when her car veered into a median to avoid a car that had run a light."

It took him a minute to comprehend my words, but when he finally did, understanding dawned. "Silenced?"

I reached for his hands. "If Mrs. Fletcher learned Douglas's secret, and Darlene was the one to kill my mom, then it would follow that Darlene would want to silence Mrs. Fletcher to protect Douglas," I said.

"She was a good woman; she had a family."

"I know where she's buried if you want to visit her."

I watched as fury quickly replaced sadness. Trace pulled from my hands and, in one swipe, knocked everything from the bathroom counter. The sound of shattering glass filled the silence.

"How many goddamn lives had to be ruined?"

Every muscle in his body was flexed as his anger rolled through him. There wasn't anything I could say and I knew he just needed time to process it, so I slipped from the room and headed down the hall for the dustpan and brush.

He was still standing there with his palms flat on the counter when I returned. His head was hung low and the scrollwork of his tattoo was rigid and flexed. I knew what he wanted: he wanted to walk because he needed to cool off. He needed a fight, but he wasn't going because he vowed that he would never walk out again, but this was different. He wasn't walking out on me.

"Go, Trace." He lifted his head as his eyes found mine in the mirror.

"I'll clean this up. Go."

I could see his confusion so I added, "I understand the draw of the fight for you, it helps you cope, so go. I'll be here when you get back."

He turned, pulled me into his arms, and kissed me.

"Thank you."

"I'm sorry."

He said nothing, only kissed me again before walking out of the bathroom. I heard him moving around for a few minutes before I heard the sound of the front door closing. I cleaned up the mess and then settled into bed with a cup of tea and a book. An hour later, the phone rang.

"Hello."

"I was asked to check in on you."

"Hi, Rafe. Tell him I'm fine. How is he?"

"When he first called me, not good, but he's better now. He's always better when he gets to work out his issues on someone else's face."

"Tell him I love him."

"I will. Good night, Ember."

"Night, Rafe."

I was dreaming about pie pops, more specifically wondering if it was actually feasible to make a pie pop or if the juice would drip out of the hole where the stick was inserted into the crust? I grew rather warm in my dream, so warm that I was seriously thinking about jumping into the lake of cold milk that existed in the cake pop forest. I felt desire stirring in my belly and little shots of electricity shooting down my arms and forced myself to wake up, because I realized why I was growing so warm.

Trace's naked body was covering mine as his mouth glided over the skin of my neck and shoulder. I was still half asleep and hadn't realized that he had already divested me of my clothes until I felt him slide into me. My hips lifted as the heels of my feet dug into the mattress. I wrapped my arms around him as I trailed my fingertips up and down his back. He moved so slowly and each roll of his hips ignited a fire in me. His mouth found mine as he very deliberately brought my body to bliss and, as I floated back down, I slipped back into sleep.

I awoke the next morning to the smell of bacon and peeled my eyes open to see Trace standing before me with a breakfast tray.

"Good morning, beautiful."

"Good morning." I sat up and settled against the headboard.

"Hungry?"

"Yes."

Trace settled down next to me and handed me an egg sandwich that was loaded with bacon and cheese. I took a hearty bite and watched as he did the same before I asked, "How are you feeling?"

"Better. Thank you for understanding."

I leaned over and brushed my lips over his before I took another bite and chewed.

"This is delicious."

"I would like to visit Mrs. Fletcher's grave."

"Okay."

He held my gaze before he whispered, "Thank you." I knew the thank-you wasn't just for going with him to the gravesite, but also for looking into what happened to her.

"You're welcome."

"How was your evening?"

He asked this with a knowing smile so I answered, "Uneventful."

He looked almost hurt before he asked, "Are you certain?"

"Yes. I had an excellent dream, though."

He leaned up and looked at me with a grin. "Really, and what was this dream about?"

"Pie pops."

"What?!" He moved the tray—luckily for me I had already finished my sandwich—before his body covered mine.

"Is this sparking your memory?"

I purposely looked clueless before I said, "No."

He looked positively put out so I decided to cut him some slack.

"Any time, Trace."

"Any time what?"

"You want to wake me like that, any time."

He grinned before his mouth found mine.

Chapter Thirty

My uncle called and asked if Trace and I would join him for dinner. The place he selected was a small eatery in Midtown and when Trace and I entered we saw that my uncle wasn't alone. We made our way through the tables and as soon as my uncle saw us he stood, his guest following him.

"Ember, Trace, thanks so much for coming."

"Any time, Uncle Josh, you know that."

"I would like to introduce you both to Vincent Gowan."

I recognized the name immediately. My uncle's guest was middle-aged, late forties, and his black hair was gray at the temples. There was a warmth to his smile and a sincerity in his eyes. At first impression, I really liked Vincent Gowan.

We sat and placed our orders and then my uncle glanced over at Trace.

"Vincent is the detective who investigated your parents' deaths, Trace. Ember and I had some questions and when I tracked down Vincent he shared with me a story that I knew he needed to share with you."

"About twenty years ago, I was a rookie on the force in Bellville, Ohio," Vincent began. "I responded to a domestic-disturbance call and that was when I met Victoria. She was terrified and the huge black bruises on her jaw and cheek explained why. Like most abused women, she didn't want to talk and wanted me gone, but every time the neighbors called in a complaint, I responded with the hopes that at some point Victoria would grow comfortable enough with me to ask for help. She didn't, though, not once in the dozens of times that I was called to her house.

"One night, months after that first visit, she called me and asked me to help her children. She feared for them: feared what her husband would do to them. It was a difficult situation, since she had never pressed charges against the man, so trying to remove his children without any legal ground was close to impossible.

"I didn't know about Amanda Walsh and what she was trying to do until after she died. Victoria felt responsible for Amanda's death and she was terrified of what would become of her and her children if she went against her husband—so much so that she stayed.

"No further calls were made and the times that I would drive by the house to check on Victoria, I'd see her sometimes in the garden and she looked peaceful, almost serene, so I assumed everything had worked out. That was a mistake, a rookie mistake. Abusers don't just stop, but it was naive hope that allowed me to believe in the impossible.

"It was six years later when I actually got the call. I drove to the house and immediately knew something terrible had happened. When I heard the whole of it, I was compelled to help. The Bellville police force is very small and I wasn't much more than a rookie so any inconsistencies in my report were chalked up as inexperience. Without any hard evidence, the case eventually went cold and that was what I wanted—for this case to never be solved. I had seen her husband's handiwork and when she shared with me his sick interest in his children, I couldn't condemn her, since I would have done exactly the same in her shoes."

"What the hell are you saying?" Trace demanded as his jaw clenched hard with his anger.

Vincent leaned closer before he whispered, "That night, thirteen years ago, it wasn't Victoria Michaels who died, it was Darlene Moore."

My eyes flew to Trace's. I took his hand, which was icy cold, and held it in my own as the full meaning of Vincent's words settled over me. Darlene Moore was dead, which meant the woman we met, the one we believed to be Darlene Moore, had to be Trace's mom, alive and well. His mother was alive, and his mother did care. She sacrificed her own life to save those of her children.

"I learned in the years that followed that Darlene killed Amanda to protect Douglas and vowed to Victoria that she would do the same to Victoria's children if Victoria ever told anyone. It was then that Darlene upped the dosage that Douglas had already been feeding Victoria, keeping her in a near comatose state, but even in that condition she found the strength to fight for you— knew that you were both in danger. She didn't help you that night, because she wanted you out of the house. She wanted you away and safe so that she could do what she knew she had to in order to ensure that you were both safe once and for all. The bodies were as gruesome as they were because I hadn't wanted anyone to be able to identify the female victim. I buried the dental records and with us being as small a shop as we are in Bellville, the only other way to identify the body was through facial recognition. The fact that the body was in the Stanwyck home only furthered the belief that the victim was Victoria. And, yes, I knowingly aided and abetted. Darlene Moore was a murderer and Douglas Stanwyck was an animal. Legally I crossed a line, but morally I didn't. I called in a favor with a doctor friend to help with Victoria's withdrawals and he said it was nothing short of a medical miracle that someone who had been drugged for as long as she had wasn't brain-fried."

Trace, who had remained completely frozen, suddenly stood and reached his hand down to me.

"Would you please come with me? I have to see her."

I stood and took his hand. "Absolutely."

When we arrived at the bar in Ramsey on his bike, I turned to him.

"Do you want me to stay here?"

"No, come inside with me."

Five minutes passed and Trace made no move to get off so I touched his shoulder.

"Tell me what you're thinking?"

He was silent for a minute, and I didn't think he was going to answer, and then he said, "There's so much going on in my head but the only thing I can seem to focus on is that my mom is alive."

"She's not just alive, but she fought for you and was the one who ultimately saved you."

"No, she made sure that Chelsea and I were safe, but it was you who saved me."

I walked with Trace into the bar and as soon as we stepped over the threshold, I spotted Victoria. It took her only a moment to turn and when she did, her expression said it all. Trace had yet to let go of my hand and, when he started to walk, I realized that he wanted me to come with him.

We met her halfway and I watched as mother and son were reunited after over a decade of separation. I couldn't help the tears that fell freely down my face when Trace moved without speaking a word and wrapped his strong arms around the delicate frame of his mother. She, in turn, wrapped her arms around him, both of them crying. Trace reached for my arm and pulled me toward them as they both included me in the hug and there we stood for quite some time.

Chapter Thirty-One

The day before my wedding, I was in my room at my dad's getting ready for the rehearsal dinner as my thoughts drifted back to the reunion between Chelsea and Victoria. After our near Guinness-record-breaking group hug, Trace and I sat with Victoria for almost five hours talking. It had been heartbreaking to witness the pain in Victoria's eyes as Trace recounted the events leading up to the accident and Chelsea's condition. Like mother, like son, Victoria blamed herself while fervently telling Trace that he was not at fault. None of it mattered when the two women actually met and, though thirteen years had passed, the bond between mother and daughter was still there. In the two weeks since, the three of them had gotten to know each other and had become a family reconnected.

With all that was happening, I decided to wait until after the wedding to give my gift to Trace, especially since it wasn't completed yet and wouldn't be for another two months. I found myself to be almost as excited for that as I was for the actual ceremony.

"Ember, come down here."

My dad sounded odd so I hurried down the stairs to find him, my uncle, Trace, Lucien, Rafe, and Kyle standing in the living room looking at the television.

"What's wrong?"

Trace looked up and his eyes moved from my head to my toes and back again. He clearly liked my hot-pink bandage gown and a naughty smile curved his lips.

"Nice."

I threw him a saucy smile and he moved to pull me to him so he could get his hands on me, roaming in a manner that was not appropriate in front of his soon-to-be father-in-law.

"Stop it, you wicked man," I whispered.

"Make me," he growled before he bit my ear.

I blushed, he laughed, and then my father's voice drew our attention.

"An ethics committee has been convened to review the case files on two of the Carmichaels, the judge, and the DA."

"I wonder what prompted that?" I asked.

Lucien's voice was unyielding when he said, "It's only the beginning.

⎯⎯⎯•◆•⎯⎯⎯

With sunshine in the forecast I stood in the small room designated for the bride and studied myself in the full-length mirror. My gown had been created with embellished lace on tulle and had a sweetheart neckline, halter straps, and a fitted bodice with a flared skirt. My hair was twisted up and I wore a cathedral-length veil trimmed in beads. The only jewelry I wore were a pair of sapphire earrings my dad surprised me with and Trace's ring.

Chelsea and Victoria had been in earlier to help me dress, but now I stood alone thinking about Trace and our journey together.

Though it wasn't a particularly long one, it was certainly a very colorful one. I couldn't imagine living a day without him. From the very beginning he appeared like some kind of mystical hero and I had been lost to him. Maybe it was fate or destiny or maybe it was just two unlucky souls finally getting a bit of luck.

The soft knock at the door pulled me from my reflection and I called for my dad to enter. He pushed open the door and a big smile spread over his face.

"Ah, Emmie girl, you look exquisite."

I spoke the words that had previously only been spoken in my heart. "I wish Mom was here."

He moved to me as he reached for my hands to hold in his own. "She is, Ember. She is here with us and I know that she's smiling as she watches us. Her baby girl is getting married to a man who is very worthy of her, the man who grew from the child she died trying to save. Life works in mysterious ways, Ember, and the secret is to not think too hard on the why or how of it, and to not mourn what is no longer, but live: live hard and love hard. Your mom would want that for you."

I kissed my dad as tears filled my eyes.

"Your name will change today, but you will always be my little girl."

"And you will always be my daddy."

He wiped at his eyes before reaching for my hand and pulling it through his arm. "Let's go get you married."

The chapel was small with wooden pews lining the sides. As soon as my dad and I stepped through the doors, Trace and I locked eyes. The long center aisle reached from the back of the church down through the nave and as I approached the altar, I saw tears in Trace's eyes and knew he was seeing the same in mine. The entire service flew by and before I knew it, the priest had announced us husband and wife. Trace's hands framed my face as he lowered his head so that our lips were almost touching and then he whispered, "My beautiful wife."

"My beautiful husband."

And then he kissed me.

*E*pilogue

I had been Mrs. Trace Montgomery for three weeks, two days, nine hours, and seven minutes and I was deliriously happy. Thanksgiving was coming up and Trace and I were having everyone over. Trace, Chelsea, and I were doing all of the cooking. I was playing matchmaker and invited Vincent because there was something in the way he spoke of Victoria that gave me the sense there could be something between them.

Trace invited Charles and Vivian to Thanksgiving. I remembered the day when Victoria walked into Charles's office; the man actually cried. Who knew that there really was a heart beating in his chest? I still didn't like him and I knew that Trace didn't either. The man knew what was happening to Trace and Chelsea when they were kids and he chose to stay quiet. There was nothing he'd ever be able to do to make up for failing them so stunningly. But he would have to be part of our lives because Lucien was going to need his help with Dane.

I finished my book, which was now in the capable hands of Professor Smythe. We had rounds of editing before he helped me pitch it. Even if it didn't get published, I was very proud of it.

Lucien was picking us up in a few minutes so I could give Trace his wedding gift. He gave me mine while we were honeymooning in Marblehead and I broke down when he did. He worked with Lucien and they created a chain of shelters for battered women and children. They named these safe havens, these beacons of hope, "Mandy."

Down the hall in the office, Trace was standing by the window looking outside. I wondered what he was thinking about.

"Trace?"

He turned and a smile spread over his face. He came around the desk and pulled me into his arms.

"Hello, Mrs. Montgomery."

"Hello, Mr. Montgomery."

"I don't think I will ever get used to you being mine."

"I am, and have been since the very beginning."

He brushed his lips over mine before I asked, "What were you thinking about?"

"You, and how my life is so different from how it would have been without you. You saw past a damaged surface and found the man beneath it. More, you loved that man and allowed him the honor of loving you."

"I feel like the lucky one, Trace."

He said nothing to that, but watched me in that way of his before he lowered his head and just when his mouth touched mine, the doorbell rang.

"Damn bell," Trace growled.

I stepped back and took his hand as excitement surged through me. "It's Lucien. It's time."

Trace came with me, but not quietly as he nagged me to share my secret.

"You're going to see it in ten minutes. Patience, young Jedi."

I reached for the door as Trace whispered in my ear, "I know what I want for my birthday this year."

I stopped in my tracks, mid-motion, to look back at him. "What?"

"You dressed like Princess Leia in the slave-girl costume."

I blushed and he grinned. "Oh, yes, I am so going to buy that outfit. Hell, it doesn't have to be just for my birthday; it could be for all the days of the week that end in *Y*."

I narrowed my eyes at him and he kissed me hard on the mouth before he reached across me and opened the door.

"Lucien, my friend."

"Good morning." Lucien turned to me and grinned. "Are we ready?"

"Yup."

I blindfolded Trace, since all of our friends and family would be standing outside Everything for the unveiling. We pulled up to the curb and my eyes moved to the steel-blue sign with "Everything" written across it in black and pictures representing the stages of cooking. Inside there were twelve workstations that when completed were going to have granite countertops, Viking appliances, All-Clad pots and pans, and chef's knives—lots of chef's knives.

I climbed from the car before helping Trace out, and walked him to the perfect spot. Lucien came to stand next to us.

"Thank you, Lucien, for making this happen."

"It is truly my pleasure."

"Can I see now?"

"Remember you told me once that it wasn't every day a wish came true?"

Trace's voice held such affection as he answered, "Yes."

I removed the blindfold, stepped back, and just watched. It took him a minute for his eyes to adjust and then he just stared. I watched as his eyes took in our friends and family first and then moved to the sign before traveling to the prominently displayed bronze plaque, which read:

Dedicated in loving memory to Roberta Fletcher,
friend and teacher,
without whom none of this would be possible.

Trace turned to me. "What have you done?"

"Made your wish come true."

He pulled me to him and buried his face in my neck as his arms wrapped around me, holding me so tightly against him. "I love you, Ember Montgomery. I love you so fucking much."

"Love, my husband, is not strong enough a word."

He pulled back and framed my face with his hands. "You are my wish come true."

"And you're mine."

Acknowledgments

As Ember stated, writing can be very solitary, but working to get a book published is not. This is my first time working with a publisher and there are a few people I would like to thank.

Maria Gomez of Montlake Romance for making the call that made *my* dream come true. It was a conversation I had dreamt countless times of having and one that I will never forget.

Krista Stroever, my editor, whose expertise helped me to really tighten up and polish the story. I thought the experience would be difficult, having someone pulling your words apart and building them back up, but Krista made it painless, and I love how the story turned out.

Michelle Hope Anderson, the copy editor, whose attention to fine detail is amazing.

Receiving reviews can be tough and Christina Collie's review was no exception, but though it was critical it was also constructive. Thanks for seeing the diamond in the rough and sharing the story with your readers.

Lastly, I'd like to acknowledge my late grandfather. It's funny how certain memories stay with you regardless of how old they are.

My grandfather knew of my wish to be a writer and he also knew that I wasn't actively pursuing my dream because I was caught up in the day-to-day of a job. During a visit many years ago, he offered me some advice: "Life's too short. If you want to write, write." Such simple words, words that I had heard before, but for some reason that conversation stuck with me. He was my Professor Smythe. Thanks, Grandpa, for the well-aimed and much-needed kick.

About the Author

L.A. Fiore loves writing and losing herself in the world of her characters. When she's not writing, she can usually be found creating colorful chaos through gardening and playing the piano. She lives with her husband and two children in Bucks County, Pennsylvania, where she was born and raised.

Facebook.com/l.a.fiore.publishing